I0706210

PRAISE FOR LISA EDMONDS

"An action-packed debut with a strong, compelling heroine. Heart of Malice is sure to cast a spell on urban fantasy readers and leave them clamoring for more adventures with Alice Worth."

—JENNIFER ESTEP, NEW YORK TIMES BESTSELLING AUTHOR OF THE ELEMENTAL ASSASSIN URBAN FANTASY SERIES

"The complex magic system throughout Heart of Malice is a genuine joy to read and there's danger and intrigue throughout. The characters leap off the page and the secrets which Alice Worth carries make her a wonderful character. I can't wait to read more of this thrilling series!"

—HELEN HARPER, AUTHOR OF THE BLOOD DESTINY AND LAZY GIRL'S GUIDE TO MAGIC URBAN FANTASY SERIES

"Heart of Malice hits the ground running with the perfect blend of magic action, compelling characters, and sizzling romance. Snarky and cynical Alice Worth is a complex and flawed woman who is not simply kickass but refreshingly intelligent. Lisa Edmonds conducts the twists and turns of the plot like a maestro conductor, spellbinding the reader with her original and innovative worldbuilding, solid magic system, and a compelling backstory that haunts the main story in surprising ways. It's an absolutely delightful, one-sitting, devour it now read."

— DEBORAH WILDE, AUTHOR OF THE UNLIKEABLE DEMON HUNTER AND MAGIC AFTER MIDLIFE URBAN FANTASY SERIES

"Fast-paced and action-packed, the story created by this author is both intriguing and addictive, as is the world she builds. Her prose is lively and entertaining and laced with just the right amount of humor. [. . .] This suspenseful urban fantasy pulls the reader into an imaginative world—one that seamlessly marries reality with the supernatural—through the author's outstanding storytelling skills."

— IND'TALE MAGAZINE

"Edmonds has an eye for both detail and entertaining characters, and her story is fun and energetic. Readers will enjoy this installment and look forward to more in the continuing saga of Alice Worth."

— PUBLISHER'S WEEKLY

"It's no secret that this is one of my favorite series and that Alice is my girl. The author shook me with this book. From the story to the action to the characters, it left me with a huge book hangover. [. . .] I. Loved. Every. Minute. Of. It."

— THE LITERARY VIXEN

HEART OF THE DAMNED

ALICE WORTH SERIES
BOOK NINE

LISA EDMONDS

STORYBOOK
House

Copyright © 2024 by Lisa Edmonds

ISBN 978-1-963525-14-4

Edited by Grey Moth Editing

Cover Design By Artscandare Book Cover Design

All stock photos licensed appropriately

Published in the United States

By Storybook House, LLC

All rights reserved.

This book is a work of fiction. Names, characters, places, and incidents either are products of the author's imagination or are used fictitiously. Any resemblance to actual events or locales or persons, living or dead, is entirely coincidental and not intended by the author.

No part of this book may be reproduced in any form or by any electronic or mechanical means, including information storage and retrieval systems, without written permission from the author, except for the use of brief quotations in a book review.

This one's for you.

CONTENT NOTES

This book, as with all other titles in this series, contains scenes that depict violence, death, sex, and topics that may be disturbing to some readers.

A complete list of content notes can be found on my website at **www.lisaedmonds.com/contentnotes**

Or Scan

ALSO BY LISA EDMONDS

The Alice Worth Series

Heart of Malice

Heart of Fire

Heart of Ice

Heart of Stone

Heart of Shadows

Heart of Vengeance

Heart of Lies

Heart of the Pack

Heart of the Damned

Short Stories and Novellas

From the Ashes

Just For One Night

Blood Money

Ghosting 101

Perfectly Magical

Alice Worth and the Elite Death Machine

The Alice Worth World Novels

Mortal Heart

CHAPTER
ONE

"getting hitched" part.

I'd never attended a werewolf pack wedding before. In fact, I'd never attended *any* kind of wedding, so I didn't really have a frame of reference to know whether a pack wedding was different. This one certainly qualified as both joyful and bittersweet.

At Nan and Daniel's request, Sean, who I'd recently promoted from honey bunny to fiancé, officiated the sunset ceremony in the backyard of our home. Conducting marriage ceremonies was certainly one of the most joyous duties of an alpha—especially when the couple had survived so much hardship and found love unexpectedly later in life, as was the case with this particular bride and groom.

The entire pack had gathered for the event, including our three newest members. Two of them, twin infants Charlotte and Emily, slept in their parents' arms in the second row of folding chairs. Our most recent addition, Matthias Albrecht, a man-shaped mountain with dark hair and eyes, sat at the far end of the third row, with two empty chairs between him and the nearest fellow pack member. And though we'd all come together to celebrate Nan and Daniel's marriage, nothing could banish the tension caused by Matthias's presence.

From my seat in the first row, I caught Sean's golden gaze. His wolf lurked just beneath his skin all the time these days. He felt the tension in the air more than any of us. But when he smiled at me and the corners of his eyes crinkled, I could believe everything would be okay.

Sean turned his smile back to the couple standing in front of him with hands clasped. Not that they'd noticed when his attention wandered. Nan Lowell and my father only had eyes for each other. I wiped my eyes with a tissue.

Baby Daisy, our wolf pup, had exhausted herself playing before the ceremony and spent most of it snoozing on my lap. When I sniffled, the little black wolf with streaks of white on her shoulders and tail wiggled free of my arm so she could lick my chin. I kissed the top of her head and nuzzled her fur. She smelled like freshly washed puppy, vanilla, and sunshine.

"Before these witnesses, you have promised to share your lives in a marriage and partnership founded on love and honor," Sean told Nan and Daniel. "You've sealed your promises with your vows, symbolized by your hand-forged wedding rings made by a werewolf craftsman. So, by the authority vested in me by the Tomb Mountain Pack, the Were Ruling Council, and the State of California, I pronounce you husband and wife."

We cheered as Nan and Daniel kissed. He surprised her by dipping her backward. When the kiss ended and he set her back on her feet, they both burst out laughing. We all laughed too and gave them a standing ovation.

Ben Cooper, our pack's third, whooped. That set off a chorus of yells from other jubilant pack members. My own happiness bubbled up and over and turned into a yell of "Yay Nan and Daniel!"

Baby Daisy raised her head and added to the joyous celebration with her own little *"Aroooooo!"* before jumping from my arms to run in circles around our chairs. Apparently her nap and our exuberance had replenished her energy.

Another voice that joined in belonged to my ghost bestie Malcolm, who'd floated to Sean's right during the wedding. For the occasion he'd traded in his trademark button-up shirt and jeans for a tux, though everyone else was dressed in backyard wedding casual and only I could see him. He caught my eye and gave me two thumbs up.

When I had a chance, I stole a glance over my shoulder. Matthias had risen along with the group and applauded, but the way he went through the motions of expressing happiness without really feeling any popped my bubbles of joy like a pin.

Daniel's smile faltered when he caught sight of Matthias. Nan noticed his change in demeanor immediately. She touched his face and drew his attention for another kiss. My father's new mate had graying hair and a kindly, nurturing nature, but she was as fierce as just about any werewolf I'd ever known. She'd earned her place as our beta—the only female beta west of the Mississippi.

Ben had put himself and his new mate Casey in charge of the after-party. As Nan and Daniel accepted the hugs and congratulations of the rest of the pack, Casey turned on the music and the multicolored lights we'd strung up around the yard. Both Nan and Daniel loved classic rock, so the playlist leaned heavily into many of the bands whose records I had in my own collection. Some of my pack mates sang along and a few danced playfully while waiting for their food, which warmed my heart. Music brought us all together almost as well as food.

Finding out I shared the same musical preferences as the biological father I hadn't met until just months ago had been one of the best parts of our growing relationship. Daniel and I had enjoyed many evenings listening to records and talking. We were still figuring out how to be parent and adult daughter, but every day I loved him more.

Meanwhile, Ben and his helpers orchestrated the enormous

amount of food required for an event that involved more than twenty perpetually hungry werewolves. When the smell of meat cooking on the grill wafted over, my stomach growled loudly.

"I heard that, Miss Magic." Sean came up behind me and gave my butt a playful smack. "I told you that little salad you had for lunch wasn't enough food."

"You would have told me I didn't eat enough lunch if I'd eaten a buffalo," I shot back, but he did have a point. Not that I'd admit it, of course.

Chuckling, Sean slipped his arm around my waist as Nan and Daniel made their way over. Most of the pack had descended on the food and drinks, leaving us nearly alone near the arbor we'd set up for the wedding. The string lights transformed our backyard into a nighttime twinkly dream. Hmm. Maybe we should keep them up after tonight. Anything that made us all smile needed to stay.

As the volume of the celebration grew and the stacks of burgers and hot dogs shrank, Matthias remained near the chairs, an island of silence and solitude. He stood with his hands clasped behind his back, probably waiting for permission to leave.

Sean nuzzled my hair before shaking Daniel's hand and hugging Nan. I hugged both of them, reveling in Nan's signature rib-crushing squeeze and Daniel's loving warmth. Then the three of us shared one big hug for good measure.

I'd recently spent a week in wolf form, courtesy of a gift from a fae who owed me a big favor. That time had brought Sean and I even closer...and forged a stronger bond with my father and Nan. Though our time together had been interrupted by a violent attack, we'd run, played, and hunted as a group before curling up together in wolf form to rest and sleep under the stars. Those joyous memories lived in my heart now.

The only people who knew I was Daniel's biological daughter—and thus Nan's new stepdaughter—were Sean, Daniel, Nan, Ben, and myself. I had two step-siblings, Nan's grown son and daughter, who were also in the pack, but they didn't know my real relationship to Daniel and probably never would. My true identity was a closely guarded secret, even from many people I loved. I simply had no choice in the matter. That pain chewed at my insides particularly on days like these.

The best I could do was share extra-long hugs with my father and stepmother and keep the truth of our family ties locked away inside with the rest of my secrets.

"Congratulations again." Sean drew me closer, kissed my temple, and smiled at Nan and Daniel, who hadn't let go of each other's hands for more than a moment since the ceremony began. "We don't want to hold you back from the food."

"Not much can keep Daniel away from food," Nan teased, patting Daniel's flat stomach with her free hand and then ruffling his thick, dark brown hair. "He stays well-fed."

"I know how well you cook, so I don't doubt it." I gave them each another quick hug. "When do you think you'll be hitting the road for Utah?" Their honeymoon would be a two-week camping trip where they could run as wolves for the majority of their time away. They'd rented a swanky camper and hitched it to the back of Nan's truck for the trip.

"We'll stick around for at least an hour or so," Daniel said, squeezing my hand again. "No sense running off right away. Utah's not going anywhere."

As Sean made a joke about Daniel not wanting to start their honeymoon immediately, I glanced at Matthias again. He hadn't moved and he remained as expressionless as ever.

My stomach knotted. *Has he forgotten how to be happy? What can I do to ease his pain and help him learn to live again?*

Matthias no longer served the Vampire Court, but anyone seeing his utter lack of expression now might think he'd come here as their representative instead of as a member of our pack. His misery made me ache.

Daniel's gaze followed mine. He took a deep breath and let it out slowly, flexing the fingers of his free hand. I grabbed that hand and squeezed as hard as I could.

"We'll take care of him," Sean told Daniel, his voice quiet—but not so quiet that Matthias couldn't hear him. Of course he wanted to reassure them both. "You focus on Nan and your time together."

"Thank you," Daniel said, and traded his moment of grimness for a smile as Nan tucked herself under his arm. "I plan to do exactly that."

My father had to be the happiest werewolf in the world today, but the situation would surely weigh heavily on his mind even in Utah. Daniel had unintentionally infected Matthias with the shifter virus during a fight. And now for better or worse—and I'd be the first to admit, for mostly worse so far—Matthias belonged to our pack.

This was Daniel and Nan's wedding day. I shouldn't compound his guilt with a long face. Sean was right: we'd take care of Matthias.

That thought allowed me to set my worries aside for now so I could smile. "Let's all get some food. I'm starving."

While Nan and Daniel went on ahead to join the others, Sean took a moment to kiss my left hand. My vintage alexandrite engagement ring sparkled in the overhead twinkly lights. "I love you," he said.

Alone with my werewolf, I let myself be weary—both mentally and physically. I rested my head against his shoulder. "I love you too."

He wrapped his arms around me. Our usual pattern involved one of us expressing our love and the other saying "I know," in the storied tradition of Han and Leia. Because he knew me so well, and we shared a nascent mate bond that allowed us to sense each other's emotions, he knew my heart was heavier than it should be on such a happy day.

"I'm at your side through it all, Miss Magic," he said, resting his chin on top of my head. "There's nothing that comes our way that we can't beat together."

I tried to say *I know*, but the words stuck in my throat.

I'd chosen to help Matthias during his Change and asked Sean to accept him into our pack. After careful consideration, Sean had taken my recommendation, but most of the pack had resisted welcoming Matthias. Some were downright hostile.

Sean said everyone needed time to adjust. That was certainly true, but a hundred years might not be enough time for the pack to forgive Matthias for his role in kidnapping Daniel and me on New Year's Eve, much less accept him as a pack mate. While he hadn't been the person who'd shot me, he'd led the team, and he'd pointed a gun filled with silver bullets at Sean's head—and that was after his people had shot us full of tranquilizer darts.

I understood how they felt, and I'd fully intended to kill Matthias myself for everything he'd done. But when Daniel infected him, everything changed.

While I'd helped Matthias shift for the first time, I'd seen the brutal truth: Valas had broken him. She'd turned him into little more than a puppet in service to the Court, to the point her will became his own. Once I understood that, my fury turned to sympathy and empathy.

I too had been broken, once upon a time. I understood what it meant to not know who I was, and have no idea where to go or what to do.

I'd done the right thing helping Matthias and encouraging Sean to accept him into the pack. But as I witnessed the tension Matthias's presence caused, guilt gnawed at me as well, and I had no idea how to reconcile those conflicting emotions.

I squeezed Sean's hand. "Go put on your apron and take over at the grill, Wolf. I'll be okay."

He gave me a baleful look and headed for the deck, where the apron I'd gotten him waited, draped over the railing. It read CAUTION: HOT CHEF and everyone thought it was hilarious except Sean. But he wore it anyway. If that wasn't love, I didn't know what was.

While Sean took the tongs from Ben, I made my way to Matthias.

He watched me without expression, but I'd gotten a lot better at deciphering his body language and reading his eyes. Discomfort lurked just behind that stoic façade.

I'd hoped once he became part of the pack that he'd feel less lost and grief-stricken and angry, but instead he remained withdrawn and distant in every possible way. He lived with us, but he tended to cook for himself and rarely joined us for meals, or anything else, unless Sean or I specifically requested it. Since we respected his privacy and boundaries, we didn't push.

I wondered, not for the first time, if he resented me for talking him into living as a werewolf instead of letting him die in the wake of Valas's death.

"A beautiful ceremony," he said as I approached. "Please congratulate Daniel and Nan on my behalf."

I'd seldom heard such a lack of emotion in a human's voice. He sounded flat and devoid of feeling, very much like an old vampire. But unlike those vampires, he *did* have feelings. He'd learned to hide them—because vampires used our emotions against us, and because with vamps, lack of emotion signaled age and thus demanded respect. The humans around them tended to emulate that coldness, sometimes on purpose, but often subconsciously.

My grandfather's cruelty had forced me to bury my emotions too. And even after I'd escaped his clutches, it took me years to learn how to simply feel again—and I still struggled mightily to process feelings. Matthias and I were the only members of our pack who understood how deep those kinds of wounds went. And it was difficult, or nearly impossible, to explain that to the others.

"You should tell them yourself," I said, my voice gentle. I rested my hand on his arm. His muscles felt like steel cables, taut and hard. He didn't move away, but he didn't relax at my touch like the other pack wolves did. "They'd be glad to hear it from you."

"Would they?" He smiled without humor. "I think they all prefer I keep my distance."

"Some might, for the time being," I admitted. "But not everyone.

These are good people, Matthias. You didn't come to us in the way anyone would have preferred, but you're here and that's not going to change. Come with me and eat with the others. We can sit at our own table if you want to."

He studied me. "Is that an order?"

"No." I kept my voice even so he couldn't tell how much my heart ached. "It's a request from a pack mate."

For a moment, I thought he might do as I'd asked. My hopes were dashed when he shook his head. "Then I would prefer to return to the house," he told me. "This is a happy occasion for your pack—*our* pack," he corrected when I started to speak. "I don't want to interfere with that."

I might have protested if I didn't remember my own reluctance to interact with Sean's pack, especially all at once, in the early days of our relationship. They'd been more than ready to meet me long before I had the courage to meet them. It took time for me to get there. Matthias needed time too.

Daniel had vacated our guest room and moved into Nan's house just in time for Matthias to join our household. He lived under our protection for now, until he could find a place of his own and figure out what he was going to do now that he no longer worked for the Court.

"You don't need my permission to go back into the house," I reminded him when he didn't move. "You're free to do whatever you want at any time."

"I would...prefer directives," he said. The way his eyes tightened and the subtle shift of weight from one foot to the other were the only signs of his feelings of loss and uncertainty, before he regained that expressionless look the vamps liked so much. "You have great authority in this pack. Why not give me orders?"

"Because that's not how this works, most of the time. We're pretty sparing with the orders around here." I smiled at him, but he just waited for me to finish my explanation. "Authority takes many forms. The vamps are dictatorial. We lead by example and guide with kindness, not threats or commands."

He didn't say so, but the flash of skepticism in his eyes let me know he didn't think our way of running things was necessarily the best way. It might be one of the most jarring differences between the vamps and us—and probably a major cause of Matthias's ongoing struggle to find a foothold.

Maybe I could turn the moment into a way of connecting with him. I gestured at our pack sitting at the tables and on the deck, eating and laughing, united in camaraderie and happiness for Nan and Daniel. "What conflicts have you seen since you've joined us, other than between yourself and others? What disrespect have you seen for Sean or me or anyone else?"

He tilted his head as he considered my question. "None," he said finally, with a little nod in acknowledgement of my point being made.

"I've told you before that strength comes in many forms," I said. "At the end of the day, a group united by love and mutual respect will outlast and outfight any group brought together by threats or intimidation. We're proof of that." I touched his hand, which was as much physical contact as he generally preferred to have—at least, so far. "Go where you feel most comfortable. We'll be here when you're ready."

I didn't say it like an order, but maybe he interpreted my words that way because that was what he'd been accustomed to hearing. He turned and headed for the front door, rather than walk through the party to the back door.

Once he was out of sight, I joined the party. Members of our pack had claimed almost every seat on our deck and at the tables we'd set up in the yard. The only close friends conspicuously missing were my business partner Arkady Woodall and her current flame Ronan, a fallen angel now living as a human. Arkady was on a stakeout for a case she hoped to wrap up tonight, and Ronan had gone out of state on mysterious bounty hunter business.

Sean had already made me a plate piled high and sagging under the weight of a fully loaded burger, a baseball-sized helping of potato salad, four barbecue meatballs, and extra beans. The smell was heavenly but that was three or four times more food than I could possibly eat. Priority number one for any shifter was to ensure their mate was safe and had enough food—and "enough" was defined by shifter standards, not human. The more worried I was by the troubles in our lives, the more worried Sean's wolf became, and the more worried the wolf became, the more food ended up on my plate. At this rate soon he'd end up serving me half of a grocery store at every meal.

I thanked him with a kiss and found an empty seat at a table occupied by Ben, his fiancée and new mate Casey, and Fiona, a paramedic who happened to be dating my ex-girlfriend Jane. I'd set them up on a kind of blind date around Christmastime. I had high hopes it would work out.

With Matthias out of sight in the house, the mood lightened considerably, which left me simultaneously relieved and saddened. Our guest room where Matthias lived overlooked the backyard, but the windows were dark. Either he was sitting in there with the lights off or he'd gone to the workout room to punch the heavy bag.

My growly tummy demanded I eat. As the others talked and joked, I devoured half my burger, some potato salad, and a meatball. Sean's smile widened with every bite I took. I rolled my eyes at his goofy grin, but I didn't stop eating.

After I chatted with Ben, Casey, and Fiona, I took my plate with me and made my rounds of the other tables, checking on the rest of the pack. Plans for werewolf-style full-contact backyard football were well underway for after Nan and Daniel left, while the rest of the pack who didn't want to play would either cheer on the sidelines or relax on the deck with drinks. Every smile and hug eased the ache in my heart caused by Matthias's situation.

All too soon—at least, for me—Daniel and Nan announced their departure. We accompanied them to the front of the house for another round of hugs and congratulations and some good-natured teasing about the honeymoon.

Daniel drew me away from the others to the other side of several vehicles so we had some privacy. Werewolf ears were sharp.

"I love you." He gave me a long hug. His signature scent of warm grass and sunshine wrapped around me too and washed away the lingering tension in my shoulders.

When he let go, his eyes shimmered with unshed tears that mirrored mine. He kissed my forehead. "Remember what I said about not leaving you behind or leaving you out. We're a family now, even more than before. Nan loves you like a daughter. She has for a very long time. Even if you can't call her your stepmom, you know she is."

"I know. And she's way more than that to me." I squeezed his hand. "I'm so happy for you both *and* for all of us. I love to see our pack growing bigger and stronger."

Some other emotion crossed his features, then disappeared. Had I imagined that flash of regret? "If you need us, call me," he said. "We'll race back as fast as we can."

"Don't worry about anything except enjoying your trip." I spotted Nan climbing into the cab of the pickup and nudged Daniel. "You'd better get going before she leaves without you."

Chuckling, we returned to the front of the house. Daniel shook Sean's hand once more, murmured something in his ear, and got into the passenger seat.

They waved as they drove off down our long driveway and turned onto the road that led to the interstate. Nan honked before they disappeared behind the trees and into the night.

in anticipation of this moment. "Here, Miss Magic. Blow your nose."

I wiped my eyes and sniffled inelegantly. "It's weird that people cry when they're happy. I mean, why do sadness and happiness have the same response?"

"That's one of life's little mysteries." He nuzzled my hair to drink in my scent, which always soothed him and his wolf. That meant he had mixed feelings right now too. "Both are strong emotions. And sometimes we feel both at the same time."

Everyone else had returned to the backyard, probably to give us some privacy. I took advantage of the moment to wrap my arms around Sean's neck and give him a long kiss. He lifted me up so I could lock my legs around his hips.

He rested his forehead on mine. "Loving you is the best thing I've ever done."

"No, the best thing you've ever done is make me breakfast burritos when I'm hung over." I smiled up at him. "But loving me is the *smartest* thing you've ever done."

He chuckled. "If the Alice of a year ago could have heard you say that, what would she have said?"

"I'm not sure," I admitted. "She might have punched me and called me an idiot. Hey, it's almost the one-year anniversary of us meeting for the first time. Should we do something for that? Is that a thing people do?"

His mouth twitched. Because of the way I grew up, isolated at my crime lord grandfather's compound, I was notoriously lacking in knowledge when it came to relationships and—well, a lot of other things.

"It's a thing if we want it to be," he said, kissing the tip of my nose. "We'll call it our one-year meet-iversary. A one-year wedding anniversary is the paper anniversary. What's a one-year meet-iversary?"

Hmm. "Pizza?"

"My beautiful food-motivated Miss Magic." He put me on my feet and took my hand for the walk back to the party, which would likely go on well into the night. The only things shifters loved as much as food were pack gatherings and full-contact, no-holds-or-hits-barred, bone-breaking backyard sports. "I hereby deem pizza to be the official gift of one-year meet-iversaries."

"Sounds good, Mister Wolf." I squeezed his hand. "What did Daniel whisper to you before he and Nan left?"

"He reminded me that taking care of you is my reason for being."

What was more intense than shifter protectiveness? A shifter *father's* protectiveness. Combine that with having a shifter fiancé and sometimes it was a lot.

"*Werewolves.*" I made a little growly sound. "As if I didn't take care of myself my whole life before I met you."

"Poor Alice." Sean leaned over as we walked and kissed the top of my head. "It's tough being loved so much, isn't it."

In between one step and the next, my vision swam. I stumbled and fell. Sean caught me just before I hit the ground.

For one disconcerting moment, I became weightless, formless, suspended in an abyss, and surrounded by darkness.

I'm falling...

I flailed and tried to grab onto something—anything—to stop my fall, but my hands encountered nothing but empty air.

And then just as quickly, I found myself sitting on the front lawn, blinking up at Sean. He held my shoulders, his eyes glowing golden. In my confusion, I'd grabbed him and hung on as if my life depended on it.

"What's wrong?" He crouched to look directly into my eyes. "Alice? What happened?"

Hell if I knew. I shook my head to clear it and let go of his arms. "I'm okay, I think. I just got lightheaded for a second."

Wait...what the hell?

My hands ached. I'd gotten a manicure for the wedding—something I rarely did because working as a private investigator was tough on my hands. My nails looked no different than they had since yesterday's salon visit, but I had a weird thought that they'd somehow been longer, more like talons than human nails. When I shook my head again, the image faded.

"The last time something like this happened, you'd been hexed." Sean's voice was half growl. "How do we know for sure you're okay?"

"Well, I could ask Carly, I suppose." When I started to rise, he lifted me up and set me carefully on my feet, steadying me with a hand on my arm. "But I have her anti-magic amulet in my pocket and I feel okay."

His expression remained grave. "Call Carly, please, Alice. You're not prone to fainting spells."

Before I could reply, Matthias's snarly voice came from the porch. "Alice, are you all right?"

"Yes, I think so. Just dizzy for a second. All better now." I leaned past Sean and spotted Matthias on the front steps.

He loomed over us, his eyes glowing amber. His aggressive stance took me aback. Thanks to my help during his Change, Matthias had near-total control over his wolf. At this moment, however, he leaned forward on the balls of his feet with fists clenched, as if ready to shift. Golden shifter magic seared my skin.

"Be calm," Sean commanded, his voice resonant with alpha magic. His eyes glowed brightly as he stared Matthias and his wolf down. "There is no threat here."

We didn't know that for sure, given Sean was right and I didn't have a habit of fainting, but his voice carried only absolute authority and certainty.

After a beat, Matthias's posture changed and the shifter magic in his eyes faded to a soft glow. He didn't back down completely or anything close to it, but the prickly feeling on my arms went away.

Sean and I *did* lead gently, but sometimes orders were required. Matthias had just created one of those times.

"I'm okay," I repeated with more conviction. "Really. Thank you."

"You are welcome." Matthias returned to the porch. His frown seemed more confused than angry now. Maybe he hadn't expected Sean to order him to be calm. Maybe his wolf's reaction had startled him as much as it startled me.

Or maybe he mistrusted his own reactions so much that he needed orders to feel comfortable with his thoughts and actions. Another possible consequence of Valas's abuse, and another reason she deserved to be dead.

After a beat, Matthias opened the front door and went back inside. Whew. Crisis averted.

Ben appeared around the side of the house with Casey at his side. "Everything okay?" His gaze went to me. "Alice, you look pale. What's up?"

"She fainted," Sean said, his hand on my lower back, probably in case I wobbled.

"Have a seat on the steps," Casey said briskly in her nurse tone. That meant I had no choice but to comply.

A few minutes later, Casey determined I didn't have any lasting physical symptoms that she could detect. My blood pressure was normal, as were my pulse and breathing. My pupils dilated normally. Unsurprisingly, those facts did very little to alleviate Sean's concern —or anyone else's.

"I don't know what to think," I told them, my elbows on my knees. "I had a weird moment where my hand didn't look like my own, but it seemed like an echo of something I might have seen during a tracking spell. I feel fine now. I don't know what else to do but stay on guard, ask Malcolm to look me over, and have Carly do her thing."

"People *do* just get lightheaded sometimes," Casey reminded us. "Alice has had a stressful couple of days."

"Couple of weeks," Ben said.

"Couple of months," Sean admitted, his tone wry. His frown belied his lingering concern and his worry tingled through our nascent mate bond.

"Couple of *years*," I stated with finality. "Also, I haven't been eating or sleeping super well lately. It probably just caught up with me all at once. But I will text Carly," I added when Sean's frown deepened. "If she says I'm okay, will that be enough?"

"It will have to be," he said, in a tone that meant *not at all*. "Hopefully she can come out here tonight."

"Knowing Carly, she probably sensed us talking about her and is already on her way," Ben quipped.

The incident could be something, anything, or nothing. I had no ideas what had happened and really nothing to look into, at least for now. Maybe Carly would see something I didn't.

I sent my witchiest friend a quick text message. *Me: Had a fainting spell at home. I feel fine now but Sean would like a second opinion. Are you available for a house call?*

After a brief wait, my phone buzzed with a reply. *Carly Reese: Katy and I can be there in one hour.*

Me: Thank you.

I pocketed my phone. "She's on her way, and she's bringing Katy along too. Can I finish the rest of my burger while we wait?"

"She has an appetite," Ben said as we resumed our walk toward the backyard. "That's a good sign, right?"

Sean growled. I was about to take his hand to reassure him when he, Ben, and Casey all whirled to face the road, their eyes glowing. So it wasn't my fainting spell that had made him suddenly angry.

"Pack to the front!" Ben called, his voice edged with a snarl.

A moment later, I heard what they'd detected long before the sound reached my ears: the rumble of engines and tires on asphalt. More than one large vehicle, heading this way.

Malcolm appeared at my side. "Do we have trouble?"

My stomach churned. "Could be."

By the time four black SUVs appeared on the road and began turning into our long driveway, nearly every member of our pack had lined up in front of our house. Sean had sent Karen and Cole Williams inside with their babies and given Matthias orders to stay in the house and guard them with his life. Whether because Sean had finally issued him an order or Karen had been kind to him or both, Matthias looked ready to shred anyone who so much as looked at the Williams family wrong. Despite my concern over our visitors, seeing Matthias ready to defend the pack warmed my heart.

We watched the SUVs come up the drive. My skin tingled as they crossed my perimeter wards.

Malcolm flitted. "It's a convoy of Vampire Court soldiers."

The rest of the pack had recognized the vehicles too. Their growls increased in volume.

Magic spiraled up my arms and sparked on my hands. As I spooled more power, the ground trembled under our feet. How dare the Court send soldiers to our home?

Esme, our little house dragon, strolled through the assembled werewolves to stand next to me, her tail swishing as she eyed our visitors. She stayed in cat form, but she could turn into a small-but-deadly dragon the moment danger loomed. Esme was a pūķis, a fae creature I'd gotten as a gift while traveling in the Broken World. I didn't want anyone to know we had her, for obvious reasons, but if the enforcers were here to attack us, I'd unleash her on them without a second thought and deal with the consequences.

The front passenger doors of the second and third SUVs opened. Bryan Smith, Charles Vaughan's human head enforcer, emerged from the second SUV. Adri Smith, his sister, who was also an enforcer for Charles, got out of the vehicle behind his. Five more uniformed enforcers also emerged. I recognized a couple of them as belonging to other members of the Vampire Court who had sided with Charles during his violent takeover of the Court.

Esme hissed. Sean and I took a few steps forward. The rage of our pack pressed against my back like a tidal wave building up, ready to break at any moment.

The group of enforcers silently faced our pack as if we were two factions about to have a showdown in a Wild West town.

"We come on official business of the Vampire Court of the Western United States and its undisputed leader, Charles Vaughan," Bryan said, his tone very formal. "We are not here to attack you."

I didn't necessarily believe him, but if the vamps intended to attack, they would have come in force, and they wouldn't have just sent human enforcers. I studied each face in turn, committing it to memory and looking in vain for any hint of what they planned to do.

"You're on private property," Sean said, his voice cold. "You need to leave immediately."

"We'll leave as soon our mission is fulfilled." Adri stood beside her brother. She held two thick sealed envelopes embossed with red wax and the seal of the Court. "Our mission is to give you these documents. May I approach you and your consort to hand them over?"

Sean studied the envelopes and the woman holding them. I imagined he was trying to detect signs of danger. "And if I refuse and remove you from our property by force?"

"We've stated we're here only to deliver a message," Bryan said. "Violence doesn't seem necessary, under the circumstances."

Not that long ago, Bryan and Adri had worked together with

Charles to save my life after I was nearly killed by a werewolf. Looking at them now, however, those days seemed long gone. That made me a little sad. I'd never thought of them as friends, but we'd been friendly.

"What's the message?" Sean asked. "You have ten seconds to deliver it, and then get the hell out."

Adri approached us with deliberate steps, keeping her hands in plain view to show she didn't have any weapons. Magic sparked brightly on my hands and coiled up my forearms. The wolves might be delayed by a few seconds while they shifted, but I was ready to attack or defend the moment something didn't look right.

Carefully, Adri handed one envelope to Sean and the other to me, gave us a little bow, and retreated, walking backward to watch us until she rejoined Bryan and the others.

Our names were written on the front of each envelope in elegant handwriting I recognized immediately. My stomach knotted. *Charles.*

A phone camera clicked from the direction of the enforcers, as if someone had documented the moment. Sean snarled.

"Mr. Maclin, Ms. Worth," Bryan said. "You have been served."

THREE

I'D SURVIVED A MANSION FALLING ON MY HEAD, ONLY TO HAVE A NINETY-PAGE indictment land on me next.

Honestly, given the choice, I would have preferred another mansion collapse.

The charges named Sean and me specifically, as well as our pack *and* the Were Ruling Council to boot. The indictments alleged Sean and I and our pack had aided and abetted Valas, the now-deposed and deceased former head of the Vampire Court, during and after the coup staged by Charles Vaughan.

Charles demanded our pack and the Were Council pay restitution to the Court for our alleged misdeeds. On top of that, the charges required that Sean and I stand trial by tribunal at the Vampire Court. If found guilty, we could face up to twenty years in prison. Charles also demanded we turn Matthias over to the Court, describing him as "stolen property."

News from Northbourne Manor, longtime headquarters of the Vampire Court of the Western United States, had been difficult to come by since the night of the coup. What little we'd heard indicated Charles had focused on asserting his authority over his new territory.

I would have thought he had more important issues to deal with than targeting us for prosecution, but apparently not.

I sat on the front porch steps to skim the nearly two-inch stack of documents while Malcolm read over my shoulder and Sean dealt with our angry pack. Rage made my hands shake so badly that every so often I had to put the pages down and take deep breaths. Not that I could focus very well anyway with my thoughts tumbling over each other like socks in the dryer. A trial...prison...*losing Matthias...*

As I read more, I veered wildly between numbness and the wild impulse to head straight to Northbourne to tell Charles to his face what he could do with these charges. Only the knowledge I'd never get through all the wards and guards protecting him kept me from doing just that.

About thirty minutes after the Vampire Court convoy departed, Carly Reese, owner of my favorite coffee shop and High Priestess of the Emerald Star coven, arrived at our house with her youngest coven member riding shotgun. They found the remains of a party, twenty furious werewolves, and one mage who wanted to burn down Vamp Court HQ and salt the ashes.

The petite High Priestess was about half the size of most of the werewolves standing in the front yard, but they cleared a path for her immediately. Even in jeans and a T-shirt that read *Witch and Famous*, with her shoulder-length curly hair in a ponytail, Carly's authority and power were unmistakable.

Taller and curvier than Carly, witch Katy Clark had already seen far more nightmares than most people encounter in their lifetimes. At sixteen, she'd fled the black magic coven run by her mother and grandmother and taken refuge with Carly, who'd welcomed into her into her coven, given her a job at the coffee shop, and guided her through the journey of becoming what Katy described as "a good-ish dark gray witch."

Now eighteen, Katy had her own apartment and earned a promotion to assistant manager at the shop. Along with lifelong struggles against using dark magic for good reasons, she and I had something else in common: family drama in *spades*. Katy's estranged mother Morgan Clark, a black witch, happened to be Charles Vaughan's consort, and her grandmother was Bridget Clark, High Priestess of the Silver Thorn Coven, who'd backed his coup.

"Thank you for coming," Sean said as Carly and Katy approached the front steps, duffel bags in hand.

"Hey, everybody." Katy flipped one of her long pink braids over her shoulder and tugged the hem of her frayed punk band T-shirt. Even someone as tough as her fidgeted under the gazes of twenty werewolves.

"I apologize for the welcoming committee." Sean scrubbed his face with his hands. "We've just had some unpleasant visitors."

"So I gathered. I'll get the story later. Hi, Alice." Carly studied me. "Well, I don't see anything right off the bat that makes me worry, but we'll take a closer look." She shooed me toward the front door. "Come on. We're going to your workshop."

I squeezed Sean's hand as I passed. He squeezed back and held on for an extra beat. I wanted to be out here with him and the rest of our pack, but my well-being was more important to him than just about anything else. So I followed Carly and Katy inside and left my copy of the Court documents on the kitchen island while we went downstairs.

Our small basement served as a magic workshop for Malcolm and me. I'd inlaid three concentric circles on the floor and lined up warded storage cabinets along one wall. There was just enough room for a narrow work table along an adjoining wall and space to walk around. It felt cramped sometimes, especially compared to my previous home's basement workshop, but I made do because the house was perfect for us and we were lucky to find a house with a basement at all.

As Carly and Katy unpacked, I told them about the visit from Charles's enforcers and the indictment. Carly's expression indicated Charles should be glad she wasn't a black witch anymore. For her part, Katy called the vamps some bad names that made me chuckle despite the grim situation.

"I'm so sorry, Alice." Carly stopped setting up their altar to give me a long hug. She smelled like incense and spices. Had she been baking? Maybe she'd used cinnamon—and was that nutmeg?—in her rituals. Either way, I suddenly yearned for one of her signature blueberry scones.

And because she knew me so well, she handed me a paper bag with two scones still warm from the oven. "Take two scones and call me in the morning," she said with a smile as she went back to setting up her altar in the smallest inlaid circle.

I sat on the work table with my legs dangling and ate while they worked. Maybe Carly somehow baked magic into her scones because the tension always eased from my shoulders and my steps felt lighter after eating one.

When they finished their preparations, I kicked off my shoes and put them under the work table next to Carly's sneakers and Katy's combat boots before joining the witches in front of their altar.

Carly began with a short prayer. "I ask the Universal Energies to open our third eyes that we might see everything positive or negative inside and outside Alice's body. We ask Hecate to surround Alice, Katrina, and myself with your protection. As I will this for us, so it must be."

With a beautiful athame in her right hand, Carly invoked the circle by walking around its perimeter three times. "I cast this circle in love and trust," she murmured. The scent of parchment and cinnamon grew stronger. "I cast this circle with the elements of Air, Water, Fire, and Earth. I cast this circle with protection to keep out anyone or anything that may cause harm to us."

Together, in the center of the circle, we closed our eyes and breathed deeply to clear our minds and prepare for the work ahead. One by one, with each exhale, I let go of my troubled thoughts. My heart rate slowed. My shoulders relaxed. My jaw no longer ached.

As I breathed, Carly and Katy walked around me, chanting, the words indistinct. Some kind of sweet smoke swirled around us and filled my nose. The last of the tension in my shoulders eased away, leaving me peaceful. If only I could bottle this feeling.

Carly murmured, "Open your eyes, Alice."

My heavy eyelids resisted obeying, but I did as she'd asked. The air wavered around me, smelling and tasting of smoke and parchment.

Beginning at the top of my head, Carly and Katy passed their hands over me from about a foot away. They moved slowly with palms outstretched, first along my front, then my sides, and finally my back.

Time felt hazy too inside the circle. I might have been standing for five minutes or an hour—I really could not tell for sure.

When Carly rested her hand on top of my head and murmured something that sounded like a blessing, my awareness bobbed to the surface as if I were waking up after a particularly fantastic and reju-venating nap.

I stretched, rolled my neck and shoulders, and opened my eyes. Apparently I'd closed them at some point.

While I got my bearings, Carly walked around the circle three times counter-clockwise, murmuring her thanks. "I open this circle with our thanks to the elements. Thank you, universe, for opening my third eye, and to Hecate for protecting us."

"You're both magical," I told Carly as Katy packed up their altar. The magic and scent of parchment that had surrounded us during the examination lingered in the air, soothing me even as thoughts of Charles and his damned indictments threatened to make me furious again. "No chance you could bottle this calming magic so I could sniff it when I feel like losing my shit?"

"Sometimes you need to feel what you feel," Carly said with a kind smile. "Even if it means you lose your shit."

I snorted. "You should put that on a coffee mug. I'd buy it. I take it by how calm you both are that neither of you found anything on me?"

"We didn't," Katy confirmed. "No hexes or black magic or anything else."

Maybe I just need a good night's sleep after all, I thought. "I'm sorry for calling you out in the middle of the night."

"Don't apologize. You had every right to be worried. We're happy to be here when you need us." Carly handed me a small round amulet that smelled like cinnamon. That explained the scent I'd noticed earlier. "As you know, our world contains more kinds of magic than there are grains of sand on a beach. So keep this close to you, just in case there's something going on Katy and I can't see yet."

Darn. That added a big asterisk to Katy's pronouncement that I was hex-free. But Carly was right—some kinds of magic were beyond their sight. I'd just have to keep an eye out for any more episodes of weirdness.

Well, *out-of-the-ordinary* weirdness. I had yet to have one day of my life without some kind of weirdness.

"Thank you." I pocketed the amulet, picked up my shoes, and followed her barefoot up the stairs with Katy behind us carrying their bags. "Sean will be relieved."

"Given everything you've been through, I don't blame him for fretting if you faint." She opened the basement door, paused for a beat, and said, "Hello."

I peered around her and spotted Matthias standing near the door. He still wore the shirt and slacks he'd donned for the ceremony. I hadn't known they made off-the-rack men's casual dress clothes in that size. Imagine the look on the clerk's face when Matthias walked into the local big-and-tall men's store asking about clothes for a backyard wedding.

Matthias had left the Court with nothing, not even the clothes on his back. He'd shifted for the first time wearing his enforcer uniform and clothing disintegrated during shifting because of the magic. I'd escaped from my grandfather with nothing but singed clothes and a photo I'd stuck in my back pocket. There was something about the fact that Matthias had joined us naked and vulnerable that got me right in the gut.

"I'm Carly Reese. Friend of the pack and witch extraordinaire." Carly emerged from the stairway and offered her hand. "I don't think we've met."

To my surprise, Matthias took her hand and bowed over it. "I know of you, High Priestess. It's an honor to meet you." He released her hand and turned to me. "Most of the pack has left. Sean and Ben are out back. They asked if you could join them if you feel up to it."

"Okay." I gave Carly another hug just for good measure. "Thanks again. You want me to walk you out to your car?"

"I would be honored to escort you both," Matthias said, surprising me again. "If Ms. Reese agrees."

"Call me Carly." She smiled at him. "Please."

I knew that look. She'd spotted a man who was hurting. Maybe it was good luck that he'd been nearby when we came out of the basement. On the other hand, Carly would have told me it was no accident that they'd crossed paths. She didn't believe in coincidences.

While Matthias accompanied Carly and Katy to the car, I found Sean and Ben on the deck drinking beers. The pack had been busy while we were in the basement. The only signs a wedding and party had taken place in our backyard hours earlier were the arbor and string lights. Everything else had been packed up and put away.

I declined a bottle of beer and settled in next to Sean on the loveseat. "They say as far as they can tell, I'm fine," I said in response to their unspoken question. "Carly gave me an amulet just in case, though."

"You were down there a long time." Sean nuzzled my hair. "But we figured if there was something wrong she would have come and told us."

"I'm sure she would have." I rested my head on his shoulder and breathed in his forest scent. "Carly also met Matthias. He's walking her to her car."

"Good." Sean moved restlessly, even with me at his side. His wolf must be howling in rage. "I've requested a meeting tomorrow with attorney Aaron Riddell about the indictment. I'd like you there as well, Ben."

"No problem." Ben took a long drink from his beer and shook his head. "What a load of bullshit this is."

I could not agree more. "What about Nan and Daniel?" I asked.

"I called Nan," Sean said. "They wanted to come back, but I told them to go on. We can always ask them to return if we need them to. Right now, I don't think it's warranted. This is a legal process. Nothing happens overnight."

"I cannot believe this is happening to us. Damn Charles and the Court all to hell." I rubbed my temples. When I looked up, both men were watching me like hawks. "I'm fine," I said crossly. "I'm just tired."

"Let's get to bed then." Sean rose and drew me to my feet. We said our goodnights to Ben, who walked around the house to the front where he'd parked his vehicle.

I gave our dog Rogue a treat, which he brought upstairs to his bed by the windows in our bedroom. Baby Daisy was still sound asleep on the bed. Sweet girl. That pup could sleep through anything when she was worn out. When I kissed her head, she didn't even stir.

Meanwhile, Matthias was nowhere to be seen. He might be outside keeping an eye out for uninvited guests. Esme had vanished too. She must be hunting. We'd installed a modified cat door in the window of the workout room so she could come and go as she pleased.

Sean and I changed into pajamas and curled up together under the covers. We'd left the indictments in our office downstairs, but they haunted my thoughts like specters floating at the end of the bed.

"What are we going to do?" I murmured sleepily, my head nestled against his chest. "Charles is out for our blood. So to speak."

"I don't think there's any 'so to speak' about it." Sean growled. "What I want to know is, what does he have to gain by doing this? He can't be willing to go to war with the Were Ruling Council and our pack over Matthias and some trumped-up, baseless charges. Not to belittle Matthias, but he's a human. When have you ever heard of the Court risking so much over one human?" After a beat, he added quietly, "Other than you."

My stomach clenched. "You don't think this is about me, do you?"

"I don't know. I don't have any reason to think so yet, but Charles never does anything without ulterior motives. And he's never hidden the fact he wants you." He kissed me. "We need to figure out what he really wants. This can't just be about Matthias. That doesn't make sense to me."

"Or to me." I wriggled closer to Sean and closed my eyes. *Charles, you scheming, no-good, fangy son of a bitch. What are you up to this time?*

Sean wrapped me in his warmth and comfort, nuzzled the back of my neck, and slid his hand under my tank top to hold me with his bare arm over my tummy.

He wouldn't be able to fall asleep until I did. Well, his *wolf* wouldn't fall asleep until I did, which amounted to the same thing. So for my sake and his, I focused on breathing in his forest scent and exhaling my tension one breath at a time.

Tonight, we had nothing but questions.

Starting tomorrow, we'd track down the answers.

I AM RUNNING for my life.

The tunnel yawns in front of me, pitch black and stinking of stagnant water and human waste. I see nothing but darkness. Only by keeping one hand on the slimy stone wall can I find my way forward. Any light would alert my pursuers to my location, so I run without it.

I could flee faster if not for the heavy burden I carry around my neck in a sling, but I cannot leave it behind. Its contents are precious—not just to me, but to the world.

I have to escape. I have to live. What other choice do I have?

Even this far underground, I know everything above is burning. That will be me if I am caught. I will burn brighter than the brightest star, but I will burn. My child will burn.

I hold him close to my breast as I run, praying he will stay asleep. The medicine I gave him will keep him quiet, but for how long?

Not long, not long enough, *the monster sings mockingly in my mind.* He will wake and begin to cry. He will tell them where you are. Leave him for the fire if you want to live.

Now his voice is all around me, booming so loudly I think they will hear him in the streets above: Did you really think you could take him and run? Stupid girl. Stupid, witless, ignorant girl.

I scream and lash out, but my magic and power find nothing to burn. He is not here in the tunnel with me. I am alone here with my child.

No, not alone. Footsteps ring out behind me, pounding on the wet stone. They are closing in. I will not make it to the end of the tunnel and escape. They will catch me, and my child and I will burn.

I spin to face my pursuers. Fire erupts from my hands. My child whimpers against my breast but does not cry.

"You will not take him!" I scream, and unleash the fires of Hell...

Someone crashed into me and pinned me flat, smothering me with their weight. I lashed out again. My fist connected with a jaw in the darkness.

My attacker cursed and grabbed my hands so tightly that I couldn't move. *"Alice!"* he shouted. "Alice, stop!"

I came awake all at once with a scream, like I was shot from a cannon out of sleep into the waking world. When I opened my eyes, I found Sean's glowing golden gaze inches from my own. He'd used his body weight to hold me still. His shirt smelled singed. My hands, immobilized in Sean's grip, tingled with magic.

We stared at each other. My chest heaved as I gasped for air and my skin felt clammy.

"Alice." He released one of my wrists so he could cup my face. "Can you hear me?"

"Y-yes." My voice sounded as shaky as the rest of me. The room spun on a wild axis.

"You're hyperventilating," he said. "Breathe slowly. You had a nightmare. You're all right. I'm here. You're safe."

I tried to slow my breathing so I didn't pass out. It took a long time. Fear gripped my chest as if someone were sitting on it. I hung on to his forearms just to feel something warm, to convince myself I was here in our bedroom and not still running through that horrible, stinking sewer.

When I managed a couple of slow, deep breaths, he freed himself from my grip and ran his hands over my body, probably checking for injuries.

"I'm sorry," I said. "I didn't hurt you, did I?"

"You got me with a good right hook, but I'll survive." He exhaled and kissed my forehead. "Who was attacking you?"

"I don't know. There was someone…" I shook my head, trying to make sense of it all. "Someone powerful was after me. He called me a stupid girl."

"Your grandfather?" Sean's eyes glowed golden. "You told me he used to call you that."

"I don't know." I couldn't remember the voice anymore. Only the words echoed in my mind.

"Who was he trying to take away that you had to fight to protect?" he persisted. "You shouted *You will not take him.*"

My stomach roiled. "My…son."

Sean froze. "Alice."

Damn it, now he was even more worried. "No, my son in the dream," I clarified. "Not *my* son."

"How do you know?" His eyes narrowed. "Did you see his face?"

"No, but I'm not psychic or clairvoyant. I don't see the future." I couldn't lie still on my back anymore. I rolled to my side and curled up. Thankfully, he let the subject go, at least for now.

He knew me well enough to understand I didn't want him to hold me right now, so instead of spooning behind me he lay facing me and gently brushed hair back from my face. Only then did I spot red marks on his chin.

I touched them with my fingertips. "What's this?"

"Scratches." He caught my hand in his and kissed my fingers. "You didn't know what you were doing."

Oh, no. "I hit you *and* I scratched you?"

"You were asleep and dreaming, Miss Magic. I'm fine. In five minutes it'll be healed." Sean rested his head against mine. "I'm just glad I woke you up before you set fire to the bed. *Again.*"

Despite everything, that made me smile, which was probably why he'd said it. "I've really got to stop doing that, don't I?" I asked, my tone wry.

He kissed me then, a gentle reclaiming that brought me back fully from the nightmare to the safety and warmth of our bed. I grabbed a fistful of his shirt so he knew I claimed him too and nipped his bottom lip with my teeth. My werewolf made that deep rumbly sound in his chest I loved so much.

He cupped my face in his hand so he and his wolf could hold my gaze. A shadow moved in his golden eyes: his wolf, pacing in agitation. "You fainted earlier, and now this. Do you really believe it was just a dream?"

If only I could give him—or myself—assurances. All I had were guesses and gut feelings at the moment.

"I think so." I sighed. "I've been so stressed and anxious, with my first 'family dinner' with Moses coming up tomorrow and now this Court mess. It got all tangled up in my head and became a bad dream. I'm sorry."

"Please don't apologize." He kissed the tip of my nose. "You want to tell me about the dream?"

I told him what I remembered, which wasn't much. The memory faded like smoke in the wind.

By the time I finished talking, the last of my fear had dissipated. When I yawned, Sean moved behind me and curled around my body, his arm across my stomach to hold me close.

"No more bad dreams tonight," he whispered in my ear. "I forbid it."

"You *forbid* it, huh?" I chuckled softly. "Is that a new alpha power I didn't know about?"

"Absolutely." He kissed the back of my neck and left his lips against my skin as if he wanted my taste *and* my scent. "Only the sweetest dreams for my Miss Magic from now on."

"If only it worked that way," I said, or wanted to say. Maybe I'd just thought it. In any case, that was my last thought before sleep swept me away.

CHAPTER
FOUR

Twenty minutes before my alarm was set to go off, I woke from a sound sleep to the dulcet tones of someone punching the heavy bag in the workout room down the hall, Rogue whining at the bedroom door, Sean yelling downstairs, and the angry screeches of our house dragon.

"Well, good morning to you all too." I sighed and threw back the covers.

Baby Daisy had curled up on Sean's side of our bed for her morning nap. I kissed her little head and she sighed in her sleep.

Our pup had been a gift from Theol, the same fae who'd given me a week in shifter form. Last year, courtesy of infection with the shifter virus and sorcerer magic, my half-shifter heritage had resulted in the creation of a wolf version of me. Malcolm had named her Daisy. I wasn't able to shift, but Daisy could leap out of me in either magical or solid form. When Malcolm and I visited the Broken World, Daisy served as our companion, guard, and guide. But only hours after we returned, she'd chosen to sacrifice her life to save mine after a sniper shot me, and I'd had no way to save her.

In return for rescuing him from a Dark Fae, Theol had offered me a miracle: the ability to shift into a wolf form of my own. Instead, I'd asked him to save Daisy if he could. Moments later, Sean and I held Baby Daisy in our arms.

So Baby Daisy wasn't our offspring—she was *me*. My wolf self reborn as a pup, with dashes of my magic, shifter magic, and fae magic all blended together. What she'd be able to do when she got older, we didn't know. At the moment she was mostly just an adorable agent of chaos.

Rogue started scratching at the door, so I got up to open it. He made a beeline for the sanctuary of his doggy bed by the window.

Esme, in dragon form, flew into the room and landed on the bed, our brand-new TV remote in her claws. Well, that explained Sean's uncharacteristic shouting.

Esme's new habit of stealing and hiding everything in our house that wasn't nailed down was driving us all up the wall. Pūķis were notoriously mischievous, at least according to legend. Esme was so young when I'd received her as a gift that she hadn't yet developed bad habits. Now mischief had become as important to her as guarding us and our home.

I reached for the remote. The little gray-and-scarlet dragon hissed and took to the air, her wings lifting her well out of my reach. Aggravated, I jumped for the remote. Esme dodged my hands and darted out of the room with her prize. She flew down the hall in the direction of the workout room and the modified cat door/dragon hatch that led to the backyard.

My shoulders slumped. "Fantastic," I told Rogue. "That's the third remote this week. And I can't find any of my phone chargers either. She even got the one that was in my locked car, for crying out loud. I have no idea how she did that."

Rogue rolled over and put his paw over his eyes. *Your cat-dragon, your problem*, his body language seemed to say.

"Thanks for the sympathy, dog," I muttered. He snuffled and wiggled deeper into the bed.

By the time I emerged from the bathroom, having showered and dressed, the house had quieted except for Rogue's snoring and the incessant steady *thump-thump-thump* of large fists pounding the shifter-proof heavy bag.

Matthias spent more time in the workout room than anywhere else. Sean assured me seemingly obsessive exercise was both healthy and typical for a newly turned shifter. I had my doubts. The nonstop thumps made me edgy. I knew better than to ignore my instincts, especially when it came to pack members.

So I broke one of my most sacred personal rules and decided to have a difficult talk with a difficult person before I had my first cup of coffee of the day.

The thumps ceased before I reached the workout room. Sharp werewolf ears couldn't have missed the sound of my footsteps, though the floor didn't creak and my shoes didn't make any noise I could hear. Nothing much got past a shifter, even a new one still getting used to...well, everything.

When I got to the doorway, Matthias stood at attention, his arms at his sides. He didn't have a Court uniform any more, so he'd adopted black joggers and a dark gray T-shirt with the Tomb Mountain Pack logo as his daily attire. Maybe after so much upheaval, he found comfort in a new kind of uniform.

He'd spent more than an hour punching the bag bare-handed, judging by his swollen, bloody knuckles. That wasn't much of an injury by either werewolf or Vampire Court enforcer standards, but I didn't like it. At all. I knew better than anyone that hurting himself was a sign of the trauma and abuse that he'd internalized. I empathized because I still struggled with that myself, though not as much as I used to.

"Good morning," I said with a smile. "Want to take a break and have a cup of coffee with me on the deck?"

I'd phrased it as a question, but he accepted it as an order, as I'd figured he would. I didn't know exactly how long he'd belonged to the Vampire Court. Long enough for him to obey without question and forget what it felt like to make his own decisions, apparently. That hurt my heart more than anything else about his situation.

He followed me downstairs and waited in the kitchen while I poured two cups of the nectar of the gods. As I added cream and sugar to mine, I overheard Sean in our home office leading a video meeting with Maclin Security employees. The reassuring rumble of his voice made me smile despite my tension.

Mugs in hand, Matthias and I went out the back patio door to the deck and settled into chairs at our four-seater table. Like Sean and Daniel always did, he automatically took the seat with the best view of the entire backyard so he could keep watch for potential threats.

The chair creaked when he sat down. He'd put on additional muscle since becoming a werewolf. Shifters tended to be muscular but more lean than bulky because they ran in wolf form so much. Matthias seemed determined to be the exception.

He might be trying to compensate in his human form for his wolf's traumatized condition, which he perceived as weakness though none of us saw him that way. Maybe he thought his wolf would grow bigger and stronger and be able to hide his trauma better. Not only would that not work, it threatened to make the psychological damage he'd experienced worse.

And maybe he thought if he *looked* the part, he could convince himself and everyone else he was thriving, when he was anything but.

I didn't ask him how he was; he'd only tell me he was fine. Instead, I sipped my coffee and looked around the backyard as the late January sunshine warmed us. My gaze swept over the thick stand of trees than lined our property and hid our house from view of our neighbors over the back fence.

Hmm...maybe Esme had a stash in the woods of all the items she'd swiped from our house. I should ask Sean to sniff around if he hadn't already thought to look there. All that stuff had to be some-*where*. Esme was a dragon, after all, and what was a dragon without her hoard?

My thoughts returned to Matthias. Sean might be his alpha—a situation both had to live with but neither would have chosen—but I was the heart of the Tomb Mountain Pack. As such, I'd helped Matthias change into a werewolf without the torment a newly turned shifter usually experienced. Now I needed to help him transition from a Court possession to a pack werewolf. A Change took minutes. Relearning how to be a man with free will and the love and support of a pack would take much longer.

I didn't have a step-by-step plan for this. How could I predict what Matthias would need from me from one day to the next, or even from hour to hour? I just followed my instincts and my heart. They'd done a pretty good job so far letting me know what to do and how to do it.

"What are your plans for the day?" I asked.

He rested his coffee mug on his knee and held my gaze for a few beats before lowering his stare to the wolf's-head pendant and sword ring I kept on a chain around my neck. No shifters could meet my eyes for very long. Though I wasn't a werewolf, I had a dominant presence in addition to being Sean's consort.

"I have no plans." His carefully neutral voice and expression gave nothing away, but I recognized the aura of loneliness when I saw it.

As much as I wanted to, I couldn't be here twenty-four hours a day to provide the support he needed and relied on, though I doubted he'd admit that to anyone, even himself. He'd be okay here in our home, but *okay* wasn't the same as getting better. I ought to know.

"I could use your help with something," I said.

He straightened automatically. "Yes?"

"Charles Vaughan has targeted us. The best defense is a good offense. We need ammunition. I would like you to compile all the information about Charles and the Court you have that might be helpful to us."

"I can't accept this assignment." His expression went flat. "I can tell you nothing I saw, heard, or learned about the Court during my time there."

His tone told me his silence was not a matter of choice. "They put a spell on you?" I asked, my voice gentle. "Is it a *geas?*"

"Yes." He flinched, as if simply hearing the word caused him pain. Maybe his grimace was at the memory of having the *geas* put on him to begin with.

I'd never experienced that kind of spell, thank goodness, but I knew a *geas* caused enormous suffering and even death if violated. Most included spellwork that killed the recipient outright if someone attempted to remove the spell. It was precisely the kind of move I'd expect the vampires to make, and yet my disgust and anger made my vision go red around the edges. Magic sparked on my fingertips.

Matthias apparently misinterpreted my reaction as anger directed at him. "I am sorry," he said earnestly.

"Don't be." I touched his arm. "We'll come back to that another time. Does the *geas* keep you from gathering new information from whatever sources you can find and passing it along to us?"

He tilted his head and considered. "I don't think so."

"Digging around might be dangerous. Are you comfortable with that?"

His nostrils flared like a wolf who'd caught a scent. "I am."

Sean had told me that information—especially when it was connected to a mystery or danger—triggered a werewolf's instincts like a kind of prey. That, in addition to their strength, agility, and other physiological advantages, was a big reason so many shifters went into private investigation and security work or related careers. Wolves liked to hunt, no matter who or what they were hunting.

And maybe Matthias didn't need to be sitting around our house marinating in his own dark thoughts. He needed a mission.

Matthias wouldn't be a stranger to digging up facts and rumors. He didn't have the Court's resources at his disposal anymore, but I didn't think that would hold him back all that much. He was as intelligent and capable as anyone I'd ever met.

"Then let's see what you can find out about current conditions at the Court and we'll go from there," I said. "Whatever you need, just let us know. If you can be ready with at least a preliminary report tomorrow morning, that would be great." After a moment, I added, "By the way, Arkady is working on gathering intel too. She'll be here tomorrow morning at eight to tell us what she's found out."

He didn't react visibly, but his words sounded clipped when he said, "Then I will ensure my report is *especially* thorough and ready by then."

Last year, Matthias and Arkady had been an item for a few months—an on-again, off-again relationship that couldn't survive their very different perspectives on what it meant to work for the Vampire Court and the demands their respective jobs put on their lives.

Now Matthias's life had turned upside down. Meanwhile, Arkady was now my business partner and happily in lust with Ronan. I wasn't sure how Matthias felt about their very different situations, other than his tone indicated some raw feelings remained.

"What will you be doing today?" he asked.

I took a deep breath and exhaled. "Sean, Ben, and I have a meeting with an attorney later this morning, and then tonight I have a..." I swallowed hard. "A dinner engagement."

He leaned forward and seemed to...loom larger, as if he'd grown a foot in both height and width in that moment. His golden shifter magic prickled on my skin. "You're troubled by your dinner engagement tonight?" he rumbled. "You don't feel safe?"

The question itself didn't startle me, but his growl and sudden aggressiveness did. Everything in his body language just now reminded me of Ben, who was third in the pack hierarchy, and even Nan.

Like last night when he'd seen me faint, Matthias reacted

instantly and instinctively to a perceived threat—more intensely and more quickly than I'd expected. But what did that mean?

I could lie to Matthias and tell him I wasn't worried about tonight's dinner and maybe he'd believe me, but I didn't want to tell him anything but truth, even if a white lie would make him feel better. The Vamp Court operated on lies, manipulation, cruelty, and victimization. Our pack didn't tolerate any of those things. Sean and I had chosen to lead by example in this and every other core value of the Tomb Mountain Pack.

"Yes, I'm concerned," I told Matthias, my hands folded around my mug. Even empty, its familiar weight reassured me. "I'm meeting with a dangerous person. I can't know for sure what they'll do, or *try* to do. But I'll have Malcolm with me and we'll fight if anyone comes at us. We'll get back here safe if we have to burn the place we're going and everyone in it to the ground."

His magic no longer prickled, but he continued to lean forward and his frown remained. "If Sean approves, I will go with you," he said. "Two allies at your back are better than one."

"Thank you for offering," I said sincerely. "But this is something I have to do on my own."

"All right." After an uncharacteristic hesitation, he asked, "Are you meeting with Charles Vaughan?"

"No," I promised. "I'm not going anywhere near Charles or Northbourne."

The tension in his shoulders eased a bit. "Good." He set his coffee cup on the table and met my gaze again, this time for longer. The reason for his direct gaze became immediately apparent when he asked, "Can I ask you to be honest with me?"

From some people I might have taken that question personally, but not from him. He'd probably experienced very little honesty prior to joining our pack.

"I will never be anything but honest with you," I stated. "I might not always be able to tell you something, but if that's the case I'll say so. I won't lie to you. None of us will."

He didn't seem convinced, but he didn't argue the point. "Sean gives others in the pack orders, but rarely to me. He asks me rather than commands me. Why is that?"

That was a more complicated question than he probably thought. It also intersected with what I'd noticed about his demeanor earlier in this conversation. How to answer in a way that would make sense?

When I didn't respond immediately, he added, "I am more comfortable with orders. Requests and options are...confusing. I wondered if his way of addressing me was punishment for attacking your pack."

"Sean isn't passive-aggressive," I assured him. "He's absolutely still angry about you attacking us on Valas's orders and kidnapping Daniel and me. If you'd survived the mansion collapse but hadn't been Changed, he would have killed you."

"He has said that, yes." He didn't seem bothered that Sean had expressed that sentiment. "I would have done the same if our situation was reversed."

"You asked why he doesn't give you orders like he does the others," I said. "Two main reasons. First, he understands what you've been through better than you think. He doesn't feel sorry for you, but he knows you and your wolf. Alphas aren't the merciless killing machines some people think. They're protectors first and foremost. Part of that is treating each member of the pack as he believes they should be treated, based on who they are and what they need."

Matthias thought about that for a bit. "And second?" he asked.

This was the tricky part. How could I explain to Matthias who and what he was as a man, werewolf, and pack member?

I was suddenly reminded of my own recent epiphany about being the heart of our pack. No one could have told me I was our heart or explain what that meant. Like Dorothy realizing she had the power to take herself home without the Wizard's help, I'd had to figure it out for myself. I had to guide Matthias to a similar revelation.

"Have you noticed how Sean speaks to Nan and Ben versus other members of the pack?" I asked. "He rarely gives them orders either."

"Which makes sense, because they're his beta and third and much closer to him in dominance." He frowned. "I don't see the connection."

"Give it a minute. What would you do if you felt any member of our pack was in danger?"

"Find the danger and kill it," he said automatically.

"Why?"

"Because…" He frowned, probably searching for the right words. "Because that's why I am here," he finished.

"Most werewolves wouldn't have phrased it like that," I said. "Of course shifters are protective of their pack mates, but they wouldn't say it's their reason for being. If I asked Sean, Nan, or Ben that question, though, they would answer the same way. So would I, if you'd asked me." I rested my elbows on my knees. "Do you know what that means?"

I knew he got it when his poker face disappeared and his eyes widened. This was certainly the first time I'd ever seen Matthias startled.

"When you realize who you are, how much power you possess, and the responsibility you carry, that's when you're capable of holding up an entire mansion to protect those you love," I told him, alluding to what I'd done to keep us alive after Valas's palatial lair collapsed with us trapped in the cellar. "Sean, Nan, Ben, you, and I are protectors. It's who we are. It's why we're here."

"You believe my wolf is dominant." Matthias glanced at his knuckles. They'd healed from punching the heavy bag without wrappings or gloves, but blood had dried on his skin. He brushed it off as he thought. "I am physically strong, but my wolf isn't ready for a leadership role."

His wolf remained battered and cowed by so many years of servitude at the Court. I'd seen that for myself during his Change, and Sean could observe it every time he looked into Matthias's eyes.

"Not yet," I agreed. "Give it time. You're still healing. I wasn't ready for my role when I joined this pack either. The good news is, there's no rush. You'll get there when you get there."

We sat in thoughtful silence for a few minutes. I was about to go inside to refill my coffee when he said, "Thank you for helping me understand what I am."

"It's a lot to think about, huh?"

"Yes." After a beat, he asked, "The Court wants me back to kill me for siding with Valas against Charles Vaughan. I think they're targeting you now because I'm a member of your pack, even though Sean is on the Were Ruling Council and you have a long history with Charles. Am I correct?"

And just like that, all my rage and frustration over Charles's bullshit came roaring back. I rubbed the bridge of my nose. "Possibly. You know as well as I do there's never a simple explanation for anything the Court does—or what Charles Vaughan does."

"I thought he would allow me to live because he knows killing me would further alienate you."

I doubted it was possible for me to be any *more* alienated from Charles than I already was, but Matthias might not be wrong. "Who knows what goes through that guy's head." I rose and rested my hand on Matthias's massive bicep. "In any case, you're one of us now. Anyone messes with you, they're messing with the whole pack. That's twenty werewolves and one totally badass mage. It would be a super-duper bad idea."

A ghost of a smile made the corners of his mouth turn up. "Super duper," he agreed. "Thanks, Alice. I'll start on my report immediately. And if you change your mind about wanting additional backup tonight for your meeting, please let me know. It would be my privilege to join you."

If my meeting was with anyone but Moses, I would happily invite Matthias to join me. And I might on a different night, if the situation called for it. Not tonight, however. Tonight I had to face my grandfather one-on-one. I had a point to make.

"Thank you. Rain check." I patted his arm and headed for the patio door. "I need more coffee. Coming inside?"

"In a while. I need to think."

For the first time, hearing him say that didn't make my stomach churn.

I went inside and closed the sliding door behind me. He'd already turned to face the backyard, his coffee mug resting on his knee.

Sean emerged from the office and met me halfway to the kitchen. He wrapped his arms around me and kissed the top of my head.

"Is your meeting over?" I asked, my voice muffled by his shirt.

"Not yet. I just told them I'd be right back." He nuzzled my hair. "Thank you for talking to him."

The office shared an exterior wall with the deck. He'd probably heard every word. "Was everything I said okay?" I asked.

"Better than okay." He tipped my chin up and kissed me. "You said what he needed to hear. You're getting good at this, Miss Magic."

"I try." I smacked his butt. "Get back to work, Wolf. I've got stuff to do before our meeting with Aaron."

"Yes, ma'am." Chuckling, he returned to the office.

CHAPTER

FIVE

At ten o'clock, Sean, Ben, Malcolm, and I gathered in attorney Aaron Riddell's posh conference room on the twentieth floor of a downtown office building.

Years ago, Aaron and I had a relationship that ended when he wanted more than just something physical. Now we were close friends as well as lawyer and client. Unfortunately, I needed his legal help now more than ever.

On the table in front of Sean was a copy of the indictment filed by the Vampire Court. Ben had channeled some of his anger into organizing it in a binder with tabs. One corner was bent because he'd thrown it at the wall at some point.

"The Vampire Court sure wants their pound of flesh," Aaron said, his voice grim. As usual, the tall African-American lawyer wore a tailored designer suit that flattered his broad shoulders and athletic build.

"About three hundred pounds of flesh, or whatever Matthias weighs," Ben quipped, but without much humor and none of us laughed. "Which they can't have," he added. "These charges are bullshit. Our people were victims in Valas's plot, not perpetrators.

Matthias Albrecht, who they demand be returned to the Court as its 'stolen property,' is a person, not property. And he damn sure wasn't *stolen*. The Were Ruling Council's laws are clear about the rights of pack members once an alpha accepts them. The Court has always respected the Council's laws—even the ones they don't like."

Ben, like most of the pack, was a long way from forgiving Matthias, so I was surprised at how quickly and vehemently he'd spoken up on our newest pack member's behalf. Maybe it was the idea of calling someone "property," or that he understood that nothing Matthias had done was of his own choice, or simply that Charles was our enemy and an enemy of our enemy was at least a potential ally. Maybe his wolf instinctively wanted to help protect Matthias because his wolf was vulnerable. Whatever the reason, I was glad he didn't want Matthias turned over to the Court.

"Since the Were Ruling Council is also named in the indictment, I've reached out to their legal team," Aaron told us. "I have yet to get a response."

"Not surprising." Sean's voice was more than half growl. "The Council's priority has always been to protect their own interests. Our pack will have to do the same."

While Ben seethed openly, Sean's rage had become cold and hard and turned him nearly glacial. My hand rested on his thigh under the conference table. His muscles felt like steel.

Meanwhile, my anger and and frustration grew with every passing minute, to the point I'd eaten only a few bites of breakfast and my stomach hadn't stopped churning since we'd left the house on our way here. It wasn't like I'd expected to walk into Aaron's office and have him tell us it would all be fine, but seeing him so uncharacteristically grim really drove home the point that we were in seriously hot water.

Aaron steepled his fingers in a very lawyerly pose. "Just so I'm clear, on New Year's Eve, Alice and Mr. Daniel Holiday were kidnapped during an attack on members of your pack on the orders of Valas. A team led by Matthias Albrecht transported Alice and

Daniel to a location in Colorado where Valas held them captive. At some point during Alice and Daniel's escape and the destruction of the home where Valas had taken refuge, Valas died and Matthias became a werewolf. You subsequently chose to bring him into your pack. Is that an accurate summary of events?"

I took a deep breath and exhaled. "Yes. That's exactly what happened."

"All right." Aaron studied me. "But now, as your attorney, I need to know the rest."

And because I trusted him, and Malcolm had already ascertained the room contained no listening or recording devices, I told him the whole story.

I began with our first encounters with Matthias in his capacity as Court enforcer, continued with our kidnapping on New Year's Eve, and concluded with how Daniel infected Matthias during a fight and why we'd opted to bring him into our pack. The only details I left out were that Daniel was my biological father and that we'd killed Vlad Țepeș at Valas's mansion.

Aaron listened, only stopping me to ask brief questions. When I finished, we all refilled our coffee mugs from the pot on the table as he thought about everything I'd revealed. Sean rubbed my back as I hunched over in my chair. As clinical as I'd tried to be while telling the story, the memories still left me nauseous, angry, and shaky.

"I have some concerns," Aaron said finally, in what might have been one of the biggest understatements of his career.

I sat up and folded my hands around my coffee mug like a security blanket. Sean pulled my chair closer to his and left his hand on my lower back.

"This indictment by the Court is of course our primary legal consideration," Aaron continued. "But by your own admission, Daniel Holiday committed a federal crime by infecting Matthias against his will. That information need not go beyond this room, but it will be extremely difficult to prevent others from coming to the conclusion based on circumstantial evidence that Daniel was responsible for the infectious bite. If Matthias cooperates with prosecutors and identifies who bit him, they will file charges immediately. As you know, the mandatory sentence for infecting a human with the shifter virus against their will is life in federal prison with no chance of parole."

The thought of my father going to prison had been one of many concerns preventing me from getting a good night's sleep since our return from Colorado.

Sean rubbed my back again. "Matthias won't identify the source of his infection to anyone."

Aaron raised his eyebrows. "On your orders, as his alpha?"

"By his own decision. I didn't need to give him any orders."

"To Matthias, the bite was no different than any other injury he's ever gotten during a fight," I explained to Aaron. "He doesn't hold it against Daniel, especially since he instigated the fight in the first place by kidnapping us."

"But if he's subpoenaed—" Aaron began.

"If subpoenaed, he will testify the bite occurred during a physical fight involving a lot of combatants," Sean said. "Which is true. There's no way to know for sure who was responsible. The destruction of the house where this occurred means no one will ever know all the people who were there. Unlike a vampire's bite, the shifter virus can't be traced from the person who was bitten back to who bit them. Theoretically, it could have been anyone."

Theoretically, my father might not spend the rest of his life in federal prison. Theoretically, my pack and I might not be implicated in the cover-up. Theoretically, the Were Ruling Council and the feds couldn't prove anything. *Theoretically.* I'd started to hate that word lately because it was one of only a few things standing between us and total disaster.

"That's all very true." Aaron nodded slowly. "And I admire that you've already prepared a strategy. We can discuss it more if it becomes necessary. At the moment, we need to focus on this indictment from the Court and legal strategies for how to proceed. First and foremost—"

"First and foremost, Matthias is a member of our pack, and we are not handing him or anyone else over to the Court," Sean stated. "The rest of the charges are baseless."

Aaron said nothing for several moments. I couldn't tell if he was frustrated with Sean's interruptions and counting to ten or just formulating a response.

"So, moving forward," Aaron said finally. "I've argued before the Court before, as Alice has probably told you, but I can't claim expertise. A Vampire Court proceeding is more like a tribunal. Their laws, procedures, and rules of evidence are different. If we do end up in Vampire Court, I will bring on additional counsel whose specialty is Vampire Court law. I'll need co-counsel with more experience and knowledge of their laws and rules."

"What about Matthias, in the meantime?" Sean asked.

Aaron tapped the indictment. "From what I see in the documentation provided by the Court, they have a strong legal claim on him."

Ben growled quietly. "Based on what?"

"Primarily, the contract Matthias signed when he became an enforcer for the Court. As you mentioned, he was initially bound to Charles Vaughan, who then later transferred him to Valas's 'keeping,' to use the Court's terminology."

"Valas is dead." My voice was sharper than I'd intended because I hated even hearing her name, so I tried to soften my tone and added, "She's not *keeping* anything anymore, except maybe a seat warm in Hell."

Ben chuckled, but Aaron remained grim. "That may be, but under Court law, Matthias's contract is with the Court as an entity, not with Valas herself. Valas's death didn't release him from his obligation. And neither does his new status as a werewolf, I'm afraid."

Fear and anger made my fingers tighten on Sean's leg.

He took my hand and squeezed. "I don't accept that," he stated, his eyes golden. "As a pack, we do not accept it. I'm not handing him over. We have to find a different solution."

"What about the Were Ruling Council?" Aaron wanted to know. "Will they stand with you against the Court on this? Will they endorse your refusal to hand Matthias over?"

Sean, Ben, and I exchanged glances. "That's a big question mark," I admitted. "Sean's on the Council, but in this matter he has to recuse himself from their discussions *and* their decision, obviously. At the moment, we don't know what they'll do."

"With my vote excluded, if they voted today with six members, the Council would be split three to three, I think," Sean said. "No definite decision is still a decision, though, because if they opt *not* to act, that is in effect a decision in favor of the Court and against us."

"We'll get a hearing before the Council," Ben told Aaron. "It'll be our only chance to influence them one way or the other. If they don't vote to stand with us, we'll have to fight the Court on our own—in the courtroom, or outside it."

Meaning when the Court's forces came to collect Matthias from us and we'd have to fight hand-to-hand, or hand-to-claw. To the death.

I felt sick and furious and a dozen other emotions. The mess seemed so big, so complex, that I hardly knew how to fight it. I knew how to square off against my grandfather or other enemies. You beat them with your fists, your gun, your magic, or your brains. I had no experience beating anyone with the law. As crazy as it might sound, I would rather have faced Charles in a physical fight than in a courtroom—especially Vampire Court.

Aaron leaned forward and folded his hands on the table. "Alice, Sean, Ben...I would like to tell you I have this all well in hand and you have nothing to worry about, but I can't tell you that. This situation is dire. The Court has demanded financial remunerations and Sean and Alice's imprisonment in addition to Matthias's return to their 'keeping.' They've decided to come for you with everything they've got, at least in a legal sense."

"And even if the legal way fails, they have other methods at their disposal," Ben said. "Their forces outnumber ours by a significant margin."

Half of our members thought bringing Matthias into our pack had been a colossal mistake. Maybe doing so had kicked a hornet's nest, but that didn't make it a mistake. The vamps were in the wrong here, not us. We just needed them—and the Were Ruling Council—to see it that way.

And I believed in Sean and our pack. I believed in Aaron too. As long as I believed, I had hope.

"Find us a legal reason to not hand Matthias over to the vamps," Sean told Aaron. "Prepare our defense for the other charges."

"I will do my damndest." Aaron finished his coffee and poured himself more. "And what about the Were Ruling Council?"

Sean didn't hesitate. "The Council will side with us. We will make that happen."

I wished I had half his confidence. Several members of the Council had hated me since day one. They hated Nan even more. And when we brought a former Vampire Court enforcer into our pack and blew up a century-long détente between the Court and the Council... well, suffice to say none of us would be on their Christmas card list this year.

But Sean was right—we did not accept that we had to turn Matthias over to the Court for likely execution. We didn't owe the vamps a damn cent and we didn't deserve to end up in prison. There had to be a way to protect Matthias and the rest of our pack without dying in battle with the Court.

What that way was, however, I had no idea. And judging by everyone else's expression, neither did they.

As we prepared to leave, Aaron took me aside. "I already said congratulations, but I wanted to say it again," he said with a smile, indicating my ring. "I'm sorry this Court bullshit is taking away from celebrating your engagement. You and Sean deserve to just be happy."

"We *are* happy," I assured him. "I promise we are."

"I'm glad." He grew serious. "I know your plate is full right now, but one of my colleagues, Philippa Grayson, has a client who needs a mage private investigator with your special talents."

My mouth quirked. "Which special talents in particular is she after? The legal ones? Or the ones that lead to you telling me not to give you any of the details?"

"Fair question." Aaron chuckled. "Philippa wants everything on the up-and-up. I don't know much about the case, obviously, but it sounds like she's got a…unique situation."

"That's ninety-five percent of a mage PI's cases." I pinched the bridge of my nose—a habit I'd picked up from Sean. "I don't have another case at the moment, but keeping Matthias alive and Sean and me out of vamp prison sounds like it's going to take all my brain cells."

"All three of them," Malcolm interjected. I gave him my middle finger behind my back. Over by the door, Ben saw my gesture and chuckled.

"I told her I would ask if you were available for a phone call and consultation today," Aaron said. "Reading between the lines, I think Philippa's got a problem she doesn't know how to handle, and that's why I told her I'd ask. If you knew Philippa, you'd understand how unusual something has to be for her to ask if I know a mage PI willing to consider—and I quote—'extraordinary possibilities.'"

"So of course you thought of me." I sighed. "I guess I'll accept that as a compliment."

How well would I be able to focus on a case with all this going on? Then again, maybe like Matthias I could use something else to think about besides wanting to punch Charles in the nose. I couldn't afford to not take on any clients until we sorted out the Court mess either. The indictments had just landed on us. The case might take months to go to court.

And maybe more to the point, I owed Aaron big time for coming through for me a dozen times over the years. He'd never asked me for a favor before.

"Okay, fine," I said finally. "I'm sufficiently intrigued to take her call and we'll go from there. No promises about saying yes, though."

"That's all I can ask. Thank you, Alice." Aaron gave me a hug. "Keep your chin up. We'll figure out a way to win."

"We will." This time I said it with absolute certainty because I wouldn't accept any other outcome. "And somehow, some way, we'll make Charles regret making an enemy of us."

CHAPTER

SIX

OLIVER HENSLEY HAD APPARENTLY KILLED A BARTENDER.

The question on the table was whether or not he'd *murdered* her.

"Ms. Worth, thank you very much for coming." Oliver's attorney, Philippa Grayson, sat at the head of the Hensleys' dining table to my right. "We realize it's probably quite unusual for you to meet with clients on such short notice."

Philippa wore a designer suit and her glossy auburn hair looked as though she'd just walked out of a salon. I didn't get intimidated by such things, but I'd be the first to admit my off-the-rack slacks and top, lightly scuffed boots, and leather jacket would have fit in better at a bar than either her posh office or the Hensleys' beautiful home. Good thing I wasn't here to impress anyone with my outfit.

"Not as unusual as you might think," I said. "As a mage private investigator, sometimes moving quickly is a matter of survival." And since small talk was neither my thing nor getting us anywhere fast, I turned my attention to Philippa's client, who sat across the table from me with his wife.

I'd done a quick background check on Oliver and Gracie Hensley after getting off the phone with Philippa. Oliver was a thirty-two-

55

year-old civil engineer. A year younger, Gracie worked part-time as a teacher's aide at a small magnet school. They'd graduated from the same high school and university. A perfectly ordinary couple with a nice house that appeared cozy and comfortable. And neither of them had so much as a parking ticket.

More than anything, I needed to get a better sense of who Oliver was, but he'd remained grim and pretty much silent since I arrived. His right hand was bandaged.

"How are you today, Mr. Hensley?" I asked.

"Call me Oliver." He forced a fleeting smile. "I'm glad to be out of jail and home, even if I've got an ankle monitor making sure I don't go any farther than our mailbox."

Judging by the shadows under his eyes, he hadn't been sleeping or eating much. Gracie looked no better.

Blond and blue-eyed, with a runner's lean physique, Oliver wore a button-up shirt and khakis, while red-haired Gracie had chosen a green top and beige slacks. They'd dressed up for this meeting, but it didn't take a PI to notice they'd basically just gone through the motions. Clearly, Gracie had been crying right before I arrived. No amount of makeup or eyedrops could hide her swollen, red-rimmed eyes.

Apparently I wasn't the only one not interested in small talk. "Did you get a chance to read through the materials I emailed?" Philippa asked.

"I did, thanks." I indicated my phone on the table in front of me. "I'd like to hear from Oliver what happened the day before yesterday —the day Madison Fernell died. Start when you got up that morning."

"Does he have to?" Gracie wiped her eyes with a tissue. "You've got the reports. He's already been through it so many times with so many people."

"I know." My voice remained businesslike. "But I need to hear the story directly from him."

She didn't appear to like my tone very much, but that was her problem, not mine. I was a long way from believing Oliver's version of events, much less deciding to take this case—even without taking into consideration how much was already on my plate.

Judging by Malcolm's expression and body language, my potential client faced an even more uphill battle to convince him than me. My ghost sidekick floated to my left, arms crossed, as he studied Oliver.

"It's okay, Gracie." Oliver squeezed his wife's hand, took a deep breath, and seemed to steel himself. "Ms. Worth is right. How can she know I'm telling the truth if I don't tell her everything that happened?" He glanced at Philippa. "Is it all right?"

She nodded. "Tell her everything you've told me."

With the green light from his attorney, Oliver took a long drink of coffee and settled in to tell his story. "As you probably know from what Philippa sent you, I'm a civil engineer. I work for a company called Piper Herrin downtown."

When he paused, I made a rolling gesture. "Go on."

"On the day all this happened, everything started out completely normal," he continued. "I got up as usual around five thirty, went for a run, and got to the office by eight. I had meetings in the morning, grabbed a quick lunch from a food truck in the square about two blocks from our building, and ate at my desk. During the afternoon I worked on reports in my office. I stayed at work until a little before six."

He definitely sounded like he'd been through this a dozen times, but not necessarily in the same way as if he'd rehearsed the speech. Having been in the hot seat at the cop shop myself more than once, I knew they made you tell the same damn story again and again hoping you'd slip up and change it.

"Did you encounter anyone during the day you thought was strange?" I asked, looking up from my notes. "Or notice anything at all out of the ordinary?"

Oliver rubbed his face with his non-bandaged hand. "You don't know how many times I have wracked my brain trying to think of anything. I've replayed the entire day more times than I can count. No, I didn't meet anyone on my morning run. No one came into our office who didn't work there. I only stepped outside to get lunch. The one person I talked to was the man who's been in that square selling sandwiches for the last two years. I walked straight to the square and back. I didn't talk to anyone on the way there or coming back—as far as I know."

I raised my eyebrows. "As far as you know?"

He trembled so badly he could barely lift his coffee mug. "If I don't remember hurting Madison Fernell, would I remember if I met whatever possessed me and made me do what I did?"

The shaking didn't look faked to me. Neither did the fear in his eyes when he added, "And how do I know it's not still here, hiding inside me? Jail was the worst place I've ever been, but I didn't want to come home. I was afraid I'd do something to my wife. I only let Gracie bond me out because I didn't feel safe there, even in a cell by myself."

"Don't say that." Gracie choked back a sob. "I know you'd never hurt me."

"Let's circle back to that later," I said before they got too emotional to talk. "So you got lunch, ate at your desk, and stayed in the office until about six o'clock. What did you do next?"

"I packed up my bag and left." He took a shaky breath. "On the way out of the building, I talked to three coworkers who were in the lobby, then walked two blocks to the parking garage. I took the stairs up to level five, unlocked my car, and put my bag in the back seat. I remember all of that as clear as day, down to what I was thinking about on the way to my car. But after I put my bag in my car..." Oliver closed his eyes and hung his head for a few beats before meeting my gaze again. "After that, I don't remember a damn thing. Almost two hours, totally gone. It's all a complete blank." He went quiet again.

Oliver certainly wasn't the first suspect to claim amnesia about a crime. I expected my gut to tell me he was lying, but it didn't. Instead of skepticism, my concern—and my curiosity—began to grow.

"When you came to, where were you?" I prompted.

"Some alley near the Eleventh Street bridge." He took a deep breath and let it out slowly. "I'd never been there before as far as I can remember. I don't drink, so I don't go to the bar district much. The first thing I remember after the blank is two delivery truck drivers yelling at me. I look down and I'm covered in blood and holding a knife, and I'm standing over someone's b-body. One of the delivery drivers tackled me and took the knife away."

Gracie put her head down on her folded arms, her shoulders shaking with sobs. Oliver rubbed her back and left his hand resting there. "I remember being arrested, but it's kind of a blur. I think I was in shock. Paramedics treated some cuts on my hand." He raised his bandaged right hand, which trembled. "The cops shoved me in the back of a patrol car and took me to the station. I sat in a room by myself for over an hour. I had no idea what was going on. When they finally came to talk to me, that's when I found out I was under arrest for murder."

So far he came across as legitimately grief-stricken, confused, and terrified. Could this be for real?

"What did you tell the detectives?" I asked.

"Same thing I told Philippa and you. I told them I didn't remember anything, but they didn't believe me. They really think I killed a woman I've never seen before in my life. I can't believe they think I'm a killer. *I am not a killer.*" His voice caught. "I swear I'm not. Something must have possessed me or made me do it."

"He's not the only one." Gracie raised her head and leaned forward. "There are *three* other cases, Ms. Worth. It's all been in the news. Nobody knows what's going on. The police don't know. They just keep arresting people. You've got to help us."

I had no doubt she believed in Oliver's innocence one hundred percent. Philippa had a lawyer's practiced poker face, so I couldn't tell if she bought the story or not. I supposed to her it didn't matter if he was lying or truthful—she'd defend him at trial to the best of her ability either way.

Nothing mattered *more* to Malcolm and me than Oliver's honesty, though. We had zero interest in helping a killer get away with murder.

At the moment, we had two salient and inescapable facts before us. First, Madison Fernell was dead, and from what the news reported, her death had been particularly savage.

Second, this murder fit a terrifying pattern. Three brutal assaults and now a murder had taken place in the past two weeks. Each of the alleged perpetrators claimed to have no motive, no connection to the victims, and no memory whatsoever of the attacks. Like many others in town, Malcolm and I had followed the cases in the news.

Despite our concern about the strange crime wave, we hadn't anticipated becoming involved. But now Malcolm and I found ourselves in Oliver and Gracie Hensley's dining room listening to a desperate man claim he had no memory of killing a twenty-six-year-old bartender on her way to work.

If these attacks *were* caused by something paranormal or super-natural, whoever or whatever was responsible had quickly developed a voracious appetite for brutality and blood.

"Which detectives did you speak to when you were arrested?" I asked. That information had not been included in Philippa's email.

She slid two business cards emblazoned with the police department's seal over to me.

I recognized the names immediately. "Diaz and Ferguson."

She regarded me with raised eyebrows. "You know them?"

"Yep." I tapped the cards on the table. "We go way back."

I didn't really want to think about the last time I'd seen Detective Ernie Diaz and his partner Joel Ferguson in person, which was in an interrogation room after the murder of my mentor Mark Dunlap. I'd always gotten along all right with Diaz, but Ferguson had disliked me from the moment we'd crossed paths. I wasn't sure if it was personal or not. He didn't seem to like mages or supes in general.

I returned the cards to Philippa. "So, Oliver, you told the detectives you had no memory of killing Madison. What else did you tell them?"

"I told them I'd never met her and I certainly had no reason to kill her." He sighed. "They don't believe me."

"I can't blame them for that." I made my voice and expression harsh to see how he would react. It was one thing to calmly tell a story, and very much another to show the right emotions during a confrontation. "A lot of suspects claim they don't remember anything about their crimes. The cops and prosecutors know it's a lie every time. So do juries."

Philippa didn't react, but Gracie bristled. "Hey. Don't call him a liar."

I ignored her and focused on Oliver. "I don't believe the 'I blacked out' excuse any more than Diaz, Ferguson, and the DA do. So tell me why I should believe you."

"I don't know how to convince anyone." He sagged in his seat. "All the evidence anyone can see points straight to me. I was holding the knife. I cut my hand when I...I stabbed her. I was covered in her blood." His voice broke.

While he struggled to regain his composure, Gracie leaned her head against his shoulder and held his uninjured hand in both of hers. Philippa shuffled papers.

Meanwhile, I watched him, looking for any tells that I was being bullshitted—and finding none.

Finally, Oliver met my gaze again. "Ms. Worth, I may go to prison for the rest of my life if I can't find a way to prove my story. All I can do is look you in the eye and swear I didn't know her and I don't remember anything between the parking garage and getting tackled by a delivery driver. I did not murder Madison Fernell." He said it without looking away or giving any indication he was lying.

I was no werewolf or vampire who could smell or sense deceit, but he might be telling the truth.

I wasn't the only one warming up to the idea. Malcolm touched my shoulder so he could talk to me in my head. *I hate to say it, but I kinda believe him*, he said.

Kinda, as in fifty-fifty? I asked.

My ghost sidekick waggled his hand. *More like eighty-twenty in favor of believing him. That's a big change for me. I came in here feeling ten-ninety the other way.*

He let go of my shoulder and drifted back. We tended to keep our telepathic conversations short in front of other people so I didn't sit silently staring into space like I'd gone catatonic.

"Ms. Worth." Philippa jotted something on her notepad and then tapped her pen. "Hypothetically, if Oliver is telling the truth and he was either possessed or magically compelled to do something against his will, what possible evidence might we find?"

"The first step would be to look for trace on Oliver," I said. "Unfortunately, two days have passed so we may be SOL there. Most trace fades quickly. Some magic practitioners are also capable of deliberately dispersing magic trace. If I *do* find some, I can try to capture it. In some cases, I may even be able to track it to its source or at least get some clues about whose it is."

For the first time since I'd arrived, I saw a glimmer of hope in Oliver and Gracie's expressions. I held up my hand. "That's only if I find something," I cautioned. "I'm a mage, not a magician. I can't make trace appear if there isn't any. And the law is pretty limited on what kinds of magic-based evidence are admissible at either grand jury proceedings or trials. My testimony would have to be weighed just like any other expert witness talking about evidence and its interpretation."

Gracie scooted forward on her chair in excitement. "That's something you've done before?"

"Yes, a few times." I'd tried to avoid it as much as possible because until recently keeping a low profile had been my chief concern. Even now I didn't want to make any headlines. "It's always an uphill battle. A lot of people are very skeptical about magical evidence. To be persuasive, in my experience it needs to be corroborated with other mundane—as in, non-magical—evidence and testimony."

"Which would also be your job to find," Philippa interjected. "Other than trace on Oliver, what else might we look for?"

"I'd visit the places Oliver went that day, especially the parking garage," I told them. "Again, looking for trace or other indications of magic and supernatural or paranormal influences. If someone *did* take control of him and removed their trace from his body, maybe they didn't worry about covering their tracks wherever they attacked him. I've found that to be the case before. After that, I have other lines of inquiry to pursue. We can go more into that if we decide to move forward."

"Thank you for the clarification." Philippa turned to the Hensleys. "Oliver, would you and your wife like to discuss this privately before we make a decision?"

"I don't think we need to talk about it." Despite my many caveats, Oliver looked like a drowning man who'd just grabbed a life preserver. "I have nothing whatsoever to lose by hiring Ms. Worth."

"You might." I deliberately made my voice cold. I wanted one more shot at eliciting a reaction. "Because if I find evidence that supports the charge of murder or disproves your claims, I *will* turn that over to the police."

Whatever Gracie's response to my promise-slash-threat was, I didn't notice. If Oliver reacted in any way that made me think he had something to hide, I planned to walk out of the house now and not look back.

Oliver didn't blink at all, however. "You won't find anything," he promised. "I did not do this. It might have been my body, but it wasn't *me* who killed that poor girl. Somehow I have to prove it. Please help me."

"Please," Gracie echoed. "I've known Ollie since the tenth grade. We've been married for twelve years. He's not capable of hurting someone."

At this moment, if Malcolm had asked me how certain I felt

about Oliver's honesty, I would have revised what I'd said earlier to eighty-twenty in favor of his truthfulness.

The only way I could be sure, or at least less uncertain, was to take the case and see what I could dig up. If Oliver was innocent, he didn't deserve to go to prison for the rest of his life. And most critically, someone or something might be committing terrible crimes and using unsuspecting people as puppets to do it. The thought made my stomach churn.

To make matters worse, it didn't sound like the police were interested in supernatural explanations, even with four alleged perpetrators all claiming the same thing. Those facts made Oliver's situation a perfect case for Malcolm and me—if I could find a way to deal with the case *and* the Vampire Court mess at the same time.

Before I could say anything, though, the crash of breaking glass and a heavy *thud* from the direction of the living room made us all jump.

Malcolm immediately zipped toward the sound. "Stay here," I told the others as I jumped up and ran after him.

In the living room, I found one of the large picture windows and a glass side table shattered. The cause was immediately evident: a large brick that had also bounced off the sofa and ended up on the floor. Oddly, I saw no sign of Malcolm. The reason why became apparent when tires squealed out front and a vehicle sped away.

By the time I got out the front door to the porch, the street was empty. Unfortunately for the brick-thrower, however, I had a dead guy ace up my sleeve.

Malcolm appeared at my side. "Blue four-door car with two people in it," he reported. "A blonde woman was driving. Big dude with a shaved head threw the brick and then jumped back in the car before it took off."

"Did you get the make and model of the car and the plate number?"

"No, I just waved as they went by." He sighed. "Yes, I got the plate."

He followed me back to the living room. We found Philippa waiting. "Mrs. Hensley's very upset," she said. "I told Oliver to go upstairs with her while we sort this out."

"I got a description of the car and a plate number," I told her. "My guess is it's likely to be friends or family of the victim."

"That would be the logical assumption. We'll let the police get to the bottom of it."

Malcolm gave me the information about the car and its plate number. I relayed what he said to Philippa. "Can I ask how you managed to see the car's plate from the house?" she asked as she copied the info down.

"I made it out to the yard just in time to see it."

"Hmm." She eyed me over her reading glasses. "You'd be willing to testify to that?"

"Yep."

"All right." She shut her notepad. "Once Oliver gets back downstairs, we'll call the police about the vandalism. Am I correct in thinking you're willing to take the case?"

"We need to discuss exactly what it is you want me to do and talk money, but yes," I said. "Just so I'm clear, I'm open-minded going in, but I'm definitely not as sure of Oliver's innocence as Gracie is. I meant what I said about the evidence I find—assuming I find any."

"I understand. Aaron speaks very highly of you and I trust his judgment." She leaned against the doorframe and took off her glasses. "Just so *I'm* clear, my reputation is pristine and I want to keep it that way. The only kind of investigation I'm interested in is a legal and ethical one, and the only private investigator I'd encourage Oliver to hire is an honest one. Other attorneys play fast and loose. They justify the means by the ends. I do not."

Yeah, no kidding. My impression of Philippa Grayson was that she dotted every *I* and crossed each *T* as deliberately and precisely as a surgeon making cuts.

"I did pick up on that about you," I said.

"Good." She nailed me with the kind of direct stare she probably used on witnesses during cross-examination. "So, why lie to me about seeing the plate?"

Fair enough question, given what she'd just said about shooting straight. How she'd sniffed me out, though, I didn't know.

"My ghost partner saw it and reported back to me," I said. "He can't testify under oath, but *I* can. His word is mine."

If the news that I had a ghost with me startled her in any way, I didn't see it. "All right," she said with a brief smile. In terms of friendliness, I got the impression that was as good as it was likely to get.

I spotted Oliver coming down the stairs. "Is your wife all right?" I asked.

"She will be. She just needs a minute. The last few days have been really, really hard on her." When he joined us in the living room, he saw the damage and seemed to deflate before my eyes. "People hate me now." He said it so quietly that I wasn't sure if he was talking to himself or us.

"I'm afraid so," Philippa said. She didn't quite sound sympathetic, but her expression showed disgust at the attack. "We need to inform the police about this."

Oliver took a step back as if to put physical distance between himself and the idea. "I don't want to do that. The cops already tore the house apart looking for evidence. We just got everything cleaned up and put away right before you and Ms. Worth arrived. And Gracie...I don't know if she can take more detectives coming through here and questioning us. I don't know if *I* can."

"That's what I'm here for," Philippa reminded him. "You won't have to say a word to them. You didn't witness the vandalism. Ms. Worth is the witness."

I made a face. Since I found out they were the lead detectives in the case, I'd been thinking about my strategy for dealing with my old detective buddy Ernie Diaz and his very unfriendly partner Joel Ferguson. I'd definitely wanted to keep my snooping under the detectives' radar as long as possible.

Those plans had just gone out the window—both literally and figuratively—thanks to the vandals. When Diaz and Ferguson found out a brick had landed in Oliver's living room, they'd be on the scene faster than you could say *probable cause*. They'd know from the jump Oliver hired me to find evidence that might exonerate their suspect. Just what I needed: pissed-off detectives dogging my every move.

Nothing to do but make the best of a bad situation. "Once the cops get here, how long can you keep them away from Oliver and me?" I asked Philippa.

"As long as you need." She raised her perfectly shaped eyebrows. "Why?"

"I need to see if I can find any trace on Oliver before the cops tie me up asking about the vandals. Time is ticking. Whatever trace he might still have is evaporating as we speak."

She turned to Oliver. "Are you comfortable with this plan?"

He sighed. "If you are, then I guess I am too."

"Go upstairs with Ms. Worth, then," she said. "I'll make the call to the police. Do as she asks so she can examine you, but don't answer any questions from anyone, including her, unless I'm present."

I'd been around defense attorneys enough to not take that personally. We both had jobs to do.

Malcolm touched my arm. *You good with this plan?*

With checking him for trace, yes, I said wryly. *Dealing with Diaz right after that, no, not really, but what choice do we have?*

We could walk. There are other mage detectives out there. Let them deal with Tweedledee and Tweedledum-dum.

You're not wrong, but now I want to know for myself if Oliver's story is true.

Me too. He floated back and forth. *Looks like we've got a case.*

CHAPTER
SEVEN

NORMALLY EVEN IN THIS UPSCALE PART OF TOWN A BRICK THROUGH A window would net a complainant one patrol car and a uniformed cop who stayed just long enough to ask a few questions, write up some quick notes, and take photos.

When the caller was the well-known defense attorney representing a man accused of a headline-grabbing murder, however, that meant a street full of blue and red lights, a crime scene tech van in the driveway, and a pair of grim detectives I recognized immediately after a quick peek through a curtained window. Diaz and Ferguson must have jumped in their car two minutes after the report came in.

I hadn't known Philippa Grayson long, but I had complete faith Oliver and I wouldn't be disturbed until Malcolm and I finished checking him for trace. I had a feeling a charging rhino wouldn't get past her Louboutins if she didn't want it to, so Diaz and Ferguson didn't have a prayer.

We took Oliver upstairs to the Hensleys' primary bathroom because I needed to draw on the floor with chalk. Tile wasn't my favorite medium for a circle or spellwork and I preferred to work at ground level rather than on a second floor, but we really had no other choice. At least the bathroom was big enough to accommodate the size of circle required.

Gracie blocked the bathroom doorway like a last line of defense between the police downstairs and her husband. Now that she'd cried herself out for the time being, I saw her quiet strength. Philippa's iron will was easier to spot, but maybe Gracie was no more of a pushover than their attorney.

"Is that witchcraft?" she asked as I crouched and drew the required spellwork from memory. She had a cardigan wrapped tightly around herself like some kind of purple cashmere armor.

"Nope. Totally different form of magic." I turned to finish the last section of spellwork that would contain any magic or trace we found and hopefully keep it from dissipating before I could contain it. "If you're uncomfortable around magic because you don't know much about it, I can recommend good websites to do some reading."

"Yes, please send me the links. I'd like to learn." She took a deep breath and let it out. "I want to understand what's going on."

"That's a good plan." I gave her a quick smile. "Knowledge is a weapon."

Nice to have someone be honestly curious about my kind of magic for a change. I'd had some clients recently who'd only hired a mage PI out of necessity and that made for spiky interactions. As if mage PI work wasn't difficult enough.

I rinsed chalk dust off my hands in the sink. "Okay, Oliver, take off your socks and shoes and step into the circle. Be careful not to touch any of the spellwork."

He'd stood quietly near the window the whole time I'd worked, keeping an eye on the comings and goings in their yard. With an injured hand it took him longer to remove his socks and shoes, but he moved much slower than I thought was necessary. I got the feeling he was stalling.

In my experience, the best way to handle a nervous client was honesty and compassion. "It's totally normal to be a little afraid and weirded out by this," I told Oliver as he set his footwear aside.

"Nothing I do is likely to hurt or harm you in any way, but it's going to feel strange. You'll sense waves of cold pass through you. Just stay calm, breathe normally, and try not to move. And don't go near the circle or smudge my writing."

"Got it." He moved carefully to the center of my spellwork. "How long will it take?"

"Five to ten minutes. I need to be very thorough because if you *do* still have any trace, there won't be much."

After one last check of the spellwork, I glanced at Malcolm to make sure he was ready too. While I checked for trace from the outside, he planned to search within Oliver's body—hence my warning about feeling cold. Malcolm gave me a thumbs up.

We joined Oliver in the circle. I took a moment to clear my mind and then nicked the tip of my right index finger on a tiny hidden edge on one of the charms on the bracelet I wore on my left wrist. With the blood, I closed the circle and used air magic to raise the wards that would contain any magic or trace we found.

Power and air swirled in the circle, stirred by the magic. Oliver twitched at the prickly sensation but didn't move.

Checking for trace didn't require me to close my eyes, but I did so out of habit so I saw and sensed only with my second sight. Malcolm sometimes made fun of me and said it was like turning down the radio to see better, but I'd caught him doing it too before.

I lowered my shields, opened myself to sensing trace, and raised my hands so my fingertips were near the top of Oliver's head.

Carefully, moving an inch at a time, I searched for even the tiniest wisp of trace lingering on Oliver's body. A quiet surge of cool blue-green magic nearby and Oliver's stifled gasp told me Malcolm had begun his search as well. His ability to search physically within a person because he could pass his hands through them was yet another reason we worked well together.

Since natural magic like mine was not capable of controlling or "possessing" anyone, or even compelling someone to act against their will, I knew what I *wasn't* looking for. Unfortunately, that left an almost endless list of other possibilities, including witchcraft or esoteric occult forms of magic from sorcery to wizardry and even archaic practices.

In my experience, most trace clung to a person's head, torso, or hands, especially if the magic had been used to control that person's actions and thoughts. I came up empty, however, even after two slow passes over Oliver's upper body. That didn't mean I'd have nothing to go on. Malcolm wasn't done and we still had to retrace Oliver's steps from the day of the murder. Even so, I was definitely feeling less optimistic by the second.

Until I got to Oliver's feet, that was.

Maybe our adversary hadn't been very thorough when they dispersed their magic trace, or maybe Oliver had walked through spellwork that snagged him. Whatever the cause, I found a wisp of black magic on the heel of his left foot. The threads were so thin and fragile that I doubted they would have still been there four of five hours from now.

Malcolm touched my shoulder. *He's been dragging that around like magical toilet paper.*

Now *there* was a mental image. I covered my chuckle with a little cough. *You find anything else?*

Tiny bit of trace in his heart. It looks the same as what you've got on his foot. I waited to try to get it out until you're ready with the crystal. It's not much, so I'll probably only get one shot at grabbing it. Plus it's the dude's heart, so I only want to stick my hand in there once. Can't imagine we'll get paid if our client has a heart attack before we even get a contract signed.

Not to mention that would be an awkward conversation with Diaz and Ferguson, I told him.

If I were you, I'd be more worried about explaining it to Darth Chanel.

He had a point there. I unhooked an empty crystal from my bracelet and twirled it gently in the wisp of trace. "*Contain,*" I commanded aloud.

The spelled crystal sucked in the trace. I let out a breath. "Got something," I told Oliver as I got to my feet. "You doing okay?"

"Can't say I'm enjoying this." He sighed and rubbed his arms. "But it's worth it if you find evidence that'll help me. Are you done?"

"Almost. We've got one more thing." I softened my tone and added, "There's a tiny bit of trace on your heart that I want to get."

Despite my attempt to reassure him, Oliver blanched.

"Oh my God," Gracie said, making a choked sound. "Is it hurting him?"

I shook my head. "It's like the sticky residue left behind when you take a price tag off something. I need to get it quickly, though, before it dissipates completely." I turned back to Oliver. "Put your hand on my shoulder."

Clearly puzzled, he did as I asked.

We didn't give him time to tense up. Quickly, Malcolm passed his ghostly hand through Oliver's chest, scooped out the trace, and brought it to my hand where I held the crystal. "*Contain*," he said. The tiny bit of residual magic disappeared into the crystal.

At the same time, Oliver let out a short, garbled cough and staggered, bracing himself on my shoulder to keep from falling. I stuck the crystal in my pocket and steadied him with both hands. Gracie left her post in the doorway to stand outside the circle.

"It's over," I said as Oliver wheezed. "You'll be okay in a second. Just breathe."

"Why did this happen to us?" Gracie seemed to have graduated from grief to anger. Seeing someone they loved hurting had that effect on most people, myself included. "What did Ollie ever do to deserve this?"

"It's possible he's never done anything to deserve it," I said. "Bad shit happens to good people sometimes. It's not right and it's not fair, but that's how it is. Sometimes the best you can do is try to set it right." And didn't I know that from experience.

"Is that why you do this?" Gracie asked. "Be a mage PI, I mean?"

"Pretty much." I dropped my containment wards and broke the circle. "We're done," I told Oliver. "You can step out now."

"Thank you." He walked straight into Gracie's arms and held her close with her head against his chest.

While they took a moment to themselves and Malcolm floated downstairs to check on Philippa, I cleaned up the chalk circle with a wet towel. I didn't tell them, but its trace would linger. Like a crossroads, once created, a circle was forever, even when every visible aspect of it had vanished.

I left the towel draped over the shower door and took a peek out the window. To my relief, only one patrol car remained and the crime scene van had already left. The detectives' car was still out front, though. Dang it.

Finally, Oliver kissed the top of his wife's head and turned his attention back to me. "What did you find?"

"I got some traces," I told them, letting the curtain fall back into place. "It wasn't much and I don't know what kind of magic it is yet, but it's a start."

"Can you tell the detectives?" Gracie asked, hope shining in her eyes.

"Not yet," I said gently. "Right now it's just a wisp of magic. It's not enough to help your case unless I can connect it to the source. I need to find some definitive proof of how they were able to control you without you being aware of what was happening. Or they may have wiped your memory of it after. I need more evidence."

She looked crestfallen, but Oliver squared his shoulders. "It's a start, though, you said. It's *something*."

"It's something," I agreed. "And where there's something, there's a good chance of finding more."

"A few minutes ago we had nothing," Oliver told Gracie, who wiped her eyes and managed a little smile. "Now we've got hope."

Hope was a precious thing. Sometimes it was the only thing someone in their position could hang onto.

Raised voices drifted up from downstairs. One of them I recognized as Ernie Diaz.

Malcolm appeared at my side. "Better go talk to the detectives," he said. "Tweedledee is about done getting stonewalled. And FYI, he said something not very nice under his breath when he heard your name."

Hooray. "I'm going downstairs," I told Oliver. "You should both stay up here until the coast is clear or Philippa calls you down. We'll talk more before I leave. In the meantime, you should probably contact someone about getting the window fixed, or at least boarded up."

"Good idea." Oliver took out his phone.

I wasn't the sort to care all that much about looking pretty, especially for unfriendly detectives, but I took a moment to fix my long braided hair, which had gotten windblown by the magic and power swirling in my circle, so I didn't look like a total disaster. Then I marched downstairs with all the enthusiasm of going to the dentist.

Diaz and Ferguson had squared off with Philippa in the Hensleys' foyer. Ernesto "Ernie" Diaz stood a little shorter than his partner and was stockier in build with dark hair and eyes. I guessed him to be in his late thirties. Joel Ferguson was blond and wiry and appeared to be about the same age, though Diaz was the more seasoned investigator and senior partner.

The moment I got within view, both detectives nailed me with almost identical glares.

"This is going to be *so* much fun," Malcolm muttered from behind me.

"Alice Worth." Hands on his hips, Diaz watched me come down the last few steps. "Glad to see you're alive. Last I heard, your car turned up stolen and burned. The Vampire Court said you were on a case for them and confiscated all the evidence. Ferguson here bet me ten bucks they'd offed you."

Even that rather colorful statement didn't elicit a reaction from Philippa. I needed to take poker face lessons from her.

I raised my hands in an exaggerated shrug. "Sorry about the ten bucks, Detective Ferguson. For future reference, when the vamps decide to get rid of someone, they don't leave evidence behind—not even a burned car. Or so I've heard."

"So you've heard." Ferguson's eyes narrowed. "Why you would want to associate with vampires at all, I have no idea."

"For the record, I don't work for the Court anymore. And not all vamps are bad. Just most." I turned back to Diaz. "Anyway, I'm sure Ms. Grayson already gave you the info about the car. I didn't really get a good look at either the driver or the guy who threw the brick, other than the woman was blonde and the guy had a shaved head. Not enough to pick them out of a lineup, but with the make, model, and license plate, you should be able to get them." *Especially if they have ties to Madison Fernell*, I thought, but I didn't say that. Far be it for me to tell them how to do their jobs.

"Pretty good to be able to get a full plate number," Diaz observed.

"Thanks. It's almost like I do this sort of thing for a living."

"Almost," Ferguson said.

I gave them my best smile just to let them know I wasn't intimidated, and to make Ferguson scowl.

Diaz eyed me. "What brings you to this house?"

"I was already here when the vandalism occurred," I said mildly. "*Why* I'm here isn't really relevant to my witness statement."

"We decide whether it's relevant," Ferguson snapped. "And we wouldn't ask if it wasn't."

They knew damn well why I was here. I could refuse to answer their questions, but I figured it would serve me better not to antagonize them any more than necessary. If I *did* find evidence that proved Oliver hadn't acted by choice, I'd want them to listen—or at least I'd want Diaz to listen. He'd considered my perspective on previous cases. I'd put Ferguson in the "lost cause" category long ago.

"I'm here at Ms. Grayson's invitation, as a consultant," I said.

"Consulting about what?" Ferguson demanded.

"I'm a mage private investigator, as you know," I told them. "So

I'm here to talk about magic and how it might or might not be used. I hadn't done much more than introduce myself before someone broke the window."

As I'd expected, they didn't comment on their investigation, especially with Philippa standing three feet away. But judging by the wry twist in the corner of Diaz's mouth and Ferguson's flat stare, they thought Oliver's story was one hundred percent bullshit.

Nothing unusual about a PI and the police working parallel or even different angles on a case; that was the nature of our businesses. One would think, however, that Diaz might give me the benefit of the doubt since I'd been right every time we'd crossed paths.

They probably figured at best I'd just end up agreeing that Oliver had committed cold-blooded murder. At worst, I'd muddy up their case. They couldn't tell me to back off, but they probably wanted to.

"Anything else?" I asked.

"Not at the moment," Diaz said. "If anything comes up, we have your contact information."

"And my lawyer's too, I assume? It's Aaron Riddell, in case you don't have that in your notes."

"Thank you. I'm aware." Diaz flipped his notebook closed. "See you around, Worth. Watch your back."

"You too."

Ferguson gave me one last glare and headed for the front door. Diaz studied me for an extra beat, his expression a mixture of irritation and something else—maybe curiosity about what I knew, or what I thought of Oliver's claims. I raised my eyebrows, daring him to ask. Instead, he shook his head and followed his partner outside.

Once the front door shut behind them, Philippa said, "You handled the detectives well."

"Not my first rodeo. Thanks, though." I took the crystal from my pocket and held it up. "I did find some very thin magic trace on Oliver. I don't know what kind it is yet or whether it's in any way connected to the murder, but I'll do my best to find out."

She clicked her pen to open it. "Then let's do the paperwork and get you on your way."

CHAPTER

EIGHT

AN HOUR LATER, ARMED WITH A SIGNED CONTRACT AND RETAINER, I BACKED my new-to-me gray SUV into a spot on the fifth level of a six-story garage near downtown, two slots down from where Oliver had left his car the day of the murder. According to our client, he liked to park on Level 5B so he could use the stairs twice daily for exercise. I personally found the desire to deliberately take that many stairs every day to be an utterly unrelatable statement, but to each their own.

"Realistically, what do you think we can find?" Malcolm asked as we got out. "Cuz I gotta say I'm not hopeful. Not after almost two days and a jillion cars coming through here."

"Stop manifesting negativity," I scolded. "We found trace on Oliver. If I can get a little more, I'll have enough to track, or at least have a better chance at figuring out what we're dealing with. Think positive."

He did a double take. "I'm sorry—did you, *of all people*, just tell me to 'stop manifesting negativity'?"

"I am a ray of sunshine," I said loftily. "My fiancé says so."

78

"Ray of *something*," he muttered. "Far be it for me to disagree with Sean. So, Lil Miss Sunshine, what do you see?"

In the middle of the afternoon, Level 5B was quiet, with only a few dozen cars in slots near the elevator. Their drivers were likely at work until four or five. And we were in luck; no one had parked in spot 512. The police had probably taped it off to search the area before they impounded Oliver's car as evidence. The tape was gone now, but maybe the people who usually parked on this level left it empty out of superstition. All the better for us. As Malcolm pointed out, time and traffic were not on our side.

"Keep an eye out," I told Malcolm as I crouched in the parking spot. "Let me know if anyone's headed this way."

"I got you, boo."

Searching for residual magic on pavement wasn't much different than the process I'd used on Oliver, except the garage floor was filthy and crawling on my hands and knees here was no fun whatsoever. Tiny rocks dug into my skin, and the concrete smelled like oil and exhaust and whiffs of stale urine and rotten, discarded food. Lovely.

I swore under my breath as I crept methodically around the parking spot, my shields down and senses wide open. Without my shields in place, I felt the ebbs and flows of natural magic around me as they swirled and pulsed along ley lines and through their respective elements: the peaceful green of earth magic, the cool blue of water magic, the light and almost effervescent white of air magic, and the searing orange traces of fire magic. And most of all, I sensed the siren call and seductive promise of red and black blood magic, the closest of the natural magics to dark, occult practices.

Had I chosen—or been forced down—that path, I might have been a truly formidable occult practitioner. That version of me haunted my nightmares sometimes. The temptation was never not there, though it was easier to ignore when my shields were strong.

"Earth to Alice." Malcolm's voice jolted me out of my thoughts. "You've been checking that same spot for like five minutes. You okay?"

"Yeah, I'm good." I took a deep breath, let it out, and refocused on my task. *Come on, come on*, I thought as I swept my palms and fingertips back and forth over the pavement and inched forward on my aching knees. *Give me something to work with here.*

And then right about where Oliver's driver's side door would have been, I found what I was looking for: a snarl of black magic. It looked and felt like a more concentrated version of what I'd spotted on Oliver's foot.

Carefully, I scooped up the trace, flinching as I pulled it free. Natural magic like Malcolm's and my own felt like the silken threads of a spiderweb. This stuff hurt like pulling on piano wire. The frayed spellwork dug into my skin like tiny fishhooks. If I hadn't already known this was black magic, that would have clinched it.

As much as it hurt to do so, before I transferred the magic to a crystal, I took a moment to play with the trace between my fingers. What kind of magic was this, precisely? Black magic, obviously, but who made it? Even as incomplete and broken spellwork, it didn't feel or smell like black witch magic, which had been my first guess. Not a wizard's magic, not fae, and not sorcery. Some form of esoteric occult magic, I decided.

I took an empty crystal from my bracelet and held it close to this snarl of trace. "*Enclose*," I commanded.

The crystal's spellwork flared and sucked the magic from my hand. I hissed in pain as the trace left bloody welts on my fingers.

"This magic is nasty." Malcolm floated down and halfway through the garage floor so we were face-to-face and I didn't have to crane my neck to see him. He got a close look at my wounds and flitted in place. "Jeez. That looks painful."

"It is." I flexed my bloody fingers and grimaced. "It feels like I stuck my hand in boiling water and then grabbed a handful of rusty razors."

"Very descriptive." He wrinkled his nose. "So, what do you think we've got?"

I told him what I suspected the magic might be. He frowned and studied the crystal. I couldn't see the magic when it was stored, but he could.

"Yeah, I don't think it's witchy," he said finally. "Doesn't remind me of sorcerer magic either, at least not the kind we've dealt with."

"Yup," I said.

Neither of us wanted to say the sorcerer Miraç's name aloud. That pain still went too deep.

"So we've crossed some of the usual suspects off the list," Malcolm continued. "If it's occult, it could be almost anything. Unless you can track it to who made it, all we've got to show for our work so far is your bloody hand and a couple of crystals we'll have to magically incinerate at some point."

"Not to mention my pants are filthy." *And* my knees were killing me. I stuck the crystal in my pocket. "I need to check the rest of the area."

"Let me," he said quickly. "I know what to look for. It's your turn to keep watch. Use a healing spell on your hand before those cuts get infected from parking garage grime."

The pain in my fingers caused me to use some words I saved for special occasions as I rose. Malcolm continued searching where I'd left off, floating above the floor and passing his hands through the concrete.

At my SUV, I gingerly cleaned my hands and the knees of my pants with wet wipes. The cuts really weren't very deep, but they would bleed for a while and they hurt like crazy. Unfortunately, healing spells hurt too.

With a sigh, I took a light green crystal off my bracelet and held it in my injured hand. "*Helios*," I said.

The low-level healing spell pulsed, sending waves of magic that felt like white-hot needles through my skin. I'd used hundreds of healing spells in my lifetime, from the very mild to life-saving seriously strong blood magic ones, and it hurt every freaking time. I'd built up some tolerance, but I still had to grit my teeth.

Finally, the spell let out two final wispy pulses of magic and faded. I pocketed the empty spell crystal. "All better," I told Malcolm.

"I guessed that when you stopped whimpering." He floated over to me. "Nauseous?"

"A little." I rubbed my tummy. "Dang healing spells always do that to me. I take it you didn't find anything else?"

"Nope. Not even the tiniest bit. So what do you think?"

I considered. "We don't have anything definitive yet, but the location of the trace matches where Oliver said his missing time began. Something could have grabbed him right at his driver's door."

He floated back and forth, clearly troubled. "Are we saying this is for real?"

"I hate to say it, since anything capable of forcing someone to kill against their will is really bad news, but I'm leaning that way." I took my bag out of the SUV and locked the vehicle. "You want to walk to the crime scene with me? I don't want to try to find parking over there. It's only a couple of blocks."

"Yeah, let's go." He floated along beside me as I headed for the elevator. "What, are you not taking the stairs?"

"No, smartass, I am not."

From ground level, it took us about ten minutes to walk from the garage to the alley just off Eleventh where Madison Fernell had died. Oliver said he'd lost about two hours from his memory. Where had he been during the rest of the missing time? This area had cameras everywhere, including inside the parking garage. No doubt Diaz and Ferguson or other detectives had already canvassed looking for surveillance footage. I needed to do the same, and quickly, before potentially helpful footage got erased or lost.

"You've got some pep in your step," Malcolm observed. "Nothing gets you going like a new case. Well, other than coffee."

I spotted a coffee shop ahead on the right. "Ooh, speaking of which..."

He chuckled. "You literally just skipped like a little kid."

"Don't tell anybody," I stage-whispered. "I have to maintain my reputation as a badass."

He very solemnly crossed his heart. "As always, your secret's safe with me."

A few minutes later, latte with extra shots in hand, I reached the entrance to the alley. Forty-eight hours had passed since the murder, so the crime scene tape was long gone and someone had washed away all the blood. A mountain of flowers, stuffed animals, cards, signs, and candles had taken their place. We were just two blocks from Salty's, the bar where Madison had worked. Her death had clearly touched a lot of people.

Even if the memorial didn't exist, I would have known exactly where she'd died. My blood magic tingled in an all-too-familiar way the moment we reached the alley entrance. I loved the power and uses of my blood magic, but it came with a price: namely, visceral knowledge of violence and pain. The brutality of what had happened here resonated all the way down to my bones.

Two young women sat cross-legged on the concrete in front of the memorial. One had her head resting on the other's shoulder as they sobbed. Even with time ticking away, I didn't want to intrude, so I leaned against the wall at the entrance to the alley and sipped my coffee. I saw no cameras in the alley, which had made it an ideal place for a murder, but we'd passed a number of them on the way here from the garage. Surveillance cameras were a private investigator's best friend. Well, cameras and shady informants willing to rat anyone out for the right price. I habitually kept an eye out for both.

"That thing you told Gracie about putting things right," Malcolm said suddenly. "We can try to do that here. But even if we find the answers, no matter what they are, it still won't make sense. It never does."

I wanted to disagree with him, but I couldn't. I thought of something Sean had said to me after we'd found ourselves between a shifter assassin, called an *ulfhéðnar*, and their target: *You can't make sense of senseless things.* Madison's murder was one of those things that would never make sense, even if we solved this mystery and ensured the right person or people were held accountable for her death.

"We still have to get the answers, though," I murmured, as much to myself as to Malcolm. "Maybe that's the best we can do. And save the lives of possible future victims whenever we can. That's our job."

"Makes me want to cut Diaz and Ferguson some slack," he said, to my surprise. "They deal with a hell of a lot of suffering day in and day out too. That's a ton of weight to carry."

I took a long drink of coffee. "Yeah, it is."

We waited quietly until the young women helped each other up and walked away down the alley, arms around each other's waists for support.

"I guess the weight's a little less when we share it," I told Malcolm.

He gave me a lopsided smile. "Careful with the sappy stuff, Alice. You can lose your badass rep even faster that way. Just be glad your business partner didn't hear you say that. And speaking of Major Killjoy, should we call her about this?"

"Later." I headed for the memorial. "Arkady's still wrapping up her insurance fraud case. If there's any trace here, we're running out of time to find it."

"You are not about to move those bears and flowers." Horrified, he flitted in front of me. "This is a memorial, Alice! If someone sees you, they'll flip out. They're not going to care if you're a PI."

"What do you want me to do? Sneak back after dark?" I frowned at him. "The trace in the garage wouldn't have lasted another few hours. If there's anything left here, it'll be gone by nightfall. The gifts are nice, but this is about getting justice for Madison."

"Just go easy, okay?" He crossed his arms. "Let's hope if anyone sees you, they're understanding about it."

I crouched in front of the stuffed animals and candles and lowered my shields again.

Because he was right and causing trouble at a victim's memorial was not a good look, I moved a few gifts at a time with my left hand, searched for trace with my right and my senses, and then put the items back before moving on. That made a painstaking process even more slow. Leaning over and crouching to do this killed my back, but I didn't have much choice.

Maybe I could persuade Sean to give me a massage later. I could probably make that happen, if I managed to keep him focused long enough before the massage turned into something else. Not that I'd mind some werewolf TLC tonight. I smiled to myself despite my grim task.

Magic trace often clung to places where violence had occurred or someone experienced strong emotions, but so far I'd found nothing. Good thing I wasn't the only person looking.

"Hey, what's that?" Malcolm floated down beside me and waved his hands over the area to my left. "You feel this?"

Frowning, I mimicked his movements. Even straining my senses I felt no magic, but I did experience a telltale icy chill and an echo of something I recognized. "A ghost? Is it Madison?"

"I don't think this is from her." Malcolm's uneasiness prickled through our metaphysical connection. He was much more attuned to anything to do with spirits and their energy. "I know what a new ghost feels like. This feels...old, and *really* evil. Like, something that crawled out of the bowels of the earth evil."

"Fantastic." I moved a couple more stuffed animals and candles aside so I could run my palms over the pavement.

There it was: wispy dark gray magic with a distinctly rotten feeling, like moldy bread. Definitely not the same trace that I'd found on Oliver and in the garage, but just as nasty. What the hell was going on here?

Unfortunately, there wasn't enough left to really do much with it, but I put it in a crystal anyway. Even the crystal felt unpleasant to hold once the trace was inside it. I stuck it in my other pocket and wiped my hands on my pants. This was precisely why I kept at least one change of clothes in my vehicle at all times.

"Incoming," Malcolm warned.

I rearranged the memorial gifts quickly and rose just as three people—two young women and a man—came around the corner into the alley. One of the women held a teddy bear and the man carried three prayer candles. I hoped they'd think I'd added something to the pile and simply leaned over to get a closer look at what others had brought.

We needn't have worried about their reaction, though. The moment the memorial came into view, both young women began crying and their male companion blinked back tears of his own. I moved out of the way so the newcomers could pay their respects.

Madison had clearly meant so much to a hell of a lot of people. The outpouring of grief was a very sobering reminder of just how important getting these answers was, not only for past victims and their loved ones, but anyone this killer might target next. The only thing worse than a senseless death was one without explanation or justice.

"It's so sad," I murmured.

The young woman who'd brought a bear wiped her eyes. Her face was red from crying. "She was the best. It's not fair."

"No, it's not fair at all." I crouched and busied myself with some of the stuffed animals, setting them upright while she sniffled.

"Were you friends with Madison?" the man asked.

I shook my head. "I heard about it and came by to pay my respects. Did you all know her?"

"We worked with her at Salty's," the young woman with the bear said. "I'm Kayley. I'm a server."

"I'm so sorry for your loss." I stood. "It looks like a lot of people really loved her."

"I hope they fucking fry the guy who did it," the man said, his voice tight with anger and grief. "Can you believe they let that asshole out on bail? He'll probably skip the country and do it again. Just wait."

I doubted Oliver planned to do anything of the sort, but I *did* believe whoever was responsible for Madison's murder and possibly the other crimes *would* harm others. I had no time to lose.

"Take care," I told them as I backed away. "And again, I'm sorry about your friend."

"Thanks," the girl with the bear said. Her male companion hugged her.

"Well, that sucked," Malcolm said quietly as we headed for the alley entrance.

I let out a breath. "Yup." The sooner I got away from this place, the better. My stomach hadn't stopped churning since we arrived.

With Malcolm at my side, I came around the corner, stepped onto the sidewalk—

and nearly collided with Detective Diaz.

CHAPTER

NINE

"Aw, crap," Malcolm muttered.

Diaz had apparently waited for me, leaning against the building and holding a coffee cup identical to my own. I wondered how long he'd been here and if he'd watched what I'd done at the memorial. On the plus side, I saw no sign of Ferguson. Small favors.

"Walk back to your car with you?" Diaz asked gruffly.

"I'm actually sticking around here for a while," I said. "What's on your mind, Detective?"

Instead of answering, he gestured with his cup at my engagement ring. "I noticed that earlier. I suppose congratulations are in order. Who's the lucky guy?"

"Sean Maclin."

"Right, the alpha werewolf. I met him once, back when your car turned up stolen and burned." Diaz sipped his coffee. "Best of luck to you both."

"Thanks." I drained the last of my own coffee and tossed the cup in a recycling bin. "But I doubt you tracked me down to ask me about my engagement."

"Yeah." He stared straight ahead at the sandwich shop across the

88

street. "Don't know if you're aware, but that poor girl was just about in pieces. That shouldn't happen to anybody, except maybe the person who did it."

"I can't argue with you on that point. But it's really important to know for sure exactly who that person is."

Diaz glanced at me. "Hensley's got you believing his bullshit amnesia story?"

Was he deliberately trying to rile me up, or fishing to see if I'd discovered anything? Maybe both.

"I don't believe anything yet," I countered. "I plan to keep an open mind until I have enough evidence to convince myself one way or another. As I think all investigators should do."

"You've heard that old saying that if you hear hoofbeats behind you, think horses, not zebras, right?" he asked, his tone sardonic.

"That's true, unless you happen to be in a safari park." I gestured around us. "We're surrounded by magic and supernatural beings and paranormal phenomena. You know those are as much of our environment as anything else. You're talking to a mage, and there's a ghost next to you."

Diaz glared in Malcolm's general direction. Malcolm grinned and waved though Diaz couldn't see him.

"If you dismiss even the possibility of something unknown to you being responsible for Madison Fernell's death, or any of the other attacks that have taken place recently, you're not pursuing justice. I'm not saying that's what's going on here," I added when Diaz scowled. "But I *do* think it's a prospect worth considering."

He shook his head. "In my line of work, the simplest explanation is usually the right one."

Yeah, but if he really, *really* believed there was nothing to Oliver's claims, would he be here talking to me? I didn't think so.

I shrugged. "Also true in my line of work. I just maybe have a wider field of vision."

"Make sure your 'field of vision' doesn't blind you to the probability that Hensley's a killer."

"Fair enough, as long as you don't ignore the chance he isn't."

"Do you have anything that suggests otherwise?" Though clearly skeptical, he sounded curious. Maybe he *did* remember I had a habit of being right.

The strange black magic *might* support Oliver's story, but I could think of a dozen other reasons for its presence. I'd hold my cards close to the vest until I had something substantial to report.

"Nothing tangible yet, but I've got something to dig into," I said. "And for the record, I have no interest in helping anyone get away with murder. I told Philippa Grayson the same thing. My morals and ethics don't change based on who writes me a check. I'm only after the truth—whatever it may be."

"I'm glad to hear it. I suppose I'll leave you to do whatever you need to do then." Diaz started toward a nondescript black sedan parked at the curb, then turned back to ask, "You ever think about coming to work on my side of the badge?"

Of all the things I thought he might say to me, that wasn't one of them. "Not really," I said. "Too many people need me on this side of it."

Strangely, he nodded like I'd said the right thing, gave me a little salute, and went around to the driver's side door. I watched him pull away from the curb and accelerate down the street.

"I think he's got a little professional crush on you," Malcolm said.

No one was within earshot, so I replied aloud. "As opposed to an amateur crush?"

"No-*ooo*." He made an exasperated sound. "Like, from one pro to another. He just basically asked if you'd like to join up and be his partner."

I scoffed. "Can't imagine why."

"Obviously he likes how your mind works."

"Well, his usual tag-along is Ferguson, so I feel like that sets a low bar."

"I'm sure Ferg has his good points, even if we've never seen them." He sighed. "Learn how to take a compliment, Alice."

"I don't have much experience getting compliments from the fuzz. They mostly just ignore me—or try to arrest me."

"So maybe it just takes the smarter ones a little while to figure out what's up. The dumb ones will never get it. Their loss. Come on." Malcolm nudged me with a ghostly elbow. "If you want to do some canvassing looking for cameras, we gotta get moving. Daylight's burning, and you've got that thing tonight."

My dinner with Moses. Ugh. "Don't remind me."

Looking for video would be complicated. I didn't know exactly what route Oliver had taken from the garage to the alley. On top of that, we had two missing hours to account for. All I knew at the moment was Oliver had been in the garage a little after six and then turned up in the alley just before eight, standing over Madison's body with a knife in his hand.

Speaking of the knife, I'd give about anything to check it for magic trace, but I'd have more luck persuading Ferguson to give me a foot massage than getting my hands on a murder weapon.

Gotta start somewhere. I crossed the street toward a sandwich shop. Like many of the eateries downtown, it was about to close for the day now that the lunch rush was over, and only about a half-dozen customers sat at tables with their late midday meals.

I grabbed a bottle of water from a cooler and approached the counter. "Anything else?" the young female employee asked as I handed over some cash.

"As a matter of fact, is your manager around?"

"I'll see. Hang on." She disappeared through the swinging door that led to the shop's kitchen.

"You should get a sandwich," Malcolm scolded. "You skipped lunch."

"I had breakfast," I muttered. "And look—I'm drinking water."

He sighed.

A short man in khakis and a polo shirt emerged from the kitchen, wiping his hands on a towel. I smiled, ready to launch into my usual explanation of who I was and request to see the footage from the camera out front.

"Yeah?" he asked, his tone and expression decidedly unfriendly.

I held up my PI license. "I'm a private investigator, and I wondered if I could take a look at your street-side camera footage from the day before yesterday."

"Nope."

I'd had people refuse to share footage with me for a wide range of reasons, but he'd already seemed angry before I'd made my request. "Can I just—" I began.

"I said no." The manager pointed a stubby finger straight at my nose. "You ought to be ashamed of yourself, trying to get that animal off for murder when they caught him in the act. Get the hell out of my shop."

The room went silent. Hostility crackled in the air.

"Okay." I picked up my water, raised my hands, and backed away from the counter. "Have a good day." I felt the manager's eyes burning twin holes in my back until I was out of the shop with the door shut behind me.

"What the ever-loving hell was that?" Malcolm flitted around me on the sidewalk in a whirlwind of ghostly rage. "How did he know who you were and what you wanted before you even walked in the door?"

I sighed. "How do you think?"

"Somebody warned him." He stopped mid-flit, his expression a mix of fury and realization. "Ferguson. Oh, shit, Alice. Did he call the business owners in the area and tell them not to give you access to video because you're working for Oliver?"

"That's my guess." I took a long drink from my bottle of water. "That's a first for me. Achievement unlocked, I suppose."

While Malcolm called Ferguson every bad name he could think of, I considered my options, which were limited. The police could subpoena footage. Private investigators could only ask to see video. If the owner refused, I really had no recourse.

"Ferguson couldn't have called everyone," I said as Malcolm's tirade wound down. "But the whisper network among business and property owners around here is probably in action too. We'll have an uphill battle to get any footage, more so than usual."

"Are we hosed, then?" He put his hands on his hips. "What about you-know-who?"

You-know-who referred to black hat hacker Cyanide Rose, a.k.a. Cyro, whose identity and interactions with us were so secret we never said her name aloud outside our home—even Malcolm. The feds had hunted her for years with no success, for reasons we'd never asked about and I could only imagine. She'd figured out my real identity years ago and been an ally since, even going so far as to meet me in person once in the Bahamas to pass along a warning about my grandfather. Unfortunately, I no longer had that memory, along with several others, because of a sorcerer's black magic.

"She's pricey," I said with a sigh. "But we might not have much choice thanks to Ferguson's interference." I hummed under my breath and pretended to check my phone until a group of pedestrians walked past. When they were out of earshot, I added, "And also in the category of legally spicy, since we wouldn't be able to use anything we got that way in court—or show it to Philippa Grayson."

"Legally spicy. Love it." He snorted. "People who insist on doing things super legally are such buzzkills."

I couldn't argue with that.

Just in case, I stopped at a couple other businesses on our way back to the parking garage, only to confirm that Ferguson had been a busy bee. I was right about the whisper network too. The final straw was when I walked into a shoe store just as the person behind the counter hung up her phone. She looked at me, shook her head, and pointed to the door.

"Well, it's official: we're pariahs," Malcolm sighed as we walked back to the parking garage. "If I were less secure about my own awesomeness, this would really hurt my feelings. I haven't felt this rejected since junior high. You okay?"

"No, I'm not okay. I'm annoyed." I pinched the bridge of my nose. "But not at the store owners—at Ferguson. They're all reacting to one side of the story. I can only imagine what picture he painted of me. If I were in their shoes, I'd probably do the same. Now we need a Plan B."

He patted my shoulder in ghostly comfort. Not that I could feel him touching me, but I appreciated the gesture.

By the time we made it back to the fifth level of the garage, I'd managed to get from frustrated to focused. Ferguson might be determined to throw obstacles at me, but I'd faced much worse than him, from Titans made of vipers in the Underworld to Dark Fae and even Vlad Țepeș himself. Compared to those foes, petty, closed-minded Ferguson wasn't much more than a pebble in my shoe.

But having said that...

"If I asked you to, would you go haunt Ferguson's house?" I asked as we got into my SUV. "You know, slam some doors, move stuff around, maybe touch the back of his neck a couple of times?"

"It would be my pleasure," my ghost said, rubbing his hands together. "You remember that nightmare form I used when I first showed up in your office? I've been looking for an opportunity to use it again."

I sighed. "Okay, well, it's a good option to have."

"Option?" He went from gleeful to crestfallen in a heartbeat. "Aw, come on, Alice. If anyone deserves to get scared shitless, it's the guy who just undeservedly made you Public Enemy Number One. Well, Public Enemy Number Two, behind your client. Can't I at least slam some doors and draw some wacky made-up symbols in the shower steam on his bathroom mirror to freak him out?"

"Drawing wacky made-up symbols on a mirror is how you accidentally summon a demon, or something way worse. We don't mess around with mirrors." I dug around in the bottom of the SUV's console and retrieved my latest pay-as-you-go phone. As it powered on, I grudgingly said, "Fine, yes, you can go slam some doors and maybe tickle the back of his neck."

He put his hands on his hips. "Don't call it tickling. Don't make it weird."

When the phone turned on, I found a number listed in my contacts as *Breanna-Massage Therapist.*

I could use a massage therapist, I grumbled inwardly. I unscrambled the numbers, typed the decoded number into the phone manually, and let it ring twice before disconnecting.

The phone rang less than a minute later. I answered the call. "This is Alice."

"Hello, Alice." Cyro's electronically modulated voice was male, which was another method she used to throw the feds or anyone else who might be listening off her track. "Congratulations on your engagement."

I blinked. "Thanks. How—?"

"Sean mentioned it the last time we spoke. What can I do for you?"

I explained my situation, including Ferguson's fairly successful campaign to hamstring my investigation.

"Once again, I congratulate you on bringing me a truly interesting project," Cyro said when I finished. "So if I'm understanding you correctly, you know Oliver Hensley was in the parking garage around six in the evening and then turned up in that alley just before eight, but you're not sure what route he took or where he was for those two hours? Or where exactly he crossed paths with the victim?"

"That about sums it up, yeah." I sighed. "How many arms and legs is this going to cost me? And how soon can you get to it?"

"Let me crack into it and see what I can find quickly. If I can get into the parking garage footage easily and track him leaving, I should be able to follow his path and get you some answers. If I run into roadblocks that will up the price, I'll let you know. Otherwise, same rate as the Olson job."

"Fingers crossed it's that easy," I said in relief. Malcolm held up two sets of crossed fingers to show his support. This would cut deeply into my retainer, but I could cover the cost. And more to the point, I didn't have much choice.

"Do you think Hensley's telling the truth?" Cyro asked.

"That's the million-dollar question." I rubbed the bridge of my nose. "I went into this thinking no way in hell. But now...my gut's telling me yes."

"And he's the fourth person to make this claim in two weeks. What the hell have you got running around out there?"

"Something from the bowels of the earth," I said, echoing Malcolm's description of the trace we'd found at the murder scene. "And if that's the case, we've got *two* big problems."

Malcolm frowned, clearly puzzled.

"What do you mean?" Cyro asked.

I'd been mulling the situation over since we'd left the alley. The more I thought about the evidence we had so far, the more certain I was that I was going to need some help from Carly very soon.

"If this *is* an old malevolent spirit possessing people to commit crimes, it's not hopping from person to person," I said. "If it was, we'd have a string of murders or attacks all in the same area, and we don't. Instead, we have three assaults and one murder in less than two weeks. So it's strategic. Maybe it's targeting specific people or specific situations. It's deliberate and patient. And old malevolent spirits are *none* of those things. Not unless someone very powerful is controlling them."

"Oh, shit," Malcolm breathed, his eyes wide as he realized what I meant. "Alice..."

"Controlling it how?" Cyro demanded. "Like some kind of puppet master? Who can do that? Spell it out for those of us who don't have magic and don't know that world."

"Necromancer," I said.

For the first time since we'd begun working together, Cyro went quiet.

"So if you *do* get video, don't just look for Hensley," I said. "Keep an eye out for anyone lurking in the background or going near his car before six o'clock. If the spirit is on a leash, the necromancer has to be nearby."

"Search for a lurking *necromancer*." Even her computerized voice sounded wry. "There's a new one. I'm starting to think I shouldn't congratulate you on your unique projects."

"Yeah, I got there a long time ago," Malcolm muttered.

Unfortunately, this wouldn't be my first interaction with a necromancer, but it would be my first in a long time. And if I managed to capture them and their pet spirit, it would be my first win against one. The last time I'd crossed paths with one, I'd come within a hair's breadth of ending up not only dead, but on their leash.

Rather than dwell on those memories, I cleared my throat and said, "I have to get going. I have a *family dinner* tonight that I need to get ready for." I put emphasis on the words so she'd know what I meant.

"I'm sorry to hear that. Take care."

"You too."

We ended the call. As I tossed the phone back into the console, Malcolm cleared his throat. "So. A necromancer."

"That's my guess." I pulled out of my parking spot and headed for the ramp. "If I'm right, that means we're going to have to take some extra steps to protect you."

"And protect you too," he countered. "I'm assuming you're going to call Carly?"

"As soon as I get a chance." I steered carefully through the garage's crowded lower levels. "I think we're going to need witchy help."

"I'm glad we have witchy help to call on." He flitted in place. "We're gonna need a big can of Ded-B-Gon. Necromancers are so creepy. They make my skin crawl, and I don't even *have* skin anymore."

"I guess that's our early warning system, then," I said as I stuck my credit card in the machine to pay for our parking. "We'll know who the necromancer is by the way your skin crawls when we meet them."

"Don't forget they reek of black magic and grave dirt and other nasty stuff. Between your nose and my skin and Carly's woo-woo powers, we'll find this creep and their pet spirit."

"We've got to find them fast," I said, my voice grim. "Before someone else turns up dead and another innocent pawn like Oliver ends up in jail. If I know anything about necromancers *and* serial killers, once they get the taste for blood, they'll keep killing until someone stops them."

"And as usual," Malcolm said dryly, "that *someone* is going to have to be us."

TEN

As soon as we got home, I shut myself in the office and wrote up my notes—one "official" version for Philippa Grayson and the real one for my own records. And then I poured myself two fingers of whisky, propped my boots up on my desk, and called Carly.

"Hello, Alice," she said in greeting. "I'm at the shop, but I've stepped into the storeroom for privacy and quiet. How are you?"

"I'm..." I hesitated. Where to even start? I settled on, "There's a lot going on."

"I know. I'm sorry." She sounded sympathetic. "You have some new trouble that's come up since last night?"

I'd long ago stopped wondering how she knew these things. "I do, which is why I'm calling. Have you heard in the news about the three assault cases and the murder where the suspects claim they have no memory of committing the crimes?"

"I have heard about it." She hummed to herself. "This is not the problem I thought you might be calling about. No wonder my cards have been cryptic. What's going on with these cases that involves you?"

I explained how I'd ended up digging into Oliver Hensley's story and what Malcolm and I had found this afternoon at the parking garage and Madison Fernell's murder scene. And then I told her what I thought we might be dealing with.

As Cyro had done, she went quiet for a long time after I said the word "necromancer." Like sorcerers, black witches, some wizards, and most other black magic and occult practitioners, very little good came of anything they did, even unintentionally. Darkness and ill intent beget more of the same.

"I'm sorry to bring this to your door," I said when the silence stretched out. And I *was* sorry.

I didn't need to tell her uncounted lives might be on the line or that I could ask for help elsewhere if she didn't want to get involved, or didn't want anyone from her coven involved. I'd known her long enough to know she was giving the situation careful, thorough, and knowledgeable consideration. Like Sean weighing matters related to our pack, Carly wasn't just responsible for herself or one other person, but an entire group whose lives, safety, and futures depended on her and each other—plus the lives of potential future victims. That was a lot to think about.

I used to only have to think about myself when I faced danger. That was a simpler time, but I never wanted to be back in that situation. The people around me were my strength as well as mine to protect.

If the Alice of a year ago could have heard you say that, what would she have said? Sean had asked me last night when we'd talked about how much he loved me.

Come to think of it, what would the me of a year ago have said about me believing the people I loved, who loved me too, were a strength and not a liability? Forget punching me; she wouldn't have recognized me. She might have thought I was a version of her from another reality.

When Carly spoke, her voice was heavy. "Katy has felt it."

"Uh-oh," I said.

She went quiet again. I let her think.

"Katy started to feel trouble rising a few weeks ago," Carly continued finally. "She called me in the middle of the night on January second and said something woke up."

I swung my feet off the desk and sat up. "Something *woke up?*"

"That's what she said."

I liked exactly nothing about the phrase *something woke up*. "Any thoughts on what that something might be?"

"Not at the moment," she said, to my disappointment. "She can't see it, and I won't let her try in ways I think are dangerous, so of course she's frustrated with me. I can't see it either. My cards refuse to reveal anything. I thought that was what you were calling about."

It was my turn to go quiet and think.

On the night of January second, Sean and I were on our way back to California after he'd come to Colorado as part of a rescue team to get Daniel and me back from Valas. While the others had flown back, he and I had rented an SUV and driven, with frequent stops to— *ahem*—celebrate my survival and our engagement. We'd stopped in Moab, Utah on the night of the second and spontaneously slept under the stars with a hastily purchased tent and camping mattress.

Valas had died mid-morning on a mountainside in Colorado on January first. On January second, back here in California, *something woke up*. Could these events be connected?

A lead ball of dread landed in my stomach.

Damn it all to hell and back, of course a fifteen-hundred-year-old sorcerer-vampire couldn't die without consequences. *Of course* something had woken up.

"Beyond this mysterious awakening," Carly said, as if that wasn't enough for me to process, "Katy's seen glimpses of black magic practitioners gaining strength and felt 'pops' of power in the aether. 'Little rumblings all over,' she calls it."

Well, this call kept getting better dand better. "Little rumblings? Does that include a necromancer?"

"About a week ago, at her request I led her through a scrying ritual with her bowl and she glimpsed a 'master of the dead,' which is what her previous coven calls necromancers. I woke her before the necromancer saw her."

Master of the dead was exactly the kind of phrase I'd expect black witches to use. Like necromancers, they were all about power—who had it, and who got ground underfoot. But no matter what you called them, a necromancer by any other name would still smell like grave dirt and rot.

"Did she tell you anything about the necromancer?" I asked. "Age? Sex? Physical description?"

"No. She only saw the shadow. I pulled her back immediately. She wasn't well-enough protected. If the necromancer had seen her, I might have lost her then and there."

In the matter of hours, this case had gone from "Oliver Hensley is full of shit" to "we're looking for a serial-killing necromancer." And yes that ball of dread still rolled in my tummy, but I'd be lying if I claimed I wasn't quivering with anticipation too.

"So, where does this leave us?" I asked.

"I'll talk to Katy." She hummed again—this time, a series of notes that might have been a spell of some kind because they sounded like a tune. Maybe something designed to keep any black magic practitioners from sensing us discussing their practice. "If she's willing to delve deeper into this, I will work with her, along with another coven member, to ensure her safety and ours."

"Thank you," I said, very sincerely.

"Preparing for the ritual will take time, though, and I need you to be comfortable with that," she cautioned. "I know the danger is imminent, but we will not rush anything. Lives and souls are at stake —yours, mine, Katy's, and everyone in my coven."

"I understand," I said. "If Katy doesn't want to do this, or you or your coven don't want to, I am fine with that too. I know the danger and risk involved."

"I'm not sure you do," she said, her voice kinder than the words sounded. "The masters of the dead can call upon the damned. They *walk* among the damned and carry their hearts on their staffs as they cross realms and traverse the abyss. This is not a sorcerer or a Dark Fae. This necromancer has allied themselves with Death itself. As prepared and strong as we'll be, there is no chance we'll encounter them and come away unscathed. That's what you're asking of yourself and us. When it's over, some part of each of us will not come back."

I raised my left hand and turned it so I could see the scar that ran across the inside of my wrist—a scar no magic created or wielded by the living could heal. "I've met one before," I said.

"Ah." She hummed that little tune again. "I'd like to hear that story, if you're willing to tell it."

"I'm willing, but not today." Maybe not for a long time. The memory was one of my least pleasant. I drained the last of my whisky and set the glass on a coaster. "Thank you, Carly. I'll see you soon. Let me know if Katy has any more thoughts about whatever woke up on January second."

"I will. Take care, Alice." She ended the call.

I put my phone on my desk. With my fingertip, I rubbed the little line on my left wrist. The skin turned cold rather than hot at the friction. What that strange sensation meant, I had never been sure, other than maybe it was the part of me that didn't come back from that long-ago encounter.

She'd tried to take a hell of a lot more—my life and my soul, in fact. I'd denied her both and sent her away with a wound of her own, thanks to my blood magic. And she'd never come after me again.

I had to wait on Cyro to get back to me with whatever surveillance footage she could get, and now I had to wait on Carly and Katy too. Every beat of my heart was a clock ticking down to the next attack, but I had nothing to go on for the time being other than thin trace I didn't dare try to track—not without a coven and a lot of bad-ass magic at my back.

So instead of hunting a necromancer, I'd get to spend the evening with my grandfather at his mansion, eating fancy food, turning down expensive scotch, and fantasizing about the day I'd get to kill him.

Lucky ducky me.

WHEN HE GOT HOME from work, Sean found me sitting on our bed with the lights off and the door closed. I'd curled up with my back against the headboard, my arms around my knees.

He toed off his shoes, sat next to me, and pulled me into his lap so he could wrap his arms around me. I rested my head on his chest and let his scent and warmth soothe me.

"When do you need to leave?" he asked.

"Seven o'clock." I checked the time. "My ride should be here in about fifteen minutes."

He rubbed his bristly chin on the top of my head in a very wolfy attempt to comfort me. "I'm sorry."

"I made the deal." I let out a breath. "Pretending to let Moses get close to me is part of my plan."

"I'm still sorry." He kissed my hair. "You shouldn't have to sit down to dinner with the man who murdered your parents and tormented you for twenty years. Are you sure you don't want me to come too?"

"You know you can't," I reminded him. "You're a member of the Were Ruling Council now. You can't have dinner with a crime lord—not even in secret. I'll have Malcolm with me. I'll be fine."

"It's not just about whether you'll be fine." He growled. "You know I'd do anything to spare you from this."

I entwined our fingers. "This first dinner will probably be the hardest. It'll get easier. I'm not even sure why I'm upset. It's not like I haven't faced him twice in the last month or so."

"A lot's happened in the past month. You spent a week in wolf form with me, Valas had her people kidnap you and you killed her, we got engaged, and now Daniel and Nan have gotten married. Not to mention we have two newborn pups in the pack and two new wolves, both of whom you helped during their Change with a new power you didn't know you had. We have more to protect than we did the last time you saw him." His arms tightened around me. "You can be as vulnerable as you want here with me, but when you walk out our door, you need to be your fierce, fearless self."

"Don't worry. I will be."

"I know you will." He tipped my chin up. "Have you remembered anything more about your dream from last night?"

I frowned and thought. "No, nothing. Why?"

"No particular reason, other than I'm still worried about you. No other fainting spells?"

"Nope. I feel good today." I made a face because my definition of "good" seemed to be *I'm not dying*. "Other than, you know, all the bullshit." I glanced at the clock again and sighed. "I gotta get ready."

He held me still. "I love you, Miss Magic. If you need me or the whole pack to come to Merrum Manor, you know how to let me know. And if Moses tries anything, do whatever you have to do to get yourself and Malcolm out of that house. We'll have your back no matter what."

"I know." I rose from his lap and went into the bathroom to brush my hair and touch up my makeup. "I don't think he'll try anything, though. He'll probably play nice for a while."

"It's the playing nice that makes me suspicious." Sean leaned against the doorframe. "He's made threats, for sure, but you've said it yourself more than once—he's been acting strangely since the night he engineered that meeting at Luciano's. I want to know why."

"Makes two of us." I blotted my lipstick, tossed the tissue in the trash, and checked my reflection.

I'd chosen an emerald green tank under a black cardigan, jeans, ankle boots, and my best crystal jewelry to wear to dinner. Each crystal held a spell useful for attack, defense, or healing. I also wore an amulet given to me by Carly. The spell it held, *Return to Sender*, would send any spell, hex, or curse back on the person who set or threw it. Another amulet in my pocket would buzz if I came near hidden wards or spellwork that would injure me. I might think Moses would play nice, but that didn't mean I trusted him.

After ensuring the safety was on, I slipped my Smith & Wesson into its holster, clipped it to my belt at the small of my back where it was covered by the cardigan, and turned to Sean. "Well, how do I look?"

"Do you have any idea how crazy you make me when you put on lipstick and a gun?" He nuzzled my neck. "Hurry up with dinner and get home. I have plans for us."

"Finding that missing remote?" I teased. "By the way, did you borrow my purple notepad? The one that was on my desk?"

"No, I did not." He pinched the bridge of his nose. "I'm going to have another talk with that dragon."

"Good luck with that, babe." I gave him a quick kiss. "Back soon." Our perimeter wards tingled on my skin. My ride had arrived. "Malcolm!" I called. "Time to go."

My ghost sidekick appeared in our bedroom and floated back and forth. "Ready when you are, Trouble Magnet."

ELEVEN

MY CHAUFFEUR TO AND FROM MERRUM MANOR WAS A YOUNG BRUNETTE mage named O'Neil. Until recently, she'd served as one of Moses's personal guards. He'd become dissatisfied with her performance and threatened to turn her over to his most sadistic lieutenant, Carter Kade. I'd suggested he assign her to me instead. She had no idea what hell I'd saved her from.

Since she was no longer a guard, she didn't wear a uniform, but she'd donned a navy blue jacket the same color. Under it she wore a black T-shirt and dark jeans. Dark clothes hid blood better. The Vamp Court enforcers also wore black.

"Good evening, Ms. Worth," O'Neil said as she opened the rear door for me.

"I'd rather sit up front." I went around to the passenger side. "I'm not a fan of sitting in the back."

She blocked the passenger door before I could grab the handle. "I can protect you better in the back. That's my job." A job that she had to do perfectly and according to Moses's demands to stay alive.

Still, I held my ground. "I know what your job is, but if we end up having to fight, we're going to fight together. I don't cower in the back seat while someone takes hits meant for me. Your boss knows that. If he doesn't like where I sit in the car, he can take it up with me."

Her eyes widened. She'd probably never heard anyone talk about Moses like that, or even imagined she would. And she had to know as well as I did that the vehicle was bugged. No doubt Moses was listening to us now.

"I don't want to be late," I reminded her when she didn't move. "Let's get going."

She apparently figured out I wasn't going to back down, so she opened the door.

Malcolm floated into the back seat as I settled in the passenger seat. He leaned close and touched my arm. *You trying to get her in trouble?* he asked. *I thought you liked her.*

Moses is listening, I reminded him. *Everything I do and say is part of this game we're playing. If I rode in the back without arguing, he'd take it as a sign I'm letting him make the rules. I've worked very hard to establish this as a partnership. I can't give an inch—not on anything. He will take a mile every time.*

This is a side of you I don't like to see. His voice in my head sounded unhappy. *You're cold when you talk that way.*

I'm sorry, I told him, and I meant it. *But that's the price of playing this game. He's cold and calculating, so when I'm dealing with him, I have to be that way too. You know that's not the real me, and it won't ever be. It's a role I play.*

He let go of my arm and floated back. His uneasiness had waned, but he clearly didn't like anything about the situation. None of us did.

Our drive to Merrum Manor remained quiet. I would have chatted about inconsequential things or at least turned on the radio to pass the time, but O'Neil was hyper-alert for any sign of a threat and I had to let her do her job.

When Valas had Daniel and me kidnapped from our pack land, she did it right under the noses of two of Moses's guards. I hadn't seen either of those guards since and assumed Moses had them killed for failing to prevent the kidnapping. Never mind we were taken by a team of a dozen Court enforcers against whom two cabal guards wouldn't have a prayer, no matter how well-armed or well-trained they were. Even Sean, Nan, and Ben hadn't been able to keep us from being taken.

Though most of his business interests centered in and around Baltimore, a year ago my grandfather purchased a sprawling Victorian-era mansion here to use as his West Coast headquarters. That wasn't a coincidence. Apparently, he'd tracked me to the area and formed a brief alliance with a local crime boss, Darius Bell, to draw me out of hiding. As soon as they succeeded, he had Bell killed and took over his cabal.

The moment the manor came into view, nausea surged in my stomach. I rested my elbow on the window and propped my chin on my hand, feigning boredom in case Moses also had a camera in the vehicle.

Fake it and you can take it, I reminded myself. *He can only get to me if I let him, and only if I let him see it.*

While the house itself remained largely unchanged, he'd made some modifications to make it more defensible, most noticeably a tall wall around the entire estate and a double gate, all protected by deadly black wards. We drove through the gates and wards. They sizzled on my skin and made me queasy. Some of the wards were illegal razor wards, which would slice us to ribbons if the spellwork that granted this vehicle passage failed midway through.

O'Neil parked in the mansion's garage. I opened my own door and got out as the heavy, reinforced door rolled closed. Malcolm stuck to me like glue as O'Neil led us into the house.

The manor had housed a bordello for almost seventy years until a combination of the number of ghosts that haunted its rooms and the efforts of law enforcement finally closed it down. Before he moved in and christened the place Merrum Manor after himself, Moses had the strongest ghosts captured into crystals for his mages to use for power and discorporated the rest of the spirits that had called the mansion home. One of the captured ghosts was Malcolm's boyfriend Liam.

Rather than follow O'Neil, I walked at her side with Malcolm behind us as we made our way from the garage down several mirror-lined hallways. We passed a dozen cabal guards and soldiers, but I didn't see any sign of Moses's head lieutenant, Nora Keegan. She and I had forged a secret alliance against Moses because she knew her days were numbered. Except for Kade, Moses went through lieutenants like toilet paper, and he knew he couldn't trust her long term because she'd betrayed her former cabal for him. Once a turncoat, always a turncoat. The moment she looked at him in a way he didn't like or he thought she'd outlived her usefulness, she'd be dead. For a long list of reasons, I'd never like or even feel sympathy for her, but I certainly didn't envy her.

O'Neil took us to a pair of doors. She knocked, paused, and slid the doors open about a foot. "Sir, your guest is here."

An all-too-familiar voice with a distinctly Baltimore accent responded from inside the room. "Show her in."

O'Neil opened the doors wider and stepped aside. Chin raised and expression carefully neutral, I strode into the room with Malcolm right behind me.

The mansion's formal dining room was as enormous as I'd imagined. As with the rest of the house, Moses had preserved most of the original luxurious décor, including the enormous risqué bordello painting over the large fireplace. Maybe he wanted to feel like modern aristocracy living in this plush Victorian mansion, which was very different in almost every respect from his very modern cabal headquarters near Baltimore. He certainly acted like some kind of king.

As I entered, Moses rose from his tall chair at the head of the dining table. It could probably easily seat sixteen people, but at the moment there were only two chairs. The tall chair at the head of the table was unmistakably his, and he'd set a place at his right so we'd be sitting only a few feet apart. As ridiculous as it might have looked, I would much rather have sat at the foot of the table than close enough to smell his cologne.

I'd dressed casually for the meal, since I didn't want to give Moses the impression that I'd invested time fretting over my clothing choices. Moses usually wore tailored designer suits whether he was at home or in public. Tonight, however, for only the second time in my entire life—the first being about a month ago, when I'd first come to see him here at the manor—he wore slacks and a button-up shirt with the sleeves rolled halfway up his forearms.

His attire put me more on guard. He seemed to be going over-board trying to relate to me. That was more suspicious than if he'd been his usual suit-wearing, overtly malicious self. I suddenly wondered if he'd somehow seen what I'd been wearing and dressed down to match my attire. Strange as that might seem, I wouldn't put it past him. To my grandfather, everything was a game.

Moses came around the table to meet me in front of the fireplace. His gray hair looked freshly barbered. So did his close-trimmed beard and mustache. He'd always been overly fastidious and conscious of his appearance, like he thought he was a cover model for *Crime Lord Monthly*.

He gave me an appraising look, as if wondering what I was think-ing, and extended his hand. "Good evening, Ms. Worth."

"Hey." I shook his hand briefly and resisted the urge to wipe my palm on my pants when he let go.

Moses glanced over my shoulder at O'Neil. "Wait in the hallway."

"Yes, sir." She closed the doors. I heard the soft *thunk* of a lock.

"You're not a prisoner," he said at my glare. "It's a security measure, nothing more. This room has no wards. I know locked doors won't keep you in."

"No, they won't. Nor will the house walls or the perimeter wards." I made a show of looking around. "Was there not a *more* ostentatious room available for this dinner?"

"Yes, but my lieutenants are using it for a meeting," he said blandly.

For a beat, I stared at him. Was that...a *joke?* Surely not. I had never heard my grandfather attempt to be funny a single time in my entire life.

At my reaction, the corners of his mouth turned up in a ghost of a smile. "Please pour yourself a drink at the bar."

"No thanks. Water's fine."

To my surprise, he didn't argue as he'd done on previous occasions when I refused a drink. "Then let's have a seat, Alice." He gestured grandly at the table. "The soup's already served."

Malcolm's unease prickled through our binding. He'd asked me several days ago if I worried Moses might poison me at one of these meals. But honestly, I didn't think so.

My grandfather had asked for three things in return for his ongoing protection and letting me continue to live my life more or less as I wanted: a truce between us, the occasional favor, and what he called "family dinners."

With my aunt Catherine, my mom's older sister, now dead, my grandfather and I were the last of the Murphys. He hadn't given up hope that he could get me back under his thumb, but he'd relied on gifts and promises as much as threats to persuade me to make a deal with him. That made me extremely suspicious, because I'd never known him to use anything but threats to get what he wanted. Maybe he thought he'd have a better chance if he didn't act like a total monster, though he had to know I wouldn't think of him any other way. So why play nice? I had no idea—at least, not yet.

I went around to my chair with Malcolm right on my heels. Moses pulled out my chair, got me settled, and then returned to his seat on my left. Malcolm floated behind my chair.

"Kind of you to join an old man for dinner," my grandfather said as I draped my napkin across my lap.

It's not like I had a choice, I thought. "I rarely turn down free food," I said instead.

With a dry chuckle, he took the cover off my bowl of soup before uncovering his own. "I remembered you like minestrone. It happens to be one of my chef's specialities. *Bon appétit*, Alice."

I poured myself a glass of ice water from the pitcher on the table. I despised that he somehow knew what kind of soup I liked, because he meant that I'd liked it when I was his prisoner. Back then, we'd seldom eaten together, especially after I reached my teens. Most of my meals were delivered on trays to my rooms in his compound.

Those memories killed what little appetite I had. I stared at the soup like it was a bowl of spiders.

Fierce and fearless, Sean had called me. And normally I was, even when it came to facing Moses. But for some reason, the fact he remembered something so frivolous when those years had been so horrible for me sucked the ferocity right out of me.

I had to regroup or I'd set myself back in my game with Moses to the point I'd never regain what I'd lost, but I felt paralyzed.

Some bad-ass mage I was. Sucker-punched by a bowl of soup.

Strangely, I couldn't tell whether Moses had done this on purpose or he actually thought I'd appreciate his version of thoughtfulness. Usually when he did or said something cruel, he looked right at me and I never had to wonder about his motives. At the moment, his attention was on his own meal.

Malcolm poked me in the shoulder. The cold sensation made me twitch. "Snap out of it, Alice," he hissed. "Eat the damn soup, or so help me I'll sing every last Olivia Newton-John song I know, starting with the ones you said make you queasy."

That jolted me out of my paralysis. Bless him. I picked up my spoon.

"How's business at Maclin Security?" Moses asked after a few minutes of quiet soup consumption.

"It's good." Which he knew damn well. Once we'd reached an agreement, he'd lifted his embargo on Sean's company and they were swamped with clients again. He probably knew more about goings-on at Maclin Security than I did.

"Sean and his business partner have worked very hard to build their reputation," I added. "I'm happy to see them busy again."

"As am I." Moses dabbed his mustache with his napkin and left his spoon in his empty bowl. "You like the soup?"

The question seemed innocuous, and his expression held only mild interest, but now that I'd had a few minutes to think about it, both the choice of soup and his casual reference to my past had to be deliberate. The fact I'd even entertained the possibility, however briefly, that he was actually trying to be thoughtful was laughable—only I wasn't laughing. Understanding that this was all just part of his game did put me back on solid ground, though.

"Very much." I deliberately scraped my spoon on the bottom of the bowl to get the last of the broth to show he hadn't rattled me—not much, anyway. "Compliments to the chef."

"I'll pass your kind words along to André." Moses pressed a button on the underside of the table.

As if they'd been waiting just outside, uniformed staff entered through a single door on the wall opposite my chair. They cleared our bowls and served our meals from a rolling cart. Dinner turned out to be roasted chicken with vegetables. I hated to admit it, but the food smelled heavenly.

Once the kitchen staff left, Moses rose and took his glass to the bar. "Are you sure I can't get you a drink?" he asked as he poured himself two more fingers of bourbon. "I have a single malt scotch here I'd like your opinion on."

Really, there didn't seem to be much point refusing a drink when we were already eating together. In for a penny, in for a single malt, and all that. "All right," I said.

He returned to the table and set a glass in front of me. I paused between bites of chicken to savor the smell of the whisky and take a sip. "Really good," I told him when he seemed to be waiting for my verdict. "Very smooth. A little smoky and a nice bite on the finish."

"Glad you approve."

We ate quietly for a while as Malcolm floated around the room. I sensed Moses watching me when my attention was elsewhere. I focused mainly on my food and whisky and ignored him.

Once he finished most of that second glass of bourbon, though, I figured it was time to get him talking. A seemingly casual chat was one of a PI's best methods for obtaining information. Even the cagiest people revealed things when they talked, especially after several glasses of top-shelf bourbon.

"We had some visitors at the house last night," I said.

Moses glanced up from his meal. "Oh?"

"A convoy of Vampire Court enforcers showed up. They served Sean and me with a stack of indictments an inch thick."

He set down his knife and fork. "I was aware you had visitors, but I was led to believe their visit had to do with your newest pack member."

His demeanor had flipped from nonchalant to deadly serious in a blink. I suspected it wasn't the indictments that caused his reaction as much as the fact his intel had been wrong.

"Your spies in the Court fed you bad info, huh?" I sipped my water with deliberate nonchalance. "That sucks—pun intended. It's tough to find good help willing to risk a very unpleasant death, I guess."

His scowl deepened. "What are the charges in the indictment?"

I gave him a brief rundown of what the Court had alleged and their demands.

Moses cut his remaining chicken into pieces as he listened and thought. When I finished, he said, "Well, obviously you'll hand this Albrecht over once you put up enough resistance to save face."

"We will *not* hand him over." It was my turn to put down my fork. "What on earth would make you think we'd do that?"

"Because it would be the smart thing to do?" He raised his perfectly groomed eyebrows. "He belongs to the Court. You're responsible for your own life first. Why risk it for a stranger?"

Deep breaths, I told myself. *He's just trying to get under your skin. Don't let him.*

"Matthias is not a stranger," I said coolly. "He's a pack mate. He's a *person*, not property. We don't 'return' people like they're Frisbees that ended up in our yard."

"Oh, Alice." He chuckled. "How can you say this man is a pack mate? You aren't a shifter. You're a human mage who associates with werewolves."

Despite my determination to stay calm, I wanted to knock that smug look off his face. "Our pack includes several humans. All of them are pack mates. A pack isn't just about whether you're a shifter."

"I think the Were Ruling Council would disagree."

"Some of them would," I allowed. "But not all. A lot of packs include humans. But even if ours was the only one that did, it would still be true."

He waved his hand, dismissing my argument in its entirety. "If you want to call yourself part of Sean's pack, that's all well and good. Hopefully you'll never have to defend that belief with your own blood."

"I already have, more than once," I said. Damn it, I hated him. "As you well know. Most recently last month in front of members of the Council and a hundred other shifters. I don't think anyone from the Council or any other pack will challenge me again about whether I'm part of the Tomb Mountain Pack."

"Be that as it may, you'll have to hand Albrecht over to the Court. If he belongs to them, he's their property. *Legally*," he added when I started to argue. "You know as well as I do the Court doesn't have employees like a corporation. You can't hire on and quit whenever you feel like it."

"That doesn't make it right, though. A whole lot of people the Court considers its property aren't there by choice."

"But some *are*. Have you asked Albrecht in what circumstances he joined the Court in the first place and what kind of documentation they have on him?"

I shook my head. "Not yet. I only know what's in the Court's paperwork."

"Then I suggest you have a very pointed conversation with him and get the facts." He finished the last of his bourbon. "I think you'll find you have no choice but to give him back and let the Court do with him as they please."

"Not gonna happen."

"Back to more important matters," he continued as if I hadn't spoken. "Regarding these indictments, I'll of course put my lawyers to work and see the charges are dismissed."

"Moses." I set my fork down again, this time for good, and dropped my napkin on top of it. "We have good attorneys. Aaron Riddell won't let us down." But since I had to play the game, I added, "I'll let him know he has additional resources he can call upon, if he needs to."

"I'll let it go at that for now. You see, we work well together when you allow yourself to be reasonable."

I counted backward from ten to one before I spoke so I could find my calm center again. "I don't know to what lengths Charles is willing to go to get his way on this. I can't take anything off the table right now, not even you."

Moses smiled. "Smart girl."

Stupid girl, he'd called me a hundred times, usually after having me tortured. *Why won't you just do as you're told, stupid girl?*

"I'm not a girl," I reminded him. "I haven't been one for a long time."

"That's true. You're very much a grown woman now." He dabbed his mouth with his napkin. "Interested in rumors about Charles and his Court?"

"Sure." As long as he was feeling chatty, I was all ears. I didn't take what he said at face value because cars in Hell would need snow tires before I trusted Moses on anything, but it might give me some insight on our situation. Or he might let something else slip about himself. Either way, I'd come out ahead.

"Then let's move to the conservatory." He rose. "I think we've both had enough of this room. A refill on your drink before we leave?"

I finished my whisky and left the glass on the table. "Nah, I'm good. Don't want to spoil such a good whisky by drinking more than one glass."

"Then let's go." He pressed another button under the table to unlock the dining room's doors.

O'Neil slid the doors open but didn't step over the threshold. No doubt she'd developed that habit early on, since many rooms in a cabal headquarters had the kinds of wards no one wanted to cross accidentally. "Yes, sir?"

"We're going to the conservatory. You can accompany us." He gestured for me to go ahead of him. "After you, Ms. Worth."

TWELVE

I'D ONLY TAKEN TWO STEPS INTO THE HALLWAY WHEN A FAMILIAR VOICE spoke from my right. "Well, well. Hello, sunshine. I thought that was you I saw skulking around."

I heaved an exaggerated sigh and turned. "Hi, Nora. You're still alive? Amazing."

Somehow, O'Neil managed not to gape at my flippant remark to Moses's most vicious blood and air mage. I could only imagine what she was thinking: *Who is this person who gets to talk back to both my bosses without fear, when anyone else who even looks at either of them the wrong way would be dead on the spot?*

Hands on her hips, Nora Keegan chuckled. She wore jeans, a long-sleeved shirt, and boots, with her shoulder-length dark brown hair in a ponytail. "Always a little comedian, aren't you?"

"I like to think so." Deliberately, so she knew it was an insult, I turned my back on her and raised my eyebrows at Moses. "So? To the conservatory?"

He smiled with what I might have described as paternal pride if I thought him capable of having normal feelings. My grandfather liked it when I acted like a Murphy, which was more or less short-hand for evil, pompous, manipulative, and cold.

Meanwhile, I felt Nora's stare on my back as Moses and I headed down the hall in the direction of the mansion's beautiful glass conservatory. Moses having dinner with me was one thing, but the fact he allowed me to go into his conservatory, where literally no other person alive or undead was permitted to go, had to give Nora heartburn. Not just because we would be alone in there, but because the conservatory contained Moses's blood garden.

Moses had mixed pints of his own magic-infused blood into the soil and it permeated all the plants and trees. For all the power the garden generated to maintain its own wards and feed magic to its creator, as a blood mage I could use it to turn him into crime lord vichyssoise without even much effort.

Moses had invited me into the garden to show off that he wasn't afraid of any threat I might pose. It was absolutely in character for him, so most people probably didn't think any more about it. But I did wonder as Moses unlocked the door to the conservatory and ushered me over its threshold if Nora might start thinking there was more to it than just Moses flexing. She was many things, but she wasn't dumb.

As Sean and others had pointed out more than once, there was no reason for anyone to suspect Moses's granddaughter Ava had survived the explosion that had apparently killed her six years ago, much less start thinking I might be her. But the more interactions Moses and I had, the more people close to him—like Nora—would notice how he treated me. And that might get her thinking.

The very last thing I wanted was for Nora to start thinking too much.

We left O'Neil in the hallway and made our way from the closed doors along the narrow footpath that ran through the thick foliage to a paved terrace near the far end of the garden. My own much-smaller garden at home had deadly carnivorous plants grown in soil infused with my blood and that of a slain demon. I wished I could have a garden as large as this one. Besides the obvious benefit of producing more power, as a blood mage, I enjoyed the heady, electric sensation of walking through any blood garden, even this one that buzzed with Moses's blood.

"I think these dinners are a bad idea," I told my grandfather as we reached the stone terrace.

I expected him to sit at the table, but instead he made his way around the perimeter of the paved area, examining the plants growing at its edge. "So you've said," he said, his attention on a large fern with beautiful dark green fronds.

"Not just for the obvious reasons." I flopped into one of the chairs and propped my boots on the seat of another one, crossing my ankles. "You don't treat me like you would anyone else who doesn't quake in your presence or kiss your ass. Anyone who's around us sees that. I thought you didn't *want* anyone to figure out who I am. If we want to keep our secrets secret, we should avoid interacting in person, except for the occasional business meeting."

When he didn't reply, I scowled. "Tell me that doesn't make more sense than this plan of yours for *family dinners*." I put air quotes around the words. "I have no idea what you're hoping to get out of dinners with me, but we might get something we both *don't* want— namely, someone putting two and two together. Someone like Nora."

"Do you think I fear anyone who works for me or what they might think?" He glanced at me, then resumed running his fingers along the long, thin leaves of the fern. "I've been doing this a long time. I know when someone has started thinking. And I know what to do about it."

"You said you wouldn't kill people because of me anymore, remember?" I persisted. "Killing people for thinking is the *direct opposite* of not killing them."

"I never said I wouldn't kill anyone." He moved from the fern to the plant to its right and caressed its leaves. "I said I would only kill those who forced my hand and made it necessary. You said you were curious about Charles Vaughan."

I gritted my teeth. "I'm not done talking about you killing your people because you think these stupid dinners are worth more than their lives."

"You made the deal. We agreed to terms." His expression turned cold. "I'm not interested in hearing you whine about the lives of people you don't know. I assure you I have the situation under control. Now, we can discuss the Court or you can choose another topic, but the subject of our dinners is closed."

I wanted to know what he meant by having the situation under control, but he clearly had no intention of telling me. So I switched gears back to the Court.

"I've known Charles for years," I said. "As much as anyone can say they know a vamp, I guess. We've interacted quite a bit, especially when I did investigative work for the Court. We cut ties a couple of months ago." No need to tell him *why* I'd cut ties with Charles. He didn't need to know the depths to which Charles had betrayed me. "I certainly didn't see this coup coming. I don't think Valas did either, or she would have been ready for it."

"That was my assessment too." Moses finally abandoned his plants and sat in the chair across from mine. "Like most, I'd thought Valas would rule her Court for as long as she wanted. She was a good leader. Not everyone liked her, but she had everyone's respect. Vaughan's move was quite the power play, even by vampire standards. He must have planned it for years—possibly decades."

"I can't help but think his new connection to the Silver Thorn coven made this possible. The moment Valas was vulnerable, he got Morgan Clark in bed, established her mother's coven his ally, and took his shot."

"We both know witches love power more than anything." He poured each of us a glass of water from the carafe on the table. "As I'm sure you're aware, the two members of the Court who sided with Valas against Charles are deceased."

I swallowed hard. "Yes, I did know that." The memory of seeing and *smelling* Valas bathing in Ossun and Friedrich's lifeblood would haunt my nightmares for a long time. "Are all three seats still empty?"

"Yes." He settled back into his chair and sipped his water. "From what I understand, Charles has focused on filling those seats with vampires loyal to him. Seats on a Court rarely become available, so for many vampires this is a once-in-a-millennium opportunity. Statements of interest come in every day from around the world."

"Charles will leverage this to the max." I rubbed the end of my nose as I thought about the implications. "Valas killing Ossun and Friedrich was just about the best thing she could have done for Charles. He must have thought it was his birthday when he found out they were dead. Between whoever he chooses to add and those on the Court who are already loyal to him, he'll have a stranglehold on the Court that will last for centuries, if not more."

"I think you're right." He raised his glass of water in a kind of salute. "For better or worse, Charles Vaughan has taken power and set himself up for a nice, long reign—if he can survive this transition period."

I snorted. "Big *if*."

How would this affect our pack? The indictments aside, generally speaking a stable Vampire Court benefited everyone because that made them a known quantity. Deals made would stick as long as the people who made them remained in power. Turnover meant chaos and jockeying for influence both within the Court and among various alliances and organizations like the Were Ruling Council, local cabals, and even the federal Supernatural and Paranormal Entity Agency, or SPEMA.

But we didn't know what kind of leader Charles would be yet, and that was an *X* factor the size of Alaska.

I sighed. "Okay, so there are three empty seats on the Court and Charles wants to fill them with toadies he can control. What else you got?"

"He plans to surround himself with an honor guard of dhampirs."

My eyebrows shot up. "Not even Valas did that. She had human enforcers."

"Valas relied on her great power to intimidate," Moses reminded me. "She didn't need a cadre of dhampirs—or *thought* she didn't."

"As it turned out, she probably wished she had an army of them when it all went to hell." I hummed. "Charles doesn't have Valas's sorcerer power, so he needs the dhampirs to back him up. Is Charles changing all the dhampirs himself? Of course he is." I answered my own question. "They'll be utterly loyal to him."

I didn't mean to sound so impressed. Moses, on the other hand, clearly admired Charles's strategy. "I've found enforcing completely loyalty to be a sound management practice myself."

No shit, I thought. "Anything else?" I asked aloud.

He finished his glass of water and set it on the table. "I enjoyed dinner."

"Yeah, I don't care. About the Court, I mean."

He smiled. I didn't like that smile. It seemed kindly but only evil and cruelty lurked behind it. Moses wasn't capable of anything else. I had the scars and twenty-four years of firsthand experience to prove it.

"I'll make some calls and pass on any information I get," he said.

"What do you want in return for asking around?"

"Nothing." At my obvious skepticism, he chuckled. "It's not difficult for me to get information. You're used to working with vampires. They exaggerate how much effort they put into gathering intel so they can charge a fortune in favors or work in trade. This is a phone call or two at most."

I'd often had that same thought about vampires and their business practices. It was eerie to hear Moses vocalize my own theory. "Thanks," I said. "I appreciate it."

"You're welcome."

I had a sudden thought. "Do you know what happened to Valas's daytime representative, Ezekiel Monroe? I haven't heard anything about him and he wasn't at the manor where Valas holed up—at least, not that I saw."

He rose. "Valas didn't take him with her when she escaped."

I stood as well. "So Charles got him?"

"Yes."

"Oh. Is he—?"

"Yes. You don't want the details, I'm sure."

"No, I guess I don't." My shoulders sagged. I hadn't been friends with Monroe, and he'd thrown me under the bus more than once on Valas's orders, but I hadn't wanted him dead. His apparently horrible execution really drove home the point that Charles was more ruthless than I'd thought.

I sensed Malcolm floating invisibly at my side and realized for the past several minutes I hadn't felt him nearby. I hadn't really noticed him leave, having been deep in conversation with Moses, but the fact he'd left me, even briefly, caused concern that I couldn't show until we were well away from this place.

"We're done, then," I said. "I'll tell O'Neil I'm ready to go."

"She answers to me, Alice. She won't sneeze unless I tell her to, much less leave the manor with you or anyone else." He regarded me. "If she turned against you on my orders, would you kill her?"

"Are you planning to tell her to kill me?"

"Not at the moment." He gave me a thin smile. "But it's always on the table. Would you kill her if I did?"

Hatred made my eyes hot and voice clipped. "Yes." In those circumstances, I wouldn't have a choice. It would be her or me, and it wasn't going to be me.

"Remember that every time you feel tempted to consider her an ally or friend. She's neither of those things to you." He gestured at the stone walkway. "After you, dear."

Instead of leaving, I said, "I feel sorry for you."

I caught a flash of—something—in his eyes. Maybe surprise, maybe fear. It vanished so quickly I thought maybe I'd imagined it or misinterpreted what I'd seen.

"What you just said about not considering someone an ally or friend applies more to you than to me, doesn't it?" I said. "I have allies and friends. I have *family*. I love a lot of people and they love me back. It must be so hard to live the way you do, after you've chosen a path without any of the things that make life worth living."

He nailed me with a withering stare that might have made anyone else run or cower. But with my feet back on solid ground, emotionally speaking, I just raised my eyebrows and waited.

"Three things, Alice," he said, his voice flat. "First, I don't need or want any pity from you. Second, power always comes with a price and I'd rather be feared than loved any day. And third, you have no business assuming anything about me, least of all what my choices have been. Now get the hell out."

That uncharacteristic flash of anger convinced me not only was I right, I'd also struck a nerve. He might have knocked me off-kilter with the soup and tried to put me in my place by reminding me O'Neil wasn't my ally or friend, but I'd just punched him back hard enough that he'd felt it. That was job well done in my book.

"Best idea you've had all night," I said. And with Malcolm at my back, I got the hell out.

THIRTEEN

WHEN O'NEIL PULLED INTO OUR DRIVEWAY, I WASN'T SURPRISED TO SEE Sean waiting. We often met each other on the porch. No doubt he felt more concerned about my safe arrival than usual.

What *did* surprise me was the sight of Matthias's enormous brindle wolf peering out of the darkness around the northeast corner of the house. While most new shifters reveled in their furry form, he'd shifted only a handful of times since becoming a werewolf. His aversion to his wolf form worried Sean and me because we weren't sure if he disliked being a werewolf, or he worried he couldn't control himself or protect others as well as a wolf as he did as a man.

At this moment, Matthias's wolf stared at O'Neil's SUV as if he wanted to take a bite out of the vehicle or its driver and didn't particularly care which. His eyes glowed as he bared his teeth, his ears flat against his head. I saw no sign of the cowering, limping wolf I'd met when Matthias first Changed. If I hadn't seen that version of Matthias myself, I might not have believed he was the same wolf as this fierce guardian.

A sudden thought made me pause with my hand on the car door:

What if once he comes into his full potential, Matthias is more dominant than Ben or Nan?

Meanwhile, O'Neil's gaze remained fixed on Sean and Matthias, watching for any sign of trouble. Over the past few weeks I'd assessed her to be a very capable bodyguard, though I hadn't had the opportunity to see her in action yet. If my past was any indication, it was only a matter of time before something blew up. Something always did.

Her charge from Moses was to keep me alive and unharmed, under penalty of her own especially unpleasant death. But if she turned on me, on his orders or for any other reason, I'd have to kill her.

Moses's cold voice echoed in my head: "Remember that every time you feel tempted to consider her an ally or friend."

A few hours ago, as O'Neil and I argued over whether I would ride shotgun or in the back seat, I'd told her if we ended up in a fight, we would fight together. I'd said it knowing Moses would probably hear me, because I wanted him to know I didn't cower in the back seat while someone took hits meant for me. And in response, he'd reminded me my morals didn't apply to O'Neil. I had to keep her in front of me—not because I wanted her to take bullets for me, but because I couldn't trust her at my back.

I got out of the SUV. "Thanks for the ride." I shut the door before she had a chance to respond. I wanted away from Moses, O'Neil, the whole mess.

Sean met me halfway across the yard as O'Neil made a three-point turn in the driveway and headed for the road. He wrapped me in his arms and rested his chin on the top of my head. I sensed Malcolm go inside the house.

"Do you want to talk about it, or do you need some space?" Sean asked.

I appreciated that he'd offered options when both he and his wolf probably wanted to hold me and not let go until I stopped shaking with pent-up anger. "I want to talk," I said.

He took my hand. "On the deck, with beers?"

One of the many things I loved about Sean was his willingness to go with the flow, even when I had unexpected requests. "Upstairs," I countered. "With no clothes on."

He blinked at me. "You want to take our clothes off and then *talk?*"

Okay, so maybe he didn't *always* just go with the flow. "Yes. And after we talk, we can do...other things."

"Well, in that case." He smiled. "Lead the way, Miss Magic."

Matthias had already disappeared into the night by the time we reached the porch. I hadn't sensed him shift back to human form, so maybe he would stay a wolf for a while. That made me hopeful.

When we got inside, I called, "Malcolm?"

He floated up through the floor from the basement. His expression indicated my tone had tipped him off that I wasn't happy. "Hey, Alice."

"Where did you go?" I demanded. "While we were in the conservatory, where did you go?"

Sean went still. "Malcolm." His voice sounded deadly. "You didn't leave her alone with that bastard, did you?"

Malcolm floated back and forth. More emotions than I could count flashed across his face, but when he spoke his voice was quiet. "I was gone for about five minutes."

I thought Sean would shift in pure rage. "Five *minutes?* He could have killed her in a second!" He nearly roared the words. "You swore to me you would never leave her side while she was at Merrum Manor. How could you betray Alice like that?"

"I didn't betray anyone." The more Sean raised his voice, the quieter Malcolm became. "Moses and Alice were chatting. It was friendly."

"There is nothing friendly in anything I do with Moses." My voice was quiet too, but for an entirely different reason. I hurt almost beyond belief. "I don't know what to say. I count on you to have my back the same way I have yours. Why did you leave?"

"To find Liam."

"Oh, Malcolm." I sagged against the wall. Finding out he'd left had been a punch in the gut. The grief on his face now felt like a second one. "Moses has traps and wards all over that manor. He could have captured you. We talked about this. It's too dangerous for you to snoop around."

"I had to know!" Malcolm burst out. "I had to know if he was there—if he was still alive. Well, not *alive* alive. You know what I mean."

"You know who *is* alive?" Sean cut in. His eyes glowed like golden lanterns. "*Alice* is alive. It's your responsibility to care about that and keep her safe."

"Don't you think I know that?" Malcolm shouted. I couldn't remember the last time I'd heard Malcolm yell in anger, or even if I'd *ever* heard him do so. "Leaving Alice to look for Liam was just about the hardest thing I've ever done, and you don't know what I've had to do in my life *or* my afterlife. Don't you *dare* accuse me of not caring."

"Stop, stop." I raised my hands. "Both of you, please stop."

Sean stalked back and forth across the living room. Malcolm watched him, guilt and anger warring on his face.

"Did you find him?" I asked.

"Yes." Malcolm floated close to me. "We were right about him being a prisoner. He's in a crystal in a mage's workshop in the east wing of the manor. They're using him as a power source for spellwork."

I flinched. There was a big difference between suspecting Liam was trapped and knowing it. My anger and sorrow made me feel sick. "I'm sorry, Malcolm. No one deserves that, especially Liam. I know it doesn't help, but I'm glad we know where he is."

"I want to free him somehow. There has to be a way."

"I will find a way," I promised. "Somehow I'll get Moses to hand him over. I just have to come up with a way to do it without him figuring out that it's something I need, because he'll use Liam as leverage in ways you or I can't imagine."

"I know." He hung his head. "I just couldn't wait to know any longer."

"It's okay." It wasn't, really, but nothing about any of this was okay. I might have done the same thing in his place if Sean were trapped and tormented in Moses's clutches.

Maybe that occurred to Sean too, because his fury had gone from an eleven to about an eight. But that didn't mean he could let it go. "I can't forgive you for this, and I won't forget it," he told Malcolm. "I trusted you. You gave me your word."

"I understand." Malcolm floated back. "I'll give you both some space."

"That's probably for the best," I said. I was so tired. "Good night."

"Good night, Alice." He floated back down through the floor to the basement.

Sean scrubbed his face with his hands.

"He loves me," I said. "He loves Liam too. I know he broke his word to you, but we'd be inhuman if we held his pain against him."

"Alice." He joined me by the stairs. He was so angry, but he didn't seem to know where to direct it. Malcolm, Moses, Charles, even Matthias. And me too, a least a little. Maybe he thought I wasn't supposed to have forgiven Malcolm so quickly.

"Come on." I took his hand and tugged.

He let me lead him upstairs. When we got to our room, I shut the door, stripped off my clothes, and tossed them in the direction of the bathroom. I sat on the edge of the bed while Sean undressed and put our clothes in the hamper.

"You're such a neatnik," I told him as he joined me on the bed.

"If we leave them out, Esme will steal them. That's my favorite pair of jeans. And I like how you look in that top." My werewolf settled in with his back against the headboard and held out his arms. "Come here."

I didn't need to be asked twice. I curled up on his lap, my head against his chest, and listened to his heart. Our wolf amulets hummed when they were close to each other. I'd teased that it sounded and felt like they were purring. Sean always made a show of taking umbrage to the comparison to cats, but I could tell he didn't hate the idea.

"So why talk naked?" he asked.

"Why not?" I countered.

He chuckled. I snuggled in a little closer. "You know, all this wiggling makes it difficult to remember we're here to talk," he said, only half jokingly.

"Sorry." I got comfortable and held still. "I just like how it feels when we're touching skin with nothing else between us. It comforts me. Who knows why since your skin is like a million degrees. I'm roasting."

"Skin contact is a shifter thing, and I love that you want it. Can't do much about my body temperature, I'm afraid." He let out a quiet growl. "You smell like Moses's house."

"I know. I wanted to shower, but I didn't think you'd let me shower alone. I doubt we'd be able to talk in there without getting distracted."

"Fair point." He squeezed me. "What do you want to talk about?"

I gave him a summary of what had happened before, during, and after my visit to Merrum Manor. He listened quietly, rubbing my back as I talked.

"It's not that he caught me off guard by reminding me O'Neil isn't a friend," I said after I described my interaction with my guard and Moses's comments about it. "Or that I'd thought of her as a friend. I'm not an idiot."

"No, of course you aren't." He kissed my hair and curled his fingers around my forearms. "You're home, Alice. You can let it out now."

I realized I'd wrapped my arms around my tummy because it had been churning and hurting since I'd seen that damn bowl of soup. I'd had to hide that fact until I was alone with Sean. Only now, when I was safe and warm and protected, could I let on how much tonight had taken out of me.

"Okay." I took a deep breath and exhaled. "Why am I so worked up about this?"

"I think you're remembering what it's like to be involved with a cabal." Sean rested his head against mine and ran his hands along my arms as if he could take my hurt away through osmosis. "These interactions are triggering all kinds of traumatic memories from the years when you had to be wary of everyone around you."

"That's probably true, but it's not like those memories are ever all that far away."

"Your life is different now. You've built a family around yourself of people you can trust, who'd put themselves between you and anything that might cause you harm. You've changed your perspective. It makes these interactions more jarring than they used to be."

I didn't like what he'd implied. "I've gone soft, is what you're saying."

"That is not at all what I'm saying." He tipped my chin up so he could meet my gaze. "You recognize the cabal mindset for what it is: brutal, unnatural, and inhumane. Unfortunately, that used to be your normal. You acclimatized to it because you had no choice. Now you have a different life and you're pushing back against anything that reminds you of how your life used to be. That includes forced proximity to someone who might save your life one minute and try to take it the next."

That made a hell of a lot of sense, and it went a long way toward explaining why Moses's warning about O'Neil had affected me far more deeply than I'd thought it should.

"I don't want to live like that anymore," I told him. "The life I have—the life I *want*—isn't compatible with cabal mentality. But as long as Moses and I have a truce and a contract between us, I can't escape it."

"Remember what you told me before you signed the contract with Moses: he's playing *your* game on *your* board by *your* rules,"

Sean said. "He just doesn't know it yet. That's how you're going to beat him, eventually, when all the pieces are on the board and the timing is right. No matter how many bowls of soup he serves you or what happens to O'Neil, that's what's going on. The more he thinks he's throwing you curveballs, the more he's snarled in your web."

"That was a lot of metaphors," I teased. Finally, the pain in my stomach and my uneasiness began to fade. "I get what you're saying. Okay. I'll think about that." I sighed. "Item number two: Matthias."

"I see a change in him already after your talk this morning." He frowned. "What's bothering you?"

"What happens if he turns out to be as dominant as Ben or Nan? Or *more* dominant?"

"New werewolves have entered packs for as long as there have been shifters." Sean pulled me close again. "Issues of dominance have always been settled in more or less the same ways. What problems have we had bringing all the new wolves into our pack since you joined us?"

"Not many, but none of the new wolves are very dominant. I have a feeling Matthias is...or he *will* be. You saw how he reacted last night when he saw me fall down. And then tonight when I got back he looked ready to rip that SUV to shreds. What if he's a third, or a beta? What happens to Nan and Ben?"

"Do you trust Matthias?"

I thought about that, but only for a moment. "Yes."

"Nan?"

"Of course!"

"Ben? Me?"

"You know the answer all those questions." I eyed him. "Where are you going with this?"

"If you trust us, then you can trust that we'll resolve any issues of pack hierarchy, no matter what they might be."

"Telling me to just relax and let things play out is a quick way to find yourself on my shit list, Wolf. You know that's not how my mind works."

As usual, Sean knew the right question to ask. "What are you afraid might happen?"

I opened my mouth, closed it, and tried to figure out what exactly had me in knots. "I'm worried I'll have to watch Matthias fight Nan or Ben," I said finally. "Even if it's to submission, I don't want them to hurt each other. And Daniel's still upset that he Changed Matthias unintentionally. How will he react if Matthias turns out to be more dominant than his mate?"

Sean rested his chin on top of my head again. "Knowing Nan and Ben as well as I do, and knowing Matthias as well as I can at this point, I don't think a fight will be required. If it is, it will be to submission. I can't tell you they won't hurt each other because that's not true, and I won't tell you not to be upset because you'd have reason to be upset. I won't be happy either. Unlike other packs where violence is the norm, bloodshed among our pack members is not something we encourage or experience very often."

"So how should I feel?"

"Exactly how you feel. I can't promise that everything in our pack will always be smooth sailing. In fact, I can promise you it *won't*. We will have conflicts—sometimes major ones, just like any group of people. What I *can* promise is I will do whatever I need to do to keep us all as safe, happy, and without conflict as I can. I can also promise that however this works out, we will all be fine. It just might take some time to get there."

It wasn't so much what he said as the conviction in his voice that made the prospect of letting things play out seem if not preferable, at least acceptable. I relaxed against his chest before I realized how tense I'd become. "Thanks for that," I said, rubbing my nose against the hot skin over his heart. "If you can let it play out, so can I, I guess."

"Atta girl." He kissed the top of my head. "Are we done talking? Or is there more on your mind?"

"Lots more, but nothing that won't keep." I smiled at him. "I've made you sit here naked with me for a good half hour. I think your patience deserves a reward."

"It's not so much that *I've* been naked as that *you've* been naked, Miss Magic." He smiled as his hand slid down my side to rest on my hip. "What kind of reward did you have in mind?"

I let out an exaggerated sigh and started to get up. "Load the dishwasher and do some laundry, I guess."

He rolled us over and pinned me to the bed with his body. "*Or*," he murmured, his lips moving from my earlobe along my jaw, "You could stay right here and let me do things to you that will make you blush when you think about it later."

I made a *pfffft* sound and arched my back to encourage him to make his way south of my collarbone. "As if you know how to do things that make me blush."

Teasing him like that was playing with fire, especially these days when his wolf's demands for intimacy were at an all-time high.

But fire was what I wanted, what I *needed*, and what I intended to get.

CHAPTER

FOURTEEN

 knew how good that felt on other more sensitive places on my body. The man was an artist with his mouth.

He cupped my breast with his hand while he teased my nipple with the pad of his thumb. Each little stroke sent quivers through my body. He clearly enjoyed watching me shake with every touch. Come to think of it, he was an artist in a *lot* of ways.

When his lips and teeth replaced his thumb, my hips bucked against him. He chuckled low in his throat and looked up at me through his lashes. "Don't try to rush me, Miss Magic. Perfect breasts deserve worship. But I don't want you feeling too desperate. You can show me what you think I should do when I work my way down."

With his mouth still on my breast, he took my hand and guided it down over my abdomen, past my navel, and between my thighs. I gasped, my back arching as our entwined fingers slipped over my slick, delicate skin.

"My Alice," he murmured. "Open your legs and show me how you like me to touch you."

I spread my knees wide. He rested his hand on mine so he could

137

feel every little quiver and every move I made while I pleasured myself. Mercilessly he licked, sucked, and teased my nipples until the ache of need spread through my whole body.

He surprised me by capturing my hand and taking my fingers into his mouth one by one so he could lick them clean. "You're gentle tonight," he said, placing my hand on my tummy. "Is that what you want from me? Gentleness?"

Ten minutes ago, I would have told him I wanted him to take charge and be rough. I liked pain with my pleasure, and I'd wanted handprints in all the places he was used to giving them to me and then a few new spots. As always, he would have been happy to oblige and then care for me tenderly after.

And I did still want that...or at least part of me did, and would have been very satisfied as a result. With Sean, I was never not satisfied—he made damn sure of that. But now that he was above me, looking into my eyes with that beautiful golden-brown gaze, I knew what I wanted more were soft touches and worship. He understood me and what I needed better than I knew myself sometimes.

"Yes, that's what I want," I said. "My heart hurts."

He scooped me up with one arm, moved us to the side of the bed, and settled us in with his feet on the floor and my knees astride his thighs. "Then let me try to make that hurt go away," he said, and pressed his lips to my chest over my heart. "I love you."

"I know."

He held himself steady as I lowered myself onto him slowly and gently.

The moment the heat and hardness of him pushed inside me, my head fell back and I let out a groan of pleasure and contentment. He let me take my time sliding down, his chest rumbling.

Even when he'd filled me all the way, he let me rest with my head on his chest, his arms around me holding tight while I reveled in his strength and love and the feeling of *him* so hot, so hard, so deep inside me. Our wolf amulets hummed on their chains, pressed between us as he stroked my back and inhaled my scent from the base of my neck at my shoulder.

I loved our farmhouse and the life we were building together, but the truth was, Sean was my home.

I used to think I would never love or be loved because it was too risky on so many levels. A year ago, before I'd met Malcolm and Sean, I'd still believed that, at least mostly. But there must have been chinks in my armor even then because I'd accepted Malcolm into my life and then Sean not long after. They'd had to work hard for that dubious privilege, but not too long before that, they would have had no chance at all. I had a long list of exes and would-be friends who could attest to that fact.

What a difference a year made.

The ache in my heart began to fade.

When I started to move, he let me set the pace, his hands under my thighs to guide and support me. I wrapped my arms around his neck and alternated between grinding on his lap and kissing him and sliding along his hard, hot length. He felt so good that I let out little cries that made his eyes glow golden.

Just before I came, I let some of my magic free to swirl around us in a gentle whirlwind of green and white with traces of blue, red, black, and gold.

"Beautiful," Sean murmured into my hair. "So beautiful. Come for me, love."

When I went over the edge, he slipped his hand between us to draw out my pleasure and make me shudder in his arms. I called his name again and again. My magic rolled through us in a second wave of pleasure that we shared. My head fell against his chest.

As I drifted, he eased me free of him, then drew me back toward the center of the bed, lay down behind me, and hooked my leg over his arm so he could slip into me again. Still gentle, he took control of our pace and his fingers played with me until I came again, this time with a wail.

"My beautiful Miss Magic," he said, his mouth on my ear. "Watch yourself take me. So deep, and so well."

I could barely lift my head from his chest. "So good, Mister Wolf. I feel so good."

He leaned over to take something from his nightstand, then maneuvered me onto my hands and knees. When I made a little complaining sound, he chuckled and kissed my back. "I did promise to make you blush," he said. "Don't think I've forgotten that just because we switched gears."

I wanted to know how he thought he'd make me blush while staying gentle, but decided I'd rather find out.

From behind me, I heard a soft sound, and then something buzzed. Before I had a chance to react, the buzzing moved between my legs. I nearly collapsed at the rush of pleasure. "*Oh.*"

Sean caressed my back and the curves of my backside. "More, Miss Magic?"

"More," I pleaded.

He didn't just turn up the vibrator—he moved it from sensitive place to sensitive place to make me writhe and clutch the bedding. Sometimes he replaced the tip of the vibrator with his tongue until I was reduced to a nearly incoherent, quivering mess.

But he didn't make me beg, and he didn't spank me, though the situation could have easily led in both those directions. Instead, he gently coaxed two more orgasms from me, each from a different place, and each so toe-curlingly good, until I collapsed to the bed, shaking and unable to move.

"You know, that was all very good, Mister Wolf, but I'm not blushing yet," I said when I could talk again.

His smile made heat roll through my entire body. "Oh, I know. That was the warm-up."

"The warm-up?" My eyes widened. "To *what?*"

He told me. And so help me, I blushed.

Chuckling, he lay down and drew me up his body until I strad- dled his face. "Remember, you can ask for mercy if you need it," he said, his eyes twinkling between my thighs. "I gave you a safety word."

"Yes you did." I gripped the headboard. "Shame I forgot it."

He laughed, and then he pulled me down onto his mouth. I let out a ragged cry.

Forget *artist*—he was a Michelangelo with his tongue, teeth, and lips. And he held me still with both hands on my hips so I couldn't move away, gentle but merciless in the way he wrenched moans and wails from me.

Then the vibrator turned on again. I moaned before it even touched me, anticipating how it would feel in combination with his tongue—

—and then he slipped it into a spot I didn't anticipate, and I came so hard and so fast that my scream might have reached the neighbors' homes if I hadn't gotten in the habit of putting up a *sub rosa* ward around our room to keep our sex life private. Our house-guest—much less our neighbors—didn't need to hear any of this. And I would have ripped the headboard off the bed if I'd had were-wolf strength.

As the aftershocks of that incredibly intense orgasm continued, Sean tossed the vibrator aside, rolled us over, settled my calves on his shoulders, and thrust deeply into me. Despite his obvious hunger, he held himself back, staying gentle even as his low growls let me know he was close to his own release.

I wanted his skin against mine now more than ever. I reached for him and he covered my body with his so I could wrap my trembling legs around his hips. He buried his face against my shoulder, his weight on one hand as he held me close with the other.

"Alice," he groaned into my ear, shudders wracking his whole body as he came in a series of hot pulses deep in my core. "*Alice...*"

The sound of my name on his lips and the way he moved against me gave me one final, soft release. I held him tightly with my arms and legs as we trembled together. There was nothing better than this. Nothing in the world.

He raised his head to meet my half-lidded gaze. "Marry me," he said roughly. "Be my mate."

I chuckled breathlessly. "I already said I would."

"Humor me." He rested his head on my chest. I held him close with my fingers in his hair. "I just need to hear you say it again," he murmured, his lips on my breast near one of the faint marks his teeth had made earlier. "Marry me, Alice."

To know this fierce man needed to hear me say I'd be his wife and mate because it gave him strength and comfort melted me. The way we could be vulnerable with each other without fear was more intimate than what we'd just enjoyed together. He was my port in the storm and I was his, in every sense of the word.

"I will," I said, stroking his hair. "There's nothing I want more."

I felt him smile. "Not even coffee or Carly's blueberry scones?"

"Um…"

It was his turn to laugh. "I won't force you to choose between your three great loves. I'm willing to share you with coffee and scones."

"Well, good, because honestly if not, that was going to be a deal-breaker for me."

Still chuckling, he kissed my shoulder and gave it a gentle wolfy bite. "Need me to carry you to the bathroom?"

"Mmm, in a minute." I rubbed my nose in his hair and he rumbled. His wolf always loved it when I did wolfy things. "Thanks for making good on your promise to make me blush. I need to dare you to do that again very soon."

"Yes, you do." He met my gaze with his own golden one and smiled wickedly. "Yes, you damn well do."

A CROWD *of thousands spills from the alleys and every home to jam the streets, their voices cheering. But the cheers are not joyful. They are triumphant. Violent. Frenzied.*

This is vengeance, is it not? It is a massacre.

I am not one of the marked ones, but the crowd has tasted blood and the madness spreads. Women plead for mercy for themselves and their children and receive none. The rape and slaughter is a great black crashing thunderstorm and the streets run with blood in rivers like rain. I am horrified by the perversity of it all. The smell of viscera sickens me. I lick my lips to taste the rage.

Perhaps even I can still be surprised at what a man can do to another man. To a woman. To a child.

Through the screams, I hear another kind of sound. A dull thudding and skidding. A slap of flesh on stone. It comes into focus: a severed head tied to a dog's tail, dragging through the streets as the animal runs. Only scraps of flesh remain on the skull, but I believe this is a woman I know. She sold me figs in the market. I want to grieve but my sorrow will not come.

What rises instead is something like joy.

I do not want to feel joy at this. This is monstrous. But I love it, I think. I may borrow this from them for my future enemies. They call us monsters, but it is we who learn monstrous ways from them.

I kneel in the shadows and put my mouth to the blood that runs between the cobblestones. The night is cold, but the blood is warm. I sip from the stream and lave the stones with my tongue. Gods, it is such a vile and exquisite brew...

My stomach rebelled violently. Sickness and desperation sent me stumbling in the dark from our bed to the bathroom on rubbery legs.

I made it to the toilet just in time to fall hard on my knees and vomit. Hot tears ran down my face. I had no idea if I was crying from being sick, the pain of landing on the floor, the horror of the dream, or all three.

When that misery ended, I flushed the toilet one last time and lay on my side on the cool tile. Through the ringing in my ears, I heard water running in the sink. Sean knelt beside me and wiped my face with a cold washcloth. I hadn't seen any blood come out of my mouth, but the dream felt so real that I expected the cloth to come away smeared red. He gripped my hand in both of his and sat with me until the nausea faded and the room stopped spinning.

I forced myself upright to lean against the side of the tub. Sean handed me a towel to dry my face and a cup of water to rinse my mouth. I shook so badly that I could barely hold the cup. I swore I could still taste blood.

Sean set the cup on the side of the tub. "Alice, what is going on?"

"Another nightmare." I drew my knees to my chest and wrapped my arms around my legs. "It was awful. And gross. Really, really gross."

"That's two nights in a row." He brushed hair back from my face. "This isn't like you at all."

"I know." I leaned against the warmth of his hand. "It's not enough my waking hours are full of problems. My subconscious has to get in on the act too and serve up nightmares. It's a bit rude, actually."

"Do you think you're okay to go back to bed?"

"I think so." I made a face. "After I brush my teeth."

He got me on my feet and stood beside me while I brushed and used mouthwash. By the time we got back to the bed, I'd stopped trembling.

I told Sean what I could remember about the dream, which wasn't much. "Do you think the gross part with the blood was my brain telling me I shouldn't be listening to what Moses has to say?" I asked when I finished. "Or that he's feeding me lies I don't want to hear?"

"Maybe," he hedged. "But what about the violence? You used the word 'massacre.'"

"Moses is responsible for a lot of violence. So are the vamps. Both are on my mind. It fits."

"I suppose it does." He drew me close so my head rested on his chest. "So much for my new alpha power of banishing bad dreams."

"I knew that was too good to be true. Like healthy chocolate cake or timeshares."

He chuckled and kissed my hair. "What can I do to help you sleep better? I thought the werewolf TLC would do the trick."

"Oh." I scowled. "So now you think you have a magical—"

He shook with silent laughter. "Not magical per se," he assured me. "But you tell me I'm good at what I do. Plus, I like to think there's something to that sexual healing thing."

"I'm pretty sure there is, at least most of the time." I snuggled closer and closed my eyes. "Back to sleep now, I hope. We've got early meetings."

Even safe in Sean's arms, though, it took a very, very long time for me to fall asleep again. And when I did, I dreamed of blood.

CHAPTER

FIFTEEN

A sentence I never thought would cross my mind: *I need to take Moses's advice.*

But that was exactly what I did early the next morning before Arkady's arrival to talk about Charles and the Court. I invited Matthias to the deck once more for a sunrise coffee and a chat.

I hadn't seen Malcolm this morning. He wasn't home. I thought about summoning him, but I figured he needed some space to think about what he'd found out at Merrum Manor and Sean's anger. He'd show up when he was ready.

"Did you sleep well?" I asked Matthias as we settled in.

"Yes," he said, surprising me. "I did sleep well."

At least one of us had. Thank goodness for coffee. This was already my second cup.

He'd also not been punching the heavy bag when I woke up, which was another minor miracle. I had to take that as a good sign.

We enjoyed our coffee for a few minutes. Moses had suggested I push Matthias to reveal under what circumstances he'd joined the Court. My original plan had been to let Matthias tell us when he was ready, but the Court's demands had shot that to hell. Now I had to

146

insist he talk about something he probably didn't want to share because it might be our only way to keep him alive.

But before I could open my mouth, he knocked me totally off-kilter. "You need to turn me over to the Court."

He said it so calmly, so matter-of-factly, that it took a moment for me to process what he'd said.

"Why would you say that?" I demanded.

"Because Charles Vaughan will do anything to get to me. He'll kill you all if that's what it takes. I'm the last man standing from Valas's regime."

"How do you know?"

"I have a few contacts left who survived Vaughan's purge. I didn't get much information from them, but I did get that."

The word *purge* made me feel ill. Had Charles always been so merciless? Had I underestimated him this badly? "You're not a threat to him *or* his Court."

"That's not how he sees it," Matthias said, his tone surprisingly gentle. "He can't let me live in any condition, even as a shifter. At best, it shows mercy; at worst, weakness. He took over in a coup. Someone else might get an idea to do what he did. Letting me live is like a tiny hole in a dam. It doesn't seem like much, but it leads to disaster."

I suddenly had the sinking feeling Matthias hadn't slept well because he was settling in, but because he'd decided to accept his fate. And that made me furious.

"The vampires are as inevitable as the tides, and just as useless to try to resist." He finished his coffee and set the cup on the table.

"Bullshit," I said.

He blinked. That was twice I'd startled him in two days.

"The vampires may *think* they're as inevitable as the tides, but they aren't." I put my mug down with a thud. "Valas said that sort of thing to me more than once, and guess what? She's ash. Vampires are just people, Matthias. They have fangs and drink blood and they move fast and live a long time, but they are *people*."

"You forgot that they're all snappy dressers and stuck-up twats," Arkady Woodall said from behind me. "But I agree about the rest."

The six-foot blonde private investigator climbed the steps to the deck. As usual, my business partner wore a black leather jacket, a snug gray T-shirt, jeans, and boots ideal for kicking down doors. Ronan called her his Valkyrie. She certainly looked the part of a Norse warrior.

Just seeing her here made some of the tension go out of my shoulders. What Arkady lacked in magic or other supernatural abilities, she made up for in literally everything else. Not a day went by when I wasn't glad she was in my corner, especially now with all this Court bullshit going on.

"You got any coffee for me?" Arkady asked. "Your girl is draggin' ass this morning."

I saw no hint of that, but I took her at her word. Always the smart thing to do with someone who had at least six or eight weapons on their person at all times.

"We do have coffee," I informed her. "*Inside.*"

She took the hint. "I'll go pour myself a cup and holler at Sean and Ghost Boy then while you two talk." She surprised me by touching Matthias's shoulder. "You doing okay, big guy?"

"I'm all right," he said, his tone neutral. "Thank you."

"You're welcome." She gave him a none-too-gentle punch on the bicep. "Alice is right, by the way. Fuck the vamps. You've given them enough. You don't owe them shit, least of all your life. Don't make me kick your ass." She went inside and shut the patio door with a bang.

"Well, you heard her." I picked up my coffee mug. "You don't want to get your ass kicked, do you?"

"Alice—" Matthias began.

I held up my hand. "You've told me what you think we should do. I believe you want to protect us and I'm grateful for that. Do you believe we want to protect you just as much?"

Judging by his expression, he didn't. I knew because my own face used to look the same way when Sean, Nan, and Ben told me they valued my life as much as their own and wanted to keep me safe. At the time, I'd thought so little of myself that I couldn't believe them.

I didn't know how Matthias would react if I implied that he had no self-esteem, so I didn't say that part. Even so, I wanted him to know I understood.

"We have a hell of a lot in common," I said. "Sean, Malcolm, this pack...they're my first real experience with that kind of love since my parents died. It took me a long time to accept their care and protection. I wish we had the luxury of more time for you to come to the same conclusion, but we don't. You can't take my word for it. I know that because I didn't believe Sean and Nan either when I was in your place."

When he didn't argue, I said, "Last night, when I came home and you were watching to make sure I was safe, you were ready to shred anyone who hurt me. Am I right?"

"Yes." He looked uncomfortable. "I used to feel that way about anyone who might be a threat to Valas. That was duty. Now it's different. My body fills with rage and the need to protect at the thought you or the rest of the pack are in danger. I have to act."

"That instinct is part of being a dominant wolf. And so you're ready to give yourself up to try to keep us safe." I scooted my chair closer and put my hand on his arm. "Giving yourself up will *not* keep us safe from Charles. It might hit pause on the threat he represents, but it doesn't make the threat go away. Not at all. It just leaves us with one fewer pack member to face the danger."

I could tell from his expression that he hadn't considered that perspective. His eyes glowed amber.

"And that rage you're feeling?" I continued. "The need to protect? That's how most of us feel at the prospect of Charles getting you. So no, you're *not* going to just turn yourself over to them. Not until we've explored all the options. And even then it's not happening, because, as Arkady pointed out, you've given them enough."

I figured I might as well take the plunge. "Matthias, I'm sorry to do this, but I need you to tell me how you ended up working for the Vampire Court. We have to know the facts so we can fight the vamps."

"I didn't work for them," he corrected. "Arkady *worked* for them. I *belonged* to them. I don't need to explain the difference, do I?"

"No, you don't need to explain," I said. The Court had done its damnedest to own me. I'd escaped their clutches, at least so far, through threats, bargains, and alliances. "I understand very well. Tell me why you think you belonged to them." Even the word tasted bitter.

"I signed a contract with the Court thirteen years ago." His voice was toneless. "I can't tell you exactly what it contained because of its NDA clause."

I knew all about the Court's NDA clauses. I'd even upheld my end of some of them. We could come back to the contract later. "But how did you end up at the Court in the first place?" I asked.

"I need more coffee," he said, rising. "Would you like a refill?"

Maybe he needed a minute to gather his thoughts. "Sure." I drained my cup and handed it over. "Cream and sugar, please."

While he was gone, I pulled my hair up in a ponytail and wrapped my cardigan tighter. The temperature had risen enough to be comfortable, but I shivered. Talking about vampires, purges, and owning people tended to have that effect on me.

Not to mention I still felt haunted by last night's bloody, disgusting nightmare. The experience wasn't new; I had nightmares all the time. Anyone with my past wasn't likely to dream about kittens and rainbows.

That dream, and the one the previous night about fleeing a monster with my child, had affected me more than any I'd had in a long time that didn't involve me reliving actual memories. Nothing about these recent nightmares were scenes from my past, but they'd felt real enough to be exactly that. Strange, to say the least. Maybe Carly had anti-nightmare amulets in her repertoire. A couple more of these doozies and I'd start experiencing insomnia. It had happened to me before.

When Matthias returned, he handed me my coffee before settling in with his own. I took a sip and sighed. Perfect. We drank quietly for a few minutes.

Finally, he spoke. "I was twenty-one. Young and dumb and angry. I grew up in foster care and spent a lot of time at the local gym learning how to be tough."

I wondered if Arkady knew that about him. She hadn't shared much with me about her life before she joined the army but I did know she'd been in foster care. For all their differences, they'd had that in common.

Matthias continued, "When I aged out of the foster care system at eighteen, a friend got me a job as a bouncer. When I wasn't at work, I was at the gym putting on bulk so no one would fuck with me ever again."

That was the first time I'd heard Matthias swear. Maybe he was loosening up a little. One could only hope. "Is that why you caught their eye?" I asked. "They recruited you because of your size?"

"Probably." He smiled briefly. "I'm sure it was a factor. Really, you could say I recruited myself." His voice grew quiet. "I was in love."

He didn't look ashamed, exactly, but something close to it, like he thought I'd think less of him for joining the Court for love. As if I would judge him. Most people who'd grown up in foster care would be willing to do most anything for love. Between his size and his desire to belong and be cared for, Matthias couldn't have been more perfectly suited for the Court.

"I would have followed her anywhere," he said. "And I suppose I did. The day after she signed her contract and took her oath, I did the same."

I could guess what happened next. "Your relationship didn't last?"

"No." He met my gaze. "The vampire to whom we were both

bound doesn't like his enforcers to love anyone but him. I'm surprised he allows a brother and sister to serve him, but I suppose they love him more than each other."

The pieces fell into place. Matthias had originally been bound to Charles, and I only knew of one brother and sister pair tied to Charles. "You loved Adri Smith."

"Yes." He took a long drink of coffee.

"I'm sorry," I said, because I didn't know what else to say. "I had no idea."

"Very few people do. That was a long time ago, though. Twelve years. A blink for a vampire, but much longer for us humans." He glanced down at himself. "Or for shifters, I suppose."

He could claim it was water under the bridge all he wanted, but I could tell he still cared for Adri. That meant I needed to tell him something I'd learned from Moses last night. "From what I understand, Charles intends to surround himself with a small army of dhampirs that he plans to change himself."

Matthias snarled. "Adri and Bryan are his head enforcers. He'll turn them both into dhampirs, whether they want to or not."

I wished I could disagree, but I'd been thinking the same thing since Moses told me about Charles's plan. "I don't know that for sure, but I think you're right." I touched his arm. He trembled with rage. "I'm sorry," I said again. "There's nothing we can do to prevent it. I wish there was."

We sat in silence for a long time while Matthias got his fury under control. I had a healthy amount of anger myself.

In previous conversations, both Adri and Bryan had made it clear they had no interest in giving up their humanity to become dhampirs, or what some called half-turned vamps. I had no reason to think they'd changed their minds. As much as I'd felt sick about Charles killing Ezekiel Monroe, Valas's daytime representative, I hated the thought of Adri and Bryan losing what little bodily autonomy they still had even more.

When Matthias seemed ready to talk again, I said, "Will you give us time to figure out how to fight the Court before you think about turning yourself over?"

It saddened me to see how mightily he struggled with his answer. He'd already decided we had to give in to the Court's demand. I'd managed to pull him back from the edge, but only barely and not for long, if his expression was anything to go by.

"All right," he said finally. "However this turns out, I want you to know I'm grateful. You've sacrificed a lot, and risked a lot, for me to be sitting here. I don't deserve for you to do so much."

"That's the vamps talking," I told him gently. "You deserve to live and thrive and be protected because you exist. It's not a privilege you have to earn."

He obviously didn't buy that any more than my claims that vampires were just people or that our pack wanted to protect him. Not that I'd expected this conversation to work a miracle, but I'd hoped to reassure him more.

It occurred to me then how many times Sean and Malcolm and members of Sean's pack had said these same things to me, and how long it took for me to think about believing them. I scrubbed my face with my hands. I couldn't expect Matthias to come around faster than I had, and yet I wanted him to.

Finally, I raised my head. At Matthias's concerned expression, I forced a smile. "Well, let's get inside and find out what information Arkady has about the Court," I said. "Sean and I are ready to prepare our counterattack. Charles may have started this shit, but we're going to finish it."

If Matthias didn't buy that either, he at least had the good grace not to show it.

CHAPTER
SIXTEEN

IF I'D THOUGHT THE NDA CLAUSE OF MATTHIAS'S CONTRACT WITH THE Court was a problem for our strategy for dealing with the vamps, that was nothing compared to Arkady's reaction. Matthias's refusal to disclose its contents blew up their truce three minutes into our meeting.

"God damn it, Matthias," Arkady said, swinging her feet down off my desk so she could sit up in my chair and glare at him. "Those fangy fuckers are trying to *kill you*. For shit's sake, if that doesn't wake you up, what will?"

For his report to us, Matthias had chosen to stand at attention near the bar in our office, his hands folded behind his back, as if we were his former employers. "I am very awake," he rumbled. "I gave my word of honor. What is my word worth if I choose when and where to keep it?"

Sean and I exchanged a glance. I'd let Arkady keep her seat at my desk when we began our meeting and taken a spot on the couch while Sean stayed at his desk. Sean had his hard alpha mask on, but the hard set of his jawline told me he shared Arkady's feelings. He stayed quiet, however. Maybe he thought she had the best chance of getting through to Matthias.

As usual, Arkady showed absolutely no sign of backing down. "Call me crazy, but the Court broke its word to *you* the minute Charles Vaughan decided he wanted you dead."

"I have a feeling Court contracts are one-way streets, though," I said.

She flicked an angry look in my direction. "Sure, Court contracts are *extremely* self-serving, especially the kind Matthias signed. But there are provisions in that contract that stipulate his life and service has value to the Court. They are obliged to protect him—even if it's only to avoid wasting *Court resources*." She put air quotes around the latter.

Matthias studied her. "How do you know what may or may not be in the kind of contract I signed?" I noticed he very carefully didn't admit or deny what she said was true.

"Really?" She snorted. "You know me well enough to know I find out all kinds of stuff I'm not supposed to know. I know the broad strokes of your agreement and gave that information to Alice's hunky lawyer. I wish I'd been able to dig up a copy of your actual contract. I'd give it to Sean and Alice so they didn't have to put up with your bullshit and misplaced loyalty."

He started to object, but she rose and marched over to him. "Alice saved your life, when ninety-nine people out of a hundred would have let you die when that mansion collapsed," she said, poking him in the shoulder. "On top of that, this pack is offering you freedom, a family, love, and protection. That is a million times more than the vamps would ever do."

"You are not listening to me." Matthias leveled a full-on werewolf stare at her, but she didn't even blink when his eyes glowed amber. "This is not a matter of loyalty or a debate over who treats me better. It's a matter of my word. And even if I was willing to break my word, which I am *not*, violating my NDA is a serious crime under vampire law. I would be subject to imprisonment on that alone."

"Who's to say you told us anything?" she pointed out. "Every organization has leaks. The Vamp Court is no exception. 'Unidentified sources' gave us the information. Boom. Done."

Speaking of unidentified sources, maybe Moses could get us the information we need, I thought. He was already snooping around Charles and the Court. What was one extra phone call?

Immediately after I thought that, I reconsidered. It was one thing for Moses to offer assistance without being prompted; asking him for favors was something else entirely. At this stage in our working relationship, I didn't feel comfortable asking him for anything outright.

"I don't mean to bring up old news, but this is why we couldn't stay together," Arkady said, interrupting my internal debate and drawing my attention back to their argument. "Your blind loyalty. Your absolute deference. Your inability to see grays because you think in black and white. Honestly, I hoped everything you've been through would have gotten it through your thick skull that you don't mean shit to the vamps and never have. Your value to them was only ever what you could do for them. I'm sorry you believe their bullshit, because you are worth a hell of a lot more than that. Alice and Sean and I can see it. Why the fuck can't you?"

Arkady had her back to me so I couldn't see her face, but I heard the slightest crack in her voice just then. They might've been "old news," but she still cared about him. He felt the same way, because his expression softened, just a little.

But if I'd hoped Arkady might be able to get him to talk, I was destined for disappointment. "I am sorry," Matthias said. "But I can't tell you the conditions of my contract."

For a moment I thought Arkady would take a swing at him. Matthias eyed her warily. He might be twice her size but she could knock him down if she decided to. I'd seen her flatten enforcers before. And werewolves too, for that matter.

Instead, Arkady stomped back to my chair, sat down, and thumped her boots back on my desk with enough force that I winced. She crossed her ankles and glared at Matthias. "Fine, asshole. We'll figure out how to save your bacon, with or without your help." She pulled out one of her tactical knives and flipped it in the air end over end to catch the handle each time. I knew how sharp that blade was and it took all my power not to ask her to stop.

I'd come to the same conclusion as Arkady while Matthias and I had talked on the deck. Between the *geas* and the NDA, he wasn't able to assist very much in his own defense. That put the burden on us.

If I considered the Court indictment and Matthias's situation to be a case, our newest pack member was essentially a reluctant client who didn't want to spill his secrets but still needed our help. Far from an ideal situation, but not the worst problem I'd had to deal with as a mage PI.

Thinking about this as a case switched some gears in my head. "We've been reactive," I said. "Given this all came out of nowhere, that's not a surprise. But as of this moment, I'm done reacting. We're going on the offense."

"I agree." Arkady caught her knife one final time and returned it to the sheath in her boot. "And I think we start by unraveling two things: Matthias's *geas* and what the fuck is going through Charles Vaughan's head."

Matthias's expression darkened. "There is no *unraveling* a *geas*."

She pointed at him. "False. There is always a way to unravel a *geas*. The key is in the wording. We just need a copy of it and smart people to figure out the magic words to unlock it. How did they get you to agree to it? The usual way?"

"Wait, he agreed to it?" I asked. "And what do you mean, the usual way?"

"If it's a *geas*, he had to agree to it," she said, ignoring Matthias's scowl. "It's a contract, not a curse. You can't slap one on someone like it's a parking ticket under a windshield wiper. The usual way the Court gets people to agree is to have them read their contract aloud, state that they agree to it, and give their full name. They think they're just formalizing their agreement with the Court in some fancy ceremony. And they are, but that's not all that's going on. Hidden in the wording of the contract is the *geas*. By speaking it aloud, agreeing to its terms, and giving their full name, they're accepting the *geas* whether they know it or not. And by the time that first pain hits and the spell kicks in, it's too late."

Out of the corner of my eye, I saw Matthias clench his fists. Uh-oh. It looked like Arkady had hit the nail on the head.

"So they tricked him," Sean said, his voice a low growl. "Dishonorably and maliciously."

"Probably." She kept her tone businesslike. A man like Matthias wouldn't want sympathy, even hers—or maybe *especially* not hers.

"What about the unraveling part?" I asked.

"Here's where it gets interesting. Basically, as a contract, a *geas* encourages adherence to its terms by promising rewards for obeying it and threatening suffering if you don't. And how do you get out of a contract?"

"You find the loopholes," Sean said.

"Bingo." She gave him a little salute. "Or in this case, find the loose thread to unravel it. The key is in the wording, which is why we need a copy of the actual contract and somebody who knows this kind of magic and can figure out where the loopholes or the magic words are."

I crossed my arms. "If it's a contract, then it binds both parties, right? So the Court has to have a way to end it if they needed to."

Arkady waggled her fingers at me. "Magic words."

Damn it, now we *really* needed that contract. How could we get our hands on it?

Again, I thought of Moses. Ten minutes ago I'd talked myself out of asking him for help, but now I was rethinking my position. *If it's a business deal, what's the harm?* I reasoned. After all, we had a partnership. I could offer him something in return. A favor for a favor.

Sean would not like the idea of asking Moses for help one bit, but his anger at the news that the Court had bound Matthias into this *geas* against his will, or at least by trickery, meant he wanted

Matthias freed from its conditions. In fact, as Matthias's alpha, Sean was a protector first, and now he knew this *geas* had Matthias trapped like a net.

"While you think about that," Arkady continued, "Let's get back to figuring out what the hell Charles Vaughan is plotting. We know he's virtually locked Northbourne Manor down. Most of my usual sources of info are either dead or incommunicado. Vaughan went scorched earth as soon as Valas croaked."

"Scorched earth is right," I said. "I would have thought he'd give at least some of Valas's people who'd been with the Court a long time the chance to swear allegiance, but apparently not. Even Ezekiel Monroe wasn't safe."

She raised an eyebrow. "Where'd you hear that?"

I couldn't very well say Moses told me, so I said blandly, "Unnamed sources."

"Touché. Anyway, what I've got is pretty fucking grim." She outlined some of the same information I'd gotten from my grandfather last night, including Charles's intentions to stack the Court with toadies and protect himself with a small army of dhampirs.

"He's setting the tone for his regime," Arkady said. "But in my opinion, this strategy of mercilessly wiping out anyone who was loyal to Valas and brutally squashing even the slightest hint of dissent is going to bite him right on his undead ass."

"For all her faults, Valas was old enough and smart enough to understand that a stable regime has to tolerate some dissent on key issues," Sean said. "Debate and different perspectives have value too."

"An echo chamber of people who think alike, or simply think and do as they're told, is about as stable as a two-legged chair," Arkady said. "The whole thing might work for a little while, but all it will do is breed resistance, not loyalty. In the end, whether it's next week, next year, or a decade down the road, he'll end up as ash."

I didn't want to care whether Charles ended up as ash, but I did. Even after I'd found out he'd betrayed me by subtly influencing me for years in hopes of getting me into his bed, not to mention turning me into a weapon in his arsenal, I still cared. I was such an idiot sometimes.

Speaking of Charles's arsenal… "What do you know about Charles's consort Morgan Clark and the rest of the Silver Thorn coven?" I asked. "What role are they playing in all this?"

"About what you'd expect," Arkady said. "The witches have thrown themselves wholeheartedly into the work of offing Vaughan's enemies, or potential enemies. Morgan in particular seems to be enjoying herself."

Ugh. More good news. As if a black witch needed more of an excuse to hurt people.

"What exactly is the relationship between Vaughan and Morgan Clark?" Sean wanted to know. "He named her his consort to get the coven to back him in the coup, but I can't picture Morgan's mother Bridget, the coven High Priestess, being content to stay in the back seat for long."

"You're right about that." Arkady took a drink of coffee and glared at the mug, apparently for having the audacity to not keep her coffee at the perfect drinking temperature. "This is one of the areas where I'm having trouble getting reliable intel. The vibe is that as soon as there's any kind of threat to Vaughan, whether it's real or perceived, Morgan and her mommy are going to use that as leverage."

"Which I'm sure Charles knows." I shook my head. "He's going to rue the day he got in bed with the witches—both literally and figuratively."

"It's a fucking bloody mess," Arkady said with a sigh. "There hasn't been a coup like this in a North American vampire court for a long time. The vamps want stability as a general rule."

"How are the other vampire courts reacting?" I wondered aloud. "I know enough about Elizabeth of the Chicago Court and Lucien of the Court of New Orleans to think they aren't happy. Elizabeth and Valas in particular go way back."

I sensed Malcolm cross the house wards. A moment later, he appeared in the office and floated over near me. He seemed less morose, so that eased my worry.

"Hey, everybody," he said. "Your favorite dead guy is here."

Sean's eyes glowed, but said he nothing.

"What's up, Ghost Boy?" Arkady said. "Anyway, to answer your question, Alice, the Courts usually stay out of each other's business because, as you know, they don't want other Courts sticking their noses into their own affairs. However, nobody likes to think their authority or life might be endangered, so they're watching this situation very closely."

"And watching their own Courts even more closely," Malcolm said. "Somebody might get ideas."

"Exactly." She raised her coffee mug in his direction. "It wouldn't surprise me in the least if the closest Courts released carefully worded statements that stop just short of condemning Vaughan's actions. What action they'll actually take is anybody's guess. I don't see any of the other Courts attacking, especially when there's no chance of restoring Valas to her seat. It might be different if Valas was still kicking around. Then they'd have something to fight for."

"Good thing she's toast, I guess," Malcolm said. "I mean, Charles sucks, but I think all-out war would suck more. Pun totally intended."

Pain lanced through my head and became a throbbing sensation behind my eyes. I flinched and rubbed my temples.

"What's wrong?" Sean asked.

"Headache." I grimaced and looked into my empty coffee mug. "I don't think I've had enough caffeine."

"How much water have you had in the last few days?" Arkady asked accusingly.

"There's water in coffee," I protested.

She confiscated my mug and headed for the kitchen. "You could bring me both water *and* coffee," I hollered.

"I didn't hear the magic word," she called back.

I sighed and massaged my temples. "Please?"

Sean joined me on the couch and took my hand. "Fainting, nightmares, and now a bad headache seemingly out of nowhere," he said. "Do we still think this is all just stress?"

"I think so." I rolled my neck and shoulders. "There's a fine line between reasonable concern and whatever the word is for being paranoid that you're on the wrong end of bad magic."

"Hypo-magic-ondria?" Malcolm suggested. "Doesn't exactly roll off the tongue."

Sean turned his golden gaze in Malcolm's direction. "I don't think this is the time for jokes."

Malcolm floated back and forth and didn't reply. Only I could see the way he looked at Sean: part hurt and part irritated.

Arkady broke the tension when she returned from the kitchen with a large bottle of water and two cups of coffee. When I reached for my mug, she held it out of my reach and shoved the bottle into my hand. "You drink half of this first."

I scowled. "That's extortion."

"I know. I'm a bitch." She handed Sean my mug and returned to my desk. "Anyway, we were talking about the other courts. I think a lot is going to depend on how Charles approaches them in terms of diplomacy. He'll have to establish diplomatic relations soon, if he hasn't already done so. It's gonna be real touchy for a long time, even best-case scenario."

"Why would anyone even *want* the job of being head of the Court?" Malcolm asked, somewhat rhetorically. "I mean, I get the power thing, but every word you say or don't say, and everything you do or don't do, has a million possible consequences. It sounds exhausting. And to take over by force like this? It multiplies all that by a thousand. Charles will never have a moment of peace or safety. It just seems...dumb."

I had to chuckle at that, though my head hurt and none of the others seemed to find Malcolm's observation funny. "He must have thought it was worth it," I said. "For the power."

We all sat with that for a minute. I downed my prescribed amount of water and retrieved my coffee mug from Sean.

Matthias had stayed silent for so long that when he spoke, I jumped. "The Silver Thorn coven poses a significant threat to Charles Vaughan," he said. "They're positioned closest to him. He'll probably have something in place that protects himself, but it might not be enough."

"Thought you couldn't say anything, Mr. Suddenly Chatty," Arkady said. "Changed your mind?"

"No. But even if I can't reveal what I know from my time at the Court, I can still reason based on available evidence."

"How very generous of you." She made a rolling gesture. "Any more pearls of wisdom?"

"Have you considered why Vaughan served the pack with the indictments, other than to reclaim me?" Matthias asked.

Arkady, Sean, and I exchanged glances. Malcolm looked puzzled as well. "I mean, other than the obvious?" I asked.

Matthias raised his eyebrows and waited for us to get it.

"Oh," I said. "It's not obvious at all, is it?"

"Not in my opinion." Matthias regarded us. "Vampires have been known to initiate a transaction or alliance with an attack. It's a way of testing your opponent *and* opening lines of communication."

My mouth fell open. "This mess is Charles trying to make a deal?"

"I don't know if that is the case, and I say that in all honesty," Matthias said. "But it's a perspective I suggest you consider."

"What the ever-loving hell would Charles think he could get from the pack by suing us and threatening to throw Sean and Alice in prison?" Malcolm demanded. "Or by leaning on the Were Ruling Council?"

Matthias's gaze went to me.

"Oh, hell no." I stood up. Headache or not, I wasn't going to deal with this sitting down. "He's not getting me. I have made that *abundantly* clear."

"Have you ever known a rejection to dissuade a vampire?" Matthias asked. "You have strong magic and great skill, as well as power and influence. You walk in more than one world, both literally and figuratively. I think you underestimate your value to someone in his position."

"Careful with all that flattery," Malcolm said, in an attempt to lighten the mood. "You'll make her conceited."

Matthias wasn't about to be distracted, however. "He may know more about you than you think. This is only more reasoning on my part, but as your pack develops your strategy for responding to the indictments, you should take all of this into consideration too."

"*Our* pack," I corrected him. "As if Charles is going to get anything from me. Or us. Or the Council."

"Knowledge is always power," Matthias reminded us. "If this *is* his way of initiating something, you need to know what's on the table. What he wants, and what he'll give."

"And what he'll try to take," Sean snarled. His fury had built steadily since Matthias had suggested the indictments were possibly a vampire version of an icebreaker. "He only ever takes. We know that as well as anyone. He's taken, and taken, and *taken* from Alice. He's not going to take one more damn thing."

The pain in my head, almost forgotten, came roaring back. I flinched. "Damn it." I sat on the couch and rubbed my temples. Of all the times to have a splitting headache.

Meanwhile, something Matthias had said bothered me. "What did you mean when you said Charles might know more about me than I think?" I asked. "What do you think he might know?"

"I can't speak to what Vaughan does or doesn't know," Matthias said.

Maybe I'd gotten better at reading Matthias's eyes or body language, but suddenly I felt certain there was a specific reason he'd suggested Charles knew something. "Matthias, I need you to tell me what you think Charles knows."

"I can't," he said. "The *geas*."

"You implied Vaughan knows something, and you did it on purpose." Sean's eyes glowed bright gold. "If you can do that, you can give us more."

Matthias barely had a chance to shake his head. In a blink, Sean crossed the room, grabbed Matthias by the neck, and dragged him from the office. Two distinctive kinds of shifter magic surged from the direction of the living room, followed by blood-curdling snarls. I recognized both Sean's and Matthias's wolves in the sound.

Oh no. No, no, no.

Glass shattered. The wards tingled and the house shook. The fight was on.

SEVENTEEN

THE BATTLE HAD ALREADY MOVED INTO THE BACKYARD BEFORE ARKADY, Malcolm, and I made it to the hole in the wall where the patio door had once been. The wolves had gone through the patio door and a section of the deck railing to reach the open area between the deck and the trees.

Sean's rage seared me through our bond. His wolf was enormous, mostly black with streaks of silver. Matthias wasn't much smaller. His size was a testimony to his power and emerging dominance. They moved so fast that to my human eyes they were little more than a blur. Blood splattered across the grass.

Nausea surged at the sight of Sean and Matthias hurting each other. But when I started to run toward them, Malcolm flitted in front of me. "They've gotta do this, Alice. Let them fight."

"Out of my way," I said.

Arkady grabbed my arm, and not gently. "Malcolm's right. This has been building up for a long-ass time. If it's not today, it'll be tomorrow."

I shook her hand off. "They're going to rip each other apart."

"Probably." She used her body to block me from moving forward. "You're gonna stay right here if I have to sit on you."

Matthias's wolf took a chunk out of Sean's shoulder. Sean twisted around and ripped at Matthias's side. I wanted to scream at them.

"I understand," Arkady said. "Remember, I used to sleep with the big idiot who's about to get his ass kicked because he fucking deserves it. And Sean needs to set Matthias right because your way isn't working. We've just got to let them sort it out."

"Matthias needs more time," I protested.

"We don't have it." She was unmoved. "Blame Vaughan for this too. Take solace in the fact you would have won Matthias over eventually, as long as he didn't decide to be a martyr and turn himself over to the Court with or without your permission. His life consisted of killing time until the vamps put him in the ground one way or another. Do you think that's changed just because he became a shifter? After thirteen years?"

"He's working on that. It's only been a few weeks. Nobody's expecting a miraculous overnight change."

The wolves circled each other, bleeding from a half-dozen wounds. I couldn't put myself between them, but I wanted to.

"And while we're on the topic of expectations," Arkady said, "You have to let Sean be an alpha werewolf. Stop trying to make him deal with these things like a human."

I flinched like she'd slapped me. Sean and Malcolm had said the same thing to me before, and I'd honestly thought I had stopped doing that. Even if I had the best of intentions, urging Sean to deny his alpha instincts, whether on purpose or subconsciously, undermined Sean's authority and caused friction between his human self and his wolf. In a way, my interference had led to tragedy within our pack: namely the death of a young werewolf named Caleb Jennings, who I'd been forced to kill when he attacked me, and that was a guilt I had to live with every day of my life.

"That was uncalled for," I said, my voice rough.

"Was it?" She must have decided that I wasn't going to try to get past her because she leaned against the outdoor loveseat and crossed her arms. "I'll let you mull it over and figure out if I'm really over the line or if I might see something here that you don't." She glanced over her shoulder. "Relax. It's about over."

How she knew that, I wasn't certain. Maybe a fighter's sixth sense. But sure enough, about fifteen seconds later Sean's wolf got Matthias on his back and closed his teeth on the brindle wolf's throat. Matthias went still. I sagged against the wall. At least my headache had faded.

Sean shifted back to human and crouched naked as he held Matthias's wolf on his back with his hand on the wolf's throat. Matthias whined and struggled. Golden alpha magic surged. Was Sean preventing Matthias from shifting back in addition to pinning him on the ground?

My anger caused magic to prickle and spark on my arms and hands. I wanted to protect Matthias. The man had been through enough. Maybe I identified with him more than most. I'd spent twenty years trapped in my grandfather's cabal doing his bidding and suffering every day. I'd lost everything because of him. But even in my darkest hours, I hadn't lost hope that someday I'd get away and make a new life for myself. Trapped by the Court, Matthias had no such hope. I doubted Sean or Arkady really understood what it meant to reach that level of despair.

I started toward the yard.

Arkady cleared her throat. "Alice, I was not kidding about sitting on you."

"Matthias Albrecht." Sean's growly voice resonated with alpha magic. His alpha power seared the air and made my arms prickle and sting. I smelled something odd that reminded me of the scent of hot stones. "You will tell me now what Charles Vaughan knows about Alice," he commanded.

"Sean, the *geas!*" I called. "He can't tell us! It could kill him!"

"If he could say part of it, he can say the rest." Sean glowered down at Matthias's wolf. "Shift back to human and tell me what you know."

Though I knew Sean could enforce his will on the wolves in our pack and submissive wolves from outside our pack, I had never seen him do this to anyone. He never liked to force a wolf to do anything. It just wasn't in his nature. But he'd chosen to do so anyway, to protect me. My stomach lurched.

Matthias hadn't had any free will for the past thirteen years. It didn't sound like he'd had much before that either. And now Sean was stealing it again, after I'd promised no one in this pack would hurt him.

You have to let Sean be an alpha werewolf, Arkady had said.

How badly did I want to find out what Charles knew about me? Enough to let Sean extract the information with brute force and risk hurting Matthias badly? Was that any better than what vamps did with their prisoners? Would Matthias ever trust any of us again after this? I felt like throwing up.

Golden magic swirled around Matthias as he shifted. Sean kept his hand on the larger man's throat as he stared, golden-eyed, down at our newest pack member. The hot stone smell and stinging on my arms intensified. Matthias let out a very wolf-like whine that cut through me like a blade.

"Vaughan knows...Alice can ease...a shifter's transition," he ground out through what sounded like a clenched jaw. His arms and legs twisted violently. The pain must have been excruciating.

I lost my breath as if someone had punched me in the stomach. Malcolm flitted and swore.

"How did he find out?" Sean demanded.

Matthias's limbs twisted again, much more powerfully, and I heard bones breaking. That sound, combined with his agonized snarl and whine and guttural groan, made me double over and gag. He looked like a huge broken doll.

"A Court spy was present...when Alice helped Casey shift...for the first time," Matthias said, his voice edged with both a growl and a whine as Sean's alpha authority pulled each word out by force. "They overheard...Alice explain to you...what she did and...how it was done."

Sean's snarl raised the hair on the back of my neck. I put my elbows on my knees and covered my face with my hands.

Somehow the Court had managed to not only sneak someone into our pack land, but get them close enough to us to overhear our quiet conversation after I accidentally discovered I had the ability to help during a first shift. Certainly none of us had sensed or smelled anyone. The spy must have had some kind of masking and other spells supplied by witches to hide them from all the werewolves' sharp senses. I had never set wards around the pack land because we didn't think there was a need. The acreage was wild and undeveloped and our pack hunted there in wolf form.

But why would Matthias have hinted that Charles knew one of my most closely guarded secrets? He'd also deliberately steered us to the realization that Charles might still have his sights set on me. He had to have known these provocations would lead to a fight with Sean that could have ended in his death. But *why?*

I could think of only one reason: Matthias had *wanted* to end up with Sean's hand—and teeth—on his throat. He'd *wanted* these answers dragged from him by force. He'd willingly suffered to give us this information, though it cost him broken bones and enormous agony.

Sean leaned close to stare into Matthias's amber eyes. "Who was the spy?"

Maybe he'd seen something in Matthias's expression, or sensed some emotion through their pack bond, that led him to want to know. But the moment he asked, I had a terrible sinking feeling what the answer would be.

One moment. One heartbeat. Three words. That was all that stood between Matthias and his death.

"It was me," Matthias said.

In the long silence that followed, I didn't know what Sean's reaction to this revelation would be. He'd killed before, for a variety of reasons—all justified in my eyes and legal by shifter law and custom. His wolf surely wanted Matthias dead for spying on us and giving Charles information that endangered me, and that was on top of the wolf's simmering rage for the attack on New Year's Eve.

Would his wolf's rage overwhelm Sean's ability to draw the same conclusions I had about Matthias's motivations for provoking a fight and getting Sean to force him to give us key information? My heartbeat thundered in my ears.

Instead, Sean proved yet again that he was both a good man and the best alpha any shifter could want. He released Matthias's throat. "Thank you for telling us this."

I sagged against the railing in relief. Of course he'd understood why Matthias had done this.

Then Sean stunned me by demonstrating that he understood Matthias even better than I did.

"Did you think I would kill you for this, Matthias?" Sean's voice was a blend of his wolf's growl and his own, but the words were clear enough to understand. "You put such little value on your life. If you want to throw it away, I can't stop you, but I won't have a part in it."

I gaped at Matthias. Arkady sucked in a breath. Malcolm flitted uneasily.

It hadn't occurred to me that Matthias might have had more than one motivation, but his expression made it clear Sean had guessed right: Matthias had given up information he thought would both help us *and* cause Sean to kill him, and he'd done it on purpose.

Sean rose. "Shift and heal."

Matthias's slow shift to his wolf and back took more than two minutes. I needed that time to gather my thoughts and deal with a host of conflicting emotions. Meanwhile, Sean guarded Matthias, protectiveness rolling off him in waves. No threats lurked at the moment, but even a dominant wolf benefited from the reassuring presence of their alpha, especially during shifting, when they were at their most vulnerable.

When Matthias had shifted back to human, Sean offered his hand. To my surprise, Matthias accepted it and allowed Sean to haul him to his feet.

Malcolm and Arkady followed me to the yard. I walked around the blood to reach Sean while Arkady stayed near the deck, her arms crossed as she stared at Matthias. I wondered what she was thinking. Was she surprised? Frustrated? Sympathetic? Thinking about serving him a knuckle sandwich? Sometimes she was impossible to read, even for me.

I still couldn't get past the fact Matthias had tried to goad Sean into killing him. He'd told me to hand him over to the Court earlier today, but the simple explanation of him having a death wish didn't sit right.

Maybe something else was going on here. Why try to get Sean to kill him after we'd told him several times, explicitly, that Sean would never do such a thing? It made no sense.

On the other hand, it was something someone might do if they'd spent the last thirteen years—and maybe all the years before that too—never being able to trust what the people around them said.

"I think you had a question for us," I said to Matthias. "Did we finally answer it in a way you could believe?"

He gave me a nod. "I'm getting there."

"Wait—I'm confused," Malcolm said, floating to my side. "What question?"

When Matthias said nothing, I answered instead. "Whether he can really trust us."

Malcolm gaped. "This was a *test?* To see if Sean would kill him?"

"Yes," Matthias said. "If he did, I would no longer be a danger to your pack. If he didn't—"

"—Then you'd know all the stuff Alice has been telling you about how they run things around here is true and you could really believe we'll defend and protect you." Malcolm flitted. "That was a hell of a gamble to take."

Matthias clasped his hands behind his back. If he cared that he was nude in front of us, I saw no sign of it. "Maybe so, but I learned a long time ago that words mean little. Actions reveal a lot, especially in the heat of the moment."

Arkady's poker face morphed into a ferocious scowl. "Un-be-*liev-able*," she said, in a deadly tone I never wanted to hear directed at me. "Matthias, you are a grade-A premium certified asshole."

Sean gave Matthias his alpha stare. A dark shadow moved in his golden eyes: his wolf, pacing in fury. "Do you know how close you came to dying just now?"

"Yes." Matthias met Sean's gaze, then lowered his eyes. "But I *did* think I would live, for whatever that's worth."

"Given what you just put Alice through, it's not worth much." Sean studied him, then added, "But I suppose it's something."

"Seriously, though, dude," Malcolm said, flitting in place. "Next time Alice tells you something, just believe her, okay? The only things she fibs about are how much coffee she drinks and how little real food she eats."

"Thanks," I said wryly.

Sean took my hand and squeezed. His anger still buzzed on my skin, but something felt different between him and Matthias now. Some kind of mistrust or coldness I'd sensed from the moment they'd crossed paths after Matthias's first shift had lessened considerably.

Arkady caught my eye and raised her eyebrows.

"Shut up." I waggled my sparking fingers at her. "Just...shut up. If you say it, I will zap you into next week."

Sean's brow furrowed. "If she says what?"

"I told you so," Malcolm said, and then zipped out of reach before I could get him.

I went to the steps and sat. Now that the shock of Matthias's revelation had worn off, I didn't feel angry or even afraid. I just wanted more than ever to take this fight to the person who'd started it: Charles Vaughan, who sat on his throne at Northbourne behind walls, highly trained enforcers, and—if our intel was right—a growing cadre of dhampirs.

Where do we go from here? I wondered.

Arkady turned to the house and put her hands on her hips. "Y'all got a broom and dustpan somewhere? Your deck is a fucking mess."

CHAPTER

EIGHTEEN

Sean wanted to board up the patio door opening and go to our pack land to run as a wolf for a while. Arkady said she had some possible sources of information to track down, so I asked Malcolm to go with her as backup with the promise that I'd summon him if I needed him.

I headed to Carly's coffee shop with Matthias riding shotgun.

"I am sorry for upsetting you," Matthias said about ten minutes into our twenty-minute drive. "And for the pain I would have caused if had Sean killed me."

"Apology accepted," I said. "For the record, I knew Sean wouldn't kill you, no matter how much his wolf might push him to do just that. I don't like to see people I care about inflict pain on each other, even when there's arguably a good reason. It's the aspect of shifter life I struggle most to accept."

"You have a kind heart."

"I haven't always." I hit the brakes to avoid a car that pulled in front of me and muttered a few choice words. "When Malcolm and

175

Sean first met me, I was anything but kind. Just ask them. Malcolm will give you an itemized list of all the rotten things I said and did."

He seemed to be debating what to say next. "Earlier today you said we have a lot in common. I think there's a lot more to your past than what's in your Court dossier. Would that be fair to say?"

I'd promised not to lie to Matthias, but I wasn't ready to reveal my identity. We didn't yet have the level of trust I had with Ben and Nan, who were the only others besides Sean, Malcolm, and Daniel who knew Moses was my grandfather.

"That's in the category of something I can't share with you," I told him. "Not yet."

"I understand." He appeared thoughtful.

I supposed by telling him I couldn't reveal anything, I'd implied he was right.

"I only ask because I think whatever's in your past remains a danger to you," he continued. "My wolf pushes me to find out where the threat may come from."

Dominant wolves did not have a "wait-and-see" attitude. They seemed hard-wired for seek-and-destroy.

Matthias had never overtly referred to his wolf. For most shifters, speaking of their wolves' feelings, instincts, and reactions was as natural as talking about their own. Then again, Matthias probably hadn't felt comfortable revealing anything about himself even before the Court got hold of him. Telling me how his wolf felt might be his most significant step yet toward getting comfortable in his own skin.

"You're not wrong about the danger," I said. "But at the moment, this mess with the Court is much more immediate."

"Thank you for the honesty."

"You're welcome." I turned into Brew a Cup's packed parking lot and found a space near the far end. "Carly might be too swamped to chat," I observed as we headed for the front door. "I'm glad the shop is busy, but I hope they're not out of scones. I might cry."

Matthias bristled before he realized I was kidding. Well, *mostly* kidding. I made a mental note to not joke about being upset until he got used to my sense of humor. The last thing I needed was for a newly turned shifter to go wolfy because a coffee shop had run out of my favorite pastries.

When we got inside the shop, the line to reach the register was six deep. Carly and three of her employees were working behind the counter.

I craned my neck to see if the top rack of the bakery case still contained scones. "There are four left," Matthias said helpfully. He had no trouble seeing over the heads of everyone else in line.

I debated texting Carly to ask if she could hold two scones back for me. Before I could send the message, however, my phone buzzed.

Carly Reese: Don't fret. I have some in a bag for you.

Me: You're the best.

Carly Reese: Just call me the scone fairy.

Up at the counter, Carly caught my eye and winked as she set her phone down to run a customer's credit card.

As we waited in line, I couldn't help but notice Matthias got a *lot* of attention. Some of the whispered conversations seemed to focus on his height, while most of the admiring glances probably had more to do with his physique and looks. I thought he was oblivious to all the scrutiny until he took a step toward me and leaned in, as if we were a couple.

"I apologize for standing so close," he murmured. "No offense intended."

"None taken. I get it. But I'm not going to fight anyone who tries to give you their number. That you get to handle on your own."

He appeared genuinely perplexed, either at the thought someone would give him their number or that I'd allow them to do so. I found that unexpectedly adorable and tried not to let my reaction show on my face. Something told me he would not understand.

Someone touched my arm. "Excuse me."

A young man with blond hair who'd just come into the shop rested his fingertips on my forearm. "Can I get past you?" he asked, nodding in the direction of the bathrooms.

I stepped back to make room for him to cut through the line. "Thanks," he said, and brushed my arm again as he passed. I moved further away and scowled. I sensed no magic from him, and Carly's spell detector amulet in my pocket didn't tingle, but I didn't like the way he'd managed to touch me twice.

"Very presumptuous of him to touch you without your permission," Matthias observed as the young man wove between the tables.

"Very."

"Val—" Matthias caught himself. "My *former employer* would have killed him for the insult."

"Unfortunately, out here we can't kill people for getting in our personal space. Usually I just accidentally step on their foot."

He leveled an amber stare in the direction the man had gone. "Does this sort of thing happen to you regularly?"

"Not regularly, but sometimes." I lifted one shoulder in a half shrug. "Some men think it's okay to touch a woman they don't know."

"Inadvisable and unacceptable."

"I couldn't agree more."

At the counter, Carly took our order. I requested my usual: a large coffee with room for milk and sugar. Matthias surprised me by ordering an iced tea, lightly sweetened. "A rare treat at the Court," he said at my quizzical look. He accepted the cup from Carly with an almost reverent air.

I'd never given much thought to the dining habits of the humans who lived at Northbourne, but Matthias's comment about not having easy access to something as simple as iced tea started me wondering. Did they also refuse to serve their human employees coffee? *Vampires are the literal worst*, I thought.

As Carly handed me a small paper bag of scones and totaled our order, Matthias moved aside to let two women pass and drank his iced tea.

"How is he doing?" Carly ran my card and turned the screen for me to tip and sign. "He seems less shrouded in darkness than when I saw him last."

"We're making strides." I put the scones in my shoulder bag and picked up my cup. "Thanks for keeping those set aside for us. I won't ask how you knew we were coming by."

"I just had a feeling." She lowered her voice. "Katy has agreed to help you get information about the necromancer. She's taking today and tomorrow off from work to prepare. The rest of our coven will provide protection for us. We hope to be ready by tomorrow night. A new moon would be the best night for this kind of work, but we'll make do."

"Thank you." I exhaled. "What do I need to do to prepare myself?"

"I'll text you. You'll prepare your way, with your magic, training, and strengths." She smiled in a way that would have made Malcolm flit. "We'll do what witches do in situations like this: coven up, circle the brooms, and bring the thunder."

Well, how could I not feel a little better after hearing that?

The line had gotten longer while we talked, so I moved aside to let the next customer order.

Matthias watched our surroundings rather aggressively while I stirred milk and sugar into my coffee at the little side counter. Many of the admiring stares turned wary.

"Try to look less like a bodyguard," I muttered. "It draws the wrong kind of attention."

"I'm sorry." He tried to look less serious and intimidating, but not very successfully.

"Just smile a little," I suggested. When his face didn't change, I asked, "Why can't you hear a pterodactyl going to the bathroom?"

"What?"

I repeated the question.

He looked bemused. "I have no idea."

"Because the 'p' is silent."

Still nothing. I put my hands on my hips. "Don't tell me you've forgotten what a joke is."

"Was that a joke?"

He was so deadpan that it took me a minute to realize he was kidding. I laughed and put the lid on my coffee cup. "Well played, Matthias. I'll let Malcolm know you don't think much of his ghost jokes."

"Ghost jokes?"

"Yeah. They're like dad jokes, but—"

"But because he's dead, they're ghost jokes. I get it." He followed me to the door. I gave Carly a wave on our way out to the parking lot.

"You know, something occurred to me," I said as we headed for my SUV. "If Northbourne is locked down, how are the vamps who live there getting enough blood to drink? I'm assuming there are only a finite number of humans on the premises. They can't just be drinking from the same ten people."

"You are correct." He appeared thoughtful. "They must have a way of bringing in new food sources despite the lockdown."

"Can we use that somehow?" I wondered aloud. "If blood donors are going in and out, maybe we can get some information, either from them or whoever's handling the donors."

"Perhaps."

I sighed. "You're not going to tell me how and where the Court vamps get their donors, are you?"

He glanced at me. "I doubt the answer to that is the same as when I served the Court. Many procedures have probably changed."

"I guess that's—"

Matthias stepped in front of me so abruptly that I bumped into him and nearly spilled my coffee. The young man who'd brushed against me twice in the shop stood talking on his phone near my SUV. Mr. Touchy didn't seem to notice us, but Matthias clearly thought something was up.

"Take it easy," I murmured. "He's just a guy with boundary issues until we know different."

Matthias put himself between me and Mr. Touchy as we passed. I noticed my self-appointed bodyguard give him a good long wolfy sniff. Despite the tension, I loved to see him doing unabashedly shifter things.

"What's the verdict?" I asked when we were in the SUV. "Did he pass the sniff test?"

Matthias frowned. "He smelled very clean. Maybe *too* clean. His clothing smelled new."

I eyed Mr. Touchy in the rearview mirror as he went to a very nondescript gray car that was several spots closer to the door. If that was his car, why had been close to my vehicle? "Can you see the license plate?" I asked. "I have a friend at the DMV."

Matthias found a small notepad and wrote down the plate number.

"I'm going to summon Malcolm," I said so he didn't come unglued when my ghost showed up. I tugged on Malcolm's trace.

A few moments later, my sidekick appeared in my back seat. "What's up? Have you heard from you-know-who? Are Carly and Katy ready to try to get a peek at our necromancer and their pet spirit?"

"Not yet and not yet. We've got a different problem at the moment." I explained about Mr. Touchy. "Can you double-check to make sure he didn't put anything on me or the car?"

"No prob." As a ghost, Malcolm was sensitive to both magic and electronic signals, making him ideal for the task.

While he checked me over for hidden spells, I dug my prepaid phone out the glove compartment and texted the license plate number to Zola, my contact at the DMV. "It might take her a few to get back to us," I told Matthias. "We don't know if this guy is anything to be concerned about, but better safe than sorry."

"We could ask Malcolm to follow him," Matthias said. "A ghost is an ideal partner for a private investigator."

"I've always thought so." I hummed. "Malcolm, what do you think?"

"I think if you're worried about the dude, I'd better find out why you both think he's fishy." Malcolm floated behind me. "Nothing on the car or you that I can see or sense. Arkady's fine for a bit. I'll see what I can find out about Mr. Touchy." He zipped away.

I hadn't even had a chance to put the SUV in reverse before my ghost sidekick returned. "Red flag," he said from the back seat. "The car's a rental and Mr. Touchy's been around some bad magic. He can shower and put on new clothes, but he can't get all the funky trace out of his aura with Irish Spring."

"What kind of bad magic?" I asked.

"Not sure. Definitely dark, but I'm only getting traces. I don't think he's a practitioner himself, but he must hang around someone who is. What do you want me to do?"

"Can you follow him from a distance and see where he goes?" Matthias asked. "This may be important."

"From a *safe* distance," I said. "I don't like the sound of bad magic, even if it's not him who's slinging it."

"Hey, safety is my middle name," Malcolm said. "Let me tell Arkady what's going on and then I'll follow Mr. Touchy. Stay frosty, you two." He zipped away.

"Stay frosty?" Matthias asked.

"He saw it in a movie," I explained. "It means stay on your toes." I backed out of my parking spot. Mr. Touchy stayed put and didn't follow us out of the lot.

"Where are we going?" Matthias asked as I turned out on the street in the opposite direction of going home.

"Somewhere I probably shouldn't go, but I have to see for myself."

He figured out where we were headed a few minutes later. "Is this wise?" he asked, his eyes glowing amber.

"Maybe, maybe not. I'll let you know in about ten minutes."

I hadn't gone near Northbourne Manor since the night I'd returned from the Broken World via a mirror in Valas's chambers. I'd sworn never to darken its doorstep again. And yet I found myself turning onto the county road that ran past its imposing gate, drawn by morbid curiosity and anger in equal amounts.

When we were a mile from the gate, Matthias said, "We are now being watched. Surveillance of all passing vehicles begins here."

I'd actually figured the perimeter was farther out. I glanced at him. "That doesn't fall under the *geas?*"

"It was an observation. The cameras are difficult to spot, but not impossible."

The massive estate had long been surrounded on all sides by an enormous wall that cut through a dense forest. When we reached the wall's perimeter, I was startled to see the forest had recently been cut back to leave about twenty feet cleared on both sides of the wall. Charles must have thought having trees and branches so close to the wall was a security risk.

Less surprising were the many additional layers of wards that buzzed and sizzled along the wall. Almost all were deadly black wards I recognized as witch magic. I sensed mage wards as well, including illegal razor wards.

The gate had been upgraded as well, or at least I thought so from a distance. The retractable barricades in front of the gate looked much larger. Four Vampire Court armored SUVs were stationed near the gate: one on either side of the driveway and two across the road facing the gate. That was new too. Prior to the coup, guards on foot had manned the gate house just inside the rolling gate.

"What's the goal?" Matthias asked. "Even if Charles Vaughan would meet with you, he sleeps during the day."

"I'm not going in." I slowed and turned into the drive. "This is just recon. Keep an eye out for trouble."

It was difficult to describe how different Northbourne felt now compared to when Valas was in charge. In addition to the physical changes and additional wards, even the air crackled with danger and tension. That feeling alone told me a lot about conditions at the manor.

I stopped well short of the barricades and put the vehicle in reverse in case we had to make a quick getaway. Two men in Court uniforms emerged from their SUV on my side. I recognized the taller man as Carlos, one of Charles's longtime human enforcers. We'd interacted numerous times over the years.

As my window rolled down, Carlos stopped about ten feet from my SUV. Both enforcers had their hands on their weapons but left them in their holsters for now.

"State your business here." Carlos's voice was flat, his expression even colder. I might as well have been a complete stranger. He didn't acknowledge Matthias in any way.

"Hi, Carlos." I made a show of peering through the gate—not that I could see anything but forest on the other side. Northbourne Manor was a good third of a mile from here and not visible through the thick trees. "Just wondering who Charles's daytime representative is these days."

"What use is that information to you?" Carlos's companion asked.

"The names of daytime representatives are not privileged information," I pointed out. "No one expects Charles to check the mail or answer the phone, but I got a message from him the other day and I need to know who to contact with my reply."

Neither man spoke for several seconds. I figured they were receiving instructions via their earpieces from someone at the manor. "You may contact Christine Foreman," Carlos said. He rattled off a phone number, which Matthias jotted on the notepad next to Mr. Touchy's license plate.

I'd met Christine Foreman several times. She'd been a lawyer before a rogue vampire attacked and turned her about five years ago. Once Amira, a member of the Court, brought her into her line, Christine had opted to serve the Court as its first human-turned-vamp attorney. I was surprised to hear that Charles had named her his daytime representative. She was very young in both human and vampire years for that position. Hmm.

"You should be on your way," Carlos said. For the first time, his gaze went to Matthias. "Traitors are not welcome here."

"It doesn't look like *anyone* is welcome here these days," I said. He didn't reply to that.

I took one last look at the Northbourne gate. At this moment, somewhere not far from here, Charles slept in some kind of secure chamber guarded by his most loyal people. I'd seen Charles's bedchamber at his old house only once, when I'd gone there to save him from a deadly vampire object of power that turned against him. He'd had a beautiful sunrise painted on the ceiling above his bed. What did Charles have above his bed now?

"Well, see you later, Carlos." I rolled up my window and backed out onto the empty road. Both enforcers moved to the center of the drive to watch me make a U-turn and drive back in the direction we'd come. Their hands stayed on their weapons until we were well away from the gate.

"What did we achieve?" Matthias asked.

"This probably doesn't make any sense to you." I gripped the wheel. "But I needed to see it and feel it to make it real."

"I do understand." He tapped the notepad on his knee. "And now having seen it for myself, I believe Arkady is right."

"She usually is, which is extremely annoying," I said. "But what in particular do you think she's right about?"

"Valas understood what it takes to maintain stability. For all her cruelty, she was a forceful and capable ruler. The Vampire Court would have stayed strong and secure for many more centuries under her. Charles Vaughan doesn't have her experience *or* her wisdom."

I couldn't argue either of those points. "With Valas still weakened from Miraç's curses, I think Charles saw a chance and took it, maybe without a good plan in place for keeping his power once he got it."

"Authority requires more than brute strength." He hesitated, then added, "I think this will end with Charles Vaughan's death.

Who will rule at Northbourne when the bloodshed is over, I have no idea."

"Whatever happens, I have a feeling we'll have a front-row seat to it," I said, my voice grim.

Matthias's next words left me stunned. "I think you should attempt to speak to Charles Vaughan directly."

"What? Why?"

"He brought you into the trouble at Northbourne. He's the only one who can free you from it."

There were few things I wanted less than to speak to Charles, but Matthias was right. If these indictments and demands *were* Charles trying to open a dialogue, then we needed to hear what was on his mind.

Come sunset, I'd have to make a call to the newly self-appointed head of the Vampire Court, with my fate and quite possibly the lives of everyone in my pack dependent on what I said and how I said it.

NINETEEN

WE'D ONLY TRAVELED A FEW MILES FROM NORTHBOURNE WHEN MALCOLM appeared in my back seat. "Good news and bad news," he said.

Matthias snarled.

"Sorry, sorry," Malcolm said hurriedly. "Do you want me to hang a bell around my neck, or what?"

"He'll get used to it," I said. "What's the bad news?"

"I followed Mr. Touchy for a while from a safe distance. And good thing I did, because he must have sensed or detected me. He tossed a black magic ghost grenade at the corner of Madison and Pine."

My stomach lurched. "Oh, no."

"What is a ghost grenade?" Matthias asked.

"Ball of magic designed to damage or discorporate a ghost," Malcolm explained. "I got a bit singed, but I'm okay."

"Thank goodness for that." I let out a breath and tipped my coffee cup up to get the last fortifying sip. "Did you manage to follow him after that?"

"I had to back off and I lost him about a mile later. The good news is, I did snag a little of the magic from the ghost grenade. Maybe you can figure out what kind it is."

"And maybe track it. Thanks, Malcolm." I cleared my throat. "So, Matthias and I were just up at Northbourne."

Malcolm flitted into the console area, making Matthias growl again. "You did *what?*"

"Just to take a look," I said. "We didn't have any trouble. The atmosphere is grim."

"I already told you that." He returned to the back seat so Matthias would stop growling. "But I guess there's something to be said for seeing it for yourself. Find out anything?"

"Yeah. I asked who Charles's daytime representative is, and they said Christine Foreman."

"That's an odd choice. She's really young for that kind of responsibility. And isn't she part of Amira's line?"

"That's what I thought," I said. "It doesn't make sense. For every answer we get, I have ten more questions."

My phone rang. The screen read *Bob's Bait and Tackle Calling.* Hallelujah. I really wanted to focus on something besides Court nonsense for a change.

"Now we're in business," Malcolm said, rubbing his hands together.

I answered the call using my vehicle's hands-free system. "This is Alice."

"Hello, Alice." Cyro's new computer-generated voice had a British accent. "I'm relieved you're driving away from Northbourne unscathed. You like playing with fire."

I wasn't surprised that she knew where we were, but that didn't mean I necessarily liked that she casually kept tabs on my whereabouts. On the plus side, if something happened to me courtesy of Moses, the Court, or whoever else, she could alert Sean. On the other hand, I'd never liked to be watched, even if it meant I was being watched over.

Matthias's expression turned thunderous. Whether his fury resulted from the prospect that someone had eyes on us or might have a way to tap into Northbourne's security system, or both, I wasn't sure.

And by *playing with fire* she clearly also meant my visit to Merrum Manor last night, though she didn't say so. I assumed she knew I wasn't alone in the car.

"I don't actually *like* doing that," I countered. "But sometimes it's the only way to get answers."

"Alice Evelyn Worth," Malcolm muttered. "You *live* to play with fire. Don't *even*."

I scowled, but that actually elicited a tiny chuckle from Matthias, so I let it slide.

"Any luck with that surveillance footage?" I asked Cyro. "Do you have something for me?"

"I'm not sure *what* I have, but I have something. I'll transfer all the files to your home computer, including the large video files. I'm going to send you a link to the smaller clips and still images so you can look at them now. I also created a map showing the route your client took from the parking garage to the murder scene with time stamps. As usual, once you download the files, the link will cease to exist."

"Thank you for this," I said with feeling. Yes, I paid for her time, but with little else to go on, these videos were worth their weight in gold.

"You're welcome. Stay safe." She ended the call.

Rather than wait until we got home, I pulled to the side of the road, turned on my hazard lights, and tapped the link she'd sent.

As we waited for the files to download to my phone, Matthias said, "Dare I ask who just called?"

"An expensive source of impeccably accurate information whose real identity I do not know," I said. "And whose name we don't say unless we're at home behind the wards."

"Ah. I understand." After a beat, he asked, "And the fact they know where you are and who's with you? That doesn't bother you?"

I thought about how to answer that. "I have mixed feelings, but they've become a sort of self-appointed guardian angel, and at the moment I benefit from that enough to outweigh whatever misgivings I have."

Matthias's narrowed eyes let me know he didn't share my assessment that Cyro's watchfulness was more beneficial than it was intrusive, but he let it go—at least for now.

Cyro had sent two video clips, eight still images, and the map she'd created showing Oliver's route from the parking garage to the alley.

I stared at the map for a long time.

Oliver had walked from the garage to the alley using the same route Malcolm and I had taken yesterday. Nothing too surprising about that. What had me befuddled were the time stamps.

"He didn't leave the garage until after seven thirty?" Malcolm peered over my shoulder. "Then basically walked straight to the alley, killed Madison, and got arrested?"

"Looks that way." I switched to the first still image. Cyro had taken it from the parking garage footage on Level 5. The camera was mounted above the elevator and showed a side view of Oliver's SUV parked in slot 512 from about fifty feet away. I couldn't make out much from that distance other than the passenger seat appeared empty. The time stamp read *18:18*.

The next image was taken at 19:18, one hour later. Now Oliver's SUV was the only vehicle in the camera's view on that level and the video had switched to night vision because the sun had gone down. The passenger seat remained empty, and the SUV was not on—or at least had no lights on.

"What the hell?" Malcolm muttered. "He's just sitting there?"

"Apparently." I rubbed the tip of my nose as I thought. "I assume the video will show that he got into his car and then didn't get back out."

"But why?"

"No idea yet."

The next image showed Oliver walking toward the stairs from

the direction of his SUV. The time stamp read *19:32*. He wore a suit with the jacket unbuttoned and appeared to be walking briskly judging by the length of his stride and the way his arms moved. I zoomed in on his face.

"He looks focused on something," Matthias said. "Like he's on a mission."

"Yeah, he does." I panned around the rest of the image and paused. "Is that a shadow on the other side of that concrete pillar?"

Matthias took my phone and studied the screen. "Maybe," he said finally and handed it back. "It could be a person, but I'm not certain."

Grumbling, I switched to the next image, which showed Oliver exiting the parking garage at the bottom of the stairs. The fifth image was from an exterior camera on the shoe store whose clerk had turned me away by pointing at the door. It showed Oliver on the other side of the street, walking in the direction of the alley. The time stamp read *19:41*.

The next image was also taken at 19:41. Instead of Oliver, it showed a pretty brunette in a leather jacket, tank top, and jeans getting out of a black Jeep in a parking lot I didn't recognize. The Eleventh Street bridge loomed in the background.

"Madison Fernell." Malcolm's voice was quiet. "Arriving right on time to walk from her car to Salty's Bar for her eight o'clock shift."

I rubbed my arms to ease the prickling from Matthias's anger and my own goosebumps. This wasn't the first time I'd watched surveillance footage of someone who had no idea their death was imminent, but knowing how brutally Madison would die gave me the irrational urge to shout at her to call in sick—to turn around and go home. But even if she had, the necromancer would have probably found another victim that night.

So far the pictures were giving us some answers, but not the ones I wanted the most. Maybe the rest would fill in the blanks and give us a direction to go.

The seventh image, time stamped 19:46, showed Oliver about to turn the corner into the alley. And in the final image, time stamped 19:49, Madison arrived at the alley from the other direction. Presumably, Oliver waited in the shadows, under the control of whatever deadly spirit had possessed his body.

At the bottom of the map Cyro had created, I found two final notes from her. The first read: *First 911 call logged at 19:56.* The second: *The only cameras in the alley, on the Finch and Sons' loading dock, had been nonfunctional for over a month.*

The latter begged the question of whether the necromancer knew that, or even cared if cameras were present at the murder scene. After all, all they would catch would be Oliver, as long as the necromancer stayed out of sight.

I flipped back through all the photos, but none of them contained other people except the image taken by the camera on the shoe store. A young couple had walked under the camera just after Oliver passed by on the other side of the street. They had their heads close together and were laughing. I couldn't say for sure whether one of them was a necromancer, but my gut told me they were just passing by.

Son of a bitch. Given how much trouble we'd gone through to get this footage, I'd hoped for so much more than the damn near nothing it revealed.

"Why did Ferguson even *bother* to interfere with me getting the videos if they don't show anything of use?" I muttered.

I'd been mostly talking to myself, but Malcolm said, "Just to be a dick, apparently. Don't give up, Alice. We've still got the videos to look through."

I opened my video viewing app. The first clip from Cyro showed Oliver arriving on Level 5B at just after six. In the clip, we watched him walk from the top of the stairs to his SUV, wearing a leather cross-body messenger bag over his suit. He unlocked his SUV using his key fob as he approached and put his bag in the back seat. That was the last thing he'd remembered doing before he'd come to in the alley.

As we watched, Oliver shut the rear door, reached for his driver's door, and paused. Through the vehicle's windows, we could see him looking down, but not what had caught his attention.

"Blast it," I muttered.

"That's right where we found the nasty black magic," Malcolm said. "So *something* was there that he could see because he's looking at it. Spellwork, maybe? Drawn on the pavement?"

"I got traces there, but it didn't feel like an echo of drawn spell-work," I mused. "It felt more like residual magic from a presence."

Oliver opened his door, climbed into the SUV, and shut the door. And didn't move. The vehicle did not turn on. The eerie clip ran for several minutes, but nothing happened except two other cars driving past from upper levels toward the exit. I saw no one within the camera's view lurking around.

"May I?" Matthias asked, holding out his hand.

I gave him my phone. He ran the video back to when Oliver put his bag in the car, and then went frame-by-frame—the reason I had such a fancy app for looking at videos. Sometimes clues were damn near impossible for naked eyes to see without it.

Unless, of course, those eyes happened to belong to a werewolf.

Matthias found what he'd spotted earlier and held up my phone. A vaguely human-shaped blur appeared just outside Oliver's SUV in a single frame. Malcolm flitted.

I'd hoped to catch a glimpse of the necromancer. I'd never expected to see the spirit they controlled. Dread made my tummy roil.

"Is this good news for you and your client?" Matthias asked when neither Malcolm nor I spoke.

I waggled my hand. "Moderately good news in that this could be some evidence to support his story."

"But...?" he prompted.

"But also very, very bad news," Malcolm said. "That is one juiced-up spirit."

Matthias frowned. "Juiced up, as in...?"

"As in, this isn't an episode of a fake ghost hunter show." I saved that frame at the highest resolution available. "In the real world, you're not supposed to be able to see spirits on cameras. Not unless they're full of power. And in this case, a necromancer's magic too."

"So you were hoping you weren't right," Matthias said.

"Yes and no. I like to be right, because then I know what I'm up against." I closed that video and opened the second one. "But I don't like to be right when it's a necromancer. Or a sorcerer. Or, you know, someone worse."

His eyebrows went up. "What's worse?"

Dark Fae, I thought, but didn't say, because they could hear when humans spoke of them and I had no desire to attract their attention ever again. Once was plenty.

"Don't ask," Malcolm told Matthias. "For real. Just take our word for it."

As unsettling as the first video was, it was nowhere near as difficult to watch as the second one. That video, which Cyro had gotten from the sandwich shop across the street from the alley's entrance, showed Oliver striding down the last block before the alley and then disappearing around the corner. Just two minutes later, Madison appeared from the other direction. Grim and silent, we watched her turn into the alley, her head down as she looked at her phone's glowing screen. The time stamp was 19:50:08.

At 19:54:36, a delivery truck passed the sandwich shop and turned into the alley. These must be the men who'd caught Oliver in the act, tackled him, and called 911.

"Stop," Matthias said, making me jump.

Again, he took my phone and went frame-by-frame, this time backward until he found a person-shaped blur similar to the one we'd seen in the parking garage, now at the entrance to the alley, just visible as a silhouette against the brick.

In the same frame, I noticed something else: a dark figure in a hat and long coat standing just at the edge of the camera's view on the same side of the street as the sandwich shop. In the next frame, both the spirit and the dark figure had disappeared.

"You son of a *bitch*," I breathed.

The necromancer could have summoned the spirit back from a block away or more, but they'd come to witness the murder first-hand. And if they'd wanted to be completely unseen, they would have ensured they were. Instead, they'd allowed a glimpse of themselves for the benefit of anyone who bothered to look. My gut told me this was a game to them. Murder and framing an innocent man were a *game*.

Catch me if you can, that shadow said.

Rage made my eyes grow warm with blood magic.

No, I didn't feel good at all about being right on this. Not even a little bit. Not even for Oliver's sake, because two blurs and a shadow weren't going to be enough to exonerate him. I needed the necromancer themselves, preferably the spirit too, and a mountain of additional proof the DA and possibly a jury could see and understand.

"I'm sorry." Matthias's eyes glowed bright amber. His chest rumbled and golden shifter magic tingled on my arms. "We can't make it right, but we can do our best to make sure it doesn't happen again."

Malcolm touched my shoulder. *Listen to him saying "we" all the sudden*, he said in my head. *You and I know damn well there's a direct pipeline from surviving abuse and being forced to harm others to wanting to help people.*

My ghost sidekick and I were certainly proof of that.

He'd probably make a damn good PI, Malcolm added. *You could train him, get him his apprentice hours. Put him on the payroll and give him a mission in life. Let him right some wrongs and maybe find some peace while he's at it.*

I thought about my own mentor, Mark Dunlap, who'd taken me under his wing and trained me to be a mage PI though I had zero qualifications and enough baggage to fill a container ship. When he'd asked me at the interview why I'd applied to be an MPI, I told him I wanted to help people. He'd hired me on the spot.

After four years of estrangement, Mark and I had reunited on a case last year. Unfortunately, our newly rekindled friendship wasn't destined to last long. A blood mage named Spencer Addison tortured Mark to death trying to find out what we'd uncovered about his organization.

The pain of Mark's loss hadn't faded much, but I'd finally framed the one photo I had of us together and hung it on the wall in my office. At least I could look at it now without a bolt of pain going through my heart, so that was something.

Could I train someone to be a private investigator? Could I be a mentor to Matthias like Mark had been to me? I wasn't sure.

I'll think about it, I told Malcolm.

He let go of my shoulder and floated back. Matthias was still studying the video of the minutes before and after Madison's murder.

I sent a quick text message via my burner phone to Cyro asking if she could track the shadowy figure I'd spotted in the video to a vehicle or get a look at their face. I didn't have high hopes, though. That glimpse was deliberate, and so was the disappearing act.

"Well, let's get home so we can look at these videos and images more closely," I said.

"And get this black magic off me that I got from that ghost grenade," Malcolm added. "Before my leg falls off."

I was about to tell him to go ahead and jump home to the safety of our wards when my phone rang. Matthias handed it to me. The screen read *Philippa Grayson*. My stomach lurched.

I'd told Sean the truth when I'd said I wasn't clairvoyant and I didn't see the future, but I *did* have a detective's intuition—and a survivor's sixth sense for impending danger. Both told me the shadow and their pet spirit had struck again.

I took a deep breath, let it out, and answered the call.

CHAPTER

TWENTY

The campus of Founders Valley Medical Center sprawled across a hilltop overlooking the Eldridge Art Museum, Harrington Botanical Gardens, and the newly renamed Lear Fineman Memorial Performing Arts Center. I parked in a shopping center across the street from the medical center's south entrance so we could watch the crime scene from a safe distance.

From our vantage point, I counted a half-dozen squad cars with lights flashing crowded into the drop-off zone in front of the main medical building. Yellow crime scene tape billowed in the breeze in the area of a covered walkway between buildings.

Additional police vehicles had parked at each of the private medical center's four gated entrances. Uniformed officers and security guards were checking every car coming and going. The gate-houses also had conspicuous video cameras that captured each vehicle as it entered and exited the campus. Ordinarily, that would be a big deterrent for anyone intending to commit a crime on the premises. But in this case, I suspected the real criminal hadn't passed any of the gates.

"Do we want to chance it?" Malcolm asked, hovering over my shoulder. "Looks like they're checking driver's licenses and talking to drivers and passengers."

"I don't think we could get in." I crossed my arms and studied the activity at the gate. "They're probably asking visitors whether they have an appointment and checking with the medical center staff. How do you feel about doing some recon in super-stealth mode?"

"Super-stealth mode is how I roll." He stuck his right leg over the console. "But I'd feel better if you could take this magic and put it in a crystal. It's making me itch."

Black and red threads of magic coiled around his ankle and foot. I met his gaze and asked him with my eyes if he was okay. He smiled, so I knew he was.

"That ghost grenade didn't miss you by much, huh?" I asked, studying the trace.

"Nope. I'm lucky I've got reflexes like a coked-up cat or you'd be trying to reach me with a Ouija board."

Another brief chuckle from Matthias. That was two in less than an hour, when I'd barely gotten him to smile before today.

Cautiously, I passed my fingers through Malcolm's non-corporeal form and scooped out the black magic that clung to him. The little tendrils wrapped around my fingers, leaving painful red marks that stung. I hissed in pain.

I'd wondered if the trace from the ghost grenade might match the dark magic we'd found yesterday in the parking garage and at the murder scene, but it did not. That didn't mean Mr. Touchy wasn't somehow connected to the necromancer, but this magic, while also occult, didn't feel at all similar.

I transferred the ghost grenade magic to an empty crystal—one with my strongest containment and masking spells so the magic couldn't escape or be tracked by the person who created it.

"We have two kinds of black magic to track now," I told Malcolm. "The magic from yesterday, which I'm pretty sure is going to lead us to a necromancer, and this one belonging to whoever Mr. Touchy is affiliated with."

"So you think this is *two different* problems?" He flitted. "I deserve hazard pay now more than ever."

"I'll put that on the agenda for my next business meeting with Arkady." I glanced up the hill at the medical center. "See what you can find out for us. Be careful."

"Always." He went invisible and zipped away.

"You care about him a lot," Matthias observed. "I didn't realize you were so close. My former employer said you'd bound him to you as..." He hesitated. "A servant."

Of course that was what Valas would have thought. Odd that she hadn't noticed or couldn't see the angelic magic that bound Malcolm and me together, though. I would have thought someone with her powers would have noticed the silver trace.

"I didn't bind him," I told Matthias. "How we ended up together is a long story for another day, but he's like my brother. Or as Malcolm puts it, my sib from another crib." I heaved a sigh and checked a local news site on my phone. "Not much online about the murder yet. The breaking news report just says one deceased victim who was an employee of the medical center, and one suspect in custody. No names. Nothing about the suspect yelling that he didn't kill anybody. If Philippa hadn't gotten a tip-off, we wouldn't know this might be connected to Oliver's case."

"The news will get out." Matthias's eyes glowed as he stared in the direction of the flashing lights on top of the hill. "And when it does, it'll be a circus. Even these detectives you say don't believe your client's story will have to at least consider the possibility that he's telling the truth."

"One of them might. I don't think the other ever will."

"Even if you show him evidence?" His frown deepened. "I don't understand that mindset. Evidence is evidence."

"You'd think so, wouldn't you?" I shrugged. "But all we have right now is blurs and a shadow and some nasty black magic. It's not going to be enough."

"In Vampire Court, it would be more than enough to require very thorough investigation, and certainly sufficient for reasonable doubt."

"I reluctantly stipulate than in some matters, the vamps are more advanced than humans." I rubbed the bridge of my nose. "I suppose it would be much more difficult to dismiss evidence of supernatural or paranormal involvement if you're happen to be supernatural yourself."

"That is true," Matthias said. "You know, if this *is* the necromancer striking again, it's a serious escalation. From a lone woman walking at night down an alley to broad daylight at a private hospital with tight security and probably multiple witnesses."

I'd been thinking the same thing. "Three assaults, then Madison's murder, now this. There's upping the ante, and then there's..." I waved in the direction of the crime scene tape. "It's not just an escalation in victimology and risk—it's several giant steps up in terms of visibility. This isn't one of the public hospitals. It's private. I've seen ads for this place offering an on-site spa, chauffeur services in luxury vehicles to and from appointments, and recliners with private televisions and charging ports in all waiting areas. People don't get murdered here."

"Now they do." His tone was grave. "With this, the necromancer wants to make a point. Anyone may become a victim or a killer. No one is safe."

My stomach filled with dread. "Another reason for the police to publicly refute claims of spirit possession. People would panic."

"And panicking people will do terrible and unpredictable things."

"Like what happened after the West-Addison harnad killed Mark Dunlap last year," I said, my voice quiet. "Or the riots in Cincinnati two years before that."

A telltale cold tingle on my arms alerted me to the arrival of my ghost sidekick. Malcolm appeared in the back seat.

"Thank you for the warning," Matthias said.

"You're welcome, buddy." Malcolm sighed. "Well, Darth Chanel was right: our necromancer has struck again. There's a murdered nurse up there in such bad shape that they're going off her name badge for identification until the medical examiner can confirm who she is. It looks like the killer smashed her face into a concrete pillar about five or six times before stabbing her. And before you ask, yes, I found the same nasty spirit trace we took from Madison's scene."

"So there's no doubt this is the work of the same necromancer and their 'pet spirit,'" Matthias said.

"Nope. No doubt." Malcolm floated back and forth. "The detectives think the nurse was already dead when the stabbing started. The first slam into the pillar might even have knocked her out, but they don't know that for sure, obviously. If they're right, at least she didn't feel the rest of what happened. I hope that's true. I heard the coroner say she has more stab wounds than he could count. He used the word 'butchered.'"

I closed my eyes and breathed deeply a few times to quell my nausea and fury.

As I did so, Matthias asked, "Which detectives did they assign to the case?"

"Diaz and Ferguson," Malcolm said.

"Huh?" Frowning, I opened my eyes and peered up at the hilltop. I couldn't see the detectives from here—just the yellow tape and squad cars that had probably parked deliberately to block the view of the scene. "So either they think it's connected and whoever's in charge assigned the same detectives as Madison's case, or Diaz and Ferguson were up next in rotation."

"Does this help Oliver?" Matthias asked. "Another case so similar to his?"

"I don't know," I admitted. "It all depends on how open-minded Diaz is willing to be."

Several vehicles belonging to local news stations sped by, presumably on their way to the medical center's north gate, which was its main entrance. A police department spokesperson was likely to speak to the press there, well away from the murder scene.

"The suspect they've got in custody is one of the doctors who works here," Malcolm told us. "Apparently it took three people to tackle him and take away the knife, and he hasn't stopped shouting that he has no idea what's going on. He fought so hard a security guard had to taser him. They finally got him into a police SUV and took him downtown just before we got here."

"Did you get a name?" I asked. "For either of them?"

"Yeah, I read over Ferguson's shoulder while he took notes. The nurse's ID said Stephanie Harris, CRNA. The doctor's last name is Hutton. That's all I heard about him."

Matthias did a quick search on his phone. "I see a Dr. Gavin Hutton, endocrinologist, on the medical center's website. He's their only physician with that last name." He showed us a headshot of an attractive, dark-haired doctor in a white coat.

Another search turned up a profile for Stephanie Harris, who was about forty, with short blonde hair.

"I can't tell you if that's who I saw up there," Malcolm said. "She was a mess."

"How will you find this necromancer?" Matthias asked.

I thought about how to answer that question. "We have some magic trace we found yesterday, and there may be more at this scene. But it's not as simple as tracking it the way I usually do because tracking can go both ways, even with spells designed to protect me. A necromancer or a spirit can use that trace to get to me, and through me to Malcolm. This kind of magic requires bigger, different practice than our natural magic."

"Occult magic is way different from ours," Malcolm explained to Matthias. "We can capture it and track it fairly well, but we can't wield it or guarantee our safety against it. Well, it's not that we *can't* wield it," he amended. "We don't *want* to."

"Even in a situation like this?" Matthias tilted his head. "If by using it you could find this necromancer and maybe save lives and prove your client innocent, wouldn't it be worth it?"

"I'm not an occult practitioner," I said. "Neither of us are. It's not something someone should dabble in. The only thing worse than a full-time occult practitioner is someone who knows just enough to use black magic in a half-assed way."

"Alice almost died last year because of just that situation," Malcolm interjected. "Someone who wanted her out of the way got hold of a poppet made by a black witch, and then didn't follow instructions for using it."

I almost snorted at the understatement. I'd damn near died throwing up blood and scratching myself to pieces. Carly had saved me from that hex and we'd become good friends soon after.

"Yeah, that poppet thing was bad." I rubbed the back of my neck. Tension and stress had formed knots in my muscles. "I hear you about saving lives—believe me, I do. But once you cross that line, no matter how justified you feel doing it, there's no going back. And the line keeps moving, and your view of the world and the people around you changes a little bit at a time, and the next thing you know—"

"The next thing you know, there is no line anymore," Matthias finished.

"Yup," Malcolm said. "So me and Alice, we don't go there. We don't want to have to fight our way back again."

"I understand." Matthias considered. "Do you know someone who *is* willing to go there?"

"Yes. We've asked for help. She's preparing, but it takes time. This is not the kind of thing you can mess with on a whim." I drummed my fingers on the steering wheel. "We need more of the necromancer magic and the spirit trace, though. We got so little yesterday from the other scenes. I don't know if it'll be enough for anyone to work with."

"I'll go get it," Malcolm said. "I'll be fast," he added before I objected. "As long as you get it out of me and into crystals before the bad guys sense something's up, I'll be fine."

I struggled with letting others take risks and probably always would. In this case, I didn't have the option of going up there myself, and the longer we waited to collect the trace, the more it would dissipate. We had little choice.

"Move fast," I said. "If I sense any trouble, I will yank you to me or send you into lockdown."

"I'll haul ghost ass," he promised before zipping away.

"What is 'lockdown'?" Matthias asked.

I took two crystals off my bracelet, ready to transfer the trace the second Malcolm returned. "We have a special crystal in the basement workshop, behind the strongest wards I can make, where Malcolm can jump or I can send him in case of emergency. Its spellwork is so heavy-duty, only I can release him from it. Even he can't get out."

"A wise precaution."

"We've had two incidents where I almost lost him," I said. "He's a powerful mage, and most threats and dangers that could hurt humans or shifters don't affect him because he's a ghost, but he's not invincible, even if he acts like he is. If he were discorporated, that could severely injure or kill me since we're bound. And if someone captured him, there are fates far worse than death for spirits."

"I am aware," Matthias said, his voice grim.

Of course he understood. He'd probably seen as many nightmares at the Vampire Court as I had while a prisoner of my grandfather. Maybe more.

Come to think of it, maybe Matthias would have an idea for how to get Liam away from Moses. Anyone who'd been close to vampires for thirteen years would have absorbed all kinds of tricks and strategies for getting what they wanted from someone who wouldn't want to give it up if they knew the value of the item in question.

Before I could broach the subject, however, Malcolm popped into the center console area without warning. To his credit, Matthias didn't snarl this time.

"Hurry," Malcolm said, flitting in place, both arms outstretched. "This magic is really, *really* gnarly."

The more dangerous trace was the necromancer's black magic coiled in Malcolm's right hand, which our adversary could use to capture Malcolm as long as he held it. So I grabbed that first, as carefully as possible so I didn't damage the fragment. Unlike the remnants of magic we'd found at the garage and Madison's murder scene, this trace was fresh, powerful, and potentially deadly. And also as close to a live connection to our killer and their pet spirit as we could get.

Yesterday, the faint trace in the garage had merely scraped and burned my fingers. These sizzling threads of magic sliced deeply into my hand like I'd yanked on razor wire. The pain was excruciating. I was no stranger to this kind of agony and barely flinched, but blood streamed from the cuts.

Matthias snarled at the sight and smell of my blood. His rage made his golden shifter magic sear my skin.

With my bloody hand, I picked up a clear crystal with runes etched all over its sides. "*Enclose*," I said. The magic ripped from my hand, leaving another set of lacerations that crisscrossed the first. I winced.

"Alice, what can I do?" Matthias demanded, his eyes bright amber as he trembled with the strain of holding back. "I can't watch and do nothing."

He might not experience the volatility of a new shifter, but his wolf was probably as dominant as Nan's and howling at him to get between me and this pain—to take the cause of it away and kill it with his teeth and claws or his bare hands if necessary. I knew this because that was how Sean reacted when I got hurt. The difference was, Sean had far more control over his wolf and his shifter instincts.

This magic wasn't something Matthias could kill, but I could borrow some of his strength. Maybe that would be enough to settle his wolf.

"Put your hand on my shoulder," I told him. And then I added two words that didn't come easily to me, but that he needed to hear. "Help me."

Though Matthias hadn't yet developed a shifter's need for physical contact with pack mates, he didn't hesitate to do as I'd asked. The moment his catcher's mitt of a hand rested on my shoulder, his power crackled in the air, waiting to be unleashed. His touch immediately comforted me.

Someday, this man will be an alpha, I thought.

I didn't know how I knew that, but I did. Not tomorrow, not next month, or even next year, but there would be a time when Matthias would come into his own and be ready to lead, protect, and comfort his own pack. The vision brought tears to my eyes, but they were tears of happiness, not grief.

I wondered if Sean knew yet. He hadn't said so, but he might have been waiting for me to come to that conclusion for myself. I wouldn't have been ready to hear it until now. He knew me better than I knew myself sometimes. I loved him for that, and for a million other reasons.

Because I'd never done so before and I didn't know how he would react, I drew carefully on Matthias's strength and magic to ease my pain the way Sean's alpha magic did when I let him do that for me. The pain didn't go away—it transferred to Matthias instead. His chest rumbled, but he didn't flinch or move away. Gently, he squeezed my shoulder, wordlessly encouraging me to take as much comfort as I needed. The painful prickling of shifter magic on my arms faded as his wolf settled into the role of providing support and protection.

I dropped the first crystal into my cup holder, picked up the empty crystal, and scooped the spirit's vile trace from Malcolm's left hand. The sensation was acutely unpleasant, like grabbing rotten garbage, but I let out a breath. Malcolm was safe now—or at least as safe as any of us could be.

I, however, was *not* safe. At all.

The faded magic we'd found yesterday had felt moldy and putrid. Malcolm had described it as evil that had crawled from the bowels of the earth.

I'd encountered many malevolent things—alive, dead, undead, and other—but nothing that felt like this magic. This spirit was an abomination. The closest comparison I could make was to the sorcerer Miraç, who'd tortured Malcolm and damn near killed me.

The spirit's dark gray trace coiled around my bloody, injured fingers with the sensation of something locking in place.

Before my eyes, my hand withered, twisted, and decayed. I screamed in pain and gagged at the horrible, nauseating sensation of my flesh turning dark and mottled blue-black.

Under the spirit's control, my own rotting hand closed on my throat and squeezed. Stars filled my vision as everything grew dim. Somewhere close by Matthias snarled and Malcolm shouted, but their words were indistinct. The roaring in my ears grew until I heard nothing else. I might be clawing at my own hand and throat, fighting to free myself, but my world had dwindled to only the sensation of my misshapen, bony fingers crushing my windpipe.

A man's ghostly face appeared in the gathering darkness, twisted in ferocious rage and hate. Unlike most spirits I'd encountered, this one was powerful enough that instead of the vague shape of a human body, I saw details: unevenly cut and matted dark hair, thick eyebrows, a patchy beard and mustache, pockmarked skin, and a discolored and threadbare shirt over massive shoulders. And the deadest, coldest, most predatory eyes I'd ever seen that didn't belong to one of the ancient vampires. I got the sense this enormous and evil man had been the embodiment of cruelty and death long before he'd become a necromancer's pet.

Slowly, deliberately, he dragged his spectral tongue over my face from my chin to my forehead. The violation was a vile, revolting act of possession and denigration. Fury and disgust made me shudder, but other than that I couldn't move. My body wouldn't respond, even as my brain screamed at me to get away.

The sensation of decay spread through me, and I swore I felt my bones, skin, muscles, and even my blood turning to gore and dust, as if my entire body would crumble and fall apart while I still lived.

"You's gon' die," the ghost promised in a raspy, harsh voice, displaying a mouthful of rotting teeth. "We's comin' for you. Jus' you wait, little birdie. *Jus' you wait.*"

And then he was gone.

TWENTY-ONE

WITH ONE FINAL, PAINFUL TWIST THAT DUG MY BONY FINGERTIPS DEEPER into my tender flesh, my hand released my throat. I sucked in a lungful of air, coughed, and wheezed.

Driven by pure instinct and a desperate need to escape, I fumbled to open my door and nearly fell out of my SUV. I went down hard on my hands and knees, too disoriented and in shock to feel the pain of hitting the pavement. My ears rang and my vision remained gray and blank.

I sensed movement behind me just before someone wrapped me in their arms and held me tight against their broad chest. I spooled magic to fight, but recognized Matthias's warm peppery scent and powerful golden magic before I had a chance to lash out.

He pressed something small and hard into my left palm. "Put the trace in the crystal," he told me, his mouth next to my ear so I could hear him over the roar in my ears.

At least I'd regained enough of my senses to do as he'd said. "*Enclose,*" I rasped.

The spirit's horrible, rotten magic slithered from my right hand into the crystal. I shuddered at the sensation and the resulting sharp pain that reminded me magic had cut that hand.

I didn't want to look at my hand, but I had to see if the nightmare vision of it decaying was real. As if he knew what I feared, Matthias's arm tightened around my waist. He took the crystal from me and cradled my hand palm-up in his own massive hand.

My last sight of my hand was of blackened flesh sloughing off my bones. What greeted me now as my vision cleared was grim, but not nearly as horrible as the illusion. My fingers and palm still had the deep lacerations left by the necromancer's magic and scrapes from the pavement, but the rest of my flesh was intact.

I made a sound that was somewhere between a laugh and a sob and looked around. "Malcolm?"

"He went to lockdown once you were freed by the spirit," Matthias said, his voice half growl. "We didn't know what the necromancer or spirit might do next, and I promised you would be safe with me."

I sagged in his arms, surprised and relieved that my ghost had jumped to his warded crystal. I had to credit Matthias for that minor miracle. Neither Malcolm nor I were known for leaving the other in potential danger simply to ensure our own safety. Rather the opposite, in fact.

Another silver lining to Matthias's time with the Vampire Court: he was nearly unflappable in a crisis. Even as I'd fought the spirit for control of my body and nearly strangled myself before leaping from the SUV to escape a threat he couldn't see, he'd had the presence of mind to grab the crystal I'd needed to contain the spirit's trace, hold me so I felt safe and grounded in the wake of the attack, and remind me to stash the magic before it dissipated. And he'd gotten Malcolm to safety by promising to protect me.

Keeping me in his lap so I wasn't sitting on pavement, Matthias tore off one of his long sleeves and carefully wrapped my injured hand. Meanwhile, I gingerly touched my neck and found several bloody gouges and sore spots where I'd tried to pull my hand away from my throat.

As he tended to my hand, I noticed something on the inside of his right bicep, where the skin was thinner and more sensitive: scars that looked very much like fingernail or claw marks.

For a moment, I felt displaced, as if I were in two places at once. I blinked at my bandaged hand, at the manicure I'd gotten for Daniel and Nan's wedding. Just like after my fainting spell, I saw an after-image of something like talons protruding from my fingertips. This time their blackened, pointed ends dripped blood.

The sound of my phone ringing startled me. The strange vision faded.

Matthias answered the call. "She will be all right," he said without a greeting. "There was an incident involving dark magic, but her injuries are minor. She is disoriented at the moment."

I had no doubt who'd called. Sean must have felt something happening through our nascent bond. "I'm okay," I managed to say, though my voice wobbled. His sharp ears would hear me.

Then I remembered my promise not to tell him I was all right when I wasn't, so I added, "I mean, I *will be* okay as soon as I use a healing spell."

Matthias held my phone to my ear so I could hear Sean's response.

"Alice," he said, his voice deep and growly. "I was running in wolf form at the pack land. I got back to my phone and shifted as quickly as I could. What the hell was that?" He sighed. "Scratch that. Just tell me how badly you're hurt."

"Only cuts on my hand and neck," I assured him.

"It felt much worse than that."

It wasn't an accusation, really, but he clearly didn't entirely believe me.

"There was more, but it was just an illusion," I explained. "I'll fill you in later when I see you." I had a mental image of Sean in wolf form trying to use his phone. That made me smile, though my hand

—along with everything else—hurt like the dickens and my tummy roiled like I'd just gotten off a rollercoaster.

I glanced around the parking lot. Thankfully, no one seemed to have noticed us. "Let me heal myself and figure out what we need to do now. I'll see you in a while. Don't rush home. I'm sure your wolf would like to run and hunt for a while longer. We need our alpha at his best." After a beat, I added, "Matthias has me."

"I know," Sean said. His voice had warmed considerably, as if he knew I'd said it as much for Matthias's sake than to ease his own worry. "I'll stay for a few more hours, then."

Not that long ago, I would have eaten tacks before I'd have said anyone "had me," much less allowed someone to take that role. I might be up to my ears in trouble, but my life had changed dramatically for the better since Malcolm and I had met. Even sitting in the lap of a newly turned werewolf in a strip mall parking lot with a shredded hand, weird visions, scraped knees, and brand-new nightmare fodder in the form of a scuzzy specter, I had that fundamental truth to lean on.

"I love you," I said.

I heard the smile in Sean's voice when he replied, "I know."

Once I ended the call, Matthias rose and lifted me to my feet.

Who had given him those scars on his arm? He'd consumed Valas's blood regularly, so he shouldn't have any scars. I hadn't noticed any until just now, and only because I'd gotten a close look at the underside of his arm.

Maybe Valas herself had hurt him. It was a strange place to dig your nails into someone...unless the moment had been intimate. That was a whole other level of Matthias's time with the Court that concerned me deeply. Any sex between Valas and Matthias could not have been consensual, even if he'd acquiesced. Not when she had all the power and he had none.

If Matthias guessed what I was thinking, he didn't let on. "Would you like me to drive?" he asked.

"That is not a bad idea," I admitted.

He bent his head and murmured, "We are under surveillance. Black car with tinted windows, backed into the third spot from the end, in front of the barbershop."

Anger made magic spark on my fingers. "The Court?"

"I don't believe so. The Court does not favor that kind of vehicle."

He had a point there. The black car was a standard four-door sedan. Luxury and horsepower were the only way the vamps or their people traveled.

"Is it Mr. Touchy again?" I asked.

"It's not the same vehicle, but possibly. I can't see the driver or passenger—just shadows."

"Can you see the make, model, and plate?"

"Yes. I've memorized them."

"Okay. Let's see what they do when we move."

He helped me into the passenger seat, then hurried around the SUV to climb in on the driver's side. As he shut his door, my phone rang again. The number was local but not in my call history.

Cautiously, I answered and put the call on speaker. "This is Alice."

A familiar voice barked, "Worth, what are you doing spying on my crime scene?"

Matthias rumbled.

Through the windshield, I looked up the hill again toward the medical center. Even from this distance I recognized the figure standing at the edge of the parking lot, facing us, holding a phone to his ear.

"Detective Diaz," I said. "I have no idea what you're talking about. I'm picking up my dry cleaning."

"Dry cleaning. Right. Was that before or after you face-planted in the parking lot and needed first aid?"

Crap. Apparently our little drama hadn't gone unnoticed after all.

When I didn't reply, he asked, "Have you been drinking, Ms. Worth?"

"Only coffee, Detective." I glared in his direction, though he couldn't see me through my tinted windshield. "Was there a point to this call? Should I remind you I have an attorney and your questions need to go through him?"

"I want to know how you knew to come here." His voice had gone decidedly chilly. "And don't tell me it was for your dry cleaning. I will haul your ass in for obstruction if I have to."

"I'm not obstructing you in any way. Whatever's going on up there can't have anything to do with my case, right? Oliver's under house arrest. These crimes must be unrelated. That's what your police department spokesperson is about to tell the press, I'm sure."

"Alice...Ms. Worth." Diaz heaved a sigh. "I would like to know what you think is going on."

"Yesterday you thought it was all bullshit. Or am I misremembering your words?"

"I *do* think it's bullshit." He blew out a breath. "But maybe it's not."

I had a sudden thought. "You're not having me tailed, are you?"

"No. Why? Someone following you?" When he spoke again, his brusque cop voice was back. "Wait—did something happen and that's why you looked injured?"

Before I had a chance to reply, another familiar figure joined Diaz at the edge of the parking lot. I recognized Ferguson's lanky build. "Later," Diaz said, and abruptly ended the call.

I watched him stick his phone in his pocket, exchange a few words with Ferguson, and disappear back in the direction of the yellow tape.

While I'd been talking to Diaz, Matthias had taken my burner phone and texted the license plate from the car parked in front of the barbershop. "No reply yet on either inquiry," he said at my raised eyebrows. "The delay is frustrating."

"I know. Zola will get back to us as soon as she can. I wish I had the kind of resources you're used to at the Court, but I don't." My hands and neck throbbed with pain and my knees ached. I took a mid-level healing spell from my bracelet and unwrapped my sliced hand. "You might want to get out of the SUV," I told him. "These healing spells cause pain and your wolf isn't going to be happy about it." The first time I'd used a strong healing spell in front of Sean, he'd almost lost it, and he had far more command over his wolf than Matthias.

Even so, I wasn't surprised at all when Matthias said, "I choose to stay. I have to learn control."

"Okay. Don't touch the spell or me until it's done." As much as it hurt to do so, I forced myself to close my bloody fist around the crystal. I drew on the green earth magic and invoked the spell. "*Helios.*"

Magic pulsed from the crystal. As the cuts, gouges, and abrasions healed, I locked my jaw and hunched in my seat, breathing in quick gasps and letting out measured groans so no screams escaped. Matthias's golden magic seared my arms and he growled almost nonstop, but he stayed in his seat and didn't interfere.

When the last of the spell faded, I dropped the crystal into the cupholder, bent over, and rested my head on my arms.

"Are you going to be sick?" Matthias asked.

"Thinking about it," I mumbled, forgetting that he didn't know my sense of humor yet. When I heard him rummaging in the back seat, I added, "No, I'm fine. Just—" I hiccupped "—queasy."

My burner phone buzzed. Matthias picked it up and checked the screen. "Your contact at the DMV reports both Mr. Touchy's and this new shadow's tags were reported stolen," he said. "So no help there."

"Fabulous." I found a partial bottle of water in my bag and took a few swigs. "Let's get home," I said. "I need to get Malcolm out of his hidey-hole, see what I can determine about this magic I got from the ghost grenade Mr. Touchy tossed at Malcolm, and take a longer look at those surveillance videos."

"What about these?" Matthias pointed at the crystals containing the necromancer's magic and the malevolent spirit's trace.

"Those I'm going to need help with." I touched my neck to check on my wounds, then dropped my hand back into my lap just as quickly. The gouges and scratches left by my fingernails had healed, but I couldn't stand to touch my own throat. "Contrary to what Malcolm seems to believe, I do *not* live to play with fire."

"Only certain types of fire," Matthias said.

"Okay, I'll give you that one." I leaned my head back against the seat. "Let's see if our shadow tails us home. Maybe we'll get a glimpse of them along the way. Thank you, by the way."

He frowned. "For what?"

He was probably not used to being thanked for anything, from the small to the significant. "Everything," I said.

Matthias backed out of our parking space, made a smooth turn, and pulled into traffic. "You're welcome," he said.

In my side view mirror, I watched the black car with the dark tinted windows fall in two cars behind us.

I stole a glance at the top of the hill. Diaz stood with Ferguson, his back to us. As we drove past, he turned to look at us over his shoulder. I didn't know if he noticed the black car or not. I also didn't know where we'd go from here, or what he'd do if I told him what I suspected had happened to Madison, nurse Stephanie Harris, or the assault victims.

Everything was an unknown right now, other than I was glad to have so many people at my back. That meant whatever I ended up facing—today, tomorrow, or in the future—I wouldn't face it alone. And that was worth a hell of a lot.

TWENTY-TWO

The black car followed us for a long time, but when Matthias exited for the highway that led to our quiet road, the car continued north on the interstate. We'd never gotten a better look at the driver or passenger thanks to the dark windows. At least my nausea had faded and I felt ready to tackle the trace from the ghost grenade.

On our way home, Cyro texted that she saw no sign of the shadowy figure after it left the scene of Madison's murder. I'd suspected as much, but the news was still disappointing.

Matthias parked next to the house and we went inside. The downstairs had far less daylight than I was used to. Before leaving for the pack land to run as a wolf, Sean had apparently covered the broken patio door with plywood until we could get a replacement. That meant Rogue, Daisy, and Esme, who usually took their afternoon naps in the living room, had to go elsewhere to find sunshine. My guess was the workout room.

"I'm going to let Malcolm out and see what we can find out about whoever created that ghost grenade," I told Matthias. "While we're in the workshop doing that, can you work on your documentation for our lawyers and keep an eye on things until Sean gets back?"

"Yes, of course." He headed upstairs to get his laptop.

I made coffee, told Matthias to help himself, and took some downstairs in a tumbler. I kept Malcolm's lockdown crystal in a warded box inside one of my spelled cabinets. Inside it, he was protected by three layers of blood magic spellwork, all of which allowed passage only one way and could be unlocked by my magic alone.

I put the blue crystal in my palm and let my magic swirl around it. "*Release.*"

Malcolm appeared beside me. "Alice," he said, clearly as relieved to see me as I was to see him. "Good gravy. That sucked big time. Are you okay?"

"Pretty okay." I waggled my hand. "Physically, I'm fine. Did you see the spirit who attacked me?"

"Unfortunately, yes, I did." He flitted. "That creep was so ugly his momma slapped him when he came out. I also saw him *lick your entire face.* Who the hell does that? That's just *nasty.*"

"You're telling me." I leaned against the work table and took a moment to soak in the comfort of my house wards and Malcolm's reassuring presence. "In the category of silver lining, I think that about clinches what we're dealing with. The spirit said *we*, not *I.*"

"Yeah, right before he said they were going to kill you." He flitted again. "Katy and Carly are going to have their hands full dealing with this necromancer and Mr. Nasty Ghost, whoever they are."

"When it's all said and done, my money's on Carly and Katy." I set the crystals from today's murder scene on the work table. "In the meantime, I want to see if we can track the magic from the ghost grenade."

As I took off my shoes and socks, Malcolm said, "So, ghost possession emergency aside, I think spending the afternoon with us seems to have loosened Matthias up. He really seemed to come into his own and took charge when you tried to strangle yourself. Even kinda bossed me around a little."

"He did really well." Barefoot, I took a piece of chalk and began drawing runes for the tracking spell inside the smallest inlaid circle. I preferred to do this kind of magic barefoot as a way of feeling more securely grounded. It was an earth mage thing. "Also, at Carly's shop, I treated him to a large iced tea and one of your jokes."

He perked up. "Oooh, which one? The one about the flamingo with restless leg syndrome?"

"No, the one about the pterodactyl."

His shoulders slumped. "Aw, that isn't even one of my good ones."

"Funny, that's what Matthias said too."

"Ha ha."

I'd already cut the spellwork for a strong containment ward into the circle, so all I had to do was invoke it. My carnivorous blood garden in the backyard provided the power. Even if something happened to my magic, the ward wouldn't fail and release whatever I had contained. That was a definite upgrade from circles I'd had previously.

In addition to the tracking spellwork, I added runes to protect Malcolm and me from the black magic, as well as spellwork to transfer magic into my crystal if any came back through the tracking spell. I wasn't sure the latter would work, but if I could preserve the magic that would make it easier to learn more about it and find its source.

"Tracking any kind of unknown magic is dangerous," I said. "And that goes triple for black magic. If I'm going to try, I need to use spells and wards to protect us from black or occult magic. I'm a bit rusty on those."

"If you're rusty, you probably should look at your spell books," Malcolm advised. "One or two wrong glyphs and that's how you end up with some otherworldly abomination in your basement."

I retrieved the necessary spell book from one of my locked and warded cabinets. Malcolm floated at my shoulder as I skimmed for the spell I needed.

"This one sounds fun," he said, pointing at a page with an illustration of a gigantic tentacled creature. "Do you anticipate ever facing a Leviathan?"

"Hope not, but it pays to be prepared." I flipped two more pages and found what I was looking for. I traced the glyphs with my fingertip. "Okay, got it."

"Can I look at that Leviathan repellent spell again? You know, just in case."

I flipped back to that page. As Malcolm read up on Leviathans and the magical repelling thereof, I drew a circle with chalk within my inlaid circle large enough for me to sit in. I copied the glyphs and runes for the protection spell around the perimeter.

I pocketed the chalk, took off my shirt so I had on just a tank top over my bra, and used a washable marker to draw the remaining spellwork on my body. I'd used tracking spells so often I could do this part in my sleep. The spellwork ran up my right arm, down my left, and across my chest.

Prep work done, I sat cross-legged in the circle and invoked a blood magic protection spell housed in one of the crystals on my bracelet. I'd had enough close calls with black magic of late to believe at least two levels of magical Kevlar might be required.

"Okay, I'm ready," I told Malcolm.

He floated over from my work table. "You want me to boost your protection spell or the containment wards?"

"Protection spell. I'll use the house wards and garden energy for the containment wards." Careful not to touch any of the runes I'd drawn, I moved around a few inches at a time until I felt like I was perfectly centered within the spellwork. "Here's hoping I see something that'll help us."

"Here's hoping you see it and don't get zapped." Malcolm flitted. "The ghost thing was bad enough. I'll never hear the end of it from Sean if you get fried and I let you do it."

I rolled my eyes. "So glad to hear that you're more worried about Sean's temper than my well-being."

I'd been joking, but Malcolm's expression had no humor in it.

"He's mad enough at me already for leaving you alone with Moses to find Liam. I don't need to give him any more reasons to shoot me dirty looks."

"He just needs a little time to cool off. His wolf is probably madder about it than he is."

"I don't know. Every time he hears my voice he looks pretty pissed." Malcolm shrugged. "Anyway, let's get this show on the road. Be safe."

"I plan to." I rolled my shoulders, invoked the various containment wards around us, and picked up the crystal containing the magic from the ghost grenade. The trace barely tingled on my hand. There wasn't much left. I figured I had about a fifty-fifty shot of this tracking spell working and about a twenty percent chance of seeing anything that would help us identify Mr. Touchy or his friends. It was still worth a try.

Slowly, so I didn't fracture what little remained any further, I drew magic trace from the crystal and wove it through the tracking spell. I sensed Malcolm channeling his own magic into my protection spell as the tracking spell surged, ready to be unleashed.

Not that long ago I'd done a tracking spell in my basement and ended up buried alive by a Dark Fae. I'd barely survived. More recently, I'd tracked and encountered a rare type of shifter called a *faoladh*.

This trace probably didn't lead to a fae or elite death machine of any sort, but it *would* be nice to track non-lethal magic for a change. As a mage PI and trouble magnet, to use Malcolm's term, I doubted I'd get to do that anytime soon.

I closed my eyes, inhaled deeply, and exhaled slowly as I cleared my mind.

Take nothing with you into the spell, my long-ago teacher had said. *Go alone in silence and return the same way.* It was a mage's mantra that dated back farther than anyone could trace. I hadn't thought of it in a long time, but recalling my near-disastrous previous tracking experiences reminded me I couldn't take those fears with me this time.

Finally, I found my silence. I took one more deep breath and let it out. *"Adinvenire,"* I said. *Find.*

The tracking spell surged from my body, carrying my consciousness along with it like a small boat in a rushing river.

Images, scents, and sounds tumbled through my mind and passed through me: fragments of rituals, glimpses of dark cowls covering bent heads, bones piled in a cauldron, fresh blood dripping from a cup that lay spilled on the floor. An arched door made of old wood with blackened iron hinges. Pale featureless faces around an altar where a body lay unmoving under a black cloth. And a haunting song sung by a single female voice that wove in between all the other images.

Definitely occult magic. Ancient, devastating, and soaked in blood.

I caught a glimpse of a face twisted in rage just before my tracking spell fractured. No, it didn't fracture—it got *smashed*. Deliberately destroyed.

I didn't even have a chance to brace myself before the spell blew apart.

My protection spells absorbed most of the blast, but my body still took a hit from the shockwave of magic and broken spellwork. I lost at least a full minute. Maybe two.

When the fog cleared and I opened my eyes, I found Malcolm floating above me. I lay on my back in the inlaid circle. The smell of ozone and old pennies hung heavy in the air. Our containment wards had done their job. Without them, the broken spell might have seriously damaged our house.

"Alice?" Malcolm brushed my forehead with his ghostly hand, making me shiver. "You with me?"

"Yup." I tasted blood. I wiped my mouth with the back of my hand and it came away smeared red. I had a moment of panic before

I realized my lower lip was bleeding and I wasn't in fact coughing up blood. Small favors. A busted lip I could handle.

"When the spellwork blew, the crystal hit the wards, bounced off, and nailed you right in the face," Malcolm explained.

"Of course it did." I pushed myself up with a groan. "Shit, everything hurts."

"What the hell happened?" he demanded. "You lasted about four seconds before the whole thing went kablooey. "

I told him everything I could remember from the tracking spell, including what I'd seen, smelled, and heard.

"So everything worked as it was supposed to, and then you saw a face and someone blew up your spell," he said. "Who could do that? Mr. Touchy?"

"Not Mr. Touchy. I don't know *whose* face it was, but it wasn't him." I got to my feet and staggered over to lean against the work table. "I'm gonna need a bunch of ibuprofen and a stiff drink. Why do I have neither of those things in my workshop?"

"Occult magic with blood and bones." Malcolm flitted around the room. "That sounds *sooo* bad."

"It felt..." I searched for the right words. "Archaic and very corporeal. I'm pretty sure I saw sacrifices."

"*Sacrifices?* What the hell, Alice? You remember when all we had to worry about were harnads and stolen objects of power?"

"Oh, the good old days." I put my hands on my knees. "Ugh. Now I'm nauseous."

My phone buzzed on the table. *Wolf Calling*. I swiped the green button, put it on speaker, and swallowed hard. "Hey."

"What's going on now?" Sean demanded.

"I'm okay," I assured him. "I used a tracking spell on some magic Malcolm ran into. It ended up going sideways, but I'm not hurt except for a busted lip. Matthias did a really good job today, by the way."

"I'm glad to hear it." He sighed. "I'm on my way home."

"Okay. I love you."

I pictured him on the other end, pinching the bridge of his nose. "I know," he said finally. We ended the call.

I grimaced and looked at all my smeared spellwork on the floor. By the time I got everything cleaned up, took care of my split lip, and texted Carly an update about the necromancer, Sean would probably be pulling into the driveway. He tended to ignore speed limits at times like these.

Then I'd get to tell him not just about getting slightly possessed and what I'd seen during the tracking spell, but also that I wanted to call Charles as soon as the sun went down.

And wouldn't that conversation be *so much* fun.

TWENTY-THREE

THE MOMENT SEAN WALKED IN THE DOOR, I REALIZED I WASN'T THE ONLY person with important information to share.

Once Matthias, Malcolm, and I gathered in the living room, Sean gave us the news we'd been expecting since the night Bryan and Adri served us with the Court's indictments and demands. "The Were Ruling Council has summoned us to a closed session tonight," he said. "I got a call on the way home from Drew Montgomery. Alice and I are expected, along with Ben and Matthias."

Drew was a senior member of the Council. I'd met him only once, when he attended the fight between Sean and Matthew Anderson. Sean had killed Matthew and replaced him on the Council.

"You, me, and Matthias makes sense," I said. "But why Ben? Because Nan isn't here?"

He shook his head. "Because in the event you and I end up in prison, Ben would become the new alpha."

Matthias frowned. "The Council would refuse to recognize Nan Lowell as alpha because she's female?"

Sean's expression made it clear there was more to it than that. "What's going on?" I demanded. "Are Nan and Daniel okay?"

"Yes, they're fine." His expression turned stoic. "I spoke to Nan just now and she gave me the go-ahead to talk to you. She wanted to tell you in person, but now we can't wait for them to return from their trip and I don't want them to rush back. This information does not go beyond this room for the time being."

Now my unease—and my heart rate—skyrocketed. What the hell was going on? If Nan and Daniel were fine, what wasn't Sean telling us?

"Yes, okay," I said impatiently. "What?"

"I'm sorry you're finding out this way, and right now, on top of everything else." Sean's gaze never left my face. "Nan will be leaving our pack effective immediately. She and Daniel are now a lone wolf pair. They are still associates of our pack and under its protection."

I sat down hard on the couch. Malcolm's mouth hung open. Even Matthias appeared stunned.

It took me a few beats to overcome my shock enough to speak. "Why?" My throat was so tight that I didn't recognize my own voice.

"Because Daniel and his wolf can't join our pack." Sean sat next to me, giving me space while staying near. "He can't bring himself to make those connections again. Not after feeling his entire original pack die. His pain and trauma are too deep."

My chest felt like someone was standing on it. Even Sean's alpha comfort couldn't diminish the hurt. "He decided this out of nowhere?"

"No." He let out a breath. "He and Nan and I spoke about this several times before their wedding."

"But not with me?" I wasn't sure which bit of news hurt me more: Nan's decision to leave or Daniel leaving me out of his conversations with Sean. "I don't understand."

"He didn't want to upset you if there wasn't a cause. Up until now, he still hoped he might be able to join us." Sean rubbed my back. "He sincerely tried, Alice. But some hurts go too deep."

That kind of pain I understood, even if nothing else made a hell of a lot of sense right now.

Daniel had been beyond shocked when he and his wolf fell hard for Nan. After thirty years of being a lone wolf, he'd believed he would never experience love again. Attraction, yes. Sex, yes. He hadn't lived as a monk during that time. Nan had felt the same after her sadistic former alpha killed her husband. And yet they'd found love with each other.

I'd assumed Daniel's love for Nan and the support of our pack would offer enough of a balm for him to overcome his past. Apparently, I had assumed wrong.

Suddenly, I recalled the look Daniel had given me the night of their wedding, when I spoke of our pack growing and becoming stronger. He'd known then, but he must not have wanted to upset me and then depart on his honeymoon.

"I didn't see this coming," I said, my voice tight with grief.

"I know. I'm so sorry we didn't get to talk about this together as a family, like we'd planned." Sean took my hand and squeezed. "Ben is our beta for the time being, but it's not a role he's suited for."

Sean was absolutely right. Ben knew better than anyone that he was an ideal third. The role fit him as naturally as a tailored suit. Trying to force him into acting as a beta was the proverbial square peg in a round hole.

Through my hurt, I thought of Matthias and his nascent dominance. But how long would it take for his true strength to emerge? Weeks? Months? *Years?* I had no way to predict the answer. It certainly wouldn't be hours, which was all we had between now and the Council meeting, when Ben's unsuitability to become beta, much less an alpha, would be plain for all to see.

Sean had told me long ago that when he became a werewolf, Henry, the alpha of the Tomb Mountain Pack at the time, took him into the pack because he sensed Sean was very dominant. Sean had become alpha not long after that in the wake of Henry's murder by his sadistic beta, who Sean also killed to protect the pack. While Sean's experience of becoming a werewolf had been traumatic, it wasn't anything close to what Matthias had gone through.

Matthias needs more time, I'd said.

Arkady's response echoed in my head: *We don't have it.*

It wasn't right and it wasn't fair. None of this was. Knowing it was all Charles Vaughan's fault didn't make anything better. But it *did* put even more pressure on my theoretical sunset call, which I'd barely have enough time to make before we had to stand in front of the Council. And that was even assuming I got through. The odds were slim.

I took a deep breath and put my feelings about Nan and Daniel's news aside for now. I'd have to process it, but we had bigger, much more unpleasant fish to fry. "Sean..."

"I know that tone." He eyed me. "What plan do you have that I am very much not going to like?"

Despite the tension, Malcolm chuckled. Matthias raised his eyebrows and clasped his hands behind his back. I got the impression they both wished they had popcorn for this one.

I told Sean I wanted to call Charles directly.

His expression went from incredulous to furious and back as I talked. I listed all the reasons I thought I needed to call, including the points Matthias had made about knowing what we were up against and the possibility this was a backhanded way for Charles to initiate some kind of conversation.

When I finished, Sean didn't say anything for a long time. I let him think.

"I don't know who Charles is anymore," I said after a full minute had gone by. "Maybe I never really did, and I was deluding myself to think otherwise. After what he's done to me, I never wanted to speak to him again. But the fact is, I have to talk to him now."

"Do you *want* to talk to him?" Sean asked.

"Yes."

"Why?"

"Think about it." I touched his hand. "If Matthias is right and this is the vampire version of *Let's Make a Deal*, Charles needs something but he can't ask us for it because he'd seem weak. Do you know what that means? For the first time we might have the upper hand even if it looks to the world like he's got us under his thumb." The more I talked about it, the more my instincts told me I was right. "He saves face and we come out on top, even if no one but us knows that."

Sean wasn't buying what I was selling, however. "Vaughan plays games within games. I'm not saying you're wrong, but there might be layers to this we're not seeing."

"Oh, I have no doubt there are. Anything with Charles has more layers than...than..." I searched for the right analogy. "Carly's croissants," I finished. "That doesn't mean we can't turn this to our advantage. As Matthias said, information is power. Lack of information is the opposite."

"Deep thoughts by Alice," Malcolm interjected. He floated back and forth over by the plywood, keeping his distance from Sean. "For what it's worth, I'm with her on this."

Sean looked at Matthias. "And your opinion?"

If Matthias was surprised that Sean asked, he didn't show it. "Alice should call," he said. "Mr. Vaughan believes she's a known quantity. He's wrong, and that gives her an edge. Also, I see little risk but great potential for reward."

"You think the indictments are Vaughan's way of opening dialogue," Sean said.

It wasn't a question, but Matthias answered anyway. "Yes, I think it's likely. Mr. Vaughan is in a precarious position and he's probably well aware of that fact. He may think Alice can somehow help him. It's the most likely explanation for his actions. Otherwise, the indictments are a frivolous waste of valuable resources, and to what end? To destabilize your relationship with the Were Ruling Council? To put you and Alice in prison? No doubt he still intends to reclaim me, but the rest strikes me as unlikely."

It seemed pretty damn unlikely to me too. And to Sean, who

finally looked less like he wanted to throw my plan in the sink and turn on the garbage disposal and more like he might grudgingly agree.

"The sun sets in about ninety minutes," Sean said. "We have to be at the Were Council meeting an hour after that and it takes thirty minutes to get there from here. That's not much time—assuming you can even get to him."

"I have to try."

"I know." He kissed my forehead. "Now, what the hell has been going on since you left for the coffee shop?"

Five minutes after the sun set, I shut myself in our office, poured a medicinal shot of good whisky, and made the call.

I had one private number for Charles, but I hadn't used it for months—since before my trip to the Broken World. I had zero guarantees that it still worked and not much hope that he'd take my call. This was simply the longest of long shots.

The phone rang twice, and then he answered. "Good evening, Alice."

His voice sounded exactly the same. I didn't know why I'd expected it to have changed, but I had. Maybe because he'd done things in the past month I'd once thought he'd never do.

Once upon a time, whenever he spoke my name it sent shivers of fear and desire down my spine. I felt neither of those emotions now. He'd left me gutted with his admission that he'd manipulated my feelings for years in an attempt to get me to fall for him and force me under his thumb. I had nothing left for him but anger and mistrust.

"Hello, Charles." My voice was steady. Yay me.

"To what do I owe the pleasure of this well-timed call?"

Let the games begin, I thought. "I'm sure you can guess."

"Should my attorney take this call?"

"Should mine?"

"Touché." He chuckled. "I have greatly missed our chats."

"If all you want is a chat, there are better ways to break the ice than a stack of indictments two inches thick. And I'd think you'd be too busy these days for idle conversation with the likes of me."

"And yet I have taken your call moments after waking, before I have even risen from my bed. Perhaps our conversation will not be idle."

Now I had a mental image of Charles reclining on his pillows, maybe still in his PJs, holding whatever super-secret phone this number went to. He'd kept it so closely at hand that he'd answered within seconds of its first ring. That told me a hell of a lot about whether he'd anticipated—maybe even *hoped for*—a call.

"I genuinely hope our conversation *isn't* idle," I said. "Because you know everything in this indictment is bullshit."

"I do not, in fact, know that." His tone remained maddeningly casual, as if we weren't talking about his attempt to blow up my entire life. "But all discussions on legal matters must be referred to my attorney, Christine Foreman. Shall I have her call your legal team?"

So he didn't want to talk about the indictments, but he *did* want to talk. "So, what's on your mind these days, Charles? Anything new with you since the last time we talked?"

"When did we last cross paths?" He hummed as he pretended to think. He knew damn well when we'd last seen each other. "Lear Fineman's fundraiser gala at the Aldridge Museum, was it not? Lear was a true humanitarian and philanthropist. A shame he died so tragically in that *very mysterious* fire."

"Yup, total shame." I didn't bother to fake grief for Lear—real name Llyr—a fae who'd done his damnedest to drag me and a bunch of others on a one-way trip to the fae realm. With any luck, he was currently experiencing new and imaginative tortures for pissing off the Dark Fae King.

If Charles knew the truth about who Llyr was or what happened to him, he didn't let on. "As you might imagine, my new position as head of the Vampire Court keeps me quite busy. I have little time to myself, which is why these quiet minutes when I wake are so precious to me."

At moments like this, he reminded me so much of Moses. Insincere and calculating and talking about inconsequential matters when all I wanted to do was to cut to the chase. Just because I understood the game didn't mean I enjoyed playing it.

"I understand you visited Northbourne today," he said before I could encourage him to get to the point. "Should I be flattered?"

"I thought you just opened your eyes."

"As you might imagine, I wake to a briefing of important information compiled by my most trusted servants."

"Now *I'm* flattered," I said, though I certainly wasn't. "I qualified as 'important information' just because I drove by the estate."

"In fact, it seems you stopped for two minutes and nineteen seconds and engaged one of my enforcers in conversation. And you were not alone."

"What can I say? Curiosity got the better of me." I sipped my whisky. "I wish I had time to recap my day, but unfortunately I have to be somewhere soon."

"So I see in my briefing. The Council wishes to hear from you, Sean, Ben Cooper, and my misplaced property. You are certainly pressed for time this evening."

We already knew the Court had a source of information close to the Were Ruling Council, so the fact Charles was aware we'd been summoned didn't surprise me. And if he'd tried to get a rise out of me by referring to Matthias as his *misplaced property*, he was destined to be disappointed.

"That being the case," I said, "and at the risk of repeating myself, what's on your mind?"

"I wish to hear your true account of the deaths of Valas and Vlad."

I didn't believe he'd done all this just to get the scoop on precisely what went down the night Valas had me kidnapped.

I *did* think, however, he very much wanted to know how she and her vile progeny had left this plane of existence. The list of firsthand witnesses to their deaths was pretty damn short.

"What are you offering in exchange for the information?" I asked. "I have a few thoughts, if nothing comes to mind."

"I offer not to extract the information from Daniel Holiday—or his new wife, who I am sure has heard the story in full."

I'd expected some kind of intimidation or blackmail, but had hoped for something more imaginative than threatening harm to people I loved.

But did I believe he'd follow through on the threat? My gut told me no. This felt like he was testing the waters, making a move, but not *the* move. He expected a counteroffer. We'd been down this road before, negotiating the terms of trading a drink of my blood for an artifact I needed to save Sean's life. With Charles, or any vamp I'd ever met, the endgame never made its appearance in the first five minutes of talking.

"You are disappointed in me," he said in the silence that followed his threat. "But I am already a villain to you, am I not? A monster, a boogeyman, a misbegotten creature who drinks blood and haunts your nightmares?"

That jolted me a bit, but he couldn't know anything about my nightmares. It was just a figure of speech.

As for whether he was a monster, well...maybe, maybe not. Every time I thought I had him figured out, he threw me another curveball. And sometimes he seemed to *want* to be perceived as a monster, and at other times, the comparison appeared hurtful.

"Charles, what happened that night goes right to the heart of these indictments," I pointed out. "You made accusations and filed formal charges without the facts. Do you expect me to spill everything I know when you've got this hanging over our heads? How would that not be playing right into your hands? Whether you're a villain or not is beside the point. What *does* matter is that I am not an idiot."

"I want only to hear how they died. That is not part of the charges against you, Sean, or the Council. The matter of your involvement in Valas's departure from Court grounds is a separate matter that will be settled in Vampire Court."

"How do you know if her death is or isn't part of your ridiculous charges?" I demanded. "That's like saying the ending of a movie isn't related to the rest of the plot. Try again."

"*ALICE WORTH.*" He roared my name, causing me to wince and hold my phone away from my ear. "I must know if Valas and Vlad are truly dead!"

Ah-ha. I was right: Charles wasn't just worried about threats to himself and his regime from those around him. I supposed I couldn't blame him for fretting about Valas and Vlad. If anyone had the possibility of turning back up after allegedly croaking for the second and final time, it would be those two. Were the indictment and the demand to return Matthias an attempt to assert leverage for getting the information? I didn't think that was the whole reason, but one hurdle at a time.

"I'd be happy to fill you in on all the gruesome details," I said, my voice calm. "Once these charges go away, that is."

He hissed. The hair prickled on the back of my neck at the sound.

"I'm the only one who can tell you for sure if they're gone," I added. "Daniel and Matthias were there, but neither of them were in any kind of shape to see what happened at the end. And no, Daniel has *not* told Nan the whole story, since a lot of what happened isn't details I want others to know. I'm your only source for the information you want. I assume you can still sense deception, so you know I'm telling the truth about that. Let's make a deal. You change your mind about the indictments because they're baseless anyway, and accept that Matthias is part of our pack now and not the Court's property, and I'll tell you everything you want to know about what happened to Valas and her pet."

"Dropping the charges as a whole is not an option," he said, his tone cold. "Perhaps the list of charges relating to your alleged involvement in the initial change of regime could be dismissed due to lack of evidence. The role you, your pack, and the Council played in Valas's resistance and attempt to launch a counterattack must be ascertained in court. However, your continued possession of my stolen property is a blatant and indefensible violation of Vampire Court law. You *will* return Matthias Albrecht immediately."

"No deal. All the charges have to go. Matthias is part of our pack and under our protection. Any attempt to take him by force is an attack on our pack, as well as a violation of Council law."

"I would not be so sure of the latter, dear Alice." His voice quieted, became almost a purr. "The Council's laws of protection do not extend to fugitives from justice, regardless of their shifter status."

"Matthias is not a fugitive from justice. You didn't file any charges against him—just demanded we hand him over."

He continued as if I hadn't spoken. "Your pack is harboring a fugitive from Vampire Court law. The Council will not protect him or you from the Court's attempts to recover him."

"If he's a fugitive, it's only because you've made him one," I snapped. "He was bound to Valas. She fled and he was forced to go with her."

"He did not have to flee. He had the option to stay."

"Do you think she gave him an option, Charles? *Really?*"

"Matthias made his choice."

And here I'd thought *werewolves* were stubborn.

"It's not a choice if it's not a choice." I glanced at the clock. *Shit and double shit.* I was running out of time, and I got the feeling Charles still hadn't gotten to the real reason he wanted to talk.

"Charles, you had to know this would be my only offer," I said. "If you want to find out what happened to Valas and Vlad, all you have to do is drop the indictments and forget Matthias ever existed."

"I cannot do as you ask."

"Why the hell not?" I shouldn't lose my temper, but him acting as if he had no choice pissed me the hell off. "You're the head of the

Vampire Court now. You make the rules. You call the shots. Isn't that what you wanted?"

He said nothing for so long that I thought he'd hung up. I had to check the phone screen to make sure the call was still active.

When he finally spoke, his voice had a heaviness I'd seldom heard before. "How can a woman who has seen so much, and suffered so much, and lived the life you have lived, be so naive as to think because I sit in the tallest chair I answer to no one, and owe nothing to anyone but myself?"

I sat back and finished the last of my whisky. What had he just told me?

Did he just imply the charges and his determination to take Matthias back were not entirely his decision? Was someone else pushing for this or even pulling his strings? Or was this yet another attempt at manipulating me by playing on whatever sympathy or soft spot, however minute, that I might still have for him? Was he pretending to be a victim when these charges threatened our pack and our lives?

Either was possible, but what did my gut tell me?

No matter how I looked at this situation, I kept coming back to one key fact: he'd kept this phone close at hand in case I called. And he'd let me know that, either on purpose or not, by answering the phone on the second ring.

He needed more from me than the story of how Valas died. He just couldn't ask for what he *really* desired because of his pride, and because now more than ever he had to seem invincible and fearless. Like Valas had always been.

If he needed something from me or my pack in order to make these charges and threats go away, he'd have to get desperate enough to ask. The question was, how much would the rest of us suffer before he reached that point?

Damn it, Charles. It wasn't the first time I'd thought that, and it sure as hell looked like it wouldn't be the last.

I saw only one way forward: push him further toward his

breaking point and force him to ask—and to make it worth my while to even consider helping him. I hoped when I told the people waiting in the living room what I was about to do, it would make sense to them and not just to me.

"Call me when you've changed your mind," I said. And then I hung up.

CHAPTER

TWENTY-FOUR

IF I'D THOUGHT MY DECISION TO CUT SHORT MY CONVERSATION WITH Charles was tough to explain to Sean, Ben, Matthias, and Malcolm, that was a freaking walk in the park compared to facing six angry Were Ruling Council members. The fact Sean stood beside me instead of sitting next to the rest of the Council somehow made the situation worse.

Nothing like *literally* being called on the carpet.

Sean, Matthias, Ben, and I stood on an enormous round rug bearing the seal of the Council. The head of the Council, Willa Meyers, a black bear shifter, sat in the center of the semi-circular dais with the gavel in front of her. On her left and right were senior Council members Drew Montgomery, a panther shifter, and Sarah Webber, a werewolf I'd met before. Hazel Burrows and Blake Hicks were also werewolves. The sixth Council member was Alvin Cress, another panther shifter. The empty seat on the far right belonged to Sean, the newest member of the Council.

I missed having Malcolm with me, but "closed session" meant no spectators and that included ghosts too. He waited outside in the lobby.

238

Willa's dark gaze swept over our faces before she focused on Sean. "We deplore the fact this respected body has *in any way* become implicated in actions taken by you or any member or associate of your pack."

"*Alleged* actions," Hazel interjected. "Sean has made it clear these charges are baseless. We have no reason to think otherwise."

"No reason but what we know the Tomb Mountain Pack has done in the past," Drew countered. "This pack has a well-documented history of what I'd call harmful and reckless behavior."

"We have no sanctions against us by the Council," Sean pointed out. He had his hard alpha mask on and had muted his pack bonds so as not to pass his anger on to the others. "I can only guess what you might deem 'harmful' or 'reckless,' but I dispute that assessment too."

"We aren't here to discuss any past questionable actions taken by Sean or his pack," Willa stated. "This meeting has two purposes: to hear their testimony and discuss our unified response not only to the charges made against the Council, but those brought by the Vampire Court against the Tomb Mountain Pack."

Ben stood slightly behind Sean, as our acting beta, and I stood on Sean's other side with Matthias next to me. I hadn't been sure how Matthias would react to facing six angry shifters who were strangers to him, but he didn't so much as waver and his spine remained ramrod straight. Whatever was going through his head, he had poise in spades.

The fact the Council had yet to acknowledge him, however, had me quietly seething. Drew's body language made it clear he thought Matthias was not to be trusted, as if he was a Court spy in our midst. The others looked wary at best—even Hazel and Alvin, who Sean believed would support us during the hearing.

"We've presented the facts," Sean said, drawing my attention back to his conversation with Willa. "If the Court insists on taking this matter to trial, they will lose because they have no evidence to support the charges against the Council *or* our pack."

"How do you know they have no evidence?" Drew asked.

"Because there is none." Sean's tone was flat. "I'll draw the Council's attention to the report I filed after Alice and Daniel Holiday were kidnapped from our pack land by Valas's operatives. If you review the report, you will see they did nothing to assist Valas, even under duress, and only barely survived. You should also have a copy of the official statement provided by Assistant Special Agent in Charge Trent Lake of SPEMA on the conditions his team found at the scene of Valas's death."

"Yes, we have read all your documentation." Willa studied Sean. "I may speak to your consort?"

Moments like this were always jarring for me, since Sean was never the sort of alpha to rule his pack with an iron fist, much less tell me when and where I could speak. But some packs *were* like that, which was why Willa asked.

"Please do," Sean said. "She may answer your questions freely."

If we hadn't been standing in front of the Council, I was sure his eyes would be twinkling because he knew damn well I'd say what I pleased. I missed the humor and sparkle in his eyes. I hadn't seen any hint of it since the moment the Vamp Court enforcers showed up at our house.

"Ms. Worth," Willa said, folding her arms on the table. "Everything in Sean's report on what transpired during your kidnapping is completely accurate?"

"Every word is true," I stated. We'd only omitted a few key facts. Everything else was utterly genuine.

"If that's the case, and there's no evidence against you, why has the Vampire Court targeted you and us with these charges?" she asked. "Other than their demand for the return of Mr. Albrecht, which we'll discuss later, what does the Court have to gain from this circus?"

"I'd like to know the answer to that too," I said with feeling.

"Care to speculate?" Drew prodded.

"No, I wouldn't. I don't have enough information to speculate. Your guess is probably as good as mine."

"You're a former employee of the Court, aren't you?" he persisted. "So is your business partner. Neither of you left on anything that could be considered good terms. Are these charges some form of retaliation for that?"

"With the vamps, anything is technically possible," I admitted. "But I don't think so. Arkady left the Court as amicably as anyone could, and I was never their employee. I did investigative work for them as an independent contractor only."

"You're splitting hairs and dodging the question," Sarah Webber said. She'd remained quiet so far, but everything about her body language made it clear she didn't believe a word we said.

Like other werewolves who thought alphas should only have shifters for mates, she'd despised me from the earliest days of my relationship with Sean and even participated in a campaign of intimidation trying to run me off. The fact we were now engaged had only increased her animosity.

"I'm not splitting hairs or dodging anything," I said, my voice calm and even. If she wanted to goad me into lashing out, she'd have to try harder. "I'm clarifying a misunderstanding. My direct answer is that I no longer work for the Court on a contract basis and haven't since well before Charles Vaughan took over. My agency has as much work as we can handle and the Court has their own dedicated investigators now who *are* employees."

"Where does your loyalty lie?" Alvin Cress leaned forward as he spoke. His tone wasn't angry or confrontational, but the question was certainly very pointed.

Maybe it was a fair question, given I'd begun doing work on a contract basis for the Court not long after I'd started training to become a mage PI. And I appreciated that Cress framed it that way, rather than as an accusation. His wording gave me the opportunity to make a positive assertion about my allegiance rather than simply repeating my denials about my relationship to the Court.

"My loyalty is to Sean and our pack," I said without hesitation. "As it has been since Sean and I became a couple. They are my family."

"You're loyal to Charles Vaughan," Drew argued.

"I have never been loyal to Charles Vaughan or the Vampire Court," I stated. "Ask them and they'll tell you that too. They'd probably laugh at the question."

"As if we would believe a word they say," Sarah muttered, loudly enough for everyone in the room to hear.

"We've known about your allegiance to Vaughan since you first became involved with Sean," Drew said. "That, along with your background and other very questionable alliances, have always been of great concern to the Council."

"Is there a question in there?" I asked. "I thought we were here to talk about the indictments."

Willa raised her hand to halt Drew's angry retort. "You asked Alice a question, and she answered," she told him. "We're not here to interrogate her."

"With all due respect, I think we are," Sarah interjected. "I don't believe we would be in this situation at all if it weren't for Ms. Worth's long history with Charles Vaughan and the Vampire Court. We need the truth from her more than anything else. I'd love the chance to extract it. I for one don't want to hear any more evasions or lies."

Extract it? What the hell? Did Sarah just threaten to torture me in front of the Council and the most dominant wolves in our pack? Magic sparked on my fingers and anger made my vision go red around the edges.

Meanwhile, my companions growled. The Council members on the dais responded with angry glowing stares and surges of golden shifter magic. Matthias's deep rumble in particular drew their attention.

"Keep him in check," Sarah told Sean. "If he shifts and attacks, he dies."

Sean took a step forward, putting himself physically between Sarah and us. His fury seared my skin. "Not one more threat or insult." His low growl told me this was his wolf speaking as much as his human self. "Alice is my fiancé, consort, and future mate, which you all know damn well. Matthias is a member of my pack. You will extend them every courtesy and honor to which they are entitled by the customs of the Council *and* its laws."

"Enough." Willa used her gavel to bring an abrupt end to the exchange. "We've heard your testimony regarding the indictments. Now we will turn our attention to the matter of Matthias Albrecht."

She glanced at Matthias and then looked at Sean. "Setting aside for the moment the Court's demand for his return as stolen property, we've read your statement regarding his involvement in the attack on your pack and the kidnapping of Alice and your associate Daniel Holiday. Why in heaven's name would you bring this man into your pack rather than kill him for harming your consort?"

"As far as I'm aware, the Council has never demanded a justification for anyone's inclusion in a pack," Sean said calmly. "We all know the reasons someone may join a pack. Many of those reasons do not involve pleasant circumstances."

"There's unpleasant circumstances, and then there's taking in Valas's right-hand man," Drew said. "The only reason I can think of for that decision is you have a connection to the person who infected Matthias in the first place. You must have felt an obligation that outweighed your instinct to kill him."

My stomach lurched. More than almost anything I feared my father would be implicated in Matthias's situation. I'd dreaded this moment since the night Valas died. But in a room full of shifters, with their sharp eyesight and heightened sense of smell, I could not let on that I felt afraid. Everything depended on that—and Matthias's ability to sell them on his claim that he didn't know who'd bitten him.

"You claim in your statement that Matthias can't name who

infected him with the shifter virus," Willa said. "Sean, I respect you as a man and a colleague, but I find it difficult to believe."

"You may ask him directly," Sean said. He gave no hint that the Council had brought up the subject we most wanted to avoid. "He has my permission to answer your questions."

Matthias stood with his hands clasped behind his back and feet firmly planted shoulder width apart. Not quite aggressive, but certainly not cowed or intimidated. I suspected his body language had contributed to Drew and Sarah's obvious dislike as much as anything else. Maybe they wanted him to come crawling and begging for their acceptance and protection. If the Council didn't already realize how dominant he was, they'd figure it out pretty damn quick now.

Willa turned her attention to Matthias. According to Sean, he wasn't sure which way she would vote either on backing us against the Court or in regard to Matthias's status. She and Blake Hicks were our possible swing votes. It didn't take a clairvoyant to predict Drew and Sarah would vote against us. Hazel and Alvin were likely to side with us.

If they voted against us, or the vote was tied, we'd have to face the danger the Court presented on our own, without the Council's backing. If we got the votes, however, they would express their support to the Court, which in itself might be enough to get them to drop the charges. Even if not, if the Council backed us, so would the rest of the packs in the area. That would be another big factor in whether Charles pursued the court case against us or not.

We needed four votes to keep us out of prison, and to keep us from having to fight and die to protect Matthias from Charles.

"You understand you are bound by your honor and your life to answer us honestly," Willa told Matthias.

"Yes." Matthias's voice had that emotionless tone I disliked so much—the one that reminded me and probably everyone else here of vampires. I wanted to tell him to let himself show emotion because that might work in his favor, but I kept my mouth shut.

"Do you know who infected you?" Willa asked.

I focused on breathing normally and keeping myself calm. If the Council members sensed anything from me at all, I hoped they'd chalk it up to the horrors I'd witnessed at Valas's refuge.

"The fight during which I was bitten was very intense," Matthias said. "Many combatants were involved. The amount of deadly magic thrown by those fighting made it nearly impossible to track everything that was happening. I was also seriously injured and had lost a significant amount of blood. My ability to see was very poor. I did not see the bite occur."

"Other than Daniel Holiday, what other werwolves were present?" Drew asked.

"As I said, the situation was very chaotic and my vision was impaired. I could not see everyone who was present."

Six pairs of sharp shifter eyes fixed on Matthias's face. *Breathe*, I told myself. *Show no fear. Trust Matthias.*

"Was the person who bit you Daniel Holiday?" Willa asked.

"No matter how many times you ask, my answer will not change. I did not see who bit me." Matthias held her gaze and did not look away. The other Council members stirred in their seats and exchanged glances—some wary, some thoughtful.

"I do not like to admit a weakness, Madame Councilor, but I wasn't just badly injured when I was bitten," Matthias continued. "I was dying. My service to the Court left me bleeding to death on the floor of a cellar in the mountains of Colorado with no friends or even allies at my side. I meant nothing to them then and I mean nothing to them now."

His raw honesty and the hollow way he revealed that to the Council made angry tears well up in my eyes. Everyone in the room would be able to smell my unshed tears. Not that long ago I would never have allowed anyone see me hurting for someone else's pain, much less the damn Were Ruling Council. But I had the thought that if anything could sway votes in our favor, it was real, honest, human emotion.

"You swear to that?" Willa asked.

He nodded. "I do."

If Sarah was the least bit moved by Matthias's words or my reaction, she didn't show it. "If you mean nothing to the Court, why are they demanding your return as 'stolen property'?"

"So they may execute me," Matthias told her.

"You know this for a fact?" Willa asked.

"I have no reason to think otherwise. From what little can be gleaned from conditions at Northbourne, every other person who was once loyal to Valas is dead on Charles Vaughan's orders. I was her head enforcer. I would imagine he plans to make a show of my execution."

And then, just when I was starting to breathe again, the other shoe dropped.

"What *I* want to know is how you've seemingly gotten past the initial phase of your change so quickly," Drew said. "I'm sure my colleagues want to know as well."

"That information is in our report," Sean said.

"There's no information—just speculation," Sarah argued. "You say it may be a result of all the vampire blood he'd consumed prior to his infection. That seems highly unlikely."

"He didn't just consume vampire blood," I pointed out. "It was *Valas's* blood. She had all kinds of weird powers and magic. She could heal wounds that would have killed most vamps. If anyone could transition to becoming a werewolf without all the volatility, it would be Matthias."

"No one in documented shifter history has done it." Drew wasn't buying it, and judging by their expressions, neither were several of the others. "We know of shifters Changed while in service to the Vampire Court and they experienced the full force of the volatility. Surely if Valas had been capable of sparing them that—"

"Have you ever heard *anything* about Valas that would lead you to believe she wanted to spare anyone from suffering?" I asked. "Because I don't believe it for a minute. If anything, she probably thought their suffering would make them stronger and better servants."

"I can attest to that," Matthias said, again in that hollow tone. "You did not serve her unless you had been broken very thoroughly, so she could rebuild you in her own way."

For several beats, a heavy silence filled the Council chamber. The first to break it was Willa. "The fact remains that the Court has claimed you are its legal property because of a contract you signed with them. Is this true?"

"I did sign a contract, yes," Matthias said. "I am not permitted to disclose its contents to you."

"So we've been informed." She laced her fingers together and propped her chin on her hands. "I understand your legal team is working on this, Sean, but if the contract is as the Court claims, the law is on the Court's side. Whether you have brought him into your pack or not, he must legally be returned to them."

Sean shook his head. "We won't turn him over."

"Refusing would break Vampire Court law," Drew said, scowling. "The Were Ruling Council is bound by treaty to recognize and uphold the Court's laws just as they do our own. This treaty has kept the peace between the Court and Council for more than a hundred years. We're not going to break it for *him*." He jerked his chin at Matthias, who didn't react either to his words or his tone.

Thanks to my conversation with Charles, however, Sean was ready for that one.

"The Court must recognize the Council's laws as well, as you just pointed out. Matthias Albrecht is a refugee from their jurisdiction." Sean reached into his briefcase and pulled out a large envelope. "Our pack has granted Matthias asylum status under Council law. This is the formal documentation for your records." He placed the envelope on the dais and stepped back.

Drew and Sarah let out quiet snarls. "Asylum was not intended as a way for a Court runaway to put us between him and his keepers," Sarah said.

"Asylum grants protection from persecution and death. That's both the spirit *and* the letter of the law." Sean's golden alpha stare immediately caused Sarah to lower her gaze.

He turned his attention back to Willa. "You asked earlier why I would offer Matthias a place in my pack despite the harm he's caused. I don't owe you a justification, but I'll give you one. It's the same reason I've welcomed most of the members of my pack since becoming alpha. My conscience doesn't allow me to turn my back on those who've suffered like Matthias has suffered. That shouldn't be news to anyone here. I also see greatness in him that even he hasn't recognized yet. He needs our strength and we need his. That is the purpose of a pack."

If I didn't already love this man with all my heart and soul, those words—and the fact he so clearly meant every syllable—would have sealed the deal.

I searched the faces of the Council members, looking for signs of hope. We needed four votes to ensure the Council's backing against the Court. A tie of three to three would mean they were unlikely to take decisive action in our favor, even if Willa voted with us.

"Does anyone have more questions?" Willa asked the others. One by one they shook their heads.

She turned to Sean. "Do you have anything to add before we begin deliberations?"

"No, I don't." He glanced at me. "Alice?"

It certainly wasn't protocol for Sean to offer the last word to his consort, but Drew and Sarah—the sticklers for etiquette—weren't going to back us anyway and the others might listen.

If it wouldn't mean putting myself and my pack in a mountain of danger, I might have offered my ability to help shifters transition smoothly in return for the Council's votes. I wasn't above bargaining. But the cost would be too high.

"The Tomb Mountain Pack has long been one of the strongest and most stalwart packs in the area," I said instead. "Our strength is also yours. You stand to gain nothing if you allow the Court to threaten and attack us, but you would lose a hell of a lot. Not just because we'd no longer be your strongest allies, but because once the Court knows they can bully you and the packs you represent, they'll never stop. If you give them an inch, they'll take a mile. Every time."

"Thank you for that reminder," Willa said. "If you'll excuse us now, we need to discuss these matters in private. I have a feeling it won't be a short conversation. You may as well head home. I'll call you with the results, Sean. Thank you all for speaking to us tonight."

I wasn't sure how to interpret her comment that they had a lot to talk about, and her expression was inscrutable. I really could not tell which way she'd vote. Same for Blake Hicks, who'd barely said a word during our discussion. Damn it.

I wanted to walk out of this chamber believing we'd done everything we could to persuade them to back us, but I didn't know if that was true. We'd just have to see how the vote would go. I had a feeling the next few hours, or however long we'd have to wait for Willa's call, would crawl by.

I touched Matthias's hand as we filed out of the room. He squeezed my fingers quickly before letting go. That was a victory, at least.

TWENTY-FIVE

BEN HAD DRIVEN SEPARATELY TO THE HEARING, SO AFTER A SHORT conversation in the parking lot, he left in his own vehicle to meet us back at our house to await the results of the Council's vote.

Rather than rush off to follow him, Sean and I took a moment to ourselves while Matthias and Malcolm waited by the SUV. Ben wouldn't mind spending a few extra minutes at our place playing with Daisy, Rogue, and Esme before we got there.

Because shifters preferred wide open spaces as a general rule, the Council building was located well outside the city on a quiet two-lane road, so we heard nothing but the nighttime sounds of insects and the wind in the trees nearby. I rested my forehead on Sean's chest and breathed in his forest scent as he propped his chin on top of my head. I loved the warm humming of our wolf amulets against my breastbone.

We stood quietly for a while, enjoying peace while we could. I wanted so badly to be optimistic, but I sensed something in Sean's body language that told me he didn't think the vote would go our way despite everything we'd said. Swinging one extra vote, maybe.

Getting two…not bloody likely, as our British pack member Rupert Bogton, who went by the nickname Boggy, would say.

Sean kissed my hair. "Ready?"

"No." I rubbed my nose on his shirt. "But yes."

He laced our fingers together for the walk back to the SUV. "'Bout time." Malcolm made a show of looking at his watch, which he'd added to his ghost outfit just now. "We were about to start walking home."

"We were not," Matthias said.

Malcolm side-eyed him, though I was the only person who could see it. "I was joking, dude. Trying to lighten things up."

"Your jokes will have to get a lot better to achieve that."

My ghost sidekick harrumphed. "I'm the funniest person on Team Alice and you know it."

Matthias's expression indicated he knew no such thing. Rather than argue, he opened the passenger door for me. "Thanks," I said as I climbed in.

"You are welcome." He shut my door and got in behind me while Sean went around to the driver's side. The entire SUV moved when Matthias got in. Malcolm floated into the back seat behind Sean, still muttering.

Sean kept the music at a low volume, and we said little for the first ten minutes or so of the drive back to the city. Sean rested his hand on my leg as he drove, squeezing gently and sharing his comforting alpha magic as I fidgeted. I didn't want to be edgy, especially in a confined space with two dominant werewolves who had plenty of their own emotions to deal with, but I couldn't help but replay our meeting with the Council in my head and wonder if I'd said the right things and presented our best case. If second-guessing myself were an Olympic sport, I'd have a dozen gold medals hanging around my neck.

This is why I prefer magic and a straight-up fight, I grumbled inwardly. Courtroom arguments and verbal sparring weren't my strong suit—far from it, in fact.

"We all did our best," Sean said, interrupting my grumpy thoughts. "You especially, Matthias. That kind of honesty takes an enormous amount of courage."

"Thank—" Matthias began.

Big, bad magic sizzled on my skin. "*STOP!*" I yelled.

Sean stomped the brakes instantly, which might have saved our lives—or at least saved mine, since Malcolm was already dead and the shifters were much harder to kill.

Traveling close to forty miles an hour, Sean's SUV plowed through the ward I'd sensed in the nick of time and into a billowing cloud of black magic that smelled of old blood and dark, damp earth. I immediately recognized it as the same kind that had created the ghost grenade that narrowly missed Malcolm.

Malcolm must have recognized it too, because I sensed a frisson of magic that told me he'd reflexively jumped to his lockdown crystal.

After that, everything seemed to happen both in slow motion and in between one heartbeat and the next.

One of the front tires exploded—whether from magic or something in the road, I wasn't sure. The SUV pulled hard to the right. Rather than swerve left, Sean turned into the skid and let off the brake.

The vehicle hit something I couldn't see and went airborne, rolling passenger-side down in midair. All the front and side airbags deployed, hitting us like punches from a heavyweight boxer. I felt a crunch in my face and intense pain and suddenly I couldn't breathe through my nose. The airbag chemicals burned my eyes and skin.

The wreck flung us around like rag dolls in our seatbelts before we smashed into an invisible barrier that crumpled the vehicle's front end. We spun, crashed into something else, and came to a stop —somehow, miraculously, more or less right side up on whatever shreds remained of the SUV's heavy duty tires.

Dazed, semi-conscious, and hurting all over, I slumped in my seat, held upright by my seatbelt as hot blood poured from my broken nose. My ears rang and my heart pounded. I thought I might be moaning.

"Alice." Sean's voice was ragged. "Alice? Answer me."

All I could do was groan and spit out blood. I suspected my teeth had cut the inside of my lip when the airbag hit my face.

Familiar hands cupped my neck gently but firmly. Sean, trying to keep my neck immobilized in case I had spinal injuries. "Get us out," he grated.

My foggy brain didn't understand what he meant until Matthias kicked the side of the SUV so hard that the entire vehicle rocked. He must be trying to get a crumpled door to open.

I had a difficult time putting coherent thoughts together, but the tingling on my arms caused a memory to surface.

Black magic, I remembered hazily. *Someone ambushed us…*

I fumbled with my bracelet, searching with trembling fingers for a diamond-shaped crystal. Times like these demanded all the crystals on the bracelet were distinctly different in not only color but design—especially spells like this, which I referred to as *Last Resorts* and Malcolm called *DEFCON-Ones*.

I closed my fist around the correct crystal, spooled blood magic, and grabbed the closest ley line with as much control and focus as I could muster, which wasn't a hell of a lot. Unfortunately—or fortunately, depending on how I looked at it—my training while a prisoner of my grandfather in Baltimore had included being deliberately injured as badly as I was now and then ordered me to fight with magic. The goal was to make me able to do exactly what I was doing now: utilize ley lines while seriously hurt.

At least the agony of grabbing the ley line was muted by all the rest of my pain and lingering disorientation. Silver lining, I supposed.

I took a shaky breath and invoked the spell in the crystal. *"Shield."*

With a visceral ignition I both heard and felt in every cell of my body, the powerful spell rolled through us to form a spherical ward large enough to enclose the SUV and a radius of about fifteen feet around it. The spellwork should null or at least displace natural, witch, and black magic. It wouldn't affect the wolves' magic or mine.

Sure enough, layers of black magic wards and spells fractured and broke, sending bolts of power sizzling back through my protection ward that made me jerk and flinch. The pain and jolts also had the unintended consequence of clearing some of the fog from my brain.

I forced my eyes open, blinked blearily a few times, and focused on Sean's bruised and bloody face, which was somehow right in front of mine. He'd apparently ripped the steering wheel off to get it out of the way so he could kneel on his seat and hold my head steady. My own warm blood dripped from my nose and lips and ran down my chin.

Through the broken windshield, I noticed we'd come to rest in the ditch between the highway and thick forest. The night was pitch dark thanks to cloud cover and lack of streetlights. The now-deflated airbags blocked most of my view, but I caught glimpses of shadows moving in the trees.

"Baby." Sean kissed my forehead. Even that hurt.

I was looking right into his golden eyes when gunshots rang out. Sean jerked twice. Blood splattered my arms.

Matthias broke my seat and laid me flat on my back so he and Sean could shield me with their bodies. More gunshots split the air. Bullets ripped through the SUV's cabin. Matthias grunted as one hit his right shoulder. Hot, tingling shifter blood sprayed across my face. Sean's shirt was bloody on his right side. I saw two bullet holes in the fabric. Rage made magic spark on my hands and the earth trembled below us.

My earth magic told me these bullets weren't silver, but that didn't mean they wouldn't be deadly. A shot to the heart or head would kill a werewolf just as easily as a human.

Now that I was lying down, I gurgled and choked on the blood from my broken nose. Sean swore.

"Hold your fire!" someone shouted outside. "Don't kill her!" The gunshots stopped. Black magic hit my ward and sizzled.

Whoever was attacking us, they'd come for me.

Sean and I looked at each other as I fought to get breaths around the blood in my airway. His glowing eyes were filled with rage and pain—and love.

"My Alice." He squeezed my hand gently. "Ben turned around and is coming back. Others will be here as soon as they can. Stay alive at any cost."

He locked gazes with Matthias. Something passed between them —a first unspoken conversation between an alpha and the man I believed would soon be his new beta. I sensed a comforting wave of magic through my nascent bond with Sean, as if a puzzle piece had fallen into place.

"Leave one alive," Sean told him.

And then they were gone out the door Matthias had kicked out.

Werewolf magic and fury sizzled on my skin as they shifted outside the SUV. I struggled to sit up or at least turn onto my side so I could breathe better. More gunshots rang out, this time in a panicked volley not directed at the SUV. My stomach clenched in anger and fear.

Familiar snarls split the air, and then the shouting and screaming began. The gunshots ended abruptly. I hoped that meant Sean and Matthias had taken out the people with guns first. The thick brush on the passenger side of the SUV prevented me from seeing what was going on.

I'd be black and blue all over soon and every one of my joints throbbed. This would be the worst whiplash I'd had in my life. I had to breathe through my mouth, but I could feel and move all my extremities. The only thing actually broken was my nose, so no way in hell would I stay in the SUV while Sean and Matthias were in danger. The only ways out of the vehicle were my shattered passenger seat window or the open doorway behind me, and I was far from nimble right now.

If one of the wolves had stayed behind, I would have had someone to guard me while I used a strong healing spell, but they'd both fully committed to Operation: Kill Them All But One.

So, no healing spell for me yet. I'd have to fight injured. Like my grandfather made sure I'd been trained to do.

For some reason, that made me hate him a little more.

Cursing, spitting blood, and moving as inelegantly as a newborn calf, I half-crawled, half-tumbled over my broken seat into the back. The top part of my seat was too heavy for me to move out of the way, so I had to scramble over it to reach the door opening.

Just before I made it outside, a man in a dark cloak and hood lunged out of the darkness as if he were about to dive into the SUV. We came nose-to-bloody-nose in the open doorway.

My would-be attacker was Mr. Touchy from the coffee shop.

He had a pair of spell cuffs in one hand and a gun in the other. Spell cuffs were designed to suppress the magic of the person wearing them, and they would work even inside my *Shield* ward. For all I knew, he might have even been the person who'd shot Sean or Matthias.

Mr. Touchy clearly expected me to attack with magic. Instead, I head-butted him right in the face with all my body weight. The cartilage in his nose broke with a highly satisfying meaty crunch. I liked that sound way better when it happened to someone else.

He stumbled back with a garbled yell and fired blindly. The bullet hit the front passenger door about two feet to my left. Son of a bitch. So much for *don't kill her*—this idiot almost killed me on accident.

And it hadn't gone unnoticed.

An absolutely berserk brindle wolf with a bloody muzzle rammed into Mr. Touchy with the full force of nearly three hundred pounds of solid muscle and white-hot lupine rage. The gun and spell cuffs went flying and I heard the distinctive sounds of bones breaking. Mr. Touchy made a gurgly sound of pain and fear as he hit the ground with Matthias's wolf on top of him. Matthias flattened his ears and bared his teeth three inches from Mr. Touchy's bloody face.

We wanted one of these attackers left alive. Mr. Touchy might as well be the lucky one.

I did something I rarely did and drew on Sean's alpha authority to make my words a command. "*MATTHIAS, HOLD HIM*," I shouted.

Matthias's wolf closed his teeth on Mr. Touchy's neck but did not bite down.

A berserk wolf with prey at their feet usually did not have enough self-control to listen to anything but their bloodlust, much less someone who wasn't their alpha or mate. And yet somehow Matthias had heard me and obeyed. Greatness and strength, indeed.

It occurred to me that Valas had wasted Matthias by breaking him down and forcing him into the role of head enforcer when he could have been her greatest advisor, fighter, and ally.

A wave of lightheadedness swept over me.

It was a mistake, I thought, watching Matthias pin Mr. Touchy down. *To misjudge him so greatly*.

I shook my head to clear it, and the dizziness faded.

Finally, I made it out of the SUV and stumbled on the rocky ground over to Matthias and Mr. Touchy. Somewhere in the trees nearby, Sean's wolf snarled, and someone's last breaths rattled in their chest.

With the back of my hand, I wiped blood from my mouth and knelt so I could run my fingers through Matthias's thick fur. His muscles quivered with rage and menace.

Mr. Touchy gurgled on the blood from his broken nose. Matthias's wolf kept his teeth right where they were, pressing into the man's throat without breaking the skin. Matthias would know more than most how crucial it was to not infect anyone unintentionally.

"What do you want with me?" I demanded.

"I'm here to free you." Mr. Touchy raised his hand.

I caught a glimpse of a spell crystal hidden in his fist. I had no idea what it contained and didn't wait to find out. Moving so quickly that my arm blurred, I slapped the crystal out of his hand. It disappeared into the tall grass.

"I will not be captured," I said, my voice flat.

"Mistress," he protested, his pleading eyes searching my face. "I still serve you."

What the hell does that mean? I wondered.

"Serve me in death," I heard myself say.

Another, much stronger wave of dizziness and nausea swept over me. I slumped to my side, my ears ringing as unconsciousness threatened to steal me away. Maybe I had a mild concussion from the wreck.

Vaguely, I heard someone choking nearby. Had Matthias bitten Mr. Touchy despite my order not to? What was happening? Try as I might, I couldn't see anything but vague shapes moving around me.

But I sensed it, and somehow saw it, when one by one the dead around us burned.

In my mind's eye, I watched a dark-haired man nearby burst into flame, his body collapsing into cinders. Then another. Then a woman. Another man. A second woman. And then Mr. Touchy caught fire. Matthias jumped away with a pained whine and a snarl.

Mr. Touchy died screaming. The flames hurt my skin until he too crumbled to smoldering ash.

Six people had come for me. Six had burned.

No evidence or trace left for anyone to follow. I will remain hidden.

My thoughts made no sense, and they hurt my head.

Strong arms scooped me up and carried me away. Dimly, I recognized Ben's familiar scent as he cradled me and ran. We traveled over uneven ground for a while, and then I felt myself handed over to someone whose embrace and scent I knew very, very well. Sean.

"Something's wrong," Ben said urgently. His voice sounded far away. Whatever else he said, I couldn't understand him. Voices murmured around me. They sounded angry and worried.

Slowly, the dizziness and nausea faded. I might be concussed, so I forced myself not to succumb to the desire to sleep.

Once again, I opened my eyes to find myself staring into Sean's golden gaze. "My Alice," he said, his eyes dark with fury and worry.

"Are we safe?" I asked.

"As safe as we can be." He kissed my forehead. "I think you can drop the ward."

I let go of the ley line and the *Shield* ward died.

With me in his arms, Sean stood with Matthias and Ben beside Ben's SUV. About twenty feet away, next to the wrecked SUV, I caught sight of a smoldering fire roughly in the shape of a person. All that remained of Mr. Touchy, I supposed.

I sighed. "So much for keeping one of them alive."

"They must have come prepared with some kind of spellwork that would kill them and immolate their bodies so we couldn't take anyone as a prisoner," Matthias said. "We don't even have clothing or magic left as clues about who these people are or who sent them."

Ben growled. "Who do we think is behind this? The Vampire Court?"

"No," I said automatically.

Matthias frowned. "How do we know?"

"Gut feeling," I said. "This doesn't feel like Charles's doing. Roadside ambush with black magic just isn't his style. The attack was sloppy."

Ben didn't look convinced, but Matthias nodded slowly. "I think I agree," he told them. "It doesn't feel like a Court operation."

"I'm not eliminating any suspects just yet." Sean turned to Ben. "You and I will stay and look for anything that didn't get burned or other evidence. I'll have to deal with the Council and the police when they show up—and they will."

"Shit," Ben and I said at the same time. Matthias growled.

The Council. Who we'd just left not thirty minutes ago after pleading our case for their support. What would they think of this attack, and how close to their headquarters it had taken place?

"Meanwhile," Sean continued, "Matthias, take Ben's SUV and get Alice home so she can use a healing spell and rest where she's protected. I've already got a couple of members of the pack coming to help us search the area and the rest will meet you at our house."

Carefully, he transferred me to Matthias. Generally, I didn't like to be carried by anyone other than Sean or Ben, but Matthias's arms felt surprisingly comforting. I rested my head on his chest.

Sean cupped my face with his hand and I leaned into his warmth. "I'll get home as quickly as I can," he told me.

"Okay," I said reluctantly. I wanted to stay, but I was in a lot of pain. I'd be of no use to anyone until I healed myself.

Ben touched my shoulder. Like Sean, he nearly vibrated with anger and concern. "You'll be okay, Alice. Matthias has you."

"I know." I let out a shaky breath. "I'm sorry we didn't get any information from these people before something happened to them."

Sean blinked, as if surprised by what I'd said. "Well, we might find something that didn't get burned." He met Matthias's gaze over my head. They had another one of those unspoken conversations. "Keep her safe," he said.

"I'll protect her with my life," Matthias promised.

Sean and Matthias got me loaded into the passenger seat of Ben's SUV, then had a conversation outside that I couldn't hear while they got dressed in spare clothing Ben kept in the cargo area. I leaned my head against the seat.

Finally, Matthias got in the driver's seat. Ben wasn't short, but he had to move the seat back as far as it would go. He put my bag and cell phone on my lap. "Thanks," I said.

"You're welcome." He made a quick U-turn. "Please talk to me while we drive so you don't fall asleep."

Apparently I wasn't the only person worried that I might be concussed. "Okay," I said.

I watched the side view mirror as we left the site of the ambush. Sean stood in the road next to the crumpled remains of his SUV, his golden eyes shining bright and angry like lanterns in the night. He didn't move until we drove around a curve and out of sight.

TWENTY-SIX

THE JOURNEY HOME SEEMED TO TAKE BOTH HOURS AND ONLY A FEW MINUTES. Matthias kept me talking, peppering me with questions that ranged from how Sean and I met to the differences between witch magic and natural magic and even which of the vinyl albums in my collection I played most often and why. He asked me several questions more than once—I suspected to see if I noticed he was repeating them.

"Aren't you going to ask me how many fingers you're holding up?" I asked at some point, in a tone that was probably more cranky than he deserved.

Matthias slid me a sideways glance. "Would you give me your honest answer if I did, or be a smart-ass?"

I crossed my arms and glared out the window.

When we arrived at the house, all was quiet. Pain and intermittent dizziness meant I had to suffer the further indignity of having Matthias carry me to the basement to let Malcolm out of his crystal.

When he appeared beside us, my ghost bestie took one look at me, flitted repeatedly, and ordered Matthias to get me upstairs so I could use a healing spell.

"Don't you want to know what happened?" I asked as Matthias carried me up to the second floor.

"I'll get the story from him!" Malcolm yelled from the living room. "Jeez Louise, Alice. You're beat to hell. This is not the time for a chit-chat!"

"I get no respect around here," I muttered. I stifled a wince when my foot bumped into the railing. Even my toes hurt.

Upstairs, Matthias braced me with one arm and his knee so he could open our bedroom door. "You use humor to disguise your real feelings," he said as he closed the door behind us with his foot. "And to try to keep us from worrying about you. You know we see through that, right?"

I'd known they did, but usually no one called me out on it. Well, except Carly.

"You're one to talk," I shot back. "As if you don't hide how you feel behind that whole 'I'm as tough as old boot leather' thing you do."

He raised an eyebrow. "Now you are deflecting."

I harrumphed. "I already have a therapist and a ghost sidekick who gripe about this, okay? Don't *you* start."

"All right." He glanced around the room. "Would you like to lie on the bed or go into the bathroom?"

Little did he know my jokes were more to distract myself from thinking about what was going to happen next than whether they worried about me.

"Bathroom," I said with a sigh. "I need my box of healing spells from the nightstand. Top drawer. Also, please bring me my pillow."

Matthias left me perched on the side of the tub while he went to get my box of spells. When he returned, he found me sitting on the fluffy bath mat with my back against the tub.

"Thanks." I took the box and the pillow. "I know you stuck around for that mid-level healing spell earlier, but you don't want to be in here for this one."

He crouched next to me. "Do you remember telling me that you would always be honest with me?"

I narrowed my eyes.

"If you were being honest right now," he continued, utterly unfazed by my scowl, "you would instead say you preferred I left you alone because you don't want me to see you suffering or being sick."

He had me there. I *had* promised honesty and I'd meant what I said. I shouldn't pick and choose when to follow my own rules.

And there was something about Matthias that made me feel safe telling him raw truth that I struggled to say to pretty much anyone else, except maybe Carly. Maybe it was the fact he'd been through hell too, or maybe I just knew what I said wouldn't go beyond this room. He'd become a safe place for me, as I hoped I was for him—or would be, someday.

"I don't even like Sean or Malcolm to see me use a strong healing spell," I said. "And I love them the most of anyone in the world. Not just because the effects are awful." I swallowed. "I used to have to use healing spells in front of people when I didn't want to. People who actually enjoyed watching me scream."

His expression darkened. He was probably visualizing what he would do to my tormentors given the chance.

I expected his shifter magic to sizzle on my skin, but instead when he touched my hand where it lay on top of my box of healing spells, all I felt was comfort and strength.

"I understand then why you don't want me to stay," he said. "But I would like to."

"Why?"

His stoic façade melted away. For maybe the first time since we'd met, Matthias let me see the real depth of his pain and grief, but I also saw hope and determination.

"Without hesitating, you lay next to me on the cellar floor at Valas's mansion and held my hand in my darkest hour," he said. "I've never known as much courage or kindness in my life as I did in that moment."

A sharp pain lanced through my head, causing me to flinch. I hurt so much, and it was only going to get worse before it got better. I didn't want to ever drink vampire blood again because of its side effects, but that didn't mean I didn't wish for its painless and even euphoric healing power.

"Alice." Matthias squeezed my bruised hand ever so gently. "Tell me to stay, or tell me to go, but make a choice."

"It's going to be bad," I said, my voice rough.

"I know." His amber gaze locked on mine. "That's why I want to stay."

To my surprise, I found myself wanting him to stay too. Maybe a little at a time I could replace the memories of Moses and his people watching me in agony back at his compound in Baltimore with better ones. Well, less awful ones, anyway.

So I opened the box, found a dark blue crystal containing a strong healing spell, and lay on the bath mat because I'd end up lying down anyway. Better to lie down on purpose than fall over and risk hitting my head.

Matthias lay down beside me. Thank goodness we had a large bathroom. He took up a lot of square footage.

"Same rules as before," I said. "Keep a little distance. You can't touch me until it's done."

"I'm familiar with healing spells." He touched my hand one last time and then tucked his bent arm under his head like a pillow. "But thank you for the reminder."

No sense putting it off any more. My ears were ringing again and I might be in danger of losing consciousness.

I gripped the spell tightly in my fist, pressed my hand to my chest, and closed my eyes. "*Helios*," I said, and smushed the pillow to my face.

The first pulse of healing magic sent a wave of agony through me that nearly made me pass out.

And it got worse from there.

In a near-delirium, I screamed and screamed into my pillow as magic rolled through my body from my chest up to the top of my head and down to the tips of my toes. Every wave was pure agony, but each pulse in my head wiped away my thoughts and replaced them with static.

Even worse, sudden, acute nausea surged, and I went cold and clammy all over. I'd be violently sick soon.

It took all my tattered concentration to hold onto the crystal and the pillow. In moments, I had no ability to think of anything else.

Which was why it took me an eternity to realize when something had changed.

My vision had grayed out almost immediately, but as the gray faded I found myself staring into Matthias's amber eyes. He must have taken away my pillow, or maybe I'd dropped it.

And then my agony faded, just as it did on the rare occasions when I allowed Sean to take my pain during a healing spell.

The healing spell pulsed, sending magic rolling through me in waves, but my hurt was gone. So was the debilitating nausea.

No. The sudden clarity of that thought startled me after the static that had clouded my mind. *I won't let Matthias take this for me.*

But he wasn't growling or bristling with shifter magic and his eyes weren't full of pain like Sean's were when he took the agony of a healing spell. I heard only a low rumble in his chest and saw a shadow move in his eyes: his wolf, staring back at me.

He wasn't hurting, and he wasn't sick. But neither was I.

"Matthias," I whispered. "What are you doing?"

"What I'm meant to do," he said, just as quietly. "I think."

Maybe he could do this courtesy of having consumed Valas's blood for years prior to being Changed, or maybe it had something to do with how I'd helped him during his first shift, when I'd taken his pain and pushed it away as he was apparently doing for me now.

Either way, he had magic of his own after all.

Tears spilled from my eyes. I didn't try to stop them. Matthias seemed to understand they weren't from pain or grief—just a lot of emotions all welling up at once.

And when the healing spell finished, he helped me into the shower, waited in the bedroom while I got myself clean, handed me a set of pajamas, and put me into bed. And never once did I feel self-conscious about him helping me. Maybe that was his magic too, or maybe I was too exhausted to be self-conscious about being cared for.

"Is Sean home yet?" I murmured as he pulled the covers up to my chin.

"Not yet." He rested his hand on my shoulder. "He said he will be soon. Don't worry about anything, Alice. We'll take of you."

I was made of worry these days, but not right now. Maybe Matthias took that too while he was taking the pain and sickness.

I was asleep before he closed the bedroom door.

I AM RESTING, but her cool hand pushes away the bedding and trails up my leg. Her fingertips delve between my thighs, caressing, teasing, and demanding.

I open my legs for her, as I have always done. As I always will, because her touches are like no other, and because she rules me. I am hers to do with as she pleases, and this she knows.

She commands, and I obey.

Without mercy, she demands I come again and again, and I do—on her fingers, on her lips, on a wand made of jade she warms by the fire.

I call her name and she laughs, the sound like bells, before she covers my mouth with her own. She drinks in my voice as I cry out. Her name is as sweet on my lips as her mouth.

She lowers her mouth to my breast. I know what is coming and fight to free myself, to no avail. She will not let me run.

When she slips her fingers deep within my sex and sinks her fangs into my tender flesh at the same time, I scream and come on her hand. The agony is exquisite.

I know only pain and pleasure for a very long time.

"We will rule the New World," she tells me later as I lie peaceful and sated in her arms. She laves my breasts and throat with her cool tongue, swirling my blood in languid circles, and licking it from her lips. "You and I will be its empresses, its queens. All its creatures of the night will swear fealty to us. This old world and its gods and rulers may go to blazes—I do not care."

I do not argue, but I know the new class of rulers in the New World are not like the ones we know here, who respect the authority and strength of vampires. They are different, these men of America, but she does not wish to hear such warnings. And old gods abide as much there as here. Their names and power reach me even on the shore of the old world, carried on the winds.

She does not hear these voices. I dare not tell her that I do, or that I carry within myself the accursed power of sorcery, given to me by a demon lord, and the dark arts of the warlocks of the Carpathian Mountains. She and I share a great many secrets, but not those.

Nor have I told her what I have contained in the small box hidden in my casket. He is my greatest secret and my greatest shame. My greatest joy, and my greatest pain.

Tomorrow she and I will leave all we know and sail for the New World aboard our chartered ship, the Lita Grey, *with only our most precious things and darkest secrets packed in and around our caskets. Our perilous journey is paid for, our safety in daytime ensured by our loyal guards.*

The Courts in the colonies have already been claimed, so once our ship arrives, my coterie and I will travel across America's entire wide land to the Court that has risen on its western coast. My companion and her guards will travel to the north, where another is planned near the waters of five great lakes. Our lover Lucien schemes to lead the Court already formed in a new town to the south called La Nouvelle-Orléans. Always impatient and unwilling to chance a rival's claim, he has already sailed.

The greatest young vampires of the old world, weary of its wars and known ways, thirst for what is new. And for the power that here belongs to the truly ancient among us and will never be shared.

"You have not bled enough for my taste tonight, Sala," she says, her

fangs at my throat as her fingers play between my thighs. "But we have hours yet before the sun rises. I may yet be satisfied."

"I will satisfy you," I assure her, my back arching. "Tell me what you desire."

"I must hear you call for me many more times." Her fang nicks my ear. It is a tiny pain and a promise, and I sigh in contentment. "We will be parted soon. I do not want to forget the sound of my true name on your sweet tongue."

I greatly desire the power she has all but promised. I want to rule my own Court and lead my kind in the New World. How could I not, after having witnessed a thousand years of rule and misrule in my own land?

And yet...

"Our thrones will be high, but they will be lonely," I say. "And far from each other."

"So they will." Her tongue traces the contours of my ear and she tugs my earring with her teeth. "But our rule will be long and our power unquestioned," she murmurs. "It is a dream, Sala. When we sleep at dawn, dream of it with me."

Old gods and new rulers await us in America, but I am sure I will dream of my Court come the dawn, lying beside her in the safety and darkness of this place.

The enormity of what lies before us seems less daunting knowing she will be there as well—though she will be farther away from me in America than my birthplace is from this village on the coast of France.

"I am yours for all time, Alys," I tell her.

She cups my face with her cool hand. "That name dies here, as does yours. After tomorrow, I go forth as Elizabeth."

"And I go forth as—"

She kisses me, stealing away my voice as I start to say the name I have chosen for myself, as if she does not want to hear me say it.

It is just as well. I will hear that new name spoken for a very long time as I sit at the head of my own Court, on the far-away western coast of America.

I opened my eyes, rolled to my back, and stared up at the ceiling of our bedroom. Between my legs, my thighs were wet from a passion-filled memory I'd relived even though it wasn't my own. And if I wasn't mistaken, it was at least the third such memory I'd experienced as a dream.

"Valas," I whispered.

She'd bound me months ago when it was the only way to break the sorcerer Miraç's power over me. And though she'd pretended to release the binding later, she never had, and that connection had lasted until the moment of her death in Colorado. It made sense that I had echoes of her memories and they'd begun to surface. No wonder my dreams lately had been so vivid.

I didn't want any of her dreams, but at least this one had been... pleasant. I strongly suspected I'd had at least one orgasm in my sleep.

"Thanks for that, I guess," I said aloud. Not that Valas could hear me, wherever she was. I chuckled.

The fact Valas and Elizabeth of the Chicago Court had been lovers didn't surprise me; I would have been far more shocked to find out they *hadn't* shared a bed. They'd shown no outward signs of affection when I'd seen Elizabeth visit Valas's Court last year, and yet I'd had a sense those waters ran deep. What *did* surprise me about this memory was their real tenderness and love for one another.

Was Elizabeth grieving for Valas's death, then? *Truly* grieving? I couldn't imagine loving someone for centuries and then losing them in such a way. I had little sympathy for Valas after all the suffering she'd caused, but Elizabeth's loss still resonated.

And Elizabeth's real name was apparently Alys. Now *there* was a twist I didn't see coming. The prospect that had anything to do with Valas's interest in me was almost too ludicrous to entertain. *Almost.* I made a face.

Despite the strong healing spell I'd used, a dull ache radiated from what felt like every bone and muscle in my body. Even my nose was still sore.

Sean's pillow was cold, the bedding left uncharacteristically unmade as if he'd rolled out of it quickly. I saw no sign of Baby Daisy, Rogue, or Esme either. The soft light of dawn peeked in around the edges of the closed curtains. The house was quiet.

He must have gotten home at some point, stayed in bed with me for a while, and risen early. The attack on the road had probably left him with a mountain of problems to sort out. As if we needed *more* problems. I rubbed my face with my hands, winced, and reached for my bedside bottle of ibuprofen.

It was barely seven in the morning, but my phone screen showed a text message from Philippa Grayson sent a half hour ago asking for an update. I needed a cup of coffee to face that and lots more to face everything else.

I found my robe, padded barefoot to the windows, and drew back the curtains, expecting to see the cars of several pack members. Instead, only my SUV and Ben's vehicle were out front. I hoped that was a good sign. If things were bad, Sean would probably have called for a pack meeting. I wasn't looking forward to telling Sean and Malcolm about my dreams, since anything to do with Valas tended to get everyone's hackles up, but at least we had some answers.

I dressed quickly, tamed my tangled hair, and opened the bedroom door. No sign of Matthias or anyone else, even Malcolm, but Sean's voice drifted upstairs from what sounded like the office. His tone seemed calm and I sensed no anger through our nascent bond. I also heard Matthias's low rumble.

Despite everything, now hope soared. Had the Council voted to support us? Could we have finally, *finally* gotten something to go our way?

I hurried down to the kitchen, poured a cup of fresh coffee, and added cream and sugar. The voices in the office quieted as I shut the refrigerator. Odd that they'd closed the office door, but maybe Sean had wanted to keep Rogue, Esme, and Baby Daisy inside so they didn't wake me. I loved how thoughtful he was, even when everything around us seemed to be falling apart.

I knocked. "Sean?"

"Come in," he called, his voice almost cheerful. How I'd missed that sound. He must have gotten good news.

Smiling, I opened the door—

—and came face-to-face with Valas.

CHAPTER
TWENTY-SEVEN

I SCREAMED AND LASHED OUT WITH MY MAGIC—

—or tried to.

Instead, I found myself rooted in place, my magic completely suppressed by a witchy ward drawn on the floor in chalk. I'd walked right into it.

Matthias had apparently waited for me right inside the door. He wrapped his enormous arms around my torso from behind, immobilizing me and pinning my arms to my sides. My mug hit the floor and broke, splashing my leg with coffee. Angry and confused, I fought him, but Matthias only growled and squeezed me tighter.

In my peripheral vision, I spotted Sean and Malcolm by my desk. And Carly was standing in front of me, holding an ornate hand mirror directly in front of my face. All of them looked furious, but I didn't understand why. What had I done?

Worst and most confusing of all, in the mirror it wasn't *my* face looking back at me, but Valas's—ancient, terrifying, and beautiful, as she'd looked before Miraç's curses ravaged her and reduced her to scraps of flesh clinging to decaying bones.

The surface of the mirror rippled and *pulled*.

Another scream—this one guttural and furious—came from somewhere deep in my mind and out of my mouth. I thought my skull might split apart. The agony was indescribable. My legs went out from under me, but Matthias held me up. His entire body vibrated as he snarled and growled.

Something began to tear away inside me, dragged toward the mirror like a tide drawn out by the moon. Panic made it hard for me to get a breath.

"Help me, Sean!" I screamed, fighting Matthias's grip.

Sean took a step forward, his expression equal parts fury and grief.

"Stay back!" Carly commanded, her voice strained and harsh. "Do *not* touch her!"

He staggered and braced himself on my desk to stay on his feet. Golden shifter magic seared my flesh and I heard the crunching of bones as his wolf tried to force him to shift. The pain must have been excruciating. Malcolm looked agonized too but he stayed where he was.

No one was going to help me, and I couldn't do anything but scream.

In the mirror's reflection, Valas's face twisted in rage, her mouth wide and upper and lower fangs extended as she screamed along with me—or as I screamed along with her.

Carly's mirror was strange and appeared handmade. Pieces of ancient-looking stones with strange runes carved into them ringed an oval piece of glass, which she'd etched with spellwork I didn't recognize.

My body twisted and wrenched as if a pack of wolves were tearing me apart. The haunting memory of being nearly killed by former pack mate Caleb Jennings and all the horrors I'd endured after made hot tears spill down my cheeks.

The agony seemed never-ending, and Sean wasn't providing any comforting alpha magic. In fact, I couldn't sense him or anyone else in our pack. Had he severed our nascent bond? The sensation of being utterly alone hurt me all the way to my soul.

"*Leave me be!*" I shrieked, and cursed them all in a language I didn't recognize.

But that wasn't me who'd cursed. It was her.

It was *Valas*, in my head, in my body, using my voice.

She hadn't died in Colorado—at least, not all the way. She'd been lurking in my head, waiting and watching in the shadows all this time.

The horror of that realization left me ice-cold. I made a choking sound.

Carly took a step closer, now holding the mirror just inches from my face, her expression and body language colder and more menacing than I'd ever thought her capable of being. The smell of burned paper—the scent of an angry witch—stung my nose.

"*Aanas anjah a skia,*" Carly hissed, her voice pure venom. She blew some kind of sweet-smelling dust from the palm of her hand into my face. "Get out of my friend, you *bitch!*"

The dust filled my lungs. A terrible chill rolled through my body. I convulsed so hard that I felt my joints pop.

Valas's grip slipped just a little.

As she fought the mirror's pull, I *shoved* at her with all my might, fighting to expel her from my body and mind and push her toward the mirror's ancient magic.

I caught a blur out of the corner of my eye just before Baby Daisy jumped into my hands. As Sean dove to grab her, she sank her tiny teeth into...something...in my chest and pulled at it as he yanked her away.

The tethers that bound Valas to me snapped.

Her spirit tore out of me with the same level of pain and visceral rupturing sensation as a blood mage stripping off my skin. For a moment, I was transported to my grandfather's compound in Baltimore and the stark, white, soundproof torture room where rivers of my blood had gone down a drain in the middle of the floor.

The mirror swallowed Valas's shadowy form into its abyssal depths as she screamed in pure rage.

Carly sagged and almost fell. Holding a howling Baby Daisy in one arm, Sean caught Carly just in time with the other.

"Let go," I croaked.

Matthias's grip loosened just enough for me to bend over and vomit black blood. And then I passed out.

WHEN CONSCIOUSNESS RETURNED, I found myself lying in our tub in Sean's arms, with warm, sweet-smelling water up to my chin and the nastiest aftertaste of my life in my mouth.

Oils and herbs floated on the water's surface, illuminated by the soft, flickering light provided by a dozen candles set up all around us on the edge of the tub. Someone had drawn runes all over my body. I recognized the healing and protection spellwork as witch magic, so Carly must have done all this too.

Everything felt hollow and hazy: my thoughts, my emotions, my senses—even my body and memories.

The only thing I remembered with clarity was the face in the mirror, screaming, with fangs bared. That image was crystal clear in my mind.

Valas.

Anger tried to rise, and fear, but witchy magic swept them away into the mist.

"My love." Sean kissed my hair. "I'm so sorry we had to put you through that, but it had to be done."

My throat hurt from screaming, but I managed to whisper, "I know."

He rubbed his chin on the top of my head and gently rested it there.

We lay quietly for a long time as I drifted in the haze of magic. The water stayed warm, probably thanks to Carly's spells, and Sean's body heat and magic comforted me. He hadn't severed our nascent bond after all—just muted it, or Carly had given him magic to put a barrier between us. Probably so Valas couldn't somehow use him or the pack to resist the mirror's magic. Cutting me off like that had to have hurt him even more than it had hurt me, and his wolf must have been beside himself.

When I finally felt like I could think clearly and talk, I rasped, "The Council vote?"

He let out a breath. "The first vote was tied."

I'd expected as much, but I'd still dared to hope we could persuade both Willa and Blake to vote in our favor.

I let out a tiny sound that was almost a whine. "The Council won't do anything to help us?" Then his words sank in. "What do you mean, the *first* vote?"

"Last night, they voted three-to-three regarding whether to back us against the Court, but Willa has asked for a second vote today after they discuss what she calls 'new information.' And no, I don't know what she means by that, or whether it's good or bad. She wouldn't say." He cupped my head to his chest. "But they voted four to two to affirm Matthias's asylum status. He's now legally protected under shifter law. Willa and the Council's attorneys are drafting a letter today to send to the Court."

For a moment, I couldn't speak, and not just because my throat hurt. "He's safe?"

He pressed his lips to my hair. "For now, he's safe."

The news wasn't what I'd hoped for. With another vote looming over whatever mysterious new information the Council had received, we still had plenty to worry about.

But I would take this win. I couldn't wait to hug Matthias—or pat him on the arm. Whichever he preferred.

With that out of the way, now Sean and I had something even more unpleasant to talk about.

"I didn't know Valas was there," I said hoarsely. "Just this morning I realized these dreams I've been having were Valas's memories, but I thought they were just echoes she'd left behind when she died. I had no idea she'd found a way to stay alive by hiding in my body." I took a deep, shaky breath. "How long have you known?"

"Only since last night." His voice now had a growly edge and shifter magic prickled on my skin. His wolf was deeply angry.

"How did you figure it out?"

"Ben was the first to realize something was wrong. When he arrived at the ambush scene, he heard you say things that didn't make any sense. And then later when you and I were talking, you seemed to be misremembering—or missing—some events that had just happened, like that you'd spoken to the man Matthias's wolf captured. We sent you home with Matthias, and then we called Carly."

"So Carly checked me over while I was sleeping and found Valas hiding?"

When he didn't reply immediately, I craned my neck to look at his face. "What? Tell me."

A muscle moved in his jaw. "Carly has known about Valas since the night of the wedding."

I sucked in a breath. "But she told me she didn't see anything."

"She lied." He nuzzled my hair. "She had to. If she'd told you then, she had no way to get her out of you. Valas might have killed her, or killed you. Or killed all of us."

I'd spotted no clue whatsoever that night that anything was amiss, and I'd certainly had no reason not to take Carly at her word when she said she hadn't found anything. Carly had fooled me completely—and fooled Valas too, apparently.

"I understand why she couldn't tell me, but she could have told you and Malcolm," I protested.

His long, quiet growl told me his wolf agreed, but he said, "She didn't think she could take the chance. All it would have taken was one unguarded moment and we might have given ourselves away.

You can sense emotions through our nascent bond, and I know you feel Malcolm's reactions too. Valas knew everything you did."

For almost a month, she'd lurked inside me. I had to assume she knew all there was to know about me now, from the fact I was Moses's granddaughter to my ability to help shifters through their Change, and everything in between. She'd shared intimate moments like sex with Sean and probably every thought I'd had. She'd even been present when Sean asked me to marry him. I'd wanted that moment to belong to us alone.

Absolutely gutting, and none of it could be undone. I didn't even know if it would ever stop hurting.

"Is that why Carly put something calming in this water?" I demanded. "So I'd be sleepy and less upset when I woke up?"

"Yes." He held me gently but firmly when I tried to get up. "We didn't know how you'd react when you got this news."

Valas had thoroughly violated me, and now Carly's potions were stealing my emotions and suppressing my magic. I couldn't even feel angry about not being able to feel angry, and that made me try to get out of the tub. I wanted control of my body again.

"I understand why you want out of the water, but listen to me for a second," Sean said, and held on when I tried to pull away. "We had to do what we thought was best for you. Please don't be angry at Carly. She worked hard to make that mirror and all these potions and spellwork to get Valas out of you and help you recover. She's been asleep for hours in Matthias's bed. He had to carry her there after she finished making this bath."

That was the closest to a scolding as I'd gotten from Sean in a long time.

"Okay," I said, my voice quiet. "I understand."

He squeezed me gently. "I'm angry too, Alice. My wolf is furious. But I understand why Carly made these choices. She knows how vicious and merciless Valas is. We had no margin for error with any of this. She waited to tell us until she'd figured out a way to extract Valas without killing you, and then we had to make a plan to catch you *both* totally off-guard. It was our only shot at capturing Valas and saving you."

"You sure as hell did catch me off-guard." I recalled Carly's strange handmade mirror. "Where's the mirror?"

"Carly has it in a box with wards, inside another box with wards. She said she'll hand it over when you've recovered."

I had so many questions about the mirror and how Carly had known Valas had hitched a ride in my body, but I'd ask her later.

"I saw Valas die," I said. "I watched Vlad stake her with her own arm. Her body burned and turned to ash right in front of me. I *saw* it, Sean." I sighed. "At least, I thought I saw it."

"You probably did see it." He laced our fingers together and drew me closer. "Carly can tell you more, but she says Valas transferred her *skia*, or shade, to your body. Her body ceased to exist, but her spirit survived."

"Of course it did. She's like a cockroach. You just can't kill her." Realization dawned. "*Oh.*"

My tone put Sean on high alert. "What?"

"She kidnapped me to summon Vlad, but that wasn't the only reason she wanted me." I moved restlessly in the tub. "She knew her body couldn't hold together anymore, even if she spent her remaining years in a bathtub full of ancient vampires' lifeblood. She didn't just want my magic and my connection to Vlad. *She wanted my body*. And when she got a chance, she separated her shade from her body and shoved it into me, just before Vlad staked her."

"Carly thinks so too." He wrapped his arms around me and tucked my head under his chin. "I'm sorry about everything, Alice. You didn't deserve this."

We were both still angry about Carly keeping us in the dark about Valas's *skia*, and Sean's wolf would hold a grudge against Carly about that for a long time, but she'd probably saved my life, body, *and* soul at great personal cost—all after I'd asked her to help track down a serial-killing necromancer and their pet spirit.

"Carly does these things because she loves you," Sean said when

I went quiet. No doubt he sensed my guilt and sadness, even as muted as they were. "And she knows you'd do the same for her without even hesitating. In fact, she told me to tell you not to kick your own ass when you woke up. You couldn't have known Valas's shade was hiding inside you. We all got outsmarted by a vampire who's had more than a thousand years to learn all the tricks. But she's trapped now in that mirror and you're free of her."

I barely heard those last few words.

Maybe Carly's calming potions had started to fade, or maybe a revelation of this magnitude was simply enough to overwhelm the limits of those potions. For whatever the reason, the thought that popped into my head just then made me go cold all over and my heartbeat thunder in my ears.

Sean went very still. "Alice?"

"The child," I whispered. "The son. Sean, the dream I had about being chased though the tunnel, when I almost set the bed on fire... that was Valas's memory, and *she had a son*."

And for all her deadly devotion and determination to keep both herself and her child alive from whoever had chased them in that memory, her feelings later about her child were certainly mixed.

How had she put it in the dream? *He is my greatest secret and my greatest shame. My greatest joy, and my greatest pain.*

"Based on the dream I just had last night, I think she brought him to America with her, contained in some kind of box," I said as Sean stared at me. "What if he's around today, somewhere? What if he's just as bad as her? What if..." My voice trailed off. I didn't even know where to start to begin untangling this confounding revelation.

"How could a vampire have borne a child?" Sean asked. "It's not possible."

"Valas isn't just a vampire," I reminded him. "She told me once that like me, she's many things masquerading as one. She has magic and powers unlike any I've ever known."

In the dream about Elizabeth, Valas had described herself as having the powers of a sorcerer, thanks to a demon lord, and what she'd called *the dark arts of the warlocks of the Carpathian Mountains.*

I shared that information with Sean. "Vlad was a warlock before she made him a vampire," I added. "It makes sense that she spent time in that part of Eastern Europe. She could have studied their practices and found ways to gain those powers."

He nodded slowly. "So, if any member of the undead could produce a child, it would have been Valas. But who the hell was the father?"

"Good question," I said. "Something tells me it wasn't a simple human who crossed paths with Valas once upon a time in ancient Constantinople. Valas must have used every kind of magic she had to get pregnant. Whoever fathered that child, she chose him very carefully."

Sean looked grim. "What if the father was Vlad?"

Ew—now *there* was a mental image I didn't need. Vlad's body was twisted and monstrous, and I could only imagine in my worst nightmares what his clothing had spared me from seeing. Even the thought of having sex with such a creature made me nauseous. But I had no doubt Valas wouldn't have let Vlad's misshapen form stop her if she wanted a child that combined her powers with his.

Then again, Vlad might not have had anything to do with this child. This was all speculation.

We didn't know much about Valas's mysterious son—much less what form he was in or even whether he still existed. But my gut told me he *did* still exist, and that before long we'd find out why Valas had brought him to the New World locked in a box.

We always seemed to be lucky that way.

TWENTY-EIGHT

Usually a dunk in witchy potions forced me to shower and soap myself more than once to scrub away odors one usually encountered in dumpsters. Unfortunately, my investigations had led me into dumpsters more times than I cared to think about, but at least literal dumpster smell was easier to wash away than stinky potions. Happily, this bath actually left me smelling good, so all I did was a quick shampoo and rinse-off in the shower.

When Sean and I emerged from the bathroom wrapped in towels, I found Baby Daisy sleeping on our bed. The list of questions I wanted answered, disasters that needed addressing, and things I had to do was a mile long, but right now I had to lie down next to our wolf pup and cuddle her with my nose buried in her soft, thick fur. Her scent was an automatic mood-lifter.

And because his wolf needed comfort and the shifter urge to snuggle with his future mate and our baby was so strong, Sean abandoned his stated intent to get dressed right away and curled around us both.

"She helped get Valas out of me," I murmured, though I probably could have yelled and Baby Daisy wouldn't have stirred. "I don't know how she did it, or how she knew how to do it, but she sank her teeth into Valas somehow and pulled."

"She follows her instincts, like any wolf." Sean nuzzled the back of my neck. "We know she has magic in her. A fae made her from your wolf, and you're full of magic. There's no telling what this pup will be able to do."

"Well, she performed a miracle today, but why do I feel like her personality and fae magic are going to bite us on the butt someday?" I asked wryly.

"Because that's how miracles work, and pups too." He kissed my shoulder. "Lots of good, lots of uncertainty, and lots of near-disasters. Just like everything else, we'll get through it because we won't have to get through it alone." He moved toward the edge of the bed. "Come on, babe. Malcolm and Matthias are downstairs waiting on us. We need to strategize. And judging by how frequently your phone has buzzed, I think your client is looking for an update."

"I'm sure she is." I caught his hand as he started to rise. "Is Matthias our beta now?"

"On paper, not yet." He kissed the tip of my nose. "But the entire pack felt it last night when he stepped up during the attack."

"I felt it too," I said, to his obvious surprise. "Like a puzzle piece falling into place."

"That's a good description." He drew me to my feet and gave me a little push toward the closet. "Reactions from the pack are mixed, as you probably guessed, but a pack isn't a democracy and Matthias isn't subject to popular vote."

"But someone could challenge him?" I asked as I emerged from the closet holding a pair of jeans, a tank top, and a shirt.

"Technically, yes. But I don't think anyone will." He tossed his towel into the bathroom and started opening dresser drawers. "They might not like it, but Matthias is coming into his strength quickly. His wolf has found a reason to stand tall. He fought well and obeyed both your commands and mine. They know he'll be a good beta." He pulled out an undershirt, shut the drawer, and eyed me.

"Alice, we're in a hurry. Stop staring at my ass like you've never seen it before."

"It wasn't your ass I was staring at." I scowled. "And besides, I'll look where I damn well please, Wolf."

"Look and get dressed at the same time, then."

I stuck out my tongue, grabbed a bra and undies, and headed for the bathroom. He smacked my towel-covered butt when I went past. I winced.

His expression immediately switched from playful to serious, and his eyes glowed golden. "Are you hurting?"

I gave him an incredulous look. "Sean, I got mildly possessed yesterday afternoon and then was in a car wreck at forty-plus miles an hour last night. I used a high-level blood magic healing spell after that, and I just had an ancient vampire-sorceress forcibly exorcised from my body. Of course I'm hurting." I kissed his jaw and rubbed his chest so he'd make that growly sound I liked. "But a couple of ibuprofen will take the edge off and I'll be okay."

"Alice." Sean pinched the bridge of his nose. "What kind of lives are we living when I more or less forgot that yesterday you got *mildly possessed* by a ghost?"

"Hey, a mild possession is basically just your average Thursday for a mage PI."

That wasn't exactly true, but at least I got him to smile for a second.

I'd apparently been unconscious for almost three hours after expelling Valas from my body. That wasn't too bad—honestly, I'd expected to have been out much longer. But that meant it was nearly noon on a day when I'd planned to have accomplished a half dozen things by now, including several connected to my client's case.

Once I got dressed and braided my hair, I picked up my phone and confirmed I did indeed have a bunch of texts and one missed call from Philippa Grayson. I let her know via text that I'd gotten into a car accident last night but was now healed and back on my feet. I assured her I'd send a full update within a few hours once I ran down some leads.

I could practically feel the disapproval radiating from my phone when she texted back a terse *Thank you*. Not that I blamed her. I always tried to give my clients my full attention, but at the moment all our problems pulled me in a dozen different directions at once.

I also had a missed call around three in the morning from Detective Diaz, but he hadn't left a voice message or sent any texts. What was that about? I put him on my call-back list for later.

When Sean and I emerged from the bedroom, the house was quiet and the door to Matthias's room was closed. "She's still sleeping," Sean murmured. He probably heard Carly breathing. "She said not to wake her or she'd turn me into a chinchilla."

My heart hurt that Carly had gone through so much to help me, to the point that she had to sleep it off. "Well, you'd be cute as heck," I said, trying to lighten the mood for both of us. "But I don't think I'd want to be a chinchilla's mate."

He kissed my palm and held my hand while we went downstairs.

We found Matthias and Malcolm in the kitchen. Matthias appeared to be making a fresh pot of coffee. I hoped it had my name on it. I could use some breakfast too, come to think of it. Or lunch. Or both. I was starving. Apparently having an exorcism worked up an appetite.

When we reached the bottom step, Malcolm zipped over to me and flitted, clearly nervous, angry, and unhappy. "Alice! How do you feel?"

"I'm okay," I promised. "I mean, I feel like shit, of course, but I'm okay."

Matthias snorted quietly. Even Sean's mouth twitched.

But Malcolm wasn't in the mood for jokes. "I don't know how I didn't see her in there," he said. "I'm so sorry. I feel like I let you down again."

"You didn't." I took a step closer so I could sort of touch his hand because he obviously didn't buy it. "I promise you didn't let me down. We had no way of knowing what she'd done. Valas didn't want to be found, and she knew how to hide from you, Sean, me… everyone. She was all but impossible to see."

He crossed his arms. "If Carly could see her, then it wasn't impossible."

"Well, Carly's extra special. And like Sean said, Valas has had a long time to learn every trick using kinds of magic you and I have only read about. She's more than a thousand years old. You're only what, twenty? There's no shame in getting tricked by someone five hundred times older than you."

Malcolm eyed me. "First of all, that was shameless flattery about my age to distract me, and it worked. And second, you are terrible at math."

As I tried to come up with a good retort, Matthias approached me with a mug of coffee. He looked about seventy-five percent less grim than I was used to seeing.

I couldn't help it; I hugged him. He hugged me with his free arm and patted my back somewhat awkwardly but didn't pull away.

"You're safe with us now," I said, claiming my coffee mug from him. "I mean, you were before, but now it's all legal and official."

"Thank you both for granting me asylum and persuading the Council to affirm it," Matthias said. "But legal and official doesn't necessarily mean they won't still try to get to me."

"You know she used to refer to you as Mr. Sunshine, back when we first met you?" Malcolm asked, hands on his hips. "Guess how you got that nickname."

"I do recall that, yes." Matthias folded his hands behind his back. "I assumed it had to do with my radiant personality."

Malcolm's incredulous expression forced me to hide my smile behind my coffee cup.

"What smells so good?" I asked.

"I put a breakfast casserole into the oven when we heard you moving around upstairs," Matthias said. "It should be ready in ten minutes."

I gaped at him.

"You'll have to forgive Alice," Malcolm said with an exasperated look in my direction. "She's in a much worse pre-coffee condition than usual, and I think she's having trouble picturing you, of all people, making a casserole. Making a hole through a brick wall seems more your style."

Matthias raised his eyebrows. "I am a man of many talents," he rumbled. He turned back to me. "What else can I get you?"

Normally being fussed over made me self-conscious, but in the wake of...well, everything, I didn't mind a bit of fussing, especially since it gave Matthias's wolf purpose.

"Thank you for the offer, but coffee and food is all I need for now." I took my mug to the kitchen island and slid onto one of the tall chairs. "Thank you all for helping Carly get Valas out of me. That experience was highly unpleasant, but I'm obviously very glad to not be giving her spirit a piggyback ride anymore. And doubly glad Carly stuffed her into that cool mirror where we can keep an eye on her."

When Matthias's expression turned grave, I touched his arm. "You're one of us now. You aren't going back to the Court, or to her. I don't care that she's apparently still kicking. As far as I'm concerned, no one but us needs to know that."

He studied me. "If Charles Vaughan finds out, he will obliterate everything in his path to get that mirror. He won't care who's in the way. Not even if it's you."

"I know." I squeezed his arm and let go. "But only five of us know the truth, right? You, Sean, Malcolm, Carly, and me. If we stash that thing where no one will find it, inside the best wards we can create, and no one breathes a word of it, Charles won't find out."

"Those people who attacked us on the road knew Valas was inside you," Sean said. "They came for her. Ben heard the man you called Mr. Touchy say 'I'm here to free you' and you—or probably Valas, actually—told him 'I will not be captured.' We found a spell crystal in the grass near him that Carly thinks was meant for Valas to transfer into."

"I don't remember that conversation," I said with a sigh. "I remember feeling really dizzy once I made it out of the wrecked SUV, but everything's blurry until Ben handed me to you. I wonder if Valas wiped it from my memory or I was just concussed."

"*Just* concussed," Malcolm said with a sigh. "Listen to her. *Just* concussed."

Meanwhile, I was thinking about what Sean had said. "She probably didn't want to risk leaving my body," I said, my hands wrapped around my coffee mug. "I guess that's what she meant by 'I will not be captured.' She thought they were trying to trap her in the crystal."

"Maybe they were," Malcolm suggested. "We don't know who those people were or what their motives might be."

"Ben told me Mr. Touchy said 'Mistress, I still serve you.'" Sean put his hand on my back to comfort me. "That seems like something a devotee would say."

"Maybe they *were* her followers, then," Malcolm said. "They might have been trying to help her and she misunderstood their intentions. When in doubt, kill them all, I guess. Vampires."

"She must have told these people whose body she planned to jump into," Sean said. "Otherwise, how would they have known who to look for?"

I recalled my abbreviated tracking spell from yesterday and had a thought. "Yesterday, before someone broke my spell, I caught glimpses of occult rituals when I tracked the magic from the ghost grenade Mr. Touchy tossed at Malcolm. Those rituals felt ancient and very bloody."

"In other words, entirely consistent with what I'd imagine Valas's own practices to be." Malcolm flitted. "You said someone busted your tracking spell. Was it Valas trying to keep you from seeing what was going on in those rituals?"

I closed my eyes and tried to see the enraged face I'd glimpsed just before my spell broke. But try as I might, it remained more of an impression than an image.

"I don't know," I said, opening my eyes again. "She's capable of doing it, but I just can't say for sure."

"Great—another mystery," Malcolm said. "So six of these people are dead. But are there more out there? Are they going to come after Alice again, not knowing Valas isn't in her anymore? What will they do when they find that out?"

"Great question." I finished my coffee and let Matthias take the mug. "I'll add that to my list of things to worry about."

"How long's that list now?" Malcolm asked dryly.

I held my thumb and index finger a few inches apart. He snorted.

"And speaking of mysteries," I said, "any more murders that look like they might be connected to our necromancer and their pet spirit?"

"I've been following the local news as best I can," Matthias said from the coffee maker. "There were a couple of murders in the city last night. Two of them I doubt are related to the necromancer." He handed me my refilled mug. He really did know how to make my coffee exactly how I liked it. A man of many talents, indeed. "According to news reports, one was a domestic situation and the other seems to be gang-related. But in the two other cases, the killers apparently cut their own throats immediately after committing murders."

"*Two* murder-suicides?" I set my mug down after a single sip. "What times did these take place?"

"Both of them at about two fifteen in the morning, about six blocks apart. I don't have any details—just what's been in the news."

I thought of Diaz's three a.m. phone call. If I'd needed a sign these twin murder-suicides were related to our case—other than my gut instinct, that was—that call clinched it. And judging by the grim expressions on both Matthias and Malcolm's faces, they shared my feeling.

The oven buzzed. As Matthias donned oven mitts that strained to fit his enormous hands, my phone rang. I recognized the number immediately. Ugh—just what I needed.

"Back in a minute." I slid off the chair, hurried upstairs, and shut myself in our bedroom, far from Matthias's sharp ears.

I answered just before the call went to voice mail. "What do you want?"

Moses's dry chuckle grated on my already frayed nerves. "Charming as always. Do highway ambushes by crazed zealots always make you this rude?"

"Yep, every time." I kept my voice sarcastic to hide the way my stomach lurched.

How the hell did he know about the wreck? And what did he mean by "crazed zealots"? I categorically did not want Moses anywhere *near* this mess with Valas. Much like Charles, my grandfather would stop at nothing to get his hands on that mirror.

My best bet was to play dumb and see what information I could get out of him. "Crazed zealots?" I asked, feigning confusion. "Is that who attacked us? I thought it was something to do with the Court."

"If you're referring to Charles Vaughan, my sources inform me he was furious about the ambush. He apparently wants you to stay alive."

His tone indicated he'd bought my dumb act, so I stuck with it.

"Well, he *would* say that, wouldn't he?" I scoffed, though I knew damn well Charles hadn't had anything to do with it. "We're supposed to be fighting this out in the courtroom, not on some backwoods country highway. He has to pretend he's playing by the rules, at least until he thinks he can get away with coming after us directly."

"Alice, use your head," Moses snapped. "A Court operation would not have been so sloppy. Why wreck your vehicle but leave you all alive? This wasn't Charles Vaughan. Those people were connected with a cult calling themselves Disciples of the Sun. What they might want with you, I don't know, but I have people trying to find out."

I patted myself on the back for convincing Moses I suspected Charles and getting him to tell me who he thought had attacked us.

"Well, if it *wasn't* Charles, then it's a hell of a coincidence," I said, feigning skepticism. "How do you know about this cult, anyway?"

"I put my best people on it. I was highly motivated to find out who tried to kill you."

Ugh. Of course he wouldn't tell me how he knew. I wasn't going to beg him for that info. We'd just have to do our own digging into this supposed cult.

"At least I know it wasn't you," I said to Moses, in a tone that would have made Malcolm roll his eyes. "The attackers didn't smell like a pompous Baltimore racketeer."

He sighed. "I called to make sure you were all right."

"Right. Like you care." I snorted. "And as if you don't have eyes on my house telling you I got home alive last night."

"Judging by the reports I got, the condition you were in last night didn't convince me you'd recover. You were seen being carried into the house—not by Sean, but by your new werewolf. You haven't left your home today. The witch Carly Reese arrived in the middle of the night and still hasn't left." He raised his voice. "These facts *might* have led me to believe you were seriously hurt, maybe dying."

Huh. Maybe he *did* care. I doubted it, but he sure was selling it with that last bit and his tone.

Given the twenty years of misery he'd inflicted on me, I really didn't care if he cared now—except it presented an opportunity I'd waited for. As long as I didn't blow this, I could take a shot at gaining something important.

"Okay." I let my voice tremble. "Look, it was bad, okay? I don't like anyone knowing when I'm vulnerable, as I'm sure you'd expect. Someone like me, with my list of enemies, can't let on when I'm not at my best. The wreck was bad and those people, whoever the hell they were, tried to capture or kill us when just wrecking our SUV going fifty miles an hour didn't get the job done. So yeah, I needed a lot of help to recover, and yeah, Carly's still here because she's recovering from helping me. At the moment, however, other than being sore from the wreck and all the magic, I'm good to go. So thanks for asking, or whatever."

During the silence that followed, I tried to determine whether he'd bought my scared and vulnerable act or not. I really couldn't tell, but I decided to keep going.

"But speaking of my case..." I blew out a breath. Time for a big gamble. "I have a problem, and maybe you could help."

"How so?" His voice sounded guarded but intrigued.

The key to bullshitting someone like Moses was to commit fully and not let even a hint of nervousness or uncertainly creep in. To pull this off, I had to go all in.

"I think I might be up against something really nasty with this case I'm on," I said. "To reel the bad guys in, I'll need big wards. I have to have sources of power that aren't connected to my house wards or blood garden, but I'm an earth mage, so that's all I've got here. I can't use pack magic, and Carly's only able to offer me a little of her kind of magic to protect me. I need...something else." I made my voice tremble a little and cleared my throat. "Sources of power that are self-contained, that I can link together and put where I need them."

"Ava Selene," Moses said, feigning shock and horror, "are you asking me for what I think you're asking me for? After all those years of telling me I'm a monster for using them?"

I hated that he'd used my real name, but I couldn't let him distract me from selling him on this request.

"You *are* a monster, but I'm after a much worse monster than you," I said, and it was actually true. "Am I proud of this? No. Do I hate myself for asking you for help? Yes." I swallowed hard, because my apprehension about the necromancer was very real. "But sometimes there's no such thing as a practice being always good or always bad. Sometimes it's just necessary."

After everything I'd been through with Sean and Malcolm, and everything I'd put them through, I didn't like how much I still believed that. Malcolm and Sean both believed some things were always wrong, no matter what, and in theory I agreed. But theory wasn't real life. My life and soul and the people I cared about were on the line. People were dying because a necromancer enjoyed dealing out death and using a monstrous spirit to commit murder.

In theory, I'd never wanted to say one word to my grandfather ever again, or share his table, or drink his scotch, or chat in his conservatory, or ask for his help, or request that he loan me weapons I'd always believed were inhumane. And look where I'd ended up: doing all those things within the last few days.

Sometimes, like now, I had to do what was necessary and hope for forgiveness, or at least understanding.

"When do you need them?" Moses asked.

I made sure none of the hope I felt showed in my tone when I asked, "What's the price?"

"If you need them to keep you alive, then there's no price," he said. "Come to the manor this afternoon and choose which to take."

I'd thought the taste in my mouth from puking black blood after Carly exorcised Valas was bad, but that was nothing compared to the taste in my mouth right now. *Remember this feeling the next time you think about asking him for something*, I told myself.

I didn't try to hide the tightness in my voice when I said, "Thanks."

"I'll see you in a few hours. Be safe." He ended the call.

I tossed my phone on the bed like it was moldy.

Sean must be feeling a tornado of emotions through our nascent bond right now. He'd probably guessed right away who'd called. I'd have to figure out what to tell him, and more importantly, what to say to Malcolm. I didn't want to get his hopes up, but he deserved to know what I was doing.

The smell of Matthias's breakfast casserole had reached the bedroom, but my appetite had evaporated. I had to eat something, though, or I'd have to deal with a couple of unhappy werewolves *and* a disapproving ghost on top of everything else.

Matthias had baked something for the same reason Sean loved to cook: a dominant wolf wasn't just a fighter and protector, but someone who wanted to ensure his pack was well-fed *and* safe. Fight and kill one minute, throw a casserole together the next. Nan had done the same. And even her late predecessor, Jack Hastings, for all his faults, had too.

Thanks to the number of crises in our lives at the moment, Matthias had found his place light-years faster than I could have hoped or even imagined. That didn't mean he and his wolf had healed—not by a long shot—but I believed he was on the path to healing. Sean, Malcolm, and I were on that path too. So were Carly and Katy. Maybe we could heal together.

Something Arkady had told me recently popped into my head: *Do you know how someone who's been beaten down finds their strength? They get the chance to be the strength for someone else.*

I'd gotten the sense she was talking about herself when she said that, but when I'd asked, she'd changed the subject. Her insight certainly applied to Matthias and his battered wolf.

As happy as I was about the Council affirming Matthias's asylum status and his rise to beta, I couldn't shake the dread I felt thinking about the next twenty-four hours. Assuming Katy and Carly would be ready by tonight, we'd be facing a necromancer and their nasty pet spirit in a battle that would force me to rely on not just my own magic and abilities but the witches' too—while risking their lives and souls.

On top of that, my visit to Merrum Manor later today would either give Malcolm something he wanted with all his heart or fail my friend in a way I'd never forgive myself for, even if he did forgive me.

Oh, and Charles still needed something big enough that he'd threatened to put Sean and me in prison, and now we had a thirteen-hundred-year-old vampire-sorcerer in a hand mirror.

At least we had casserole and coffee and each other. That counted for something.

TWENTY-NINE

I opened the bedroom door to find Carly waiting for me in the hallway. I only jumped a little.

Her clothing was wrinkled from sleeping fully dressed and her eyes had shadows, but she was smiling.

"You've really got to stop lurking behind closed doors," I said, and walked into her open arms.

She hugged me tightly and for a long time, smelling of all the herbs and potions she'd used to extract Valas and help me recover afterward.

"I'm so sorry I had to keep that secret from you and the others." She rubbed my back before releasing me. "It hurt me to lie to you, but I had no choice."

"I know," I assured her. "Sean explained everything—or mostly everything. I was upset at first, but I understand why you couldn't tell anyone. You fooled me completely. I have a lot more respect for your acting skills now. Your magic and abilities too. I had no idea you had exorcisms on your résumé."

"A High Priestess has to have a pretty big skill set." She touched my hand. "I know you're angry and hurting about this violation and it's probably dredged up all kinds of past traumas you and I have been working on in counseling sessions. We'll talk through this soon. You don't have to sit with it right now, but try not to pretend it didn't happen."

"Sean and I talked about how and why she'd hidden inside me when I woke up in the tub," I said as she led me to the doorway of Matthias's room. "I'm a long way from working through it, but talking about it right away helped."

"I knew he'd take good care of you, and I'm proud of you for not burying your feelings like you used to do."

"Thanks," I said, with a wry smile. "I'm trying to do better."

"And you *are* doing better. I'm proud of you for that too. Let's talk about this."

Carly touched a rectangular wooden box with a hinged lid and runes carved on every square inch. It measured about twenty inches long by ten inches deep and ten inches wide. She'd put it on Matthias's nightstand, but I sensed and smelled its powerful witchy wards from the doorway.

"I made this mirror myself using pieces of *lapis manalis*, stones that cover entrances to the underworld," she said. "To get the stones, I had to call in a lot of favors and ask a friend to fly here from Belgium on a moment's notice with the stones in her carry-on." She held up her hand when I started to speak. "I'm not telling you this to make you feel bad, though I know you'll feel bad no matter what I say. I'm saying it because I need to teach you everything there is to know about this mirror, from its making to its potential, because it's now an object of power. Protecting it and keeping it secure is a matter of life and death for everyone connected to you *and* me."

I had no doubt that was not an exaggeration. If Valas escaped, she'd rain vengeance on all our heads. Not only that—Carly had created one of the rarest kinds of magical objects: a true object of power. Capturing and containing Valas was only one of its uses. That alone would be plenty to make it not only supremely dangerous but also worth killing for, as Matthias had pointed out.

As an object of power, now it would be worth a lot more, which meant Carly was right: I needed to know everything there was to know about the mirror. All my other obligations would have to wait.

"I'd like to see the mirror, please," I said quietly. Not just because I needed to learn its powers, but because I had to face the horror it contained.

She picked up the box. It looked surprisingly heavy—so much so that I almost offered to have Sean carry it for her.

"We're going downstairs to your workshop," she said. "I won't open this box without your strongest wards around it."

My phone rang. It was Diaz calling again.

I heaved a sigh. "I have to take this," I said, to Carly's obvious displeasure. "I'll try to be quick."

"Alice." She shook her head and carried the box toward the stairs. "I'll be in the workshop whenever you're ready."

I felt another headache building—the kind of pressure-from-the-inside, skull-busting headache that came from being pulled in so many directions at once. And I was so, so tired.

I pinched the bridge of my nose.

Damn it, Diaz probably had info that was time-sensitive about the necromancer we wanted to catch. What was I supposed to do?

As Carly made her way slowly down the steps to the main floor, I leaned against the wall and answered the call. "This is Alice." Hopefully I didn't sound as exasperated as I felt.

"Worth." Diaz's strained voice made me think he hadn't slept since the last time we'd spoken. "I want to see you."

"Detective—"

"I'm not asking," he snapped. "One hour. Pick a place where we won't be seen. Not your house. Somewhere in town."

"I can't meet in an hour," I told him. "I have something I have to do right now that can't wait."

"There is *nothing* you could be doing that's more important than solving this case quickly."

You have no idea, I thought.

I gritted my teeth. "I assure you I want this person caught every bit as much as you do. I'm working on that, but I still have something I need to do before I do anything else. A lot of lives are on the line with this too."

A grim silence was the only reply to that.

"Okay." I let out a breath. "Make it two hours. I'll try for that. Let's meet in the south parking lot at Fields Park. There's no cameras there except one at the gate going into the park. But I need something from you."

"What?"

I took a deep breath and took my shot. "Bring me the knives from all the murders we think might be connected."

"*What?*"

I held the phone away from my ear while Diaz yelled at me about chain of custody, his career, the district attorney, his lieutenant, and a lot more besides.

When he paused for breath, I cut in. "Detective, you can leave them in evidence tubes. I will wear gloves if you don't want my fingerprints on the containers. I won't be able to get as much from them as I would if I touched them, but I understand you have to preserve and protect your evidence. Sign them out, bring them with you, let me see if I can get *anything* that will help us, and put them back. Only you and I will ever know."

"Worth..."

This time Diaz's weary tone made me swallow hard. He'd had to look at the victims up close. Had probably attended their autopsies. Maybe made the death notifications. Put up with Ferguson's bullshit and probably pushback and pressure from his bosses too.

"I wouldn't ask you this if I didn't think it might make the difference between catching this person tonight or not catching them," I said. "I might not always follow the law, but I respect people like you who work hard to uphold it and save lives and bring murderers to justice. I am asking you respectfully to try to bring me those knives so I can help you put an end to this killing spree."

"Do you know who's behind this?" he grated.

"I have a strong suspicion," I said. "I think I'm close to finding them. And I promise you will be the first person I call when I do."

"Two hours. Fields Park south lot. I'll do the best I can." He ended the call.

I stuck the phone in my back pocket. "Me too," I said to no one in particular.

Back downstairs, only Sean remained in the kitchen. No sign of Malcolm or Matthias. I poured myself another cup of coffee and grabbed a bottle of water from the fridge.

"Alice, food?" Sean said, pointing to a plate piled high with casserole.

"I have no appetite," I told him wearily. "I'm sorry. I know your wolf worries and drives you up the wall about this. I'm just sick to my stomach right now and I can't even think about eating a bite. I promise to try when Carly and I are done downstairs, before I go… run errands."

"Given these two phone calls, I'd like to hear about your errands." He scrubbed his face with his hands. "I love you."

He said it in that tone when I sorely tested his patience.

"I know you love me." I gave him a kiss. His body nearly vibrated with anger and worry. "Carly is going to teach me all about that mirror so I know how to keep it secret and safe. Then I'm meeting Detective Diaz to talk about the case and maybe get my hands on the murder weapons."

"Looking for magic trace on them?"

"Yes." I sighed. "After that, I'm off to Merrum Manor. I'd like to take Matthias with me."

Sean studied me. "Matthias and not Malcolm? Why?"

"A couple of reasons." I explained why I was going and what I hoped to get. "I can't risk taking Malcolm this time," I added as Sean processed what I'd told him. "Matthias will guard me with his life. He might not have magic, but he's got plenty of FAFO energy, as Arkady would say."

"FAFO?"

"Fuck around and find out."

"Ah." He kissed the tip of my nose. "How much do you plan to tell Matthias about your dealings with Moses?"

"I'm thinking about that. I'll figure out the answer by the time we're headed that way."

"Okay." He caressed my butt rather than smacking it. I didn't hate that. "Get to class, Miss Magic."

"Yes, sir, Mister Wolf." I headed for the basement door.

When I arrived in my workshop, I found Malcolm and Matthias watching Carly draw spellwork with chalk in my largest inlaid circle.

I opened my mouth to ask Matthias to go upstairs, then thought better of it.

"I need to face her too," Matthias said quietly. "Carly says it's all right with her if it's okay with you."

That explained why Carly was prepping my largest circle for wards. Squeezing the four of us into either of the smaller circles when Matthias took up a significant percentage of the basement as a whole would be borderline hilarious and definitely uncomfortable, even if one of us was a ghost.

"We have a couple errands to run after this," I told Matthias in an undertone as Carly continued to draw spells. "I'd like you to come with me, if you're available. I'm going to meet semi-secretly with a homicide detective about the murders, and then I need some supplies for tonight's ritual."

Carly flicked a glance up at me and then went back to work, her expression unreadable. I wondered if she could tell I was up to something. Ugh. Probably.

"What about me?" Malcolm asked, floating back and forth next to us with his hands on his hips. "I thought *I* was your errand buddy."

"You are," I assured him. I'd tell him about my plan to visit Merrum Manor after we got done learning about the mirror. "But today I need you to stick close to home and keep an eye on things, unless I summon you. Build your most heavy-duty wards on this basement before Katy gets here for the ritual tonight."

"What am I keeping an eye on?"

I used my chin to indicate the wooden box containing the mirror, which Carly had left on the work table. "That thing. I need your best ideas for containing it not just with spellwork, but physically. We're sitting on a nuke."

"Well, when you put it like that." He flitted. "You just *had* to end up with a vampire-sorcerer's spirit inside you, didn't you? It couldn't have been just the spirit of a funny retired car salesman with a ton of good stories."

"You know that's not how things work around here." I drank some water to help dilute the coffee in my otherwise empty stomach. "Thanks for making the casserole, Matthias. It looks amazing."

"Not amazing enough to eat, apparently," he rumbled, and gave me a look so identical to Sean's disapproving stare that I chuckled and almost snorted water out my nose.

Carly sat back on her heels and studied her work. "I think I'm happy with this."

I set my water on the table and stood outside the circle. "What kind of spellwork am I looking at?"

"A smaller, focused version of my umbrella spell." She rose and grimaced. Drawing spellwork on the floor made muscles ache. "The concept is to keep anyone from seeing what it is we have or what we're doing with it, even if someone is scrying or using their Second Sight to see." She held my gaze, then did the same with Malcolm and Matthias. "Above all, no matter what, this mirror and what it contains should not even be *glimpsed*."

I'd just called the damn thing a nuke, but now I was thinking it was something way worse and way more volatile than that. "Understood."

"Understood," Malcolm echoed. He looked every bit as unhappy as I felt.

"Shoes off," Carly said. "Wait to get in the circle until I tell you."

Matthias and I removed our shoes and socks and left them over by the table. Malcolm changed his ghost attire to have bare feet to make me smile.

"Come this way," Carly said.

We lined up at the spot in the spellwork where she wanted us with me in front. She dipped her fingertips into a small pot of fine powder that smelled like freshly burned wood and hints of something sweet. Matthias's nostrils flared and he inhaled deeply to get a good whiff.

"Bend your head," she said to me.

I did. She ran her fingertips over the crown of my head, on my hair, and murmured something. "Step over the spellwork," she said.

I did as she asked and moved to the far side of the circle. Carly repeated the process with Matthias, but he had to nearly crouch so she could reach the top of his head. She chuckled, then murmured the same incantation before telling him to step into the circle.

I wondered how she would dust Malcolm. As it turned out, despite not being able to see him, she passed her fingers directly over the top of his head the same way she'd done for us and then invited him into the circle.

"How *does* she do that?" Malcolm muttered when he reached my side. I shrugged.

Carly dusted her own head, then stepped over the spellwork. My skin tingled. Matthias let out a little growl but didn't move.

In the center of the circle, Carly had prepared an altar cloth with the box in the middle. Around it, on the cloth, she had placed seven candles—one each at the corners of the pentagram and one on the left and right sides of the box.

Ever the teacher, Carly explained the altar's arrangement to us. "The purple candle at the top of the pentagram is for spirit. The blue candle in the top right corner is for water. Red in the lower right is for fire. Green in the lower left is for earth, and at the top left the yellow candle is for air. On the right side of the cloth, the black candle will draw negative energy, and the white candle on the left brings in positive energy. I've brought two athames today, each cleansed by moonlight and spring water on the new moon. I will use the selenite athame for opening and closing the circle. The other is made from obsidian and will be for our protection."

While the selenite athame was clearly ceremonial, that obsidian edge looked perfectly capable of being used in both symbolic and very real ways.

"Sit around the altar, please," Carly said.

Matthias and I sat. Malcolm floated down and sat cross-legged across from me.

She took a beautiful athame from the altar and walked around the circle three times. "We call upon Archangel Michael to hide us from the people and spirits we are trying to see with your shield. Use you sword to cut down anyone or spirit that tries to see around your shield. Bathe us in your white light to protect us from anyone or spirit that might wish us harm. Let your light shine into the eyes of those who follow the creature contained in this mirror so that they might turn from their dark practices, or that they may at least run from your righteousness and might."

I kept my reaction off my face, but the invocation left me conflicted. By sharing some of Ronan's memories, I'd seen a being I believed to be the Archangel Michael. Those glimpses of bladed wings haunted me. And Michael had tortured and imprisoned Ronan for a century, sentenced him to a mortal life among humans, and carved the record of his trial into his skin, all in retribution for breaking angelic law, and all without caring how many lives Ronan had saved by drawing his celestial sword in battle.

To say I mistrusted Michael was an understatement. I didn't like people who hurt my friends, even if they happened to be archangels. Or maybe *especially* if they happened to be archangels who were supposed to be the good guys. Then again, righteous didn't necessarily mean good. I'd done a number of things in my life I considered righteous, but I couldn't really argue they'd been *good* by most people's definition.

I supposed for all our sakes I had to put my distrust aside if Carly wanted Michael to protect us and hide the mirror from those who might look for it, but I did it with serious misgivings and a lot of internal grumbling. Come to think of it, that was how I did most things these days.

All my misgivings and grumbling would have to wait, though. Right now, we had work to do.

CHAPTER

THIRTY

 making the candles flicker. I sensed a strange crackling overhead, but I couldn't see anything.

Carly caught my eye and winked. "Umbrella."

She knelt opposite me and set the athame on the cloth in front of her. "Let me explain the wards on the box," she said.

Malcolm and I listened and watched as she walked us through the spellwork on the outer box. Matthias paid close attention too, though he didn't have magic. Like me, he knew knowledge was a weapon—he'd said so explicitly just the other day. So of course he'd want every weapon in his arsenal.

When Carly opened the outer box, she revealed a smaller, flatter box inside. It too was covered with spellwork. All of the spells were for containment, nulling energy directed at the box, or hiding the contents of the box. She walked us through all those spells as well.

Inside that box lay the mirror, wrapped in linen with amulets tucked between the layers.

"The spelled linen keeps her from seeing anything if she surfaces

305

and hides the mirror from all eyes," Carly explained. "And the amulets are backup protection and magic to keep the mirror intact."

I had never seen anything with so many layers of protection and concealment. Not even my warded storage here in my workshop had that much. My tummy roiled.

Carefully, Carly unwrapped the linen, setting each amulet aside in the box, until she revealed the mirror itself. I braced myself to see Valas, but the glass was dark and empty.

I'd been too distracted earlier to really study it closely, but despite what it contained and being made of broken pieces of ancient stone, the mirror really was lovely. Carly had somehow fitted the stones together like a mosaic in a ring around the glass. She'd also inscribed spellwork on every square inch of the glass. Her spellwork was beautiful, like a spiderweb strung across the surface. I liked to think of the runes as fancy prison bars.

Beyond the glass, darkness yawned. The abyss reminded me of the mirror in Valas's chambers I'd used to travel to and from the Broken World, but that glass had felt miles deep—so much so that I experienced vertigo just standing near it. This darkness didn't feel as deep, but when it came to magic and portals, looks and impressions were absolutely deceiving.

"The stones are pieces of *lapis manalis*, as I already told Alice," Carly told us quietly. "You can research those on your own. The spellwork is the strongest, most powerful, and most deadly spell I know."

Both Matthias and I moved back.

"Where does that mirror go?" Malcolm asked, also in an undertone. Something about looking at that mirror in those boxes made speaking in hushed tones feel necessary, like we were afraid we'd wake something, or were in the presence of something that was fragile in a very bad way. "Is she trapped in the mirror itself, or is that like a pit on the other side of the glass? Or is the glass a portal to what I hope is a super-duper nasty place she can't get out of?"

I'd very much wondered that myself.

Carly's smile made the little hairs on the back of my neck prickle. "It's a pit, and it's a portal," she said. "Minerva forgive me, I'm rather proud of what I made to hold Valas."

I made a sound that was definitely not a gulp. "Yes?"

"You know of Tartarus?"

"The land of the super-damned?" Malcolm flitted. "The Hell that's below Hell? *That* Tartarus?"

"That one," Carly said, with more than a little smugness.

My eyebrows shot up. "You sent her to *Tartarus?*"

"I haven't sent her anywhere." She indicated the mirror. "On the other side of this glass is a pit. Its bottom is very fragile, like an eggshell. Any violence, any magic, any *anything* will break it. Beyond it lies Tartarus."

"Valas is in this pit," Matthias rumbled. "But if she attempts to escape it, or attack us, or do anything besides exist, she'll break the barrier. She'll cause her own fall."

"Not just fall," Carly said, with a smile like a cat who'd just cornered the tastiest of mice. "*Fall.*"

We all stared at her.

Malcolm was the first to regain his power of speech. "Damn, Carly. Nice. I didn't know you had it in you."

"I contain multitudes," she said. Her smile faded. "I was inspired by our situation involving the necromancer and their spirit, who they've called back across the abyss from the land of the damned to cause suffering here. I don't send anyone to those depths myself, but I can put the choice in her hands. She may exist for eternity in this pit if she behaves. If she doesn't..." She pointed down. "It's a long, long drop to the bottom."

"I don't know anyone who deserves this fate more than her," I said. "Except maybe this necromancer and their spirit."

"I'd certainly be happy to cast *that* spirit back to Tartarus." She reached for the linen wrapping.

Valas's face appeared in the glass.

I jumped. Magic coiled around my arms.

Malcolm flitted back so quickly he almost hit the circle Carly had drawn. He stopped himself just in time.

Matthias snarled. Golden shifter magic seared my skin. I heard bones crunching as his wolf tried to force him to shift. Somehow he maintained control and stayed human. But his fists clenched until his knuckles popped and turned white.

Carly didn't so much as twitch.

The last few times I'd seen Valas, she had been in various stages of nightmarish decay because of the sorcerer Miraç's curses. I'd nearly died trying to remove those curses when I returned from the Broken World. In fact, I thought I *had* gotten them all out of her, but either I'd missed some or he'd hidden additional spells designed to activate if someone managed to remove the first set. Miraç had been highly motivated to ensure Valas suffered greatly and for a long time before her final, true death.

Valas's long, black hair swirled around her narrow face, stirred by the powerful magic on the mirror's reverse side. Her dark eyes reflected the glowing symbols and glyphs of Carly's spellwork. She would forever appear to be in her mid-twenties, but no one would ever mistake those cold eyes for anything but ancient. In spirit form, she wore no clothing, and her pale skin stretched over her bones. I couldn't see anything of her body below her collarbone, but she appeared whole, intact, and as powerful and deadly as ever.

To see her beautiful and predatory again, as if Miraç's curses had never reduced her to scraps of flesh on bone, and as if Vlad hadn't staked her with her own arm, left me gutted. But because she would use my despair against me, I fought to hide my reaction.

Malcolm kept his distance near the circle's perimeter, but both Matthias and I stayed put once the initial shock of Valas's sudden appearance wore off. Meanwhile, Carly's streak of staying utterly unflappable in situations that caused the rest of us to become highly flapped continued.

"Caroline Althea Reese," Valas said, smiling to show her unusual upper and lower fangs. "High Priestess of the Emerald Star Coven. I must congratulate you on such a fine entrapment. In a thousand years, no one has caught me so well. I never thought anyone would have the skill or the gall."

"The long-lived always do tend to underestimate humans, regardless of our knowledge or skill." Carly's expression gave nothing away—no fear, no anger, nothing for Valas to feed on. "You understand your situation?"

"I do." Valas's smile hadn't waved. "It is a fine puzzle. I shall enjoy solving it."

She didn't say she'd kill us all if she escaped, and yet the implication was clear. A lesser vampire would have threatened, but Valas promised.

Her dark gaze went to Matthias. They locked eyes for a long time, as Valas tried to intimidate him with her unblinking stare and my new pack mate and his wolf beheld their longtime tormentor in her prison. I wanted to take his hand, but I got the sense he wanted to do this on his own.

"I have made few mistakes in all my long centuries," Valas said at last. "I see much, Matthias Albrecht, but I did not see your depths. I cannot help but wonder why."

"Your field of vision is wider than most." Matthias's voice was heavy with more emotions than I could identify. He probably felt about Valas much the same way as I felt talking to my grandfather. "But you aren't without blinders. You're so sure of yourself and what you know of the world that you miss what's right under your nose, such as Charles Vaughan's ambition."

I wondered why he'd chosen not to reply to her comment about his potential and strength and instead redirected the conversation toward Charles. To make her angry so she'd break the barrier and fall to Tartarus? Or because he wanted her to know what she thought of him no longer mattered? Maybe both.

If he'd wanted to get her to lash out, however, it didn't work. She simply smiled and moved her gaze to my face. "Ah, lovely Alice. My chariot."

As if my existence was merely for her use and she hadn't violated me in the worst, most despicable way.

Rage made me want to throttle her through the glass, but that wasn't possible—and like Moses she'd just use my anger against me. So I kept my expression blank and promised myself I'd get to punch the heavy bag later.

"What a divine experience, sharing your body and mind," Valas purred. "So many secrets you carry. And so many fears."

Maybe she knew all my secrets and fears—and maybe she didn't. She lied even more smoothly than I did. The fact she bragged about it made me wonder if it was true, or if this was just a bluff to mess with my head. Could go either way.

"Is this where you tell me you'll use them all against me when you escape?" I asked, feigning boredom. "How cliché."

"No. I am not as simple at that. I am fathomless." Her smile grew. "No one in all existence knows you as well as I, mage who calls herself Alice. Imagine what I know." She drew so close to the mirror's surface that I almost expected her breath to fog the glass. "Imagine what I will do with what I know, and what I know you are capable of."

Really, if she'd seen my memories, she knew I'd faced things in the Underworld and the torture of a sorcerer and I wasn't easy to intimidate, even by her. And she might think she knew me, but like Carly, I too contained multitudes. I wondered if that was a line of poetry. Carly had a habit of quoting poetry. I'd have to ask her.

"That knife cuts both ways, Sala Veli," I said, and gave her a smile of my own. "I know some of your secrets too now. But before I put you at the back of the closet under a bunch of shoe boxes, I have one question." I leaned over the mirror. "*Who's the daddy?*"

Her eyes went full black, and her mouth opened as if to scream. And then she vanished.

"Did the barrier break?" Matthias demanded. "Did she fall?"

"No." Carly drew the linen across the mirror's surface, placed an amulet on top of it, and continued the wrapping process. "She controlled herself enough to keep it from breaking, or the spellwork would have let us know she'd fallen." She glanced at me. "Did you intend for her to break it?"

"Not necessarily." I shrugged. "But I wouldn't have shed a tear if she had."

We watched as Carly re-wrapped the mirror and closed both boxes before blowing out the altar candles. She opened the circle, then placed the box on the work table.

Meanwhile, Malcolm had stayed quiet since Valas showed her face. Maybe seeing her spirit trapped had unsettled him more deeply than us. I'd have to talk to him about it when we were alone—that and why I was going to Merrum Manor this afternoon. That was going to be a tough conversation on multiple levels, but apparently this was the day for difficult talks.

"Where will you keep the box?" Carly asked me.

"Somewhere very secret and safe." I pointed to my cabinet with the strongest and deadliest black wards. "I'll keep it in there until we make a plan for its permanent location. My first thought is to put it in a safe, fill the safe with cement, and drop it dead center of the Bermuda Triangle."

"That is one option, but not one I'd recommend." She started to pack up her altar. "So, she had a child?"

"I think so. I had dreams that were actually Valas's memories. There was a son."

"Oh, dear." Carly heaved a sigh. "We'll have to deal with that then, won't we?"

"Probably," I admitted.

As she put her things in a bag, Carly asked, "Any questions before I leave?"

Malcolm cleared his throat. "Yeah, I have a question. *Caroline?*"

◦ ◦ ◦ ◦ ◦ ◦ ◦ ◦ ◦ ◦ ◦ ◦ ◦ ◦ ◦ ◦

ONCE WE SAW CARLY OFF, I discovered Sean had channeled his frustration into digging into the mysterious Disciples of the Sun Moses had claimed were responsible for attacking us on the highway. The briefing didn't take long.

"Not much out there but rumors," Sean told Malcolm and me over coffee at the kitchen island. Matthias had gone outside to walk around and work through some emotions on his own. "No website, no social media presence. They don't seem to have much interest in recruiting new members publicly. I reached out to several people I thought might have information and all they've heard is whispers. They're like shadows, this group. I'd give a lot to know how Moses dug this up—if he really did."

"I hate to say it," I said slowly, "but my gut says he was telling the truth about who he believes is responsible. Now, whether he's got reliable intel, I don't know."

"Well, we know they came for, uh, *her*," Malcolm said, gesturing at the basement. "For whatever reason, she didn't want to be taken by them—at least, not like that."

"What kind of group is this?" Sean wondered. "The name sounds like a cult, but we don't actually know."

"They're definitely occult practitioners," Malcolm said. "When Alice tracked the magic we got from Mr. Touchy, she saw occult magic and arcane rituals that looked ancient. And we saw that magic in action on the roadside."

Again, I closed my eyes and tried my damnedest to recall that face, but all I got was a vague shape. Only their fury was clear in my memory.

"I really don't know," I said finally, my shoulders drooping. "It might have been whoever leads the group if they sensed me nosing around. They made it clear I was trespassing in their lair. I definitely got booted out abruptly and with considerable *oomph*."

My skin prickled with Sean's angry reaction to my description of how the tracking spell ended. He loved me completely and he had my back no matter what, but neither he nor his wolf liked anything about the danger I faced daily as a mage PI—much less the unique and increased dangers of adversaries like necromancers, Dark Fae, and sorcerers.

"I'll keep looking for information," he said, and rubbed my back. "If my sources all come up dry, we can see about casting a wider net, but we need to be careful. Six people died last night trying to ambush us, but we don't know how many people are involved in this group. We can't assume they won't try again, or know how they'll react if they find out she's no longer—" he growled "—within you."

I can guess, I thought. Judging by their expressions, Sean and Malcolm could too. Once they regrouped from the ambush, these Disciples of the Sun might be really pissed off—and highly motivated to find Valas.

Malcolm wanted extra hazard pay. I probably deserved some too. Too bad I was the boss in this setup and the boss wasn't currently offering raises or bonuses, even if we had more danger circling than usual.

Best I could do was a reassuring smile for Malcolm and a couple of ibuprofen and another cup of coffee for me.

THIRTY-ONE

By driving like the proverbial werewolf out of hell, Matthias and I arrived at the south lot of Fields Park three minutes before the two-hour mark.

I'd let Matthias drive because I remained wary of possible after-effects from having Valas dragged out of me. If a day or two went by and I didn't have any dizziness, I'd call myself okay, but for now I trusted a highly trained and very pissed-off werewolf to be my chauffeur and backup.

He backed into a spot well away from the single camera that pointed at the gate into the city's largest park. From here, I could easily see the hill in the park where late one night almost a year ago I'd killed a half-demon serial killer who'd preyed on young women he picked up in bars. When I'd set myself up as the killer's next victim to trap him, I'd certainly had no idea how fateful that night would be.

"Alice?" Matthias asked. "Are you all right?"

Oops. I might have been staring into space a little too long. I tore my gaze away from the otherwise utterly unremarkable hill. "Yeah, sorry. I had a nasty case once that ended in this park. It brings back memories." I craned my neck with a grimace. I was still sore from... well, everything. I had no idea what vehicle Diaz would be driving to our clandestine meeting, other than I doubted it would be his official car.

"Do you think he'll have the knives?" Matthias asked. "That's a big ask. If he gets caught, that's his job, his pension, and probably prison time."

"I know. All I could do was ask. If he can't do it, or won't, then we'll have to work with what we have."

A dark blue SUV with tinted windows backed into the spot next to us. The window rolled down a few inches, enough for me to recognize Diaz in the driver's seat.

"I'll be back," I said to Matthias. "Honk if you see trouble."

He glanced at me. "I will do more than honk."

I slipped out my door, hurried around to the passenger side of Diaz's SUV, and hopped in.

Diaz gripped his steering wheel, staring straight ahead as I shut my door. No, he hadn't slept since I'd seen him last. Nor had he showered, though he'd changed his shirt and maybe splashed his face with water. He looked exactly like who he was: a homicide detective trying to catch a spree killer, whose partner and superiors probably thought these cases weren't connected at all, much less committed by something supernatural. A detective forced to demand a mage private investigator's help, only to be asked to commit a felony.

"I'm sorry," I said.

He finally looked at me. "For what?" he asked gruffly.

"Everything."

"Not your fault."

"I'm still sorry, though. Why did you want to meet?"

He scrubbed his bristly face. "I want to know what you think is going on. No bullshit, no evasiveness, no 'You'll be the first person I call.' I want to *know*."

If I were in his shoes, I'd do anything to know—to have some kind of facts to hang onto instead of guesses and evidence that made no sense.

"I'm almost certain it's a necromancer and a very evil spirit they are controlling," I said. "The spirit possesses a victim, who then commits the crimes like a kind of puppet, with no memory of what they've done. The necromancer may choose the target, or maybe the spirit does. That I'm not sure of yet. But it's deliberate and very controlled."

Diaz sat with that for well over a minute. "What evidence do you have?" he asked finally.

I explained why I thought a necromancer was involved. And then I showed him the still images from the two videos where the spirit could be seen. He stared at those for a long time, moving my phone to different angles and zooming in and out.

"How'd you get footage?" he asked as he handed me my phone back. "Ferguson said he'd done his damnedest to keep you from getting your hands on any."

"I'm going to choose to dodge *that* question," I said. "I know Ferguson really despises me for some reason, but even for him, that was a shitty move."

"I know. I told him not to do that again. Our time needs to be spent investigating, not on playground bullshit."

"I appreciate that. And one more thing about the spirit...I met him in person. Well, sort of. You remember when you saw me fall out of my SUV yesterday?"

"Yeah." He studied me. "It possessed you too?"

I waggled my hand. "Only kinda. It got partial control, created some unpleasant illusions, and threatened me. Then it disappeared. What you saw was the aftermath. I was a little freaked out."

"Understandable. But how do I know it's not possessing you right now?"

"Well, that's a fair question." I frowned. "I'm not sure what to tell you, other than it's *not* possessing me and I've recently been checked for possessions."

Now it was his turn to frown. "Is that a common problem for you?"

I snorted. "Usually no, but the last couple of days have been kinda wild."

"You're telling me."

We shared a sigh.

I thought the news about the necromancer might freak him out, but Diaz actually looked a little better now. No less haggard, but he had more energy, and his gaze seemed sharper instead of tired and dull.

"What do you plan to do about this necromancer?" he asked.

"I'm putting together a team to track them and trap the spirit. We're meeting tonight. That's what I meant when I said you'd be the first person I'd call, and I still mean that. The moment I have a name for you, I will tell you. But you can't go up against the necromancer yourself. You will die, and then it'll get worse."

"Worse than death, huh?" He processed that. "So, what do you intend to do? This person, whoever they are, has to face justice."

"And they will," I promised. "But their pet spirit has to be trapped first or it will be free to kill at will. Then I have to lock the strongest pair of spell cuffs I have on the necromancer before I drop them on the steps of the jail, along with all the evidence."

"That sounds like a goddamn mess."

"Yep. It's going to be. But that's the best-case scenario."

He reached behind me, to the floor behind the passenger seat, and put a gym bag in my lap along with a pair of latex gloves. "Glove up," he said.

I let out a breath and grabbed the gloves. Skin contact with the murder weapons themselves would have been worth its weight in gold, but that was simply not an option.

Diaz had risked everything to let me touch these evidence tubes, even with gloves on. That was even more pressure not to fail in our mission.

Inside the bag were four knives, each in its own clear evidence tube marked with an orange biohazard sticker because of the dried blood on the blades. Red SEALED EVIDENCE—DO NOT TAMPER tape secured the lids, initialed and dated by a crime scene tech. Each knife was secured in place with its point in a foam block at the bottom of the tube.

I immediately noticed two of the knives appeared identical. While the other two were the type of generic, mid-range tactical knives that would have caused Arkady to roll her eyes, the matching set were expensive daggers—the kind favored by occult practitioners.

"Those are from last night," Diaz said, indicating the daggers. "Two simultaneous and nearly identical murders six blocks apart. Each involved a couple. The male partner killed his female companion. Both couples were walking to their cars after leaving the same bar at closing time, but they walked basically in opposite directions. In both cases, bystanders intervened, but too late to save the female victims. Several good Samaritans got minor injuries trying to subdue the killers. The killers cut their own throats immediately after."

"There were witnesses?"

"About a dozen between both scenes." He ran his hands through his hair, making it stick out before he self-consciously smoothed it down. "The statements vary because not one of them was sober, but several of them reported the killers acted 'like robots.'" He put air quotes around the words. "I'm not sure any of them will remember saying that once they sobered up, so they'll be useless as witnesses at trial, but I'm inclined to believe them—especially given what you just told me."

I eyed the daggers, turning them this way and that, as I thought about Diaz's description of the crimes.

"This is another serious escalation," I said. "Yesterday afternoon it was a nurse at a busy, exclusive hospital with lots of security, killed by an endocrinologist in broad daylight. Last night, two couples in the bar district." I waved the daggers in their tubes. "Now four victims, matching weapons, and the murders happened at the same time?"

"As far as we can tell, if not the same second, the same minute."

I pondered that. "The necromancer wants us to know these crimes are connected *and* related to black magic. These knives are commonly used in occult rituals, while the other two are generic and practically untraceable. The only thing they could have done to make it more obvious was to leave a note."

"But how could they commit two murders at the same time?" Diaz demanded. He glared at the daggers. "If you're right and this is a necromancer and their 'pet spirit,' how did they kill two—no, four—people at the same time?"

I could think of only one possible explanation, and it meant I needed to text Carly right the hell now. "There might be two spirits," I said. "I've never known a necromancer to be able to control two at the same time, but I think that's what we're supposed to figure out from this evidence."

"Are you saying this asshole *wants* us to know he's got two murdering ghosts?"

"He *or* she," I corrected. "Yes, I do. In fact, I think they've gone to great lengths to let us know, with these matching daggers and murder-suicides. They're not trying to hide it. They're *flaunting* it."

"Son of an ever-loving *bitch*." His face turned bright red. "They're taunting us."

"Yeah, I think so."

"But *why?*"

He wasn't going to like my answer.

"If I had to guess," I said, "it's because they can."

The longer these knives were missing from the evidence room, the more chance their absence would be noticed.

So while Diaz processed his rage, I set my own anger aside and took a good, close look at the daggers, as if I could find the answers on the blades.

They appeared handmade, as most ritual blades tended to be.

That made them unique and easier to identify than the mass-produced knives used in the first two murders—if we found more made by the same hand. Most practitioners had a signature style as well as magic. I'd never encountered someone whose handmade implements weren't consistent in design, regardless of their purpose.

The difference between these daggers and Carly's lovely handmade athames, which weren't designed for bloodletting, much less killing, was jarring.

"I hear your wheels turning," Diaz said. "What are you seeing when you look at those knives? I know what my evidence techs say about them, but I need your thoughts."

Maybe Malcolm had a point about Diaz liking how my mind worked. I decided to take the compliment this time.

I told him my thoughts on the making of the daggers.

"These knives have characteristics that make them easily identifiable as black magic implements," I added. "Look at the wavy and irregularly shaped blade with twin razor-thin edges. The hilts have four spines facing away from the person wielding the knife, which could be dipped in poison."

"They weren't," Diaz interjected. "At least as far as our techs could tell."

"Good to know. Also, notice the three black crystals inlaid into the handles. Three is an important number in many forms of magical practice. What if anything these crystals hold, I'm not sure, and I don't know that I'll be able to tell without touching them. And I wouldn't do that anyway without serious precautions."

"This is all good information." He jerked his chin at the daggers. "Anything else?"

"Even in their tubes, they feel perfectly balanced in my hands, so their maker is meticulous and highly skilled." I demonstrated by balancing a tube on my index finger. "I'd say these daggers took months to make."

"That's patience, too," he mused. "Focus and discipline. Cold-blooded."

"Yep."

Since they had far more potential as clues than the mass-produced knives, I studied the daggers from all angles and in the sunlight. I wanted to wring every last drop of information from them I could from sight alone before I got to magic-related clues.

Then I saw it.

I squinted and held each of the tubes one at a time at an angle a few inches from my eyes. Was I seeing what I *thought* I was seeing?

Holy shit...maybe the answers *were* written on the blades.

"Diaz," I said slowly, "I see words on these blades."

"What? Something the techs missed?" He practically snatched one of the tubes from my hand. "Show me," he demanded.

"You won't be able to see it. It's written in magic. The trace has already faded to almost nothing. In a few hours, it will be gone."

With a curse, he handed it back. "What the hell does it say?"

"Big," I said.

"What the fuck does that mean? Big what?"

"This one says *Little*." I showed him the other blade. "*Big* and *Little*. Does that mean anything to you?"

"Not a damn thing." He pounded his fist on his steering wheel. "Not a goddamn thing. What kind of game is the necromancer playing with this?"

"I don't know. Those words have no significance in any practice I'm familiar with."

He held the tube at arm's length between his thumb and index finger. "What if they're, what do you call it, magic words?"

The situation was too grave for me to chuckle. "Invocation words," I corrected. "No, those would be terrible invocation words. The idea is to choose words to invoke spells that aren't commonly used. To invoke a spell requires intent as well as magic and the 'magic word,' but that doesn't mean spells can't be accidentally triggered. That's one of the reasons practitioners use Latin or other rarely spoken words as invocation words."

"Good to know." Diaz looked thoughtful. "Do you think the

necromancer made these daggers expressly for these murders, or adapt them for it?"

"Good question. I'm not sure if I can tell you that from the daggers themselves."

"Just trying to get a handle on this asshole's mentality. How long they've been planning this bullshit."

"I get that," I said. "Here's my two cents. Profile this necromancer as a serial killer with an extremely short cool-down period between crimes. They get off on power, and the ultimate form of power is control over life and death."

"That tracks."

"They also crave notoriety. They want their crimes talked about in headlines and hushed voices. They want the fear to be palpable. And now they've killed six people and the police department *still* claims the murders are unrelated. The police spokesperson denies there's supernatural involvement, even after what happened last night. If you know how this kind of person's mind works, you know what's about to happen if those denials continue."

"They'll have to up the ante again." He tried to drink from his take-out coffee cup, but it was empty. With a curse, he crumpled it and threw it into the back seat. "They'll have to make it so obvious and public the department can't deny it any longer. There might be a bloodbath."

"I'm afraid that's the next move. Unless..." I swallowed. "Okay, hear me out. What if someone leaked what we just figured out?"

"Let the public know a homicidal occult practitioner is killing random targets using equally random targets?" He looked horrified. "The city would panic."

"Which feeds the necromancer's ego," I pointed out. "Fear is what they want. Maybe it keeps them from killing again for a while."

His mouth twisted like he'd just bitten into something sour.

"Look, I'm not saying you should do it," I said. "It might be the worst idea I've ever had, and believe me, I've had some doozies. I understand what happens when people panic."

"Last year's anti-vampire riots. Cincinnati two years before that."

"Yes. But the mayor could order a curfew. The feds could get involved, like they did last year. Authorities could try to control the panic. Meanwhile, the necromancer basks in the fear, and my friends and I try to spring our trap while their guard is down."

He'd seemed better for a while, once he knew what was going on, but now Diaz looked worse than when I got into the vehicle. Malcolm would have said that was one of my many gifts.

"I'll think about it," Diaz grated. "Meantime, what are you going to do with those knives?"

"I've been handling them all while we've been sitting here." I held up the one that had apparently killed Madison Fernell. "This one has nothing on it. It's been too long since it was used. No inscriptions on it that I can see. The knife from the nurse's murder yesterday has some trace. The daggers from last night have the most. I'm going to try to draw the trace from them."

"Is that dangerous?"

"Not for you."

"What do I need to do?"

"Just stay where you are. You don't have to do anything."

As he watched, I trailed my fingertips back and forth along the length of the tube containing the doctor's murder weapon, gently pulling the magic on the handle toward me. Through the gloves and the tube, it felt like trying to draw nails to a weak magnet that was just a little too far away. It would work—it would just take time.

After nearly five minutes, I had it.

It was the spirit who'd licked my face yesterday; no doubt about that. And entwined with that faint trace was that of the necromancer. Both were too faded to be useful for tracking, but at least I had confirmation of who'd forced the doctor to use the knife. Only one spirit's trace, too, not two.

I repeated the process on the dagger marked *Big*. This trace was much fresher and cut my fingertips when I drew it from the dagger. Diaz grimaced at the sight of my sliced fingers. I sensed the necromancer again, plus the same spirit trace as the nurse's murder. It didn't feel any less revolting today than it did yesterday.

On the second dagger, however, I sensed the same necromancer, but a different spirit. And this one contained even more vileness and hate than the first. Another set of slices drew blood from my fingers.

As soon as I started bleeding, I let Diaz handle the tubes so I didn't get any blood on them. While he put them back in the bag and zipped it up, I wrapped my hand in a bandage I'd stuck in my pocket for exactly this purpose.

"Dangerous work you do," he said, returning the bag to the back seat.

"Yes, it is—and more often than you'd probably think."

"What did all that tell you?"

I let out a breath. "I sense one necromancer and two very malevolent spirits who must be acting under their control."

"You're sure?"

"One hundred percent."

"Okay." He tapped a zipped document holder on the floor at my feet. "Take that. Burn it when you're done. No one sees what's in there but you."

"Understood." I picked up the folder with my good hand. "I'll keep you in the loop. If you decide to engineer the leak, I'd appreciate a heads-up so I can ensure all my people are gathered before any kind of curfew goes into effect. Give me at least a couple hours to get organized."

"Roger that." He touched my arm. "Thank you, Ms. Worth. I don't know how all this will work out, but I want you to know I respect you."

"Back at you, Detective." I opened my door and hopped out with the document holder. "Stay safe."

"I fully intend to."

As I shut the door, I thought of the old saying about what paved the road to Hell.

I certainly hoped our collective good intentions would pave the road back to Hell tonight for those two spirits—and not for any of us.

THIRTY-TWO

By the time I made it back into the passenger seat of my SUV, Diaz had already headed for the lot's exit, leaving a spray of gravel behind him.

I honestly wasn't sure if he'd take my suggestion and leak the information about the necromancer or not. He had to weigh a lot of possible outcomes—and figure out how to do it without anyone knowing it was him. When all this mess was said and done, the man still needed and wanted his job.

Matthias's gaze went to my bandaged hand. "You're bleeding again."

"Yup." I sighed, stuck Diaz's document folder under my seat, and leaned back against the headrest. My fingers throbbed and tingled with residual magic. "Welcome to the reality of working as a mage PI. The phrase *blood, sweat, and tears* has never been more accurate."

"I've seen all those from you in the past twenty-four hours." He rested his massive hand on the gearshift but didn't use it. "You have a healing spell?"

Aargh. It was like having another Sean or Malcolm around. "Yes," I said, in a tone that was definitely not peevish.

Under his amber gaze, I unfastened a low-level spell from my bracelet and used it. This one took about thirty seconds and left me only mildly nauseated.

Once that was done and I stuck the used crystal in my pocket, he shifted into gear and drove toward the lot's exit. "You said you needed supplies for tonight's ritual," he said. "Where are we going now?"

Well, here we go, I thought. "Merrum Manor," I said aloud. "You know how to get there?"

"Yes." His tone couldn't have been more neutral, but shifter magic sizzled on my skin.

"We'll talk on the way," I said.

My promise did not appear to lessen his tension whatsoever.

The trip to Merrum Manor from Fields Park took more than a half-hour. As Matthias drove, I told him what I'd figured out while talking to Diaz. I also texted the information about the two spirits to Carly.

When I told Matthias I'd suggested Diaz leak the information about the necromancer, he turned thoughtful. "I think that's a sound strategy," he said finally. "It's a gamble, and no doubt the repercussions will be far-reaching, but I suspect you're right about the necromancer craving fear and attention. If they don't get it, they'll escalate sharply again, and with two spirits under their control, the consequences might be catastrophic."

"That was my thought. Diaz said he'd let me know what he decides and give us warning."

"Good." He flicked a glance at me. "And now, we're going to the residence of Moses Murphy for ritual supplies because...?"

"It's a complicated situation," I said. "And there's far more going on than I can tell you right now. But the short version is that I am going there to pick up some crystals containing spirits to use as sources of power during tonight's ritual."

If he was surprised or dismayed that I planned to use ghosts for their magic and power, he didn't let on. "Is this where you went for dinner a few nights ago?"

I suddenly had the feeling keeping anything from Matthias would prove exceedingly difficult—especially since I was unwilling to lie to him. "Yes."

"You asked me to go with you instead of Malcolm this time. Why?"

The tummy ache I'd had since the moment I'd asked Moses about getting these crystal intensified sharply. Not because of Matthias's question per se, but because of the weight on my shoulders.

Part of me had wanted to go to Merrum Manor without telling Malcolm what I planned to do, because if I failed to free Liam but he didn't know I'd tried, I wouldn't break his heart today. But I'd only considered it for about two seconds before I realized there was no way I could do this without telling him the truth.

When I'd pulled Malcolm aside to tell him my plan, his reaction had been hope, worry, anger, gratitude, fear, and back to hope again, all in about four seconds.

"I told you I'd try to get Liam back for you," I'd said as he flitted around the office. "I'm sorry it's taken so long. This is the first and best chance I've had."

Almost too overcome for words, he'd extracted a promise from me to keep Matthias and myself safe above all else, then retreated to the basement workshop to stay busy until we returned with either good news or bad.

"Alice?" Matthias prompted, bringing me back to the present. "If you can't tell me, I understand, but—"

"No, I'm going to tell you." I squared my shoulders. "You're with me on this mission today for two main reasons. First, you're intimidating as hell and I don't want anyone to fuck with us."

He gave me a quick smile. No doubt he knew I'd deliberately referenced his comment from the other morning about putting on bulk to dissuade others from messing with him. "And the second reason?" he asked.

I took a deep breath and told him about Liam.

Matthias's reaction to the story was utterly predictable: anger and resolve. "We'll get him back for Malcolm if it's at all possible," he stated, in the tone I'd come to realize signified a vow. "Short of endangering you, of course."

"I don't mind a bit of danger," I reminded him. "I live to play with certain kinds of fire, remember?"

"Moses Murphy is the kind of fire I would expect you to avoid, given you're not anything close to the simple mid-level mage you claim to be." He pondered that for a minute, then said, "This man is the danger to you that my wolf had sensed before."

He didn't phrase it as a question, but I answered anyway. "He and his organization are a huge threat to a lot of people. Our pack is no exception. At the moment, he and I have an agreement that keeps me and those around me in less immediate danger than we could be."

"But by no means safe."

"Not even remotely. It's a détente, and a precarious one." After a beat, I added, "Watch out in particular for two of Murphy's lieutenants, Nora Keegan and Carter Kade. If we cross paths with either of them, they're likely to try to goad one or both of us into a confrontation, though they go about it in very different ways. Just pretend you're a duck and let whatever they say roll right off your beak."

"I..." He cleared his throat. "I don't think that's quite the right metaphor."

I waved my hand. "Beside the point. Just don't let them get your hackles up. They're not worth it. They're the walking dead. Murphy will kill them both someday. It's only a matter of time."

When we pulled up to the outer gate, it rolled open for us to drive into the small courtyard between the gates. The wards had been opened for us to pass. Once we'd crossed the gate, a guard in uniform pointed for us to back into a spot next to a familiar black SUV. O'Neil stood at attention in front of it, waiting to take us to the manor.

"Go ahead," I said at Matthias's glance. "They wouldn't lower the wards on the second gate for anyone. We have to ride through in one of their vehicles."

"I do not like this." His manner and tone had switched abruptly to the cold formality he'd had while associated with the Court. I decided to call it Matthias's bodyguard mode.

"Me neither, but it's part of the deal." I put my hand on his where it rested on the gearshift and turned my head so no one could read my lips. "I will tell you this: none of these wards or walls will keep us in if it comes to that."

Matthias parked as directed and we got out. "Hello, Ms. Worth," O'Neil said, opening the front passenger door of her vehicle for me.

No fight over putting me in the back seat. I couldn't decide if that was a win for me or for Moses.

Matthias towered over O'Neil while she shut my door, standing just out of reach while still using his bulk to send the message of why he'd come with me. He climbed in behind me as O'Neil went around to the driver's seat. As soon as he shut his door, she pulled forward and turned the SUV to face the inner gate, which rolled open as the retractable barricades slid down into the ground.

The wards on the inner gate scraped across my skin like a dull-edged razor as we crossed. Matthias rumbled until we were through and on our way up the long driveway to the manor.

If Matthias hadn't liked riding in one of Moses's vehicles, he liked us pulling into the garage and the door rolling closed behind us even less, judging by the prickling of shifter magic. O'Neil kept one eye on him at all times as we got out and followed her into the manor.

Instead of leading us toward the east end of the house, where the dining room and conservatory were, O'Neil took us to the north wing and a small but well-warded workshop that seemed to be a shared space rather than single mage's work area. Most of the magic I sensed felt like traces of wards in various states of construction.

Maybe this workshop was a kind of classroom where mages honed their ward-building skills.

It didn't surprise me that Moses hadn't allowed us into his most secure workshop area, but it did worry me. Malcolm had reported Liam was in a crystal kept at the other end of the manor.

"Take your time," O'Neil said at the door to the workshop. "When you're ready to leave, press the button near the door."

"This door will not be locked when we are inside," Matthias rumbled. "No wards either."

"No lock, no wards," O'Neil assured us. "The button activates a notification that you want to leave. I'll ensure our path to the garage is clear and then open the door. My employer prefers your visit to be free from distractions and anything you might consider a potential threat."

I had no doubt she was parroting Moses's exact words there—to the point I almost heard what she said in his voice. Did Moses not want me seen visiting today? Or what was his real motive for almost sneaking me in and out? Damn it, did everything have to be a game with him?

"Sounds good," I said. I reached for the doorknob, only for Matthias to beat me to it and open the door. He looked inside, gave me a nod, and stepped over the threshold first.

When he was satisfied the room was safe, I entered. O'Neil shut the door quietly behind me.

The room had the standard features of a mage's workshop, from three concentric circle inlaid into the floor to work tables and cabinets—all made of wood, the kind of building material usually safest around magic—and no decorations. The only item on the wall was a control panel near the door that had the *Request Exit* button O'Neil had mentioned plus several others, including two large red and orange toggles for emergencies.

Working with magic wasn't all that different from working with explosives. One wrong move could do a lot of damage. My grandfather's cabal headquarters near Baltimore lost an entire wing when I was a teenager because of an accident involving dangerous magic and an idiot who opened a door to a workshop without ensuring the mage inside wasn't working on something volatile. A dozen people died in the explosion.

On the work tables were nearly two dozen crystals, laid out neatly in wooden saucers. My heart pounded.

"What do you want me to do?" Matthias asked. "Guard the door?"

"I think we're safe enough in here." I bit my lip. "Just stay next to me, okay?"

He didn't ask why. Maybe he didn't need to.

Please let Liam be in one of these, I thought. *Please let me bring him home to Malcolm.*

Nothing to do but look for him.

I wondered if Moses was watching. I didn't see any cameras, but I had to assume he was. So whether I found Liam or not, I couldn't let on that I had any mission here but what I'd told him.

With Matthias close by providing protection and comfort, I studied the crystals very slowly, one at a time. I held my hand over each to make sure it contained a spirit and not a trick or trap, and then I picked up the crystal and lowered my shields to get a clear sense of the amount of power and kind of magic of the spirit it contained.

The ghosts were aware in their crystals—aware of being used and reused for seemingly eons by Moses's mages for their power and energy. An endless cycle of regaining their power, then being drained for spellwork and magic almost to the point they'd cease to exist, and then another cycle of regeneration and depletion. Again and again and again, until they finally went wraith and could no longer be used and then a blood mage would discorporate them, allowing them to pass on to whatever waited for us beyond this realm of existence. It wasn't a fate I'd wish on my worst enemy—except maybe Moses himself.

I hated every moment of this terrible task. Each of these spirits was a person just like Malcolm. In fact, any one of these spirits could have *been* Malcolm if Moses had ever managed to trap him. That was a big reason I'd been so angry when Malcolm snuck around the manor a few nights ago while I talked with Moses.

Even worse, the sorcerer Miraç had used Malcolm for power in this same way, and had used my stolen magic and memories too. The trauma of that had given us nightmares and made this kind of work doubly unpleasant.

I couldn't help my harsh breaths or the tears that stung my eyes and threatened to spill down my cheeks. I held them back because Moses was watching and probably listening too, and because my tears would upset Matthias's wolf. I'd save them for when I was alone later with Sean.

I wanted to take all the ghosts with me and release them to freedom, or discorporate them so they could have peace, but I doubted Moses would let me take all twenty. He might want me to stay alive, but I'd have a hard time convincing him I needed the combined power of twenty spirits. Every one of the crystals I'd handled so far contained a strong mage ghost, each worth almost as much as a diamond the same size.

Twenty ghosts. Twenty souls in torment. Twenty more reasons to hate Moses and the mages who worked for him by choice.

In the fifteenth crystal, I found Liam.

I recognized his magic immediately, since I'd used some of it once to help Malcolm. His crystal buzzed on my palm, surprisingly strong—more so than most of the spirits I'd sensed so far. Probably because before Moses captured him he'd been tethered to the nexus of power near the manor and had resided within its walls for a hundred years.

I'd feared finding him reduced to erratic wisps and surges of power, meaning he'd gone wraith, but instead he felt strong and steady. I had no way to know for certain until I let him out, but I had more hope now than ever before.

My heart leapt into my throat, but I made sure not to react except to nod as if I thought his power and magic would work with mine and then set the crystal aside with the others I planned to take.

When I finished, I had chosen twelve crystals. A little more than half. Trying to walk out with all of them wouldn't fly, but twelve seemed reasonable. That was two circles of six. The numbers made sense for both mage and witch rituals.

I transferred the crystals to the small zippered pocket inside my cross-body bag. Walking out of this room and leaving the other eight behind hurt my heart, but I had done what I could do for the twelve in my bag. I'd have to live with that.

Matthias put his hand on my upper back. "Are you all right?"

"Yes." I made sure my voice was strong, even while my stomach churned. We weren't out of this yet. I wouldn't even be able to take a deep breath until we were in my SUV and well away from the manor.

At the door, Matthias pushed the button to request departure.

"One moment, please," O'Neil said through the intercom.

We waited. My heartbeat pounded in my ears.

The door swung open about a minute later. "We're cleared to leave," O'Neil said, stepping aside.

Matthias went into the hallway first, then motioned me to follow.

The walk back to the garage entrance seemed to take four times longer than the walk in. I watched O'Neil's body language for any indication that something might be up—that Moses planned to spring a trap—but saw nothing to make me suspicious. Still, I couldn't shake the feeling it had been too easy.

Don't jinx yourself, I scolded myself. *Nothing about this has been "easy." You're just used to disaster striking. Maybe this time it'll be different.*

We came around the last corner with O'Neil in front and Matthias at my back.

Carter Kade, Moses's former head lieutenant, stood in the hallway between us and the door to the garage. So much for a clear passage.

Tall, blond, and muscular, he seemed to have put on even more bulk since I'd last laid eyes on him. He'd held Arkady prisoner as part of Moses's ploy to get me to meet with him in person at a neutral club called Luciano's. Arkady had knocked him out cold with one punch in retaliation for groping her. That memory at least was pleasant, unlike all the rest of my encounters with Kade. Several months ago, he'd shot Ben full of silver bullets, nearly killing him. I'd managed to save Ben's life, but not by much.

Kade had no idea I was really Ava Murphy. Back in Baltimore, for nearly ten years, my torture sessions had aroused him. He couldn't touch me then because I was off-limits, but he never hid how much he enjoyed watching me scream and bleed, even in front of Moses. Kade's enjoyment of torturing women in particular had only grown in the interim, from what I'd heard. His sadism and loyalty had made him Moses's favorite lieutenant until Nora Keegan came along.

He'd expressed interest in me every time we'd crossed paths, but I felt certain Moses had told him I wasn't to be touched. Judging by the way he looked me over, though, his interest hadn't waned.

O'Neil's expression indicated she liked his appearance in the hallway even less than I did. Interesting. She'd stopped us at least fifteen feet from him. She probably knew his reputation as well as I did.

"This path was cleared on Mr. Murphy's orders," she said. She carefully kept her tone neutral and not confrontational, since Kade held a much higher rank, but I detected a note of suspicion.

"Did anyone ask you a question?" Kade's cold gaze moved from me to O'Neil in a clear attempt to stare her down. "Senior staff are exempt from those orders."

To her credit, O'Neil kept her chin up and spine straight. "You might not have seen the code issued, sir, but this clear passage is designated Level One. I apologize, but I have to ask you to vacate this hallway until we've passed through."

Kade's expression darkened and he took a step forward. Behind me, Matthias growled low. Shifter magic prickled on my skin.

"You," Kade spat, "don't ask me to vacate anything, O'Neil. Do you want another demotion? Or would you like a position *under me?*"

O'Neil stood her ground, but she flinched at the clear implication. "No, sir, I wouldn't want a demotion," she said, carefully sidestepping his threat to have her transferred to his command. "But I am under strict orders from Mr. Murphy to escort these guests from the manor without allowing anyone to have contact with them."

She isn't your ally or your friend, I told myself. *What happens to her isn't your problem.* Except I wasn't wired to be that cold. I never had been, even when necessity forced me to pretend.

By standing up to Kade, O'Neil had walked into a minefield. So I tossed a grenade straight at him.

"We don't have time for this," I said, my voice flat. "We need to leave. You don't like being told what hallway to be in, take it up with your boss. O'Neil is following *his* orders."

"You've always got a smart mouth, Alice." Kade advanced on me, his face twisted in the mean look I recognized because I'd seen it back in Baltimore. It meant he was about to hurt someone. "Every time I see you, you've got something to say. You feel big and brave when you've got your pet wolves with you. But someday you'll be by yourself, little girl. And then I'll put something in your mouth that'll shut you up."

At that threat, I expected Matthias to step forward or say something, but he didn't. I'd warned him about Kade and he'd listened to the warning. That didn't mean he wouldn't reduce Kade's number of attached limbs to zero given the opportunity. He'd have to wait his turn, though. Sean had already called dibs if I didn't kill Kade first.

"We're on a schedule," I said, injecting both boredom and impatience into my tone. "We're here on business and we don't have time for interference, which is probably why this passage was *supposed to be* cleared. So scat."

Kade's eyes narrowed as if he was trying to figure out why I wasn't scared of him or his threats. Everyone else always was, except probably Nora. My defiance had to be both infuriating and puzzling.

Maybe this confrontation had silver lining. If he started thinking too much, maybe Moses would let me kill him.

Hmm. Maybe Malcolm was right and I *did* like to play with fire.

Finally, Kade smiled in a way that made me itch between my shoulder blades, put his back to the wall, and made a grand sweeping gesture. "Then by all means, don't let me keep you."

He clearly had no intention of obeying the directive to depart, so O'Neil had to decide whether to ask him again to leave the hallway or walk us past him. After a beat, she chose the latter and led us on toward the garage.

Kade's eyes stayed locked on me as we approached. I didn't really fear that he'd figure out I was Ava, but he definitely wanted to know what kind of deal Moses and I had that allowed me apparent *carte blanche* to come and go from the manor with O'Neil as my designated bodyguard. I doubted many others had that privilege.

I might think he couldn't lay a finger on me, but my instincts told me to be cautious. Matthias also kept a wary eye on him until we'd reached the garage door.

In the end, Kade stayed where he was with his back to the wall until we'd gone out to the garage and O'Neil shut the door behind us. She let out a breath loudly enough for me to hear it.

Now that the immediate danger was past, I didn't understand what had just happened. Kade had openly defied Moses's order to clear the hallway. Why? To see me? To try to goad one of us into an altercation? To see how O'Neil would react? Were we being tested somehow? And if so, why, and by whom?

Matthias had his Vamp Court poker face on, but I could tell he had the same questions.

Our drive from the manor to the gate was ominously silent. O'Neil took us through the inner gate into the courtyard and backed in next to my SUV.

When we got out of the vehicle, I asked O'Neil, "What was that about?"

"I don't know, Ms. Worth," she said, her expression grim. She started to say something else, then changed her mind.

I wondered if she was worried about what might happen when she returned to the manor, if Kade might try to harm her. I wondered too, but there wasn't much I could do about it either way. She worked for Moses. Her life was in his hands. I'd managed to get him to assign her as my bodyguard when he became dissatisfied with her performance as one of his personal guards, but ultimately her fate wasn't in my control. And like it or not—and I *didn't*—what Moses had said the other night was still true: I couldn't trust her.

Blast it.

This whole thing felt like some kind of manipulation, but I didn't know what kind or why it had happened—at least not yet.

As soon as Matthias and I had settled into my SUV and he'd started the engine, the outer gate rolled open. We pulled through the gate and onto the road, leaving O'Neil standing next to her vehicle. The gate began rolling closed again the moment our rear bumper cleared the opening.

A mile later, with Merrum Manor finally out of sight, I let out a sigh of relief and dropped my bag on the floor at my feet. "We made it."

Matthias shook his head. "I'll agree with you when we're back at the house and you're behind your wards."

"Fair enough." I bent to look in my bag for sunglasses and noticed a large brown envelope tucked in next to the document folder that Diaz had given me.

"Stop the car," I said.

Matthias immediately hit the brakes and pulled to the shoulder. "What is it?"

I pointed to the envelope. "That was *not* there when we arrived at the manor."

With a snarl, he picked up the envelope and gave it a deep sniff. "No scent," he said, his voice half growl. "I don't smell anyone unfamiliar in this vehicle either. Whoever got in and left this, they used some kind of spells to mask their scent." He handled the envelope carefully. "It feels like paper."

The last envelope full of paper I'd gotten was the Court indictments.

Gingerly, I took the envelope from Matthias. By all appearances, it was a generic, mass-produced document envelope with a self-adhesive flap—no fancy wax seal, nothing written on the outside. When I held it up to the sunlight, I saw the shadow of paper inside. Maybe about thirty pages or so. What the hell?

I tore it open, peeked inside, and sucked in a breath.

"What is it?" Matthias demanded.

I didn't know what to say.

Sean had asked me the other night if I trusted Matthias, and I did. But in this moment I truly didn't know how he might react to what I held in my hand. He wouldn't hurt me—of that I was sure—but other than that, this could go a lot of different ways.

Not to mention, how the hell was I supposed to explain how this item had ended up in our vehicle without lying or divulging the real nature of my relationship to Moses?

I still suspected the encounter with Kade was some kind of test, and now I thought this might be another. I didn't like games and tests were juvenile. But I'd talk to Moses about that later. For now, I had a highly agitated beta werewolf to deal with.

"Matthias," I said carefully. "We'll talk about what's in this envelope when we get back to the house. Until then, I need you to take my word that it's not anything dangerous. Let's just drive."

"That is not very reassuring." His eyes glowed bright amber. "Someone broke into this vehicle without our knowledge and left an item you're worried about describing to me."

"I know." I touched his arm. "Please trust me and drive us home. Malcolm needs to know if Liam is all right, and then you and I will talk about what's in the envelope, I promise."

Reluctantly, he eased back onto the road and resumed the drive, but his tension blazed on my skin. I couldn't blame him. And I cared about him deeply—enough to feel sick that he was agitated. But I also knew we needed to be at home with Sean when I told him what I had, because he'd need his alpha and our counsel.

In fact, he might need more than that.

I sent a quick text message to Arkady asking if she could come to the house right away.

Her reply came back almost instantly. *RKD: I'm about done with this invoice and report for the insurance fraud client. One hour?*

Me: Perfect.

RKD: Give me a clue what this is about so I know what weapons to bring.

After a beat, I responded. *Me: I need your brain and your ability to reason with Matthias.*

RKD: Oh boy. I'll bring my brain. No promises.

I also texted Sean to let him know what I'd gotten from Moses and that I'd asked Arkady to come over for the discussion with Matthias. He said he was in a video meeting with a client and after that one with Maclin Security staff but he'd be done in about an hour.

I thought about angrily texting Moses, but changed my mind. This needed to be a phone call, or better yet, a face-to-face conversation. So I stuck my phone in the cupholder and drank some lukewarm coffee instead.

Matthias growled as he drove.

Damn it, Moses, I thought, scowling out the window. *What the hell are you up to?*

THIRTY-THREE

THE MOMENT WE GOT INSIDE THE HOUSE, MALCOLM ZIPPED UP THROUGH THE floor from the basement to hover right in front of me. "Do you have him?"

I held up the crystal I believed contained Liam. "I have him. He feels strong."

Malcolm's expression made my heart ache. If Liam was still strong, he had a good chance of escaping from the crystal intact and thinking clearly. He'd likely emerge profoundly traumatized, though. The odds of him being the Liam we had known before were slim to none. Malcolm knew that better than anyone.

"What do you want me to do?" I asked. "We have options..."

"No." He shook his head. "We need to release him, and then he gets to decide what he wants. We don't have the right to make any choices for him."

"Fair enough." I turned to Matthias and met his bright amber gaze. "Arkady should be here in about forty-five minutes. That gives me enough time to help Liam. Are you all right in the meantime?"

"Not particularly." He flexed his hands. His joints popped. "Give me a project."

I'd been giving this some thought on the way home as well, in between grumbling inwardly about Moses's games and wondering if Diaz was going to leak the information about the necromancer.

"Research the process of becoming a licensed private investigator in California," I said. "And prepare a report for you and I to discuss later."

Matthias tilted his head. "I will." He sounded thoughtful. Not exactly jumping up and down with excitement at the prospect of a career change, but definitely intrigued. I'd take it.

He headed upstairs to get his laptop. Meanwhile, I heard Sean in the office hosting another video meeting with Maclin Security staff. He'd started working from home more and more and doing installations and personal security less. He'd always enjoyed the field work far more than paperwork and running meetings, which were more his business partner's forte. All the threats around us must make him feel as if he needed to be close to home. If it didn't bother him, it shouldn't bother me, but it did.

Malcolm zipped back and forth between me and the basement door. "Alice," he prodded.

"Sorry. Got lost in thought." I grabbed a bottle of water from the kitchen and we went downstairs.

In the workshop, I created a strong ward in the largest circle. We didn't know what Liam's condition would be when I released him, so I wanted to give him plenty of space, in addition to a shield that would protect him if one of Moses's mages had bound him. My plan was to create the impression Liam and the other ghosts had discorporated during tonight's ritual and then they would be free.

While I finished drawing the spellwork, Malcolm floated over to look at Liam's crystal where I'd left it in a little wooden bowl on the table. "I can feel him," he said, his voice quiet. "I'd almost forgotten how he feels to me. Like being home."

I joined him by the table to put down my chalk and take off my boots and socks. "I'm sorry it's taken so long."

"Don't you dare apologize." His expression turned fierce. "You risked everything to do this for Liam and me. As far as I'm concerned, you never have to apologize for anything ever again."

I raised my eyebrows.

"Okay, maybe not ever again," he amended. "But, like, for the rest of today you get a pass." He flitted. "This feels like a first date but a million times worse. I'm so nervous."

"Me too." I brushed his ghostly hand with my fingertips. "Are you ready?"

"Yes." He made a face. "No, but yes."

"I get that." I took Liam's crystal and a second one charged with energy from my house wards that would be his new anchor to the middle of the circle. I set the anchor in the spellwork I'd drawn and rose. "At the very least, he's going to be disoriented when I let him out. First priority is to give him time to get his bearings and calm down. Then we'll go from there."

"Okay." He squared his shoulders. "Ready, for real."

The ward I raised around us would both protect and contain Liam in case he came out panicked and tried to flee on instinct. The crystal buzzed and pulsed on my palm, as if the ghost it contained sensed something was going on. Maybe he felt my magic and the wards around us. He might even have recognized them.

I spooled earth magic and let it roll through the crystal in my palm, hoping it would reach him like a kind of warning of what I was about to do. I didn't have a release word for Liam like I did for Malcolm and his lockdown crystal, so I'd have to break the binding spell that held Liam inside.

The crystal buzzed three times. Was that a signal that he sensed me? I hoped so.

I closed my eyes, took a deep breath, and broke the binding spell with a single blow of blood and earth magic combined.

With a shout, Henry Liam Ashe appeared in front of me, his eyes wild with fear and anger.

I knew from official records that Liam died of influenza at age twenty in 1910 while working at the brothel once housed in the manor my grandfather now owned. He looked the same as the last time I'd seen him: curly red hair and green eyes, wearing a shirt, vest, trousers, and cap, per the fashion of his day.

As I'd expected, he flitted away from me instantly and hit the barrier of the ward, ricocheted back and forth in the circle a few times, and then flitted around us in a whirlwind of ghostly panic.

"Liam," Malcolm said, his voice calm and gentle, with none of the conflicting feelings I sensed through our binding. "Liam, I'm here. You're free. I'm here."

Liam came to a stop about six feet away from Malcolm. They stared at each other for a long time as a dozen emotions flashed across both their faces.

"Malcolm?" Liam asked finally. "How…? When…?" He flitted several times and looked down at himself, as if searching for the spell that had tethered him to his crystal. "I'm not bound anymore?"

"No." Cautiously, Malcolm floated closer. "Alice rescued you from the mages who captured you. You're free now. You're safe."

"This is some kind of trick." Liam backed away, his gaze flicking back and forth between Malcolm's face and mine. "It's a trick, isn't it?"

"It's not a trick, I promise." Malcolm held out his hand. "I'm here. You're really here."

"Where am I?"

"This is Alice's new workshop. You remember that cute were-wolf, Sean? He and Alice bought a house together. Feel the magic around you. Nobody can fake Alice's weird magic and my wards."

I scowled. My magic was not *weird*.

Slowly, Liam floated over to Malcolm and touched his outstretched hand. "How long has it been?" he asked, his voice rough.

"A few months." Malcolm laced his fingers through Liam's. That gave me a little pang because I couldn't hold either of their hands that way. "I'm so sorry. We came as soon as we could."

"It's all right," Liam said, though it wasn't and we all knew it.

Now that he was free and calm, I wanted to give them privacy and space. "Liam, that crystal is powerful enough to serve as an anchor for you so you won't need to return to the manor ever again," I said as he and Malcolm continued to look at each other. "When you're ready, I'll do the binding spell for you. You're one hundred percent safe inside this ward in the meantime."

He nodded and forced a brief smile. "Thank you for saving me, Miss Alice."

I left them murmuring to each other and went upstairs. I found Matthias and Arkady in the living room, each working on their laptops at opposite ends of the couch. Arkady had her giant water bottle next to her and Matthias had a cup of coffee. The silence felt... almost comfortable.

"You got here fast," I said to Arkady as I went to the kitchen to fill my own coffee mug. "What happened to an hour?"

"I decided I could write up the report here just as well as I could at the office." She glanced up as I settled into a chair with Diaz's zipped document holder and the mysterious envelope that had shown up in my SUV. "What you got there, business partner?"

"One's confidential. The other, I'll let you know when you're done writing that report so we can get paid."

She toyed with the hilt of one of her knives. "You sure you want to keep me waiting?"

I pointed. "Type."

She harrumphed and turned to Matthias. "You believe this shit?"

He kept his eyes on his laptop screen. "I am not involved in this disagreement."

"Chicken. See if I back you next time." She went back to typing.

I took a drink of coffee, set my mug on the side table, and unzipped the document holder. "Oh," I said involuntarily.

"What?" Matthias started to put his laptop aside.

"It's okay. Sorry." I cleared my throat. "Extremely confidentially —as in, this does not go beyond this room—Diaz gave me copies of all the autopsy reports. He put a full-color eight-by-ten photo of Madison Fernell at the murder scene on top."

"Asshole," Arkady muttered. "He might have given you a heads-up on what was in the folder."

I could only speculate as to why he hadn't, and why he'd deliberately left a very graphic photo as the first thing I'd see. Possibly he'd wanted to jolt me with the image. Maybe that didn't say anything good about him, or maybe he'd wanted to give me a visceral reminder of what was at stake if we didn't succeed tonight. I didn't hold it against him. I wouldn't have made it through the autopsy of one of these victims, much less six.

The office door opened and Sean emerged, empty mug in hand. He noted Arkady and Matthias working on their laptops, gave me a satisfied look, and bent to kiss the top of my head before he saw the document holder and its contents in my lap.

"Oh, babe," he said, his voice and expression grim.

"Yeah." I took his hand because his touch gave me strength. "Are you done with your meetings?"

"Almost. I need a refill and about ten minutes, and then we can all talk." He squeezed my hand. "How's Malcolm?"

"Overwhelmed." I managed a smile. "He and Liam are down-stairs. I can't imagine how they both feel right now. It's going to take a long time to work through it all."

"For sure." He headed for the kitchen and the nearly empty coffee pot. "Just enough for one cup," he said as he filled his mug. "At the rate we drink coffee around here these days, we need a full-time barista."

"Ooh, a promotion for our part-time barista," I said with a wink at Matthias. He grumbled under his breath, but he seemed to take my teasing in stride.

For the next ten minutes or so, I went through the autopsy reports and photos and took notes on a notepad I kept on the side table. In particular, I looked for any clues to the spirits' or necromancer's identities, similarities in wound patterns, and anything that might fall in the category of the killers' signatures.

Profiling the victims didn't give me much to work with. Madison, the nurse, and the two young women killed last night had little in common in terms of physical appearance. The nurse was forty-one, while Madison and the two most recent victims were in their twenties. Two of the victims were brunette, one was blonde, and the fourth had red hair. Different body types, different heights, different ages. Three of the four victims were in or near bar districts when they died, but I wasn't sure if that was significant or not. I still believed the necromancer targeted the nurse at the private hospital to show no one was safe.

The male victims who'd died by their own hand, though not by their own choice, were also very different: a short man with dark hair and a tall man with blond hair. I felt reasonably certain the victims weren't chosen because of their appearance. I did, however, think women were the primary target and the men an afterthought.

The alleged suicides also felt like an escalation as well as a significant shift in *modus operandi*. With the first five known crimes, the necromancer wanted to enjoy forcing someone to commit a violent attack or murder and then face the legal, psychological, and personal consequences. By having the men kill themselves last night, though, the necromancer had apparently switched gears in terms of what kind of suffering they wanted to cause. Now the men's families and friends would bear the brunt of the emotional impact after these alleged murder-suicides.

If the necromancer chose the targets and controlled the spirits, which was my theory, women were the primary targets. That gave me some insight into the necromancer's motivations. The spirit who'd appeared to me had seemed gleeful about killing, and I'd gotten a decidedly sadistic *and* misogynistic feeling from what he'd said to me and that disgusting spectral lick of my face. A general hatred of women seemed to be a factor in the murders.

The choice of weapons also fit. Stabbing was up close and personal. Visceral. Bloody. Assertive and dominant. The slice and stab of a blade was a primal act of violence and penetration into unwilling flesh. It wasn't enough to me to say for certain I believed the necromancer to be a man, but statistically the vast majority of murderers were male, and the crimes had a distinctly misogynistic feel.

The autopsy reports and photos showed just how frenzied the killings had been. Each woman had more than thirty stab wounds. Madison had the most, at fifty-four, probably because her killer had longer to inflict wounds before being interrupted. The hardest pictures to see were those of the victims' hands and arms showing the injuries they received while trying to fend off their killers. They'd all fought so hard, but to no avail. According to the medical examiner, Madison had wounds that indicated the blade of the knife had gone right through the palm of her hand and into her forehead.

In the end, my review of the reports and photos accomplished a couple of things, but the price was terrible nausea and white-hot rage combined with sadness. I now had more insight into the perpetrators' mindset, M.O., and level of sadism, and a strong sense that hatred of women lurked at the root of these crimes, which was something I might be able to use later. I also had an all-consuming desire to send these spirits back to Hell where they belonged and have the necromancer cold and dead at my feet—preferably in pieces so their corpse could be torn apart by carrion birds.

The only way to exonerate Oliver and the other supposed killers was to turn the necromancer over to Diaz and the D.A. for persecution, but I didn't want the necromancer alive in prison, even if it was the black hole of the federal ultra-max supe prison in Colorado Springs.

I thought of the photos I'd just seen, and I envisioned doing monstrous things to this necromancer. And not only could I envision it, but I knew I was capable of carrying it out.

What did that mean? If *monster* was what you did, not who you were, did that mean I really was a monster, despite all my denials?

"Alice."

I looked up. Sean stood in front of my chair, his eyes golden. I hadn't heard him come out of the office or noticed him approach. Behind him, on the couch, Matthias watched me too. Even Arkady had closed her laptop to eye me. Apparently I'd been radiating fury and grief for a while.

"Well, that sucked to look at." I closed the document holder and set it aside with a sigh.

"Alice," Sean said again. He crouched in front of my chair and took my hands. "You didn't need to look through every page yourself. We could have helped."

I started to say Diaz had given me the file in confidence, but I didn't bother because that would have been the most transparent bullshit excuse. They all knew I'd done it because I didn't want them to have to see what I'd seen and read what I'd read.

"I fell on that grenade," I admitted, alluding to Sean's long-ago accusation that I did that continuously without considering that I didn't have to. "I had to know it all—all the gory details. I want to know who we're up against, what makes them tick."

"We all do." Arkady put her laptop aside, leaned forward, and rested her elbows on her thighs. "You're not the only person here who can 'read' crime scenes, you know. I was PsyOps. Matthias here can analyze scenes with the best of 'em. Don't be an asshole and keep all the bad shit to yourself. Maybe we have ideas and insights too, you know."

"That's a fair point." I sighed. "I'm still getting the hang of this team thing."

"You're getting better." Sean squeezed my hands and rose. "What did you learn?"

I gave them a rundown of my notes and thoughts.

"I didn't get anything from the reports that will make it easier to track down the necromancer per se," I finished as they thought about what I'd revealed. "But insight into how a perpetrator's mind works is an advantage. If nothing else, when we face them, I know what buttons to push."

"We may need every advantage we can get." Sean held out his hand. "Can I have the other envelope, please?"

I handed it over. Matthias shut his laptop and put it on the coffee table, his gaze fixed on the envelope. Arkady scooted to the edge of her seat.

Sean slid the stack of papers out to skim through them and confirm what I'd told him about the envelope's contents.

"We have no reason to think this isn't what it seems to be?" he asked me, glancing up from the page.

"No reason," I said. I hadn't spoken to Moses yet, but my gut told me this was the real deal. "I think it's exactly what it looks like."

"I'll get right to the point, then. Matthias has waited enough." Sean met and held Matthias's gaze. "We've come into possession of what appears to be a copy of your contract with the Vampire Court."

Arkady blinked twice. As far as I could recall, that was only the second time since we'd met that I'd seen her appear startled. She and Carly were the most stoic people I knew, though for much different reasons.

Slowly, Matthias rose. He'd so steadfastly and even angrily defended his NDA about the contents of the contract and all but asked us not to try to get hold of it or find out what it said, and now we had the real thing in hand. No doubt he was keenly aware of our concern about how he'd react.

Arkady stood too and moved to the side so she could watch all of us. Clearly she wondered if Matthias would be angry.

To my surprise, Matthias turned his glowing gaze on me. "Alice, did you go into debt with Moses Murphy to obtain this document?"

Instead of angry, he sounded and appeared very, very worried— almost to the point of looking sick.

"No, I didn't," I said, my voice firm. "There's a note on the document telling me I'm expected to create some wards at a business

Murphy owns in the city in return for the copy of your contract. And I didn't ask for him to get it for us; he took the initiative."

Matthias absorbed that. "But how did Murphy know you wanted a copy of the contract? And why would he give it to you in exchange for making wards? He has his own mages for that kind of work."

"I'm kind of wondering that myself." Arkady had flushed in anger. I'd never seen that reaction from her. Usually her fury was cold, not hot. "What the hell's going on here, Alice? I knew you had dealings with Moses Murphy, but this is a whole other level. That contract should not have been possible for him to get. Northbourne is locked down tighter than an ant's asshole. So that packet of paper there cost him a goddamn *fortune*. No way in hell do you pay for that with wards." She took a step toward me, her expression darkening. "No way in hell does Murphy risk making an enemy of Charles Vaughan and the Vampire Court for *wards*."

Before I had a chance to reply, Malcolm drifted up through the floor from the basement. He'd either felt Matthias's shifter magic sizzling or heard the tone of our voices change.

He scanned our faces. "Uh, guys? What's going on?"

"Alice has some explaining to do," Arkady told him, her flinty gaze never leaving my face. "Something about Moses Murphy."

Malcolm started to reply to her, then apparently changed his mind. *You gotta tell them*, he mouthed to me before disappearing back into the basement.

Torn about what to do, I looked at Sean.

"Your secrets are safe with them," he said. "And they're in no more danger if they know versus if they don't. I think you know that."

I *did* know. If I'd believed Matthias and Arkady were any safer being near me but not knowing the truth, I would be deluding myself. If things went sideways with Moses—*when* they went sideways—they'd be his targets regardless. They had to know the truth so they understood the situation clearly.

I'd wanted Moses to be dead before I had to bring anyone else into our confidence. But like most things in my life, that hadn't gone according to plan at all. And then he'd forced my hand by giving us the contract.

Nothing to do but say it. Matthias and Arkady were waiting, and if I didn't spit it out, Arkady looked ready to turn me upside down and shake me by my ankles until I talked.

"My real name is Ava Selene Murphy," I said. "I am Moses Murphy's granddaughter."

THIRTY-FOUR

THE FIRST PERSON TO SPEAK WAS, UNSURPRISINGLY, MY BUSINESS PARTNER.

"Well, fuck me." Arkady put her hands on her hips. "That explains a *lot*."

Matthias studied me, his head tilted. I could only imagine all the thoughts and realizations crashing in his brain at the news.

Arkady's visible anger at me evaporated, replaced by her usual wry cynicism. "I didn't have *find out my business partner and bestie has a whole secret identity* on my bingo card for today, but I guess here we are anyway."

"I guess so," I said with a sigh. "You're taking it well."

"I get why you didn't tell me sooner. That's the kind of secret that's tough to share, and I've got plenty of those myself. And honestly, I'm way more pissed at myself than I am at you."

"What? Why?"

"Because I should have figured it out sooner." She scowled. "I got that you aren't who you say you are. That part's kinda obvious to someone who puts clues together for a living. Sussing out that you're the mysterious Murphy granddaughter everyone thinks is dead is a *much* bigger leap."

I cleared my throat. "For the record, Sean figured it out about six months ago, with way fewer clues than you've had."

Her eyes narrowed.

"It's okay," Sean said, feigning sympathy. "You can't expect to out-hunt a werewolf."

"*Anyway*," she said icily, "I want the whole damn story, but we don't have time for that today, what with murderous necromancers to find and witch rituals to set up and so forth." She marched up to me and poked me not-at-all gently in the chest with her index finger. "But don't think for a minute I don't know the reason you didn't tell me this before now. You're still trying to protect everyone around you, even though like Sean just said we're in the same amount of danger either way."

"Well, when you put it like that, it makes me sound bad," I said.

"You're not bad. You're just—" She rubbed her face with her hand. "Jeez. I don't even know *what* you are. I'm going to have to process this for a while. If even *half* the stuff we think we know about how Murphy runs things is true, I can't even begin to wrap my brain around what you've been through. No wonder you're..." She trailed off.

"Deeply traumatized?" I suggested.

"Overly protective and hyper-independent?" Sean interjected.

Malcolm poked his head up through the floor. "A hot mess express?"

Matthias crossed his arms and eyed me before rumbling, "Funny?"

"Good call," Malcolm said approvingly. "That which does not kill us makes us funny as hell." He disappeared back into the basement.

Arkady sighed. "Yeah, you're all those things and a whole lot more."

Sean kissed the top of my head. "Told you it would be okay," he murmured into my ear. I kissed his jaw.

"Anyway, you wanted me over here because—?" Arkady prompted.

"Like I said in the text, we need your brain." I tapped the contract. "You said a *geas* can be broken by unraveling the spell and the key is in the wording. We just need to crack the code."

"Code-cracking *is* one of my many talents. *However...*" She turned to Matthias and met his amber gaze. Something passed between them—a kind of understanding between former lovers who might be finding a way to be colleagues, if not friends. "I know what Alice and Sean want, but nobody's gonna try to crack jack shit unless it's what *you* want. They'll have to go through me to try."

As much as I wanted Matthias free of the *geas*, I for one would not be trying to go through her. Alpha werewolf or not, Sean didn't look excited about the prospect either.

"So it's your call." Arkady's voice had a gentle note I'd rarely heard before. "Do you want me to try to crack the code or not?"

"I'm not ready to answer," Matthias said. "It's not just that trying to remove the *geas* might kill me, though that's a big concern in itself. I don't know what other things might happen if you fail...or if you succeed. This is a big decision."

"Had you not thought about getting out of it someday?" Sean asked. "Or did you truly believe it wasn't possible?"

"I didn't know it was possible," Matthias admitted. "And since I learned it was, I didn't believe anyone would be able to get a copy of the contract."

"Fair enough." Arkady's mouth quirked. "I did tell you I was trying to get a copy, though. Knowing me as well as you do, you didn't think I could make it happen?"

"I thought you had the best chance of anyone," he said, rather diplomatically. "But obviously the Court is extremely highly motivated to keep documents of this nature secure. How Murphy accomplished it, I don't know."

"Probably the usual combination of money and threats." Arkady shrugged. "Throw enough money at something and threaten to break enough bones and the impossible magically becomes possible."

Hearing them talk casually about Moses felt jarring, though I wasn't sure why. I knew my true identity was safe with them, but maybe I felt like my secret had spread a little too far for my comfort. A year ago, no one had known who I was but me. Now the list of those in the know was up to eight people—and possibly also two vampires who could not remotely be called trustworthy.

Carly would probably tell me this uneasiness was more about my need to control my environment than anything else. I supposed those counseling sessions were paying off because I found myself psychoanalyzing myself almost as much as Carly did these days.

I was about to change the subject away from Moses when my phone buzzed in my pocket and saved me the trouble. The screen showed a text message from Diaz: *Pizza arrives at 1800.*

"Diaz is going to leak the information about the necromancer at six o'clock," I told the others. "That's two hours from now. I fully expect widespread panic and for the chief of police and SPEMA to order a curfew, among other things."

Sean nodded grimly. "I think you're right. What time should we expect Carly and Katy?"

"They're witches, so of course they want to begin the ritual at midnight," I told him. "But if there's a curfew they'll have to be here before that. The big X factor is what level of chaos this information causes. We'll have to see what the police and SPEMA do after the news breaks."

"And in the meantime?" Arkady wanted to know. "I mean, you're about to go up against some real nasty hombres. If we were doing this my style, I'd be cleaning my guns, polishing my knives, warming up with some cardio and difficult blade throws, and getting in the zone by firing up my favorite ass-kicking playlist and envisioning the many creative ways I'm going to unalive the bad guys. What does a mage do to prepare for battle?"

"I make a pot of coffee." I dug a piece of chalk from my pocket and held it up. "And then I draw."

I SPENT the next three hours in my basement, drawing spellwork on myself with marker and then crawling around on the concrete floor using up nearly an entire box of chalk to complete the intensive and intricate spellwork Carly had requested for the ritual.

About an hour into that project, I took a break to create the binding spell that secured Liam to the anchor crystal so he would be safe without needing to stay inside a ward. Once we were satisfied that the spellwork was strong enough that he couldn't be tracked or stolen back by one of Moses's mages, he and Malcolm left "to talk about ghost stuff," as Malcolm put it. They planned to return before the ritual began.

At a little after seven o'clock, I'd just finished the last of the wards Carly wanted when Sean opened the basement door and called down that the news about the necromancer had spread like wildfire.

I wiped chalk dust off my hands with a towel and trudged upstairs on aching knees to watch the red-faced chief of police and the assistant director of the local SPEMA bureau host a chaotic press conference. They denied and condemned the rumors emphatically, but announced a city-wide curfew of nine p.m. for public safety.

Arkady had plunked herself on the couch, sitting cross-legged as she surfed local news sites on her phone. She looked up as I settled into my usual chair with a mug of coffee. "If the necromancer wanted fear and chaos, they've got it now," she said. "I sure hope however Diaz got the word out that he did it in a way that it can't be traced back to him because the chief looks ready to string somebody up by their balls."

As far as I could tell, none of the news agencies and local bloggers claimed the police or SPEMA were the source of the information about a necromancer. Several cited "an independent investigative team" as the party that had determined the killings were connected and the work of a necromancer and malevolent spirits under their control. I guessed that was who Diaz credited—or blamed—for coming up with the idea a necromancer was involved. As long as no one down at the cop shop suspected I might be the "independent investigative team" in question, we should be fine.

"I haven't seen this much ducking and dodging since middle school dodgeball," Sean said as the chief restated some version of *We have no information or evidence that substantiates these rumors* for the umpteenth time. He stood next to my chair with his arms crossed. "All these denials could drive the necromancer to do something to prove the chief is lying."

"We knew doing this was no guarantee of anything," I said. My voice sounded as tired as I felt. Three hours of creating and drawing spellwork was no joke. "All we can do is hope this is the attention the necromancer has been craving and they'll hit pause on the killing until we can get them."

Without warning, Sean confiscated my coffee cup. "Hey," I protested. "I need that."

"What you need is food and rest." He held the mug out of my reach. "You have time before Carly and Katy get here to at least take a power nap. Go upstairs to bed and we'll stay quiet down here. You can eat when you get up."

"There's no way I can sleep with all this going on," I protested, then reconsidered. "At least, not by myself."

"Daisy is up there already," Sean pointed out. "She's perfect for nap-time snuggling."

"She is, but I think I need your snuggling more." I yawned to emphasize the point. "Pretty please?"

"Might as well go cuddle with your boo," Arkady told him. "I think Matthias and I can hold down the fort for a while."

Sean got the long-suffering look he often had when Arkady was around. I couldn't tell for sure if she phrased things deliberately to elicit that reaction, but I wouldn't put it past her. Her number one love language was giving people shit, and I supposed it said something about all of us that we adored her for it. Well, mostly.

We left my coffee mug on the kitchen island and went upstairs. I heard the shower running in the guest bathroom. "Matthias punched the bag for a long time while you were in the workshop," Sean said at my inquisitive look. "He thinks while he punches."

"I get that." I squeezed his hand. "He's going to be okay, I think. Eventually."

"He will." He kissed the top of my head and shut our bedroom door to block the low murmur of the television downstairs. "You get a lot of credit for that, Miss Magic."

I didn't feel that I'd done all that much, but I was too tired to argue. I crawled onto the bed fully clothed except for my bare feet and curled around Baby Daisy. Sean toed off his shoes and spooned behind me, his arm around my tummy to hold me close as he nuzzled the back of my neck.

Exhaustion made my arms and legs feel like lead, but as the minutes passed, sleep didn't come despite Sean's comforting warmth and Baby Daisy's snuffly snoring.

Every time I closed my eyes I saw the photos in the file Diaz had given me. And I heard the spirit's raspy voice on repeat: *We's comin' for you. Jus' you wait, little birdie. Jus' you wait...*

I let out a sound that was part groan and part whimper.

Sean kissed my shoulder. "Shh. Rest, love."

"I can't." I turned my head so I could see his face. His expression was grim. I hated to see him look like this, especially when I knew I was the main cause of his worry.

"It all just spins in my head like there's a puzzle here I haven't solved yet," I said. "Like somehow I've missed something, or something hasn't clicked into place that's important."

He didn't say anything for a while. I could tell he desperately wanted me to rest. The shadows moving in his golden eyes told me his wolf was extremely unhappy too because I was exhausted, and when I was exhausted, I wasn't at my best. I had to be at my best tonight—my life and many other lives depended on it.

"Let's solve the puzzle, then, so you can close your eyes," he said finally. "What's bothering you?"

What *was* bothering me? Everything, sure, but something in particular nagged at me. My instincts were trying to get me to figure something out.

What didn't we know? Well, we didn't know the identity of the necromancer yet, but I believed we would discover that tonight. We also didn't have the identities of the spirits. I wasn't sure that mattered all that much. The mission there was to capture them and send them back where they belonged. Names weren't required for that.

Or were they?

"Maybe these spirits aren't just puppets controlled by the necromancer," I said, mostly to hear the thought aloud. "That's how I've been thinking of them, but I could be wrong. It doesn't *feel* right to call them puppets or pets. There's a power dynamic here that's more complicated."

"This is your gut telling you this?" Sean asked. "Or your magic?"

"Maybe both?" I thought about it more. "When one of the ghosts threatened me yesterday, he said *We're coming for you*. I thought he meant himself and the necromancer, so I didn't really think about it all that much. But that was before I knew there were two spirits. Now I think he meant himself and the other spirit, which means they have a sense of themselves as individuals with purpose, not the mindlessness of normal summoned spirits. Maybe that's why those words keep popping into my brain every time I have a minute to think. My subconscious, or my gut, or whatever you want to call it, is trying to tell me the identity of the spirits is important in some way and they aren't just pets or pawns. I think this might be closer to some kind of partnership between the necromancer and the spirits. There's a give and take."

The more I talked it out, the more this sounded right, and the less I liked where this train of thought was headed.

That must have shown on my face, because Sean raised up on his elbow. "How does that change the situation?"

"I don't think it's going to be as simple as capturing the spirits and then sending them back to Hell like we planned. They're powerful in their own right and apparently capable of having intention and making decisions. That means if we sever their binding to the necromancer, they won't be mindless and easy to catch. We may need their full names."

"How would you get that information?"

"I do not even know." I rested my head on his bicep. "The necromancer has it, obviously, but they're not likely to tell me or anyone else. And we have to trap the spirits before we take on the necromancer, or we up the danger level of that meeting by about a hundred times."

"So it's like the worst version of the chicken or the egg conundrum." His expression turned wry. "You need the names of the spirits from the necromancer to capture them, but you can't confront the necromancer before you capture the spirits."

"That's about the size of it." I sighed. "Well, I feel a little better since I figured out what's bugging me, but now I'm wondering how to get out of *this* mess."

He ran his nose along my hairline to my ear and kissed me gently. "We figured out what was bugging you, but I suppose a nap is still not happening?"

"I wish I could, but I don't think so." I cupped his face with my hand. "I'm sorry. You love me so much, and yet I can't even take a nap when it would take a little of the edge off your stress. I'm the worst fiancée ever."

"Maybe so, but I knew what I was getting into." He kissed the tip of my nose and held up my left hand with our fingers entwined. "I bought this ring with the biggest, dumbest, goofiest smile on my face, and I didn't even care what the clerk in the store or Malcolm thought. I could not have looked less like an alpha werewolf in that moment if I'd tried. And the other night when I watched Daniel put

Nan's ring on her finger at their wedding, all I could think about was the day I get to have that moment with you. Nothing is going to get between us and that moment, or any other moment of our lives, if I can help it—necromancers and their murderous spirits be damned."

I blinked at him. "You took Malcolm with you to buy my engagement ring?"

Sean's patented long-suffering look returned. "*That* was what you heard out of what I just said?"

I laughed and drew him down to me for a kiss. "I heard every word," I promised. "I'm just trying to focus on the funny part so I don't get sniffly."

"That's fair." He sighed. "I will admit Malcolm helped me choose the right ring. The tough part was listening to him give advice while not letting on to the clerk that a ghost was helping me shop."

"Welcome to my life," I said dryly. "It's tricky having a ghost sidekick sometimes, but I wouldn't trade it for anything."

My perimeter wards tingled in a way they hadn't in a very long time. I sat up abruptly. What the hell?

My confusion deepened when I looked out the window. The sun hadn't even set yet. Seriously, *what the hell?*

Sean was off the bed and on his feet instantly. "What's wrong?"

"Vampire," I said. "In the yard."

I had a strong suspicion who it was, too. I'd wondered when Charles would get desperate enough to talk to me. The answer, apparently, was tonight.

Sean's eyes blazed gold, and then he was gone—out the bedroom door, down the stairs, and judging by the crash from the direction of the living room, through the plywood that covered the already broken patio door, all before I made it to the upstairs hallway.

"Shit, shit, shit," I muttered as I ran.

THIRTY-FIVE

When I got to the living room, it was empty. The welcoming committee had apparently already assembled outside to confront our visitor. To my surprise, I didn't hear fighting, though I wasn't sure if that was good or bad.

I caught a glimpse of myself in the mirror near the stairs and winced. Not that I was particularly vain, but my hair had come loose from its braid, my eyes appeared almost bruised because of deep shadows, and chalk dusted my wrinkled clothes. I looked about as good as could be expected for a woman whose day started with an exorcism and hadn't gotten much better from there. Oh, well. Anyone who showed up at the house uninvited on a day like today got what they got—even the newly minted head of the Vampire Court of the Western United States.

I couldn't help my clothes or my shadowed eyes, but I unbraided my hair on the way to the patio door and combed it with my fingers so it hopefully looked casually tousled and less like I'd stepped out of a wind tunnel, or just rolled out of bed after a desperate but unsuccessful attempt to nap.

Out on the deck, Sean stood at the railing facing the trees. Matthias and Arkady had taken up positions to the right and left of him on the far sides of the deck. Arkady had blades in both hands and spun them reflexively, ready to throw.

I joined Sean at the railing. Bryan stood in the grass about ten feet from the deck, a white handkerchief in his hand. Judging by the expressions on my companions' faces, they didn't find a signal of truce reassuring whatsoever, but they hadn't attacked yet.

Belatedly, I realized Bryan was still human and not a dhampir—not yet, anyway.

I scanned the trees. "Where is he?" I asked, without bothering with a greeting.

Instead of answering my question, Bryan said, "On behalf of Charles Vaughan, I request a parley, under the rules set by the Were Ruling Council."

Were Ruling Council rules and not Vampire Court rules? Why? To play games with us? Or for the same reason Charles had answered my call last night in less than two rings?

Or maybe because meeting under the Council's parley rules meant we couldn't attack our visitors unless they became an immediate threat. And with the Council breathing down our necks right now about so many potentially deadly problems, violating one of its longest-standing sets of rules wasn't an option, even more than usual.

No one was more aware of that fact than Sean. A muscle moved in his jaw. "Parley granted," he said finally. "Show your face, Vaughan."

Charles stepped clear of the tree line. He also carried a white handkerchief with something embroidered in crimson thread in one corner. Probably his initials.

As always, the slim, dark-haired vampire wore a tailored suit with a crimson tie and pocket square as a nod to the official color of his Court.

I hadn't really expected him to look any different, but maybe I'd thought he would have adopted some sign of his new position, like a sash. Or a cape. Despite the tension, the mental image of Charles dressed like a movie vampire caused a bubble of laughter to rise. I squashed it just in time and bit my lips to keep from smiling.

Damn it, I was so tired, and the vampire who'd betrayed me so badly so many times was in my fucking. Back. Yard.

"I apologize for the intrusion," Charles said, his softly glowing eyes focused on Sean. "And I thank you for accepting our request for a parley."

"For a head of a Vampire Court, you don't travel like we'd expect," Sean said. "Sneaking through the woods instead of arriving with an entourage in luxury vehicles."

The corners of Charles's mouth turned up, as if he knew Sean had used the word "sneaking" deliberately. "I cannot pretend to be here on official business, as you might have guessed."

"If you're not here on official business, there's no reason for us to parley. We don't have any personal business with you." Sean studied him. "You can leave the way you came. Back through the woods, to wherever you've parked your car."

Utterly unperturbed by the dismissal, Charles pointed at the trees to his left. "Are you aware there is a sizable cache of odd household items in a hollow tree stump about fifteen feet in that direction?"

Oh, blast it—Esme's stash of stolen stuff. I'd forgotten to ask Sean to look for it in the woods.

"Thank you for that information." Sean flexed his hands. "Now, with all due respect, leave our property."

"I acknowledge your demand that I leave," Charles said smoothly. "And I will before long, but before I do, I beg your leave to speak privately to Alice. I have information for her, and answers to the questions she asked of me a few nights ago."

"No way in hell are you speaking to Alice alone," Sean stated. "Parley rules or not, you've run out of chances to have that privilege."

"You speak for her?" Charles raised his elegant brows. "Or is that Alice's decision?"

I sighed. "Charles, don't play that game with us again. You know damn well Sean doesn't speak for me, just like you know damn well we didn't help Valas during your takeover or after it."

"Perhaps I do know these things," he said, which floored me because he'd denied it so vehemently just a day ago. "Perhaps the time has come to settle those matters, in light of...certain questions."

"What certain questions?" I demanded. "Stop talking in riddles. I am *so* not in the mood for games. What's changed between last night and tonight?"

He took a step toward us and ignored Sean's growl. "I woke well before sundown today," he said. "And I do not know why. I thought perhaps you might."

When my wards had alerted me to his presence, my immediate thought had been that it was too early for him to be awake, much less arrive here, but I'd figured he'd gotten his hands on some kind of magic or strong blood that had allowed him to wake early.

"You're lying," Sean said.

I studied Charles's expression and body language. Just beneath the façade of cool detachment, I saw real uncertainty and disquiet.

"I actually don't think he's lying about this," I said. "When did you wake?"

"Well over an hour ago." He glanced at the western horizon. "And I stand in the fading sunlight even now without burning."

"Is this your witches' doing?" Sean demanded. "Would they have done it without your knowledge?"

"This is no witchcraft." Charles shook his head. "The witches of the Silver Thorn Coven do not have this power."

"How many vamps woke early?" I asked.

"Our information indicates the phenomenon has affected all the vampires within a radius of more than a hundred miles."

"In a radius?" I asked. "A radius with what in the center?"

His expression gave me the answer before he said the words. "Northbourne Manor," Charles said.

Of *freaking* course Northbourne was the center. We had no idea what artifacts and magic practitioners the vamps had on its grounds —and apparently even Charles didn't know either. I squeezed my fists until my nails bit into my palms.

"What do the witches say?" Sean asked. He still didn't believe Morgan Clark and her coven weren't somehow involved. I couldn't blame him.

"They say something is stirring, but they cannot see what it is," Charles told us. "Those who have looked see nothing but darkness, my consort tells me. And the powers and energies they use are growing. Even the High Priestesses of the black witch covens worry."

Katy's words to Carly popped into my head: *Something woke up*.

Charles's glowing gaze locked on me. Either his intuition was in fine form tonight or something had shown on my face. "You know of this," he said, his expression fierce. "Speak, Alice."

"Information isn't free," I said.

He hissed. Sean stiffened and Matthias took a few steps forward, his eyes glowing amber.

"You came here to make a deal, didn't you?" I asked calmly. "So let's deal."

"It is not that simple," Charles ground out. "I have already told you I do not answer only to myself."

"From where I'm standing, it's super simple," I countered. "You have something I want, I have something you want. In fact, you need more from me than answers about why you woke up unusually early today, don't you?"

"Perhaps." His eyes silvered. "This is a dangerous game you play, Alice Worth."

Every fiber of my being rang like church bells when he said that. I had him. For the first time since we'd met, I really, truly had him.

"Dangerous games? I don't know if you've heard, but I live for that shit," I said. "Now, I am expecting guests soon, so we have about an hour to make a deal." I gestured at the broken patio door. "Come inside and have a seat at my table, Charles."

I didn't know what it was I had that he was so desperate to get, but I had every intention of extracting the absolute maximum amount of payoff in return.

Sean's expression was like granite. He knew as well as I did we had the best chance right now to deal with the Court's indictments because we—or I—had Charles on the ropes. That didn't mean he liked anything about having Charles in our house, much less sitting next to me, but it wasn't like I could leave the head of the Vampire Court standing in the open in my backyard. That would just be courting trouble for everyone.

Without a word, his expression cold, Charles climbed the steps to our deck, followed by Bryan. I met them halfway to the patio door. Sean, Arkady, and Matthias watched Charles and I study each other.

Try as I might, it was no use pretending Charles and I didn't have six years of history and a lot of intimate moments between us. We'd never slept together—not for lack of trying on his part—but intimacy took many forms. We had revealed parts of ourselves and secrets to each other that we'd shared with very few others.

When I'd discovered a few months ago the depths of Charles's betrayal, I had asked Sean how I could know which of my thoughts and emotions about Charles were real and which weren't. At the time I'd thought everything about my interactions with Charles was false. With some distance, however, I'd reconsidered. Many of our interactions were completely engineered by him to manipulate me, but my heart told me some were real.

Charles had loved me and maybe still did, in his own way. He thought because he loved me that gave him carte blanche to do whatever he felt was necessary to make me his, and whatever was necessary for me to be safe—or as safe as anyone could be with all the threats that surrounded me. And he himself would always be a threat to me, no matter how much he loved me, because his love was a kind of possession. It was destructive and lacked morality. When it came to people and things he wanted, the ends would forever justify the means.

He didn't just want my heart and my body; he wanted my magic and skill, too, very much like Moses did. Charles wanted me to want power the same way he did, to want to rule at his side as if we were of the same mind, but we weren't and we never would be. He'd told me once that he'd give me the world. Then and now I knew it wouldn't be worth the price I'd have to pay. And I didn't want the world anyway.

During his confession, he'd revealed he wanted me at his side for another reason: because I made him feel more human. He wanted to recapture the feeling of being alive after more than two hundred years of existing as a vampire. As much as I wanted that for him, I didn't want the burden of being his conscience or making him feel human. I didn't want love to be a burden on me. I didn't want to love someone I couldn't trust with all my heart and soul.

At the same time, Charles's love for me was just real enough that it had probably prevented him from doing what most vampires would have done in his designer shoes: break up my relationship with Sean by any means necessary, even if it meant killing him. I didn't think Charles deserved a medal for doing the right thing, but I had to imagine he'd entertained the thought and must have decided against it. Surrounded as he was by ruthless vampires who knew he wanted me, that had to have been a difficult decision to make and live by as he watched Sean and me fall in love, buy a house together, and get engaged.

He'd never have those things, ever, and that did hurt my heart. Despite everything he'd done to me, even the betrayals that were unforgivable, I didn't want him to have no hope of having the love and family I had. I didn't hate anyone that much except Moses.

Sean didn't need me to be his moral compass, or to make him feel human. His love was selfless and good. Charles's love was conditional and full of dangers, and I couldn't love him back. No, it wasn't that I couldn't—I *wouldn't*. Because that wasn't the kind of love I really wanted, and not the kind I'd come to realize I deserved.

Maybe Charles had come to that conclusion too, because when our gazes met I read sadness there, along with anger and a lot of other emotions. Despite everything, I didn't like that I was the cause of that sadness. Some part of my heart still hurt for him.

Bryan spoke. "Since we are here under parley rules, I would like a word with Matthias alone."

"Why?" Sean asked.

"It's a private matter."

Matthias exchanged a glance with Sean. "I'll speak to him," he rumbled in response to Sean's silent question, then turned back to Bryan. "But I reserve the right to share what you say with my alpha."

"I accept that," Bryan said.

At Charles's nod, the two men went down the steps to the back-yard and disappeared around the corner of the house. I wondered what the hell Bryan had to say to Matthias that was so secret.

I led Charles to the patio door and ran my fingers along the door-frame to grant him onetime passage through my wards. I'd certainly never anticipated letting Charles into my house, much less watching him unbutton his suit jacket and sit at my humble dining table.

Sean and Arkady stayed close by, just in case Charles decided to violate the rules of parley. I didn't think he would, but I'd been wrong about him before.

"Coffee?" I offered, heading to the kitchen to reheat the mug I'd abandoned to go upstairs with Sean. "A beer? I might have some wine." Call me petty, but I wasn't going to offer him my good scotch. He didn't deserve it.

I expected him to decline. Instead, he surprised me by saying, "A beer, please, Alice." At my expression, he added blandly, "When in Rome."

Once my coffee was ready, I got him a bottle of local craft beer, uncapped it, and brought our drinks to the table. Sean took the seat next to me and we faced Charles together. Arkady stood with her back to the wall and kept a wary eye on both our guest and the open patio door.

"Okay, Charles," I said, my hands wrapped around my mug. "Before you start talking, I really have one big question for you. *What the actual hell?*"

THIRTY-SIX

Charles smiled to flash his fangs. "Can you be more specific?"

I ticked items off on my fingers. "In the first place, a freaking coup. Hooking up with Morgan Clark and her coven. Executing everyone loyal to Valas—even Ezekiel Monroe. Filing all these charges against Sean, me, and the Were Ruling Council when you know it's all lies. Turning your enforcers into an army of dhampirs against their will. Stacking the Court full of puppets who are loyal to you." *Sending Matthias into our pack land as a spy to get information about me you have no right to have,* I thought, but didn't say aloud. "Trying to get your hands on Matthias to execute him. Honestly, Charles, I don't know who you are anymore. I suppose I never really did if you could do these things. And I can't imagine why you'd think you could commit such atrocities and then waltz up to my door asking me for favors with that much blood on your hands."

"I'm surprised at you, Alice." He shook his head with feigned disappointment. "Repeating these rumors as if they were true, when as you yourself said it would be out of character for me to do such things."

I scowled. Games again. Games and more games. God forbid we

ever had a single conversation that didn't consist almost entirely of bullshit on his part. We knew he was here to ask us for something, but apparently his strategy for that involved starting on the offensive.

Charles had to have seen and sensed my growing anger, but he kept going. "Is it possible you are gullible enough to believe such an obvious tissue of lies? Or are you still so ready to believe the worst of everyone you know?" He glanced at Sean. "After all, that has happened before."

Sean growled. "For someone who's come to us asking for favors, you're making poor choices by insulting us and dredging up our past conflicts."

"I don't think he can help himself." I sighed. "Charles, don't tell me it's all lies. We have information from multiple sources."

"I did not say it was *all* lies," he countered. "But the worst atrocities you accuse me of committing are simply misinformation. Allow me to prove it."

He took out his phone and hit a few buttons. After a pause, he said to the screen, "I am with Alice Worth. She wishes to see proof that you are still alive." He turned the phone so I could see who he'd spoken to via video chat.

"Hello, Alice," Ezekiel Monroe said.

Valas's longtime daytime representative and attorney looked exactly as he had the last time I'd seen him: long gray hair held back with a gold and ruby clasp at the nape of his neck, wearing a designer suit with the same signature crimson tie and pocket square Charles wore. His real age was rumored to be somewhere close to seventy-five, but he looked only about fifty thanks to years of drinking Valas's blood. He appeared to be in his spacious office, sitting at his desk, with shelves of legal texts and a small bar with glasses and bottles in the background.

Moses had told me Monroe had died very unpleasantly. Arkady had heard the same thing. And yet here he was, neither dead nor undead, and I was getting madder by the second.

"How do I know you're not held prisoner and forced to speak to me?" I demanded.

Monroe raised his perfectly trimmed eyebrows. "I don't have any way to prove that other than my word, which of course you won't take. But the rumors of my terrible death are all exaggerated, I assure you—much like the other rumors you've heard. Charles will explain."

"Yes, he damn well will," Sean said, his voice cold.

"Thank you for your time, Ezekiel." Charles ended the call and placed his phone neatly on the table in front of himself. "Satisfied?"

Despite five years of dealing with him—and a lifetime of interacting with vampires—his audacity left me speechless for several beats.

I glared daggers at him. "Of course I'm not satisfied! Why on earth would I be? You had better start telling us the truth right the hell now or I will pull the plug on this parley and use my wards to eighty-six you out of here so fast your fangs will spin."

He chuckled. "A vampire ejection ward? In all my years, I have never experienced one. The novelty would almost be worth forcing your hand into using it."

While Sean had on his hard alpha mask, Arkady appeared very much in favor of activating that particular ward. She'd gone ice cold in what I assumed was rage at Charles's revelation that he'd spread misinformation about goings-on at Northbourne. She prided herself on gathering accurate intel. Very possibly, sources she'd previously considered trustworthy had given her the bad information.

And speaking of sources...how would Moses react to finding out his supposed intel was mostly or all lies and that he'd unknowingly passed those lies on to me? No doubt some heads would roll over that. My grandfather did not react well to losing face. Looking foolish or easily duped was not something a man in his position could afford.

"So which rumors are true and which aren't?" I asked finally. "And I want the truth, Charles. So help me, if you lie to me now, you can take every request you want to make of me, fold them until they're all pointy corners, and—"

"No need to utter the remainder of that threat. I comprehend." He toasted my words solemnly with his beer, took a drink from the bottle, and returned it to the precise center of its coaster. "I deposed Valas in a coup—that is true. But I did not execute Ezekiel Monroe. I have turned only those enforcers who willingly agreed to become dhampirs. Bryan can attest to that. I am seeking to fill three empty seats on the Court, but not with 'puppets,' as you say. I seek vampires with a vision of leadership and rule that will ensure the stability of the Court now and well into the future. I learned many things from my predecessor, and among them was the necessity of hearing different perspectives, especially on matters of great importance."

Arms crossed, I leaned back in my chair and studied his face and body language. I expected my bullshit radar to ping, but instead he seemed to have morphed from his earlier cockiness to open and earnest—*seemed* being the key word.

"That all sounds good, theoretically," Sean said. "But I'll believe it when I see it."

"I expected skepticism." Charles raised one shoulder in an elegant half shrug. "I have spoken with Elizabeth of the Chicago Court and Lucien in New Orleans. We recognize that our Courts stand at a crossroads. We must decide what our role will be in these difficult and complex times. We cannot expect to live and rule as we have for centuries, or even as we did in the past few decades. Vampires are eternal, but the world changes at the blink of an eye. We cannot simply stand like rocks in a fast-moving river, or we will be dissolved and swept away."

Hoo boy. I tried to imagine Charles's conversations with his new peers, especially knowing what I did now about Elizabeth and Lucien's long, intimate history with Valas.

"What do they think about recent events?" I asked. "I can't imagine they're happy about what you've done."

"Certainly not happy," he acknowledged smoothly. "But I believe they understand. Valas could no longer rule and her condition worsened by the hour. You saw her yourself and know that to be true. And so I made the choice that seemed best for all concerned."

I found that statement to be highly debatable, but we had bigger issues to address. "Well, you did what you did and it's done. And then for whatever reason, you let rumors spread that you were holed up at Northbourne committing atrocities while you filed baseless charges against Sean, me, our pack, and the Were Ruling Council. I want an explanation of both."

"It is a trick as old as time." Charles took another sip of his beer. "A magician's favorite. Draw the audience's attention to the left hand so they do not see what the right is doing."

"Which part is the trick?" I demanded. "The rumors or the indictments?"

"Both."

Judging by Sean's snarl and the way his magic seared my skin, I had the feeling only the parley rules kept him from leaping over the table and trying to separate Charles's head from his body.

I was entertaining the same fantasy myself. My chest ached. It hurt so much to be thought of as insignificant, and fury burned in my gut like I'd swallowed hot coals.

"What is your right hand doing, then?" My voice was quiet—but deceptively so. My eyes were warm, meaning they glowed with blood magic that seared the air.

Charles's gaze turned wary. He'd once lost half his throat to me and though the wound healed quickly, he'd likely never forget how close he'd come to losing his head and dying on the spot.

"I cannot tell you every secret," he said, and had the grace or good sense to at least act regretful. "But as an act of good faith, I will share what I know that pertains to you and your pack."

Maybe I didn't deserve to know Court secrets—hell, even members of the Court weren't privy to what the head of the Court knew—but whatever Charles knew that involved us, he should have already revealed. I deserved that much.

"Everyone else's lives are just a game for you, aren't they?" I demanded. "Every time I accidentally think something the least bit positive about you, I get reminded what kind of person you really are. Do you have *any idea* what you have put us through with these charges? Do you know how much danger we're in because of you? You're playing dice with our lives, Charles, and you just don't care. We're all just means to an end."

"You say I do not care as if it is a fact." He leaned forward, suddenly angry. "Do you think I made these decisions lightly? Because I did not. Has it occurred to you that I might have done it for your benefit as well as mine?"

"What?" I gaped at him. "Did it occur to me that the legal expenses we've incurred, the strain and stress we're going through, the threats made against us by Council members who've been waiting for a chance to turn against us, and every sleepless night were *for our benefit?* No, it did not. In fact, I find it absolutely unbelievable that you did this to help us in any way, shape, or form. But the fact you're making that claim on the night you've come here looking for favors makes all the sense in the world."

"How little you think of me." Charles held my angry gaze with his own. "Perhaps you will think differently when I tell you Moses Murphy demanded I file these indictments against you."

Shock left me speechless.

"He was quite persuasive," he continued. "I need not list the threats he made, but I am sure you can imagine. Despite my many misgivings, I thought it in both our best interests to acquiesce."

"But why?" I asked, my voice tight with rage.

"It seems he wishes to have you reliant upon him for protection against the wicked vampires and the mercurial Were Ruling Council."

I didn't want to believe him, but I did. My gut told me every word was true. How completely on-brand for Moses to strike up secret alliances to manipulate me. He'd done it before.

My heart sank as I thought of the Council's impending second vote Willa had requested "in light of new information" they'd received. Was that information coming from Moses?

Sean, however, clearly wasn't ready to buy Charles's explanation. "Prove what you say is true," he said.

"Our understanding was not written down. I have no contract to show you." Charles showed us his pale, empty hands. "But I believe you may have received a document today I provided as a sign of good faith that I would uphold my end of the bargain. He gives you the contract and emerges the hero of the day, yes?"

"Not at all." I drained the last of my coffee and set the mug on the table with a bang. "Murphy is no hero. I knew he had ulterior motives for giving me the contract. I just hadn't figured out what they were yet."

"What happens if Murphy finds out you've told us this?" Sean asked.

"I am certain he will attempt to have me killed." Charles flashed his fangs again. "So I must ask that you not reveal that we have spoken of this. Murphy plots and plans as ruthlessly a vampire. I would respect him for it if he were less odious, and if he did not target you, who I wish to...not harm."

I didn't comment on that last bit. "And the reports from North-bourne you claim are rumors?"

"There was no wholesale slaughter of Valas's supporters. The actual casualty count from the coup and its aftermath stands at less than twenty, not counting those who perished at the mansion in Colorado, for which I do not have accurate data. All died in battle—none on a scaffold. I would provide our own Court records if I thought you would find them persuasive."

"Even if that's true, why let these rumors spread?" I demanded. "They make you sound like a monster."

"I know, and I like the situation much less than you do. But as I said, the rumors are merely temporary misdirection. The truth will come to light soon, once the gates of Northbourne are open once more." He folded his hands on the table. "I have no desire to be thought of as a merciless and evil man, but I have little choice at the moment."

"Because Murphy wants you to seem that way?" I asked.

"Because Moses Murphy is only one of my many concerns." He regarded me. "As I am sure you have already surmised, I have taken a position of great power. Now I must establish myself as a leader worthy of loyalty and longevity. I choose not to do this by fear, as some might expect, but by offering a vision for the future that not only vampires endorse but also the Council and local, state, and federal authorities. I plan to set the tone for the American Vampire Courts in the twenty-first century."

"Oh, is that all?" I snorted. "That's a relief. I was worried you might have bitten off more than you could chew."

His smile was indulgent. "My coup might have seemed sudden and spontaneous to you, but I have been planning for a long time what I might do given a chance. And I am well aware that everything I do will be greeted with the utmost skepticism and even hostility, even from vampires who have a long view of things. There would be no use in suggesting changes to the ancient Courts elsewhere in the world, but the Courts of America are not as fully entrenched in the past. We look forward more often than back. Even Valas looked ahead, despite her many long centuries. My vision is not so different than hers—save a few key respects."

I had a lot more questions since he seemed to be in such a chatty mood, but our time was running short. Carly and Katy should be arriving in about fifteen minutes, and I very much wanted Charles gone before they walked in the door.

"Okay, so we've heard your explanations, and we'll think about whether we believe you," I said. "It's time to get to the point."

"If I may say one more thing before we move on." He studied me. "I understand your pack has granted Matthias asylum, thus ensuring neither my Court nor any other can reclaim him. I am glad to see you took my advice."

I gaped. "*Your* advice? You never said any such thing. You said—" I cut myself off and scowled as realization dawned. "You said he was a fugitive from justice and demanded we hand him over as such."

"Indeed, I did say that." Charles raised his eyebrows. "Which gave you the idea to use the Council's asylum laws to protect him, did it not? Had he no such protection, my Court would have to reclaim him or lose face, and another Court could step in and take him as a discarded asset. Now he is safe, as you have legally outmaneuvered me. No one needs to know I gave you the idea."

I didn't need to ask why he hadn't just made the suggestion outright. I would have assumed he had an ulterior motive, or that he knew it wouldn't work, because why would he *try* to give us a way to keep Matthias safe? One glance at Sean told me he'd come to the same conclusion.

I didn't want to thank Charles for anything, but if what he said was true—and damn it, it did ring true—then he'd done us a massive favor.

"Thank you," I said, and tried not to sound begrudging. "I assume you did it because you want something, though, so what is it you need from us so badly that you left the safety of Northbourne and snuck up to my house through the woods waving a white flag?"

Charles plainly didn't like that I'd phrased it that way, but I didn't like anything at all about the entire situation, so he could just deal with it.

"I wish to strike a bargain." He leaned back in his chair, his hands folded on his slim abdomen. Instead of the overly formal tone he usually adopted while negotiating a deal, he was clearly going for a more casual, just-between-us approach. Much like Moses's attempts to relate to me better by dressing down to have ostensibly easygoing chats, Charles's body language put me even more on alert.

"We're not striking any bargain that doesn't include dropping the charges against us," Sean said. "So let's start there."

"Please hear me out. If we can stipulate for the moment that the charges are the result of Moses Murphy's desire to leave Alice no ally but himself, I propose we continue the process of navigating these legal waters, at least for now. If Murphy believes you are wholly dependent on him, he is less likely to try to harm you on other fronts. Privately, you and I have the understanding that the charges are baseless and unsubstantiated. If a tribunal is held at the Vampire Court, I will be pleased to fully exonerate you, your pack, and the Were Ruling Council due to the utter lack of evidence."

"There's more at stake here than the tribunal and you know it," I shot back. "The Council may be moments from turning its back on us if you're telling the truth about Moses. If we lose the Council's support altogether, I don't know if there's any chance to get back in their good graces regardless of the outcome of a tribunal. Two or three of its members might not be fans of us right now, but that's better than making enemies of the Council as a whole. Sean could lose his position on the Council too, and that could mean people's *lives*. Come on, Charles. You can't expect us to go along with this!"

"I hear your objections and I sympathize with your situation." He raised his hands. "May I finish outlining my proposal?"

I made a rolling gesture.

"I mentioned that my vision for the future of my Court is different from that of my predecessor in a few key respects. One of my goals is to make the Court a more visible and effective presence as a judiciary body that can balance the legal concerns and responsibilities of vampires, humans, shifters, and others alike."

"Why?" Sean asked. "And don't try to tell us it's for the good of humanity."

"Human jurisprudence is ill-equipped to handle cases involving nonhumans," Charles said. "You know as well as I even the Supernatural and Paranormal Entity Management Agency struggles to properly adjudicate nonhumans because federal laws, much like local and state laws, are rooted in deep human distrust of any evidence or testimony involving the non-mundane."

"I knew this was really about you." I glared at him. "What better way to demonstrate this new interest in justice than by putting a mage and the strongest and largest werewolf pack in the area on trial for alleged crimes against the Court?"

"The subterfuge is for your benefit as well as mine," he argued. "Can you not see that? Murphy is appeased, you understand you are under no real threat of imprisonment, and the Council and everyone else will see you and your pack are truly as innocent of wrongdoing as you claim. There will be tension until then, yes, but—"

"*Tension?*" Sean rose, his eyes golden with fury. "Vaughan, you self-centered son of a bitch."

Charles stood as well. "I do not pretend I am not self-centered. I most assuredly concocted this plan with my own needs in mind, but I weigh Alice's situation as well. You may not believe me, but whether she is at your side or mine, I do not wish her dead. Murphy knows this and he leveraged it to force me to file the charges. Alice's freedom and her life were at stake if I refused." He turned his attention to me. "He smiles to your face and lays traps all around you. I must appear to be the worst of those traps or he will make another."

Just once in my life I don't want to have to choose the lesser of two evils, I thought. *Just once.*

Maybe Charles sensed my bitterness, or maybe it showed on my face. "If only the world we inhabit offered us clear and easy moral choices," he said quietly. "But I have lived long enough, and you have experienced enough, to know better. We live in shadows. We find few bright lights of pure goodness where we dwell."

"Someday I'll be out of the shadows, but not yet." My voice sounded as hollow as I felt. "Sean and I will discuss your proposal. What else do you want?"

"I require the full and truthful account of the deaths of Valas and Vlad," he said. "In return, and by way of lessening the burden upon you caused by the indictments, I offer a boon you may use at any time, for any favor of me you require."

Well, that was a much more complicated request than it had

been yesterday. Yikes. I kept my gaze locked on his and ensured I didn't look down toward the basement, where Valas's mirror was stored in my most heavily warded cabinet.

"I'll consider it," I said blandly. "Anything else?"

"I believe you are now aware that I know you recently discovered the ability to ease a shifter's Change and bypass the months of volatility that normally follow an infection."

Sean's fury scoured my arms. "How the hell do you know what we know?"

Charles glanced at the patio door as Matthias stepped through the broken opening. His cold and distant expression immediately caused me to stand up.

"Bryan has chosen to wait outside, where he cannot overhear what is said in here," he said tonelessly. "With your permission, I'll remain outside with him to ensure he keeps his distance."

My gut twisted in anger and fear at Matthias's defeated body language and and obvious pain. What the hell had Bryan said to him?

"Stay with Bryan," Sean said, his voice curt.

Matthias ducked back through the broken door. Once his footsteps crossed the deck and went down the steps, I turned on Charles. "What the hell did Bryan say to him?" I hissed. "I swear, Charles, if you told him to threaten Matthias—"

"I did not," Charles cut in. "Whatever was said between them, I can only guess."

"Then take a damn guess. I want to know what's hurt him."

"Alice," Charles said gently. "Let him tell you himself. It is not my place to say."

Blast it. "Then tell us how you knew we found out about your little spy operation," I snapped.

"Matthias will explain the particulars, but I will say that the spell that binds him works in such a way that I know what he was forced to reveal to you." He glanced at Sean. "I did not think you had it in you to cause one of your pack wolves that much agony, but you continue to surprise me."

Sean didn't reveal that it had been Matthias's idea. Instead, he took a step toward Charles. "Alice's new ability is the most dangerous secret about her that exists," he ground out. "You know every shifter group in the world would kill us all to get her. Others would kill her because they'd see her as a threat, and they would slaughter everyone in their way. It would likely make her the target of an *úlfheðnar*. Vaughan, you cannot speak a word about Alice's ability to *anyone*. No one can know. And you can't ask her to try to use that power for your benefit."

"I am not asking her to do so," Charles said, to my surprise. "I understand the danger as well as you do. I would as soon walk into the sun as make Alice a target for a shifter assassin. I simply ask that she use this ability only for wolves in your own pack, and only in a way that does not arouse the suspicions of the Council or anyone else."

I stared at him. "Why?"

"For the reasons Sean has just stated." He started to reach out, as if he wanted to touch my hand, but thought better of it and folded his hands behind his back once more. "And because you know as well as I do that Murphy would see your ability for what it is: the ultimate power. His ticket to gain control of anything and anyone he wanted. All your people would be dead and you would be his prisoner once again—this time, for good."

Charles had never come out and said he knew my real identity, but in my gut I'd known he knew because this wasn't the first time he'd made an oblique reference to my past.

"If he tried to use me in that way, he'd become the target of everything we just said," I said.

He studied me. "Do you think that fact would even give him pause?"

No, it wouldn't. Not even for a second. He'd send an army to kill everyone I knew and take me to his compound in chains. And then

I'd have no choice but to end my own life using the spell I had carved on my right femur.

"I hate you for knowing this about me," I said.

He flinched. And it wasn't feigned. I'd landed an uppercut straight to his jaw, but I couldn't feel the slightest satisfaction about it.

"I want to kill you for hurting Alice," Sean added. "But that will be her privilege, not mine."

Charles sighed. "I will leave you to discuss who gets to wield the stake, then." He gave us a courtly half bow. "Please give my proposal due consideration. I believe we would make good allies against a man who has no loyalty for anyone but himself."

"Pot, meet kettle," I muttered.

He busied himself buttoning his suit jacket and ignored my dig.

Well, I'd give him something he *couldn't* ignore. I spooled power and grabbed my house wards. "*Banish*," I said.

With a swirl of magic, a *whoosh* of air, and a shout of surprise, Charles flew backward out the broken patio door and disappeared. I heard what sounded like the deck railing breaking as his body went through it.

I winced. "Oops."

"It's okay." Sean kissed me on the top of my head. "Ben's been asking me for a project." He drew back to look into my face. "Are you all right?"

"No." I gave him a weary smile. "But tossing him out of the house felt good."

My phone rang. As Sean and Arkady went out to the deck, presumably to ensure Charles and Bryan were leaving, I checked the screen. It was a local number, but not one from my address book. Now what?

With a sigh, I hit the green button. "This is Alice."

For a moment, I heard nothing. Then I realized someone was crying. "Hello? Who's this?" I asked.

"Alice." Her voice sounded choked. "It's Gracie Hensley."

Oh no. "What's going on?" I demanded. "Are you okay?"

"No." She sobbed. "Ollie tried to kill me and then he tried to kill himself. He's locked in the bathroom. Please help."

Oliver had worried at our initial meeting about the possibility of hurting his wife. She'd reassured him—and us—that he wasn't capable of hurting her or anyone else. And I'd agreed.

But now he'd attacked his wife, seemingly out of nowhere. Why?

My stomach sank. Could he be possessed again?

"Is he talking to you?" I asked, trying not to let on what I was thinking. "Did you have any conversation?"

"Yes." She sniffled. "I asked him why he was doing this and he said he didn't know. I asked him if he remembered what he'd just done and he said yes, and this time he'd done it on purpose. I think he's having some kind of breakdown."

Everything we'd heard about those who were possessed was that they acted like automatons, or "robotic," to use Diaz's term. The manual strangulation was a different M.O. too. So probably not another possession.

So if that wasn't what set him off, what was it? A breakdown, like Gracie thought?

The only reasonable explanation I could think of was the lingering effects and trauma of experiencing possession and Madison's murder had pushed Oliver over the edge. This attack was more blood on the necromancer's hands, as far as I was concerned.

I ran to the patio door and looked for Sean. "Call 911," I told her as I spotted him in the backyard with Matthias and Arkady. "You need to call the police and an ambulance."

"Please, no. I don't want him arrested. I need your help."

Sean caught sight of me in the doorway and left the others on watch to jog back to the deck. "Did you call Philippa?" I asked.

"No!" she wailed. "I don't trust anybody but you not to call the police. Please come. I'll pay you whatever you want. I need you to tell Oliver he's not a killer before he hurts himself again."

My wards tingled out front, signaling Carly and Katy had arrived.

My phone said it was ten minutes until nine. The citywide curfew began at nine. And we had a life-or-death ritual to set up and get ready for before midnight. All those pressures made my skull feel like it would explode.

"Alice, please!" Gracie's voice cracked. "There's no one else who'll help us. No one else understands."

"Okay," I said, because what else could I do?

Shit, shit, shit. I had absolutely no idea how to get myself to their house without being stopped for violating the curfew that I'd hoped the chief of police would declare after Diaz took my advice and leaked the information I'd given him. Best laid plans and all that.

"I'll get there as soon as I can," I promised. "Just keep talking to him so he's not alone with his thoughts. Tell him I'm on my way and I can prove he's not a killer."

"Thank you." She started crying again, and then she ended the call.

"How are you going to get to their house?" Sean asked, his voice and expression grim.

"I have no idea yet," I said. "But it's only the second or third impossible thing I've done today, so I'll just have to figure it out."

THIRTY-SEVEN

Generally speaking, I made it a personal policy not to piss off powerful witches, even gray or white ones. And though I'd seen Carly angry and fierce while facing down adversaries, I'd never been on the receiving end of a harsh word from her—even when I'd said or done things that even I had to admit probably deserved either a reprimand or a minor hex.

To be fair, Carly wasn't exactly angry at me when I left her and Katy at our house to set up for the ritual, but she was capital letters NOT HAPPY, despite my promise to be back well before midnight. I departed with my tail between my legs, metaphorically speaking.

"Carly's going to give you the hiccups for two days," Malcolm predicted as Matthias drove us as speedily and stealthily as possible toward the Hensleys' house on the city's posh west side. "Maybe an itch on your back that you can't scratch no matter what. Or make it so caffeine doesn't have any effect on you anymore."

I sucked in a breath and clutched my travel tumbler of coffee to my chest. "Don't *even* say that. Not even as a joke."

"*Does* caffeine affect you anymore, actually?" Matthias rumbled.

"From a purely scientific perspective, you consume it in quantities that might require medical study...or an intervention."

"Once again," Malcolm said haughtily, "I must remind you that *I* am the comic relief on Team Alice."

I put my tumbler in a cup holder and crossed my arms. "Neither of you are funny at all."

"I think you are both quite funny," Liam said from where he floated next to Malcolm in the back seat.

"Whose side are you on?" Malcolm demanded in mock outrage.

They all were trying so hard to cheer me up despite their own heavy hearts, and I had one of those moments when I felt I didn't deserve this much care and support. At least I recognized those moments for what they were now instead of letting my past trauma damage my current relationships like it once did.

"Thank you for that," I said with a tired smile. "And for coming with me."

"As if we'd let you go without us," Malcolm scoffed. "Especially since Sean had to stay behind to try to talk to the Were Ruling Council. I hope he can resist the urge to dismantle the storage building with his bare hands after what Vaughan told you. At least Carly brought him scones. How she finds time to bake with everything else going on, I have no idea."

"I think she bakes *because* there's so much going on," I said. "We've all got our coping mechanisms."

"Hers just happens to be yummier than most," he agreed. "Or so I imagine. The scones *look* tasty, anyway."

"I can attest to their tastiness," Matthias said.

He'd spoken briefly to Sean while I was getting ready to run out the door and probably shared what Bryan had told him. We'd jumped right in the SUV after that and I hadn't had a chance to ask him anything. He'd obviously put it away to deal with later. Hearing him joke about my coffee consumption had eased my worry a bit, but I sensed he remained deeply troubled. I'd have to wait to talk to him until we had privacy.

Meanwhile, we had two ghosts in the back seat instead of the usual one because Malcolm had wanted to come with me to the Hensleys' and Liam didn't want to be separated from him, even safe behind our wards at home. Despite Liam's obvious anxiety about the possibility of being reclaimed by one of Moses's mages, he seemed to be doing fairly well. He'd only been imprisoned in a mage crystal for a few months, but to him it might have felt like eons.

He and Malcolm hovered quietly for most of our drive. I didn't sense tension between them, but I wondered about the silence. Maybe they'd talked for all the hours between when I'd released him from the crystal until I'd summoned Malcolm home to tell him about Gracie Hensley's phone call and they were just talked out for the time being.

To lessen our chances of being caught violating the curfew, I'd activated the *Look Away* and obfuscation spellwork I'd etched into the wheel wells of my recently purchased vehicle. They basically encouraged anyone who spotted us to ignore us, but we weren't invisible by any stretch of the imagination. It was, as I'd told Sean and Arkady before we left, simply the best I could do.

The curfew only applied within the city limits, so we'd seen several vehicles on the road on the way into town from the house. Soon, however, we were one of the few signs of life on eerie empty streets. Matthias drove slowly with the SUV's lights off, ready to pull to the curb the moment we spotted law enforcement or a SPEMA vehicle. I had a story prepared if we did get busted, but by some miracle we made it to the Hensleys' house without crossing paths with local cops or the feds. Most of the homes we passed were dark with curtains drawn, as if the occupants feared lights might attract the attention of the necromancer or spirits we planned to track and trap.

As soon as Matthias put the SUV in park in the driveway, I jumped out the passenger door and ran. My footsteps were the only sound on the empty street, so I cut across the lawn with Malcolm and Liam right behind me. I noticed the window broken by vandals had been covered with plywood.

The moment my boot touched the porch steps, the front door flew open to reveal Gracie in the doorway. Crying had made her face and eyes red, and angry dark marks on her throat showed where Oliver had tried to strangle her with his bare hands.

"Just you," she said to me, her eyes wild with fear as Matthias came up the sidewalk. "He'll only talk to you."

"This is my trainee," I lied. "He'll keep out of sight, but he can't stay outside." And he wouldn't, if I was any judge of his facial expressions.

"Okay," she said faintly as Matthias joined me near the door. His head brushed the support beams of the porch ceiling. At least his eyes weren't glowing, so she'd probably just think he was the biggest damn human she'd ever seen. Hopefully we could deal with the situation without her knowing there was a nearly seven-foot beta werewolf in her house on top of everything else.

She stepped aside so we could get inside and shrank back as Matthias passed. "We're here to help," he said kindly, his voice pitched low so it wouldn't carry farther than the entryway. "Alice will take care of your husband. Do you have a first aid kit so I can help you?"

Up close, I spotted small bloody gouges and scratches on her neck that looked exactly like the ones I'd made on myself when one of the spirits forced me to squeeze my own throat. I pushed away that memory before it could distract me from what I needed to do.

"Tell me what happened," I murmured to Gracie, who looked lost. "Give me the details."

"We were going to bed early because of the curfew. I thought we could watch some TV or a movie and try to get his mind off things. But as we lay there, he started looking more and more angry, and then he got very quiet, and then all of the sudden—" she took a ragged, sobbing breath "—he got on top of me and put his hands around my neck and squeezed. He looked so angry. I thought he was going to kill me. I was about to pass out, and then he let me go."

Matthias made a low rumbling sound that thankfully she didn't notice.

"Did he tell you why he attacked you?" I asked.

"He said he thought he was a killer, but then he couldn't go through with it and now he doesn't know who he is anymore. He just sat on the edge of the bed and cried while I tried to get my breath back. I thought he'd be okay, or he'd eventually be okay. But then he realized how much he'd hurt me."

What an absolute nightmare. "What did he do then?"

"I was kind of in a daze, like I was in shock. He went downstairs, got a knife, came back, and tried to cut his own throat right in front of me."

"Oh, jeez," Malcolm muttered.

"I managed to get the knife away from him." She held out her hand to show me several deep cuts on her palm. "I don't think he cut anything major on his neck, but he was definitely bleeding."

I kept my voice gentle because she looked so skittish. "Thank you for telling me the story. I'm so sorry about all of this. Let Matthias take care of you. Where is Oliver?"

"Our bathroom upstairs. I hear him in there moving around, but he won't talk to me." She swallowed hard and flinched. Her throat would be sore for a while, probably. "I have a first aid kit in the downstairs bathroom."

"Get the kit and stay down here with Matthias," I said. "I'll talk to Oliver and let you know when I think it's a good time for you to come upstairs."

She headed down the hall, sniffling.

"Thank you for offering to help her," I said to Matthias in an undertone. "Sorry to fib about why you're here, but it was easier than explaining. Try to keep her calm. Liam, do you mind staying down here while Malcolm and I go upstairs? Just to keep an eye on things while Matthias is busy."

"Yes, ma'am." Liam flitted uneasily. "I'll do my best."

Malcolm touched Liam's hand reassuringly and followed me toward the stairs.

We crossed paths with Gracie carrying her first aid kit. "It'll be okay," I said, and hoped it was true.

She gave me a sniffly smile and followed Matthias toward the kitchen. Liam stayed right behind them, looking around nervously.

"Liam's okay," Malcolm assured me as we climbed the steps to the second floor. "He's just worried about the necromancer and the nasty ghosts. And Matthias too, a little, though he knows he can't actually do anything to him. The dude's just...gigantic."

I couldn't argue with that. The only person I knew who was as tall and muscular was Ronan. If Liam thought Matthias was intimidating, he'd be petrified of a giant fallen angel, even if he *was* mortal now. I made a mental note to reassure him about Ronan before he returned from whatever mysterious bounty hunter business had taken him out of state for a week.

The condition of Oliver and Gracie's bedroom sobered me instantly. Just a few days ago, the room looked straight out of a designer's portfolio. Now it was a testament to the violence Gracie had endured. Most of the bedding was on the floor and blood splattered the sheets. Bloody handprints and smears along the wall and a dresser indicated where Oliver had staggered from the bed to the bathroom. I spotted another smear of blood on the bathroom door and a smudge on the handle.

The silence in the bathroom caused a ball of dread to form in my stomach. I laid on the floor and peered through the tiny gap under the door. Drops of blood on the tile floor led to a pair of bare feet on the rug near the exterior wall. Oliver was probably sitting on the side of the tub. I took a deep breath and let it out before I rose.

"You good?" Malcolm asked.

I nodded grimly. Unfortunately, Oliver would be far from the first person I'd had to talk back from the ledge. My own experiences on ledges helped me empathize with those who found themselves in such misery and hopelessness that death seemed like the only answer.

If nothing else, I hoped my evidence, while not yet sufficient to persuade a human court or D.A. to drop the charges against him, might be enough for him to accept that he wasn't a killer. Then he and Gracie would need counseling to try to repair the damage done to their relationship.

"Oliver?" I called. "It's Alice Worth. Are you okay?"

For several moments, I didn't get a response. When it came, his voice sounded rough. "Go away."

Very quietly and gently so he couldn't hear me doing it, I tried the door handle and confirmed it was locked. "Hey, Oliver," I said, making my voice as kind and sympathetic as I could. "Gracie called me and asked me to come over and talk to you. You did the right thing and let her go. She's going to be okay."

No answer this time, but at least he hadn't repeated his demand that I leave.

"I know you're really angry and upset right now," I continued. "And I understand that. I can't imagine how you're feeling. But I have good news. I have evidence I can show you that proves you weren't responsible for what happened to Madison Fernell."

"I killed Madison. I stabbed her over and over again and I cut her throat."

"Your body did, but *you* didn't," I countered calmly. "If you'll let me in, I'll show you proof."

If I could get within reach, I could drop him with a sleep spell so he wouldn't be a threat to anyone, including himself, until I could reach Philippa Grayson and hopefully get him inpatient treatment and professional counseling.

"There *is* no proof," Oliver grated. "You're trying to trick me. It's not going to work."

"If I show you some proof, will you open the door for me? I'll give you space. I'm only here to talk."

"What about that guy downstairs? What's he here for?"

Dang it. I'd worried that he'd seen us arrive from the window. "He's an apprentice private investigator. He's just keeping Gracie company." I didn't tell him Matthias was also giving Gracie first aid. No sense bringing up her injuries. "I asked him to stay downstairs. It's just me here at the door."

"You say you have evidence." His voice remained rough and suspicious. "What kind of evidence?"

"I've got some evidence at home that we're going to use to locate the person who's really responsible for Madison's death. I plan to get them into police custody tonight. I've also got some photos and video on my phone that show the spirit that possessed you."

Another long silence. I didn't like the feeling of that silence. I suspected Oliver was in a very dark place.

"If I show you the photo of the spirit, will you let me in to talk to you?" I asked.

"Okay," he said reluctantly.

On my phone, I opened the image taken from the sandwich shop's surveillance video that showed the spirit leaving the alley after the murder. "Here's one picture," I said, and slipped the phone under the door.

Bare feet crossed the floor toward me. A shadow appeared under the door as Oliver bent down to take my phone.

I gave him a moment to look at the photo, then said, "You see it, right? There's another video taken in the parking garage from when the spirit latched on to you. By themselves, it's not enough for the D.A. to dismiss the charges against you, but once we catch that spirit and turn the person in who controlled them, you'll be exonerated." I hoped. "You're an innocent man, Oliver. Can I please come in and talk to you face-to-face now?"

The lock clicked and then his footsteps retreated. "It's open," he said. Now he just sounded tired.

I let out a breath and touched Malcolm's ghostly hand. *Go check on Matthias and Liam, I said. Let Matthias know I'm talking to Oliver. We'll come downstairs when he's calmed down and cleaned up.*

You sure? he asked, clearly unhappy. *I know you don't think he's possessed again, but dude's already been violent once tonight.*

I know, but I think we're done with that. If there's a problem, I'll let you know.

Reluctantly, he zipped away.

I turned the door handle, slipped inside, and shut the door behind me.

In a bloody T-shirt and pajama pants, Oliver stood in the middle of the bathroom about where I'd drawn my circle the other day to check him for magic. His chin nearly rested on his chest and his shoulders were hunched in what I supposed was despair. As Gracie had described, his throat showed several shallow knife wounds that had bled profusely but hadn't nicked either his carotid or jugular. On a couple of cuts in particular, less than an inch or so either way and he'd be dead now.

"Hey, Oliver," I said gently. "It's going to be okay."

He avoided my eyes and said nothing. His expression was so devoid of emotion that my uneasiness came back with a vengeance. Was he in shock after seeing the image of the spirit, or because of what he'd done to Gracie? Or both? He might even be experiencing some kind of breakdown.

"I'm sorry this happened to you," I said, keeping my voice kind and calm. "Like I said, I can't imagine how you feel, but there is a light at the end of the tunnel now. I promise you are not a killer."

Oliver's head remained bowed, but for the first time, he flicked his gaze up to me. "But what if I am?"

For a moment, another face appeared superimposed over his like an out-of-focus photo or afterimage. It flashed in and out so quickly that I might have chalked it up to my imagination or some kind of strange aftereffect of the concussion or my recent exorcism...

...except I knew that face. I'd seen it just yesterday hovering only inches from my own.

My stomach dropped.

My phone. He'd taken my phone. I saw its outline in his pajama pocket. Son of a *bitch*.

Fury and dread gave way to cold focus as I spooled magic.

Oliver smiled and put his finger to his lips. "Shh, little birdie," he said, his voice a rough blend of his own and the spirit's. "Be quiet, or everyone in this house dies."

THIRTY-EIGHT

This wasn't the first time my best-laid plans had blown up in my face. In fact, it wasn't even the first time *today* it had happened.

Back at my house, Carly and Katy were prepping their altar, mirrors, spellwork, and according to Carly, actual-factual divine forces to protect us as we faced the spirits and the necromancer.

At this moment, trapped in the Hensleys' lilac-scented bathroom, I had pretty much none of those things. And my backup team were all down in the kitchen, utterly oblivious—at least for now—to what I faced.

I didn't let go of my magic, but I forced myself to be calm so neither Malcolm nor Sean would sense I was in trouble until I had a plan. As much as this spirit enjoyed killing, I had no doubt he'd try to make good on his threat.

"Who are you?" I asked.

"You's don't need my proper name." He forced Oliver's mouth into an unsettling, uncanny rictus of a smile, like a robot mimicking human expression. "But we know *yours*, little birdie. Alice...Evelyn... Worth." His grin stretched Oliver's lips until he looked like a dog or a wolf baring its teeth. "Whore name if I ever heard one."

I'd been called worse by people in my own family, not to mention a Dark Fae and other very scary things, so that insult didn't faze me much. "What can I call you, then? I can't very well just say *Hey psycho.*"

His atonal laugh made the hairs prickle on my arms. I hoped Matthias couldn't hear it from downstairs. "Call me Little," he said. "That's what they all called me. I got a lot of names."

I recalled the mysterious words etched into the blades of the weapons used in the murder-suicides last night. "So if you're Little, where's Big?"

He chuckled. I liked that sound even less than his laugh. It held so much malevolence and unmistakable threat of intimate violence that my skin crawled. I had to resist the urge to back away.

"He's having his own fun," Little told me, with another chortle. "We each got our own lil' hobbies, you know."

More bad news, if true. I didn't think the spirits were more dangerous off their master's leash than on it, per se, but the fact they were capable of making plans, controlling themselves, and being devious instead of flailing mindlessly and jumping from host to host or screaming in an alley meant they had been on our side of the abyss a while as well as being incredibly powerful. So the necromancer had been planning this crime spree for a while.

In the meantime, Little's speech patterns, voice, and overall demeanor had clued me in that he wasn't from our time. How long ago he'd lived and how long he'd been dead I didn't exactly know, but there was something distinctly out of place about him.

"What are *your* hobbies, then?" I asked when he seemed to be waiting for me to respond. I needed to buy time to hatch a plan. "Besides the obvious, I mean."

"Robbin' and stealin' always kept coins in our pockets and food in our bellies," he said, with obvious pride. "But mostly we like the killin'. There's other pleasures we want that we's been missin' for a real long time, though. We aims to enjoy ourselves. We jus' have to figure out how to control cocks as well as we control hands and feet."

Fury and revulsion made my magic sizzle and guts churn. "You won't be doing any such thing," I said, my voice cold. I wasn't sure about the physiological aspects, but given enough time and opportunity, they might actually be able to follow through on this new, monstrous threat.

He grinned again. "I think I want to start with you, Alice Evelyn Worth. Can you stay quiet 'til I'm done so I don't have to kill your friend and this one's sweet lil' wife? I bet you can." He leaned forward. "But I hope you don't," he added in a whisper. "I want blood on my cock. Ain't nothin' better in this world or the next."

The full horror sank in of what he and "Big" planned to do to me and whoever else they wanted to victimize. The threat formed images in my head that went straight to some of my biggest and deepest fears. Nausea surged. My hands trembled.

During my years as my grandfather's captive, he'd threatened to use me as breeding stock if he found the right sire for my offspring. My consent was never a factor in the equation.

In my line of work, I'd faced similar threats to Little's before too —but never with the added complication that if I fought back, I'd endanger the lives around me.

Little grinned at me. His ghostly rotten teeth shimmered in front of Oliver's perfect smile. "What do you say, little birdie? Will you scream?"

I took a moment to think of Carly, who'd insisted I draw the spellwork for tonight's ritual on my skin under my clothes well in advance so the magic had extra time to bond to me. If she'd foreseen this moment, she would have told me, but maybe she'd gotten some kind of inkling I might need the spellwork ahead of schedule. She'd halfway gotten me believing there were no such things as accidents when it came to things that mattered.

And she would have told me the fact Little, in Oliver's body, was standing right smack in the middle of the circle I'd drawn the other night wasn't a coincidence either.

I'd wiped away the chalk days ago, but the echo remained. It would only be a fraction as powerful, well-warded, and solid as mine at home, but it would be enough to get the job done—I hoped.

Little's smile twisted into a snarl. "I asked you a question. Are you gonna scream, lil' birdie?"

"No," I said.

As if I'd given in, I went to my knees right in front of him, making sure I was inside the perimeter of the circle.

He smirked down at me. "Not so proud now, are you? You look real good there on your knees. I think I'll make you crawl behind me wherever I go until I'm done with you."

Another flash of memory surfaced—this one worse than the last. Moses had taken me to see my parents' bodies after he'd burned them alive. By the time I knew they were gone, nothing remained but ash in the shape of two people who'd held each other as they'd died.

He'd made me stand next to the ash until I couldn't stand any longer, and then I'd had to crawl behind him out the door of my parents' home and down the sidewalk to his car. I was eight years old.

I'd curled up in the back seat of Moses's car, as far away from him as I could get, and sworn I would never crawl for anyone ever again.

For this half-baked plan of mine to work, timing would be everything. I sliced my finger on the hidden edge of one of my crystals and waited for blood to well up. A weak echo of a circle needed a good dab of blood to invoke. I'd practiced this scenario repeatedly too, both during my captivity in Baltimore and since moving to California.

Little reached for the waistband of his pajama pants.

I pushed love and trust as hard as I could through my nascent bond with Sean and touched my bloody finger to the circle. "*Enclose,*" I said.

The circle flared weakly, but I figured Malcolm and maybe even Matthias would feel it and come running. I didn't have much time.

Little made a snarling sound.

With my earth magic, I grabbed the spellwork written on the

skin over my heart. The smell of parchment and damp earth filled the circle, swirled by witch magic and my own power. Something detached inside me. The sensation reminded me of Carly's mirror pulling Valas out of me and my stomach lurched.

No time for nausea or second thoughts.

I lunged at Little—or it felt like I did. My *ka*, my astral self, slipped free of my body as easily as shedding a cloak. Nothing so terrible should feel so effortless. The deceptive simplicity and terrible power of the spellwork made me respect and fear Carly's magic even more.

In fact, Charles, Moses, and the world at large should be grateful Carly was on the side of good.

As my physical body slumped to the bathroom floor, my spectral self dove through Oliver's body. I wrapped my arms around Little's ghastly, ghostly form and ripped him out of Oliver. My client collapsed and hit the floor in a heap.

Little thrashed in my grip, howled in rage, and, of all things, tried to bite my face. Reflexively, I kneed him in the groin and his howl became a screech.

Huh. I couldn't believe that worked. I filed that away to tell Malcolm about later.

I gripped Little tighter, took a deep breath, and hummed five notes.

The circle crackled and the floor yawned open beneath us. I heard Malcolm yell my name just before Little and I plunged into absolute darkness.

THIRTY-NINE

WE FELL FOR A VERY, VERY LONG TIME, OR SO IT SEEMED. OR MAYBE IT would have been more accurate to say we fell a very, very long way. Time had no meaning in the cold and dark.

Nor was I sure we were plunging down per se. The sensation was of movement, but after the initial drop through the bathroom floor our route could have just as well been in any direction. The sensations in my spectral body were all very confusing. I decided to call it *down* just to make myself feel better.

While my memory of my time in the Underworld remained clear, I had no recollection of either my fall into that place or my return from it to the Broken World. We'd only known that some time had passed during each passage and the journeys had been rather bumpy, judging by minor damage to our backpacks and bodies.

Unfortunately, I couldn't say the same for my trip to Tartarus. In my spectral state, I was aware of every moment. I didn't sleep. I didn't feel hunger or thirst. I simply *was*, for a long, long time.

Little fell at a rate greater than mine—enough to keep me out of his reach and vice-versa. He was returning to the place he belonged, while I was an intruder in this realm. At least he eventually exhausted his repertoire of curses and threats and lapsed into sullen silence.

I hummed the whole way down.

Every time I felt a bump, or my fall slowed, I repeated the little five-note tune Carly had taught me, and the plunge continued. Little, on the other hand, didn't need a spell to travel between our world and the place beyond the abyss where his damned soul had been sent to spend eternity.

Linear or even coherent thought proved surprisingly difficult in this eerie, icy darkness. I came to understand, at least vaguely, that I was passing by other places as if I were in an elevator traveling from a penthouse to the basement through every floor in between. With each "floor" or barrier I passed, my mind became foggy. By the time I'd regained my ability to think, I'd forgotten what I'd thought about prior. Moments felt granular and disconnected from each other instead of flowing in a stream like I was used to.

During a rare moment of clarity, I wondered if Valas would someday take a similar fall. Part of me wanted her to stay trapped in Carly's eggshell pit behind the mirror so I knew where she was. I had faith in Carly's ability to construct an escape-proof prison. If Valas fell to Tartarus, on the other hand, I couldn't keep an eye on her. She was too strange, too powerful, and too full of unknown magic for me to feel sure she'd be trapped there. If anyone might find a way out of its abyssal depths, it would be her.

At least I could feel reasonably certain she wouldn't have help getting out of Tartarus if she fell, even if a necromancer tried to summon her back. For all their power, a necromancer must possess bone, blood, or flesh, or at least an item that contained part of the *ka* of the deceased to summon their spirit back from Tartarus. Valas's spirit might have survived the events that took place in Colorado by hitching a ride in my body, but nothing of her body remained. I'd seen it burn to ash.

Then another wave of confusion hit and those thoughts drifted away.

Sometime after that—maybe an hour, maybe a day or a year—Little abruptly blinked out of existence, and in the next second, so did I.

I had no time to register my own lack of existence, which was just as well.

We arrived in Tartarus without warning or dignity. In my experience, this kind of travel usually ended that way.

And of course I landed face down in dirt. All the saints and sinners forbid I *ever* land in *any* realm in *any* other way than face down in dirt.

This dirt tasted like licking a battery, and it was black and mixed with ash. So was the air, in fact. And it was so fucking *cold* that it seared my skin like I'd dropped into a cryogenic freezer—or at least what I imagined one might feel like. I gasped reflexively and sucked in a lungful of ashy Hell-dirt that sent me into a violent paroxysm of coughing. Within moments of arriving, my bones ached from the cold.

I won't survive here, I thought, and nearly laughed at myself. I could almost hear Malcolm say, *Duh, Alice—I'm pretty sure that's the whole friggin' point.*

Right about the time I rounded up enough working brain cells to realize I actually had physical form now, someone huge, heavy, and screaming profanities jumped on my back and punched me so hard in the back of my head I was surprised his fist didn't come out my forehead.

I went limp as if he'd knocked me unconscious, hoping he wouldn't hit me again if he thought I was out. Not that much of an exaggeration, truth be told. My ears rang and everything went out of focus.

I had little magic in this place; my power was natural and came from the air and earth of the human realm. Little and I and every other denizen of Tartarus had physical form, but not the same kind we'd had in my world. That meant my blood magic had very limited use, but it wasn't useless. And most importantly of all, Carly's magic came from universal energies, meaning it was just as strong here as anywhere else.

Dimly, I thought about the fact somewhere far, far from here, the people who loved me were scrambling. They'd know where I'd gone and why because Malcolm had witnessed me fall and take Little's spirit with me. We'd had a plan for how the night would play out, but that had gone to Hell, quite literally, and now we'd all have to work out Plans B, C, and D. And possibly E through G.

First things first: I had a job to do, if I could manage to do anything but see stars and dirt.

I stayed limp and motionless as Little ground my face deep into the cold, black, ashy soil. He held me there until he was apparently satisfied that either I wasn't conscious or I'd chosen not to fight him anymore. Then he took his enormous weight off me and flipped me roughly onto my back.

When he loomed over me, I saw him clearly and in the flesh for the first time. As when he'd appeared to me as a spirit after the murder at the hospital, his face was twisted in fury and disgust. Even over the heavy stench of old batteries, blood, coals, and burning wires that pervaded everything in this place, he reeked of hate. His eyes shone with hunger, but not for food. He craved death in the way most people wanted food, shelter, and love. His thick body, all muscle and rage, trembled with his obvious desire to kill me with his bare hands. I felt his appetite for death as clearly as I felt the roughness of the dirt under me.

He wore tattered clothing that placed his living years at least a few centuries before my own: an almost shapeless shirt made of thick material that had worn through in several places and pants in a similar condition. His gnarled feet were bare. I spotted rope marks on his ankles and wrists and another around his thick neck that formed a V-shape at the base of his skull. Whoever he was, he'd been bound hand and foot and hanged for his crimes before his soul landed here in Tartarus, where by all rights he should have stayed.

Where he *would* have stayed if it weren't for the necromancer who'd summoned and unleashed him on the living once more.

He saw me looking at him and spat in my face. "Cunt. Whore."

Those were not words I liked. So I did what any reasonable person would do in that moment: I pulled a weapon and stabbed him right in the heart.

He screamed and fell backward onto his ass in the dirt.

My weapon was about twelve inches long and resembled a stake more than a dagger or sword. It came with me to Tartarus courtesy of Carly's spellwork, and I'd pulled it from my thigh where the spellwork had been hidden under my jeans. I had never wielded any kind of weapon that was nothing more than a two-dimensional drawing on my skin only moments before, but it was definitely handy—and the only kind of weapon I could have brought with me to this place.

Still woozy from that punch to the back of my head, I lurched to my knees and plowed my shoulder into Little's chest. We landed on the ground in a tangle and flurry of punches and kicks. He hit my cheek with his elbow hard enough to snap my head back, and I scratched his face so deeply I left gouges that oozed thick blood. As he cursed and tried to shove me away, I pushed blood magic out my fingertips to form blades and drove them into his gut.

Despite his nickname, Little was easily double my size and weight. To lessen his advantage, and because it had worked well before, I tried to knee him in the groin again. He managed to partially block my blow but I still made enough contact that he howled and tried to roll to his side to protect his sensitive bits. I needed him on his back, though, so I drew back my arm and landed an uppercut to his square jaw that hurt like hell and probably broke my hand, but my form and strength when I delivered that punch would have made Sean proud. All those hours punching the heavy bag and sparring were paying off.

While Little was dazed, I grabbed the hilt of the strange weapon Carly had designed and put all my weight into driving it the rest of the way through his torso. It grew longer as it plunged deeper into his chest, and it took every bit of leverage and force I could muster with both hands to get its point through his innards and ribcage and out through his back to stake him to the ground. Little's gurgly scream made me grin.

The moment the point slid into the dirt, spikes spiraled out down the length of the now almost three-foot-long stake, tearing through his flesh and pinning him to the ground with a flare of parchment-scented witchy magic. Little tried to wrench himself free, but the spikes and stake held fast.

With a sound that was almost a roar, Little punched me in the face so hard that I went down in a heap. The blow *should* have knocked me out pretty much instantly. In fact, I lay still for a beat, fully expecting to lose consciousness. Instead, I got the uncanny feeling this place denied its inhabitants any kind of escape or temporary relief—even right hook-induced unconsciousness. No rest for the wicked, indeed.

The best I could do was roll out of his reach and let him flail on his back like a dying roach. Sick to my stomach and dizzy, I sprawled on the dirt and blinked blearily up into dark, stinking nothingness.

The smell of this place never abated. If anything, the stench got worse. It reminded me of melted wiring and old blood with notes of burned flesh. At least I no longer felt the painful cold, though I wasn't sure why. The black dirt clung to my skin no matter how much I tried to brush it off. I got the itchy, burning feeling it was working itself through my skin to reach my blood and bones and organs.

The sky above me, if I could call it a sky, was as black as the dirt. Far, far above us loomed a ring of reddish-orange, as if fires burned all around the edge of the black abyss in which we lay. When I tried to focus on that light, I had the nauseating sensation that the distance between the dirt under my back and the fiery barrier was eternal...as eternally deep as this place was eternally vast.

For the first time, it really sank in where I was.

Tartarus—the Hell under Hell. The deepest, most wretched

depths of any known realm, prison for all manner of damned gods, monsters, and humans. Named for a primordial deity who, according to myth, might have fathered the monstrous immortal Titan Typhon, who I'd smote with an almighty bolt of lightning in the Underworld. Luckily for my companions and me, a dragon the size of a jumbo jet had taken him away from the battlefield and re-imprisoned him. According to my research on the topic, he might be here in Tartarus.

My life took strange turn after strange turn, and yet still managed to come full circle sometimes.

I'd seen parts of the Underworld, but Ronan had assured me it bore no resemblance to Hell. The descriptions offered by myth and legend were simply that: myth. As a result, even after research I'd had no idea what to expect of this place. Hellfire had seemed reasonable. Masses of writhing bodies screaming in tortured agony had also been high on the list of possibilities. But much like the Underworld, Tartarus proved to be not at all as I'd expected.

Maybe each damned soul faced its own kind of suffering here. I'd arrived tethered to Little's spirit, so this might be his personal eternal torment. For someone who thrived on inflicting suffering and death, an eternity in a wasteland devoid of anything or anyone to torture would be a hellish fate, and one he'd certainly earned.

"Whore," Little rasped.

Now that I'd gotten him staked in place, I decided to just ignore him until he stopped talking, like I'd done during our fall. Really, my head hurt too damn much to think about anything except escape, and even those thoughts felt muted and distant. My right thigh ached and stung where I'd drawn the magical stake from my skin. My jeans felt warm and sticky there, like I was bleeding. I was surprised that I didn't particularly care about that.

This place sapped all my energy, as if the vast emptiness pulled it from me. Or was I concussed again? Was that a thing that could happen in whatever form I was in while trapped? Maybe so. If I could bleed, I could probably get concussed. And I'd kicked Little in the nuts and he'd felt it. I supposed an eternity of suffering in this place required a form that could experience pain and injury.

Little tried again to get me to respond. "Lil' birdie." He still sounded angry, but now he was also petulant, like a child. "Why cain't you just let us have our fun? What business is it of yours?"

Trying to explain morality, right and wrong, or justice to a sadistic psychopath would be like trying to fill a colander with water, so I didn't bother.

He was a murderer and a monster—as much of a monster as I'd ever met in any realm. I saw little appreciable difference between him and Typhon. At least Typhon had the excuse that he was born a monster. Little had chosen to become one and apparently relished every moment of it with no hint of conscience.

When I didn't reply, his tone changed again, to the same sneer he'd used when I'd knelt in front of him in the Hensleys' bathroom and he'd thought he was about to get what he wanted. "Big will kill everyone you love," he taunted. "He'll slaughter them all and leave the gutted corpses for you to find. He'll fill a cup with their blood and make you drink it."

"Boring threat," I mumbled. "My grandfather makes up better threats in his sleep. You're a *boring* monster."

Hmm. I usually had much better insults than that. Maybe I actually *was* concussed. Or maybe I didn't belong here and this place knew it. Maybe I was fading out of existence again.

Come on, Carly, I thought, willing her to hear me with whatever sixth sense she had that made her nose twitch when I was in trouble. *Bring me back before it's too late.*

Carly had described the spellwork I wore as a kind of bungee cord that would pull me back once I'd staked the spirit or spirits in place so they couldn't be summoned again. But that was based on the plan that I'd grab them and open her express elevator to Tartarus during the ritual we'd planned to conduct at midnight. I hoped the spellwork could at least be used as a fishing line now and she and

Katy could reel me back up. I would have crossed my fingers if I had the strength.

The ground rumbled very faintly. Everything had been so eerily still for so long that at first I thought I might have imagined the sensation. But as the vibration increased, even my cottony brain processed that something was coming—something that felt *way* bigger than us.

Unfortunately, I didn't know where the rumble was coming from, and there was absolutely nowhere in all this vast eternal emptiness to hide.

Little thrashed against his stake and cursed with renewed vigor. "The Keeper," he howled. "The Keeper is coming."

I tried to get up, or even just roll onto my side, but my arms and legs didn't want to obey. Little's howls dissolved into laughter.

I still saw nothing but darkness, but a bellow rolled through us with visible shockwaves. When the first wave hit, it reduced my hearing to a high-pitched ringing as if someone had fired a gun six inches from my head. The pain made it nearly impossible to think, but at least I couldn't hear Little's mad laughter. The ground heaved and rolled.

I'd made it almost to my hands and knees when a body appeared out of nowhere and landed right on top of me.

CHAPTER

FORTY

I recognized his magic long before my pain-muddled brain processed the sight of his face, or the fact he'd landed on me with one hundred percent of the weight of an adult man, or that I was simultaneously *so freaking mad at him* for risking himself like this, but also so relieved to see him that I would have cried if I remembered how to do that.

He rolled off me, knelt at my side, and cupped my face with both hands so he could look me right in the eye. *Alice,* he said, or I thought he said. I still couldn't hear anything. *Alice, I'm here,* he mouthed. His expression was extremely grim. I probably looked pretty rough.

Weird that he wasn't sharing thoughts with me. Maybe we couldn't do that here. That figured.

I'd only ever gotten to touch him while we were in the Broken World, where ghosts were more corporeal than in our own world. For ninety-nine percent of our time together, I couldn't so much as touch his hand, much less hug him, and vice-versa. Even so, I loved him with all my heart.

Though I'd gotten a taste of what it would be like if Malcolm were alive while we visited the Broken World, I was utterly unprepared for seeing and *feeling* my best friend really and truly in the flesh for the first time. Even if this privilege only lasted as long as we remained here, it was worth every bit of suffering to feel his touch. I leaned against his hand to soak in his warmth. He hadn't yet grown cold with the emptiness of this place.

Malcolm got me sitting up, then with surprising strength he hauled me to my feet. My limbs felt heavy as lead, and the ground heaved with the approach of whatever creature Little referred to as the Keeper. Malcolm kept us upright by bracing himself and locking his arms around me. I sagged against him, my head on his chest. The buttons on his shirt pressed into my cheek. What a simple joy to feel that sensation.

My happiness was short-lived. As suddenly as the rumbling had started, everything went silent and still, like a deep breath before a scream.

Little threw his head back in maniacal laughter I couldn't hear over the ringing in my ears.

The darkness around us exploded into fire and a thousand whirling, writhing arms or tentacles, each with a different monstrous head at its tip, all screaming.

Orange coals and fire fell like rain, pelting us from all directions and sizzling in the black dirt. Malcolm attempted to protect us with his magic. When that failed, he resorted to trying to shield me with his body as he half-walked, half-dragged me away from Little. The pain of my own burns barely registered, but Malcolm's agony seared me through our binding.

Over my shoulder, I saw the creature's arms darting toward Little a half-dozen at a time so each monstrous mouth could snap its teeth at his body. It was hard to tell from a distance, but it looked like the bites took out mouthfuls of flesh as other heads mimicked Little's laughter and screams.

Unfortunately, my hearing was coming back. The sound of the Keeper made my teeth ache and my stomach heave.

Every time I tried to speak, nothing came out. I feared madness would overtake me unless we got far enough away from the Keeper and its prey to escape the terrible cacophony.

Malcolm and I stumbled across the dirt as fast as my rubbery legs could move, but the creature seemed as vast as the darkness. The falling coals and fire did grow less frequent as we put distance between ourselves and Little—enough that Malcolm was able to move us out of the way of most of the burning debris.

My legs went out from under me. Only Malcolm's arms kept me upright.

"Hang on, Alice," he shouted, his mouth next to my ear. Hearing his voice gave me enough strength to stay on my feet. "Carly's going to haul us back together."

When? I wanted to ask, but my mouth wouldn't form words anymore. I'd lost the ability to speak.

A little at a time, I was fading away. As much as the Underworld had sensed I'd crossed the veil between life and death more than once and tried to keep me, Tartarus knew I didn't belong here. Only monsters belonged here.

If I didn't get out soon, Malcolm would return empty-handed.

Malcolm held me tighter, as if he also knew I was fading. "Time is different here," he told me in answer to the question that probably showed in my eyes. He was so grim his face seemed all hard lines and shadows.

How much time had passed back in my own world since I'd fallen from the Hensleys' bathroom?

A coal hit the side of my head and bounced off with a sizzle I heard but didn't feel. Malcolm tucked my head under his chin. We'd stopped walking at some point but I hadn't noticed. At least the rain of fire and coals had dwindled to almost nothing.

In the distance, the Keeper and Little continued to laugh and scream. I'd run out of pain and fear and even the ability to feel satisfied by Little's torment, but Malcolm was here and Carly wouldn't let us down. At least I still had hope.

I closed my eyes to rest. When I opened them again, Malcolm had gone very still, and he was looking at something over my shoulder—something in the opposite direction of the Keeper and its prey. I managed to turn enough to see what had caught his attention.

It was a figure in a hooded cloak, carrying a tall wooden staff on which hung a black heart on a hook. Black magic crackled along the edges of the necromancer's cloak and the length of their staff. And unlike our magic, theirs would work perfectly fine here in the realm of the damned.

The figure raised its head enough for me to see a gold mask and a pair of red eyes glowing under the cloak's hood. The mask covered every part of their face except those eerie eyes. Why a mask? So I couldn't see their face and use the memory in some kind of spell? Or because I might have seen them before? Or just to be dramatic? Necromancers did tend to be more theatrical than most other magic practitioners I'd met.

The necromancer raised their right arm and pointed at me, and then at an empty hook on their staff. Well, that was a clear threat, as if their mere presence wasn't enough. Little was off the necromancer's hook now—quite literally—and thanks to Carly's stake he couldn't be reclaimed by the necromancer. So now the necromancer meant to replace Little's heart with mine.

I still had no ability to speak, and barely enough energy to move, but I managed to lift my unbroken left hand and extend my middle finger just long enough for them to see it before my arm fell back to my side.

A laugh rolled across the black dirt. It wasn't accompanied by a seismic wave and it didn't come from a thousand monstrous heads, but I liked it less than that of the Keeper. The necromancer's baritone laugh was distinctly male and far more seductive than it had any right to be.

I'd learned early in my life that the most dangerous monsters didn't *look* like monsters. They looked nothing like the Keeper. They were beautiful, with easy laughter and charming smiles, and they wore designer clothes and shared funny anecdotes over cocktails or beers while they fantasized about sinking their fangs, teeth, or claws into your soft belly.

Even in my deteriorating condition, I had the vague, half-formed idea that when we returned to our world, I wouldn't be looking for this man in some dark alley or a crumbling house in the woods. Something about the way he stood and watched us told me I'd find him in broad daylight, sipping coffee at a sidewalk café or working in a corner office downtown.

"Alice Evelyn Worth," the necromancer intoned. His voice and black magic wrapped around me as sinuously as a serpent and squeezed. He'd made my name a spell.

Reflexively, I broke his spellwork with my blood magic. Over the stink of Tartarus, I caught the scent of necromancy—damp earth and rot—as the spell fractured and dissipated.

The necromancer laughed again, as if amused by my ability to defend myself. That spell hadn't been all that powerful. He'd tested me, played with me. It was a tease, and a promise, and a threat.

Malcolm held me more tightly and glared at our adversary.

"You owe me a heart, Alice," the necromancer said, his tone conversational. "I'll be coming to collect my debt."

Did I know that voice? Was there a reason my instincts had told me this man felt at home in the sunlight and worked in a posh office?

No, I didn't know this man, I decided. But I might know *of* him.

Meanwhile, Malcolm was having none of the necromancer's threats. "We owe you *something*, but it's not a heart. We owe you one of *those*." He hooked his thumb back toward the Keeper.

The necromancer chuckled. We were just giving him all kinds of reasons to laugh down here. Come to think of it, had anyone ever laughed in Tartarus before, other than Little's maniacal howls?

That was the kind of question one might have when one was about to fade out of existence while trespassing in Hell's subbasement.

Something tugged at my insides, as if a rope tied around my middle had suddenly become taut. And so help me, I might have been hallucinating, but I could have sworn I smelled blueberry scones.

Somehow, the necromancer must have seen or sensed Carly's magic too. "I'll see you both again soon," he said. The mask hid his face, but I heard a smile in his tone. I had enough of myself left to hate him for it.

"Not if you don't see us coming," Malcolm said coldly.

In the next moment, we were gone, with the Keeper's laughter, Little's howls, and the necromancer's chuckle ringing in my ears.

CHAPTER
FORTY-ONE

THE DARKNESS WAS ABSOLUTE.

Am I dead?

No, I feel safe. I wouldn't feel safe if I were dead, would I?

I wouldn't be thinking if I were dead. But I don't feel...alive.

I opened my eyes.

I lay in a small circle lit by candles, with an altar in the center. At the top of the altar, in the direction I thought was north, lay a pine branch, a green candle, and a little pile of rich, damp earth. On the right Carly had placed small brown feathers and a cone of incense. Opposite the pine branch, to the south, I saw a white candle and several white feathers. And to the left was a blue candle and a bowl of water. I didn't know the symbolism of these items, but all were elements of nature. Maybe they represented Malcolm's and my natural magic. The pine branch might have signified Sean's forest scent and been intended to soothe me.

As my vision adjusted to my surroundings, I recognized my base-ment workshop. Carly had made my little circle away from my inlaid circles, which still contained the spellwork I'd drawn in preparation for the ritual intended to capture the spirits and hopefully catch a glimpse of the necromancer.

The only light in the basement came from the candles on the altar, so everything beyond the reach of their little flames was hidden by darkness. Witch magic—white, gray, and black as night—hung heavy in the air, but I saw no sign of Carly or Katy.

I started to sit up, then found I was already sitting without having moved. When I looked down at myself, my body wasn't solid.

Oh.

I was still my astral self. My body wasn't here—at least, not yet. But I felt certain Matthias had guarded it and Carly would put me back together.

Malcolm was nowhere to be seen, though I sensed we'd returned together. Relief washed over me.

A pair of glowing golden eyes appeared outside the circle, as if someone had been sitting in the dark with their eyes closed and then opened them. I knew those eyes immediately. I'd looked into them a thousand times.

"Sean?" I said, tentatively.

He rose and moved into the flickering candlelight at the edge of the circle. He couldn't see me, but he must know where I was by the sound of my voice.

He was naked, as if he'd been in wolf form and shifted back, and then waited for my return without caring about clothes. And again I found I'd moved without moving. This time, I'd gone from sitting to standing near the circle's edge in a blink. My feet had no weight on them, though I felt the basement floor under my soles.

"Alice," he said, his voice all growl.

The anger and grief on Sean's face sent a bolt of pain right through my heart. I fluttered in place like Malcolm did when he was upset. Huh. That felt as weird as it looked.

"I'm so sorry," I said. I didn't have a throat per se, but I still felt as if I had a lump in it. "He threatened to kill everyone in the house. I didn't think I had any other choice."

"I know." His bones and joints popped and crackled with the strain of holding back his wolf's fury and pain. "Malcolm was listening through the door, waiting to hear what you'd do and trying to figure out how to help. He told me the same thing: you did what had to be done." He flexed his hands. "He also said the spirit threatened to rape you."

I'd had no idea Malcolm was nearby listening, but I was glad he'd reported everything to Sean and the others so they knew what had led to my sudden departure.

"He did make that threat," I said, "but he didn't get to lay a finger on me. And then I put him back in Hell's subbasement to get eaten alive one bite at a time over and over again by some kind of primordial horror for all eternity."

He reached toward the barrier of the circle Carly had made to keep me safe, then remembered neither of us could cross it and lowered his hand. "Don't go where I can't come for you, Miss Magic. I love you too much to be left behind."

"I know." His unhappiness made me ache all the way to my soul. "How long was I gone?"

"For us, it's still tonight. It's not even midnight yet." His eyes looked bruised. "How much time passed for you?" He obviously feared what my answer might be.

"I'm not sure," I admitted. "It felt like a really long time, I think, but time is weird when you're not in your body. Super weird when you're in another realm or traveling between them."

He knew I was making light of the situation so I didn't get lost in memories and emotions. It was, as Carly and Matthias had pointed out, my favorite defense mechanism. But it was the only way I knew how to cope for now, until I had time to process everything.

"Where's everyone else?" I asked.

"Waiting upstairs. I had to be alone down here while I waited for Matthias to bring your...body...home." He scrubbed his face with his hands. "My wolf couldn't bear to hear any voice or smell any scent but yours. Not even Carly."

I wanted so badly to hold him and never let go. "Well, I'm ready to get back in my body," I said. "Being invisible is fun and all, but I've got a to-do list that requires being out of this circle and able to touch stuff. That includes you."

He didn't smile, but the prickly sensation of shifter magic eased. He retreated into the shadows and returned with his phone in hand. He sent a quick text, started to put the phone in his pocket, and then realized he didn't have one.

I chuckled. "You need some pants, babe."

"I need more than that." He tossed the phone and I heard it *thump* on something soft that I couldn't see. "Arkady went to stay with Oliver and his wife so Matthias could bring you here."

"How are the Hensleys doing?"

"According to Arkady, she got them calmed down enough to give them first aid and talk about what happened. It probably helped that she brought them amulets made by Carly to protect against any future attempts at possession. How she got there with all the cops and feds patrolling tonight, I don't know, but she did. She said something about her Harley having some 'after-market mods' she got from Ronan. Know anything about that?"

"Not the details," I hedged. "But I think he took her shopping at an underground market that sells fae stuff. Probably the same place he bought the gear for his own Harley. You know, like his saddlebags that can hold more than they can hold?"

His eyebrows went up.

The basement door opened. "Here, Sean," Carly called. I heard a quiet rustle from the direction of the stairs.

Sean disappeared in that direction and then returned wearing a T-shirt and jogging pants emblazoned with the pack logo. "Aw," I said in mock disappointment.

"You said I needed pants." He did smile then, at least a little. "I'll spare Carly and Katy the awkwardness."

I didn't think Carly would care one bit, but Katy was eighteen and though she'd seen a lot in her lifetime, a naked alpha werewolf with...generously sized attributes and what was in my opinion a perfect ass might distract her from the work we still had to do.

Three people filed down the stairs. Carly and Katy walked in front, wearing short hooded robes and carrying candles, and Matthias followed cradling my limp body.

Oh, jeez. I'd never seen my body from a distance before. I looked...dead.

Something like panic made me flutter again, this time all around the circle a few times before I made myself go still. Sean growled softly. He'd probably sensed my reaction and wanted desperately to hold me, but we couldn't touch each other. His wolf must be howling.

Sean met Matthias at the bottom of the stairs and took my body from him. They had a short conversation in an undertone as Carly and Katy approached me.

The light from their candles illuminated something I hadn't seen earlier: the quilt from our bed, made into a nest on the floor. I spotted several items of my clothing in the nest as well. Sean must have taken them from the hamper because he needed my scent. The quilt nest had clearly been occupied by Sean's wolf. More heartache. I fluttered in my circle.

"Welcome back." Carly came to stand directly in front of me while Katy went to the work table to gather items they needed. "Malcolm tells us you had a rough time of it down there."

"It's a really bad place," I said. "But I'm glad it exists for people like Little. And Big, when we find him."

"And their master." She looked straight into my eyes. "We *will* get them, Alice."

Matthias stayed near the stairs. Maybe he was standing guard, or maybe he still felt Sean needed space. He appeared stoic, but his eyes appeared deeply troubled. It had been a troubling night, and it wasn't over yet.

Sean brought my body to my little circle. My skin appeared

clammy and gray and my breathing was shallow. Other than the rise and fall of my chest I might have been a waxen figure, or dead.

The appearance of my body gave me the uncanny feeling of having goosebumps though I didn't have flesh. I recalled Malcolm describing that sensation to me before. If nothing else, this episode had given me a lot of insight into what he experienced on a daily basis.

"So, what now?" I asked. "Do I just…jump back into my body?"

Carly chuckled. "Not precisely, no. Do you see the green amulet in the dish of herbs on the altar?"

I found myself next to the altar after only just thinking about being next to it. As much as I wanted my body back, I *would* miss this kind of quick, effortless movement. "Yep, I see it," I said.

Katy handed Carly a little cup. Carly dipped her thumb into the pot and drew a symbol on my body's forehead in a colorless liquid that glimmered in the candlelight.

"Whenever you're ready, touch that amulet," Carly told me.

I'd been ready since the moment I'd staked Little to the black dirt of Tartarus.

Almost before she finished the sentence, I touched the amulet. Witchy magic flared so brightly that I blinked—

—and found myself looking up into Sean's golden gaze.

I'd had no sensation of movement, or Carly's circle falling, but I was back in my body and in Sean's arms.

Time had passed because someone had cleaned up the little circle that had protected my astral self and put the altar it had contained away. Carly and Katy were now over at the work table murmuring to each other, and Matthias had disappeared.

"There you are, Miss Magic." Sean kissed the tip of my nose. It tickled, but I didn't mind.

Only a few hours might have passed here, but I'd been non-corporeal for long enough to make the sensations of being in a body feel strange. I ached all over again—a deep, profound ache that seemed to radiate from every bone. But now I even noticed the sensation of wearing clothing, when ordinarily I would have scarcely paid attention to the whisper of fabric against my skin. Even so, there was absolutely no place like home. That went for my body, Sean's arms, and our chaotic farmhouse.

Being cradled in front of others made me self-conscious, so I wiggled to let Sean know I wanted down. He set me on my feet with obvious reluctance, wrapped his arms around me from behind, and rested his chin on top of my head. I'd missed his scent and calming alpha magic so much.

"Thanks for making sure I had the spellwork on me already, Carly," I said. "Sorry things didn't go as planned."

She smiled over her shoulder at us, but the expression was fleeting. "Not according to your plan or mine, but there are other plans at work. Our job is to make the best of what comes our way, and we did. The first spirit is gone, you and Malcolm are back safe, and we think we know who the second spirit is."

"You do?" Startled, I tried to take a step forward, but Sean wasn't quite ready to let go, so I stayed put and leaned against his chest. "How? Who?"

"Malcolm heard the spirit who possessed Oliver call himself 'Little' and the other spirit 'Big,'" Sean told me. "I gave that information to Ben. He dug up information on a pair of cousins from the late 1700s and early 1800s called the Harpes—Micajah and Wiley Harpe. They were known as Big Harpe and Little Harpe, and historians think they probably killed dozens or even hundreds of people. It's just a theory, but—"

"But it fits," I finished. "The clothes I saw the spirit wearing looked like they were from that time. And the evil and lust for killing I feel in them...that fits too."

"If we're right, we can summon the second spirit," Carly said. "We have the name he went by and his birth name."

"Where's Malcolm?" I asked. "Did he tell you we met the necromancer down there?"

"He's upstairs talking to Liam," Sean said. "He said the necromancer wore a hood and mask."

"He did, but I think his voice sounded familiar, like I might have heard it somewhere." I told them about our interaction. "It's not much to go on," I added. "I can't even say I've met this man in person. In fact, I'm pretty sure I haven't."

"So someone you've heard talking on the news, maybe?" Sean suggested. "Or seen at an event?"

"Maybe. It's just an inkling right now. I think I'd recognize the voice if I heard it again, but that won't help us find him. He said he'd be coming for my heart, so I suppose he might seek us out if nothing else."

Sean kissed the top of my head. "Could you not casually reference the removal of your heart?"

"Sorry. Yes, okay, no more offhand comments about my heart. What time is it?"

Sean glanced at his discarded phone, which lay on the quilt nest where he'd tossed it. "Eleven fifteen."

I'd left our house at around nine p.m., driven to the Hensley home, journeyed to and from Tartarus, and gotten back in my body, all in about two hours. My sense of time was so out of whack that he could have said literally any time of day and I would have accepted it.

"Carly, what do you need me to do?" I asked.

She stirred something in a goblet and brought it to me. "Drink this, please."

I eyed the cup. It didn't smell bad, but it didn't smell very good either. "Eye of newt tea?"

"Tea, yes. No eye of newt in this one." She touched my hand. "You can't have any of the spellwork on you that you drew earlier. Broken or used spellwork isn't good."

"No, it isn't." I knocked back the lukewarm tea and handed her the cup. "But is there time to draw it all again?"

She raised her eyebrows. "Do you think you're going back?"

All over my body, wherever I'd drawn spellwork, the remaining spells broke and the magic they contained evaporated in puffs of parchment scent. Strange dripping sensations made me think the spellwork I'd drawn on my skin with marker had turned to liquid and was running down my chest, arms, and legs.

"You're not going back there," she continued as I grimaced and rubbed my arms to ease the discomfort. "Someone else will go."

"Who?" I demanded.

The answer came from behind us. "Me."

I turned to see Malcolm and Liam at the bottom of the stairs. But it wasn't Malcolm who'd spoken—it was Liam.

"No way in hell," I stated, well aware of the irony of my phrasing. "I'll go again. I just need to re-draw—"

"Alice, you're not going." Carly's expression hardened. "You won't survive another round trip. We made this decision before you woke up. We discussed it and Liam volunteered."

"I can do it," Liam said before I could protest them making a decision without me. "Miss Carly explained what I need to do and how to do it, and Malcolm told me what it's like. I'm not afraid."

"It's his choice, Alice," Malcolm added, his tone firm, which was an unpleasant surprise. "He's tethered to this house and he'll have Carly's spellwork too. He'll make it back."

They'd united in this decision, and they'd all had time to come to peace with Liam's choice, but damn it, I'd just gotten him away from Moses. I hadn't pulled off that minor miracle for him to risk himself like this—or for Malcolm's heart to get broken again. I didn't say any of that aloud, but they probably all knew what I was thinking.

"I volunteered because I don't like evil any more than you do, Miss Alice," Liam said. "We all read up on these Harpes. They don't deserve to be up here and I can help put this other one back where he belongs. Don't ask me to do nothing when I could do something."

"Don't forget that we need you here," Carly added. "You said this master of the dead knows who you are and wants your heart. He'll seek you out. We may have to fight on two fronts, and your pack isn't suited to either battle. A necromancer and this spirit are matters for witches and mages."

Sean didn't seem pleased by that assessment, because no alpha werewolf wanted to hear their pack wouldn't do well in battle, but Carly was right: this wasn't the kind of fight for our pack. If we'd needed teeth and claws or brute strength, or even superior numbers, sure—give me our pack any day. But this face-off was going to be about magic and a different kind of power.

Plus, the necromancer wanted to put my heart on a hook and walk around with it hanging on his staff as a trophy and source of power. That made any interaction with him extremely personal. If he came tonight, or whenever he came, I wanted to be here waiting.

That didn't mean I liked anything about the idea of Liam facing the kind of danger posed by Big, the fall itself, or the horrors of Tartarus, but it wasn't my call to make. And maybe more to the point, if I were in his ghost shoes, I'd be chomping at the bit to rid the world of this evil too.

"Whatever happens, get back here to us," I told Liam. "Even if it comes down to you or him, come back and we'll work out another way. We want you to stick around."

"Yes, ma'am," he said with a smile and a little tip of his cap. "I'd like to stick around too."

The cap thing was cute, so I let him get away with the *ma'am*.

This time.

FORTY-TWO

At ten minutes to midnight, six people gathered in my basement workshop: Carly, Katy, Sean, Liam, Malcolm, and me.

The spellwork was done. The altar was ready. A hundred scents and the rising power of witch magic hung in the air.

Katy sat crosslegged at the top of our circle with a silver bowl full of spring water in front of her. She usually used an obsidian mirror for scrying, but apparently she preferred a bowl tonight.

The living participants had donned amulets that protected against spirit possession and identical hooded cloaks to help hide our faces from prying eyes. Malcolm and Liam had changed their ghostly attire to match and Katy had given them anti-possession spells. Everything in the circle was designed to protect us. The rest of Carly's coven had gathered in three secret locations to provide power, shielding, and defense for us.

Carly's original plan had only included herself, Katy, and me, but Sean refused to be a bystander and Malcolm wanted to be close enough to help Liam if the situation called for it, so she'd reset the contents of the circle to accommodate six people instead of three.

Sean had left pack leadership to Matthias during the ritual, with Ben and pack member John Knightley as backup.

Matthias had taken the mantle solemnly and without hesitation, and Sean hadn't seemed to have a shred of hesitation giving it. Whatever happened during and after this ritual, and whatever decision the Were Ruling Council came to regarding its support of us, my faith in my pack had increased yet again—and the power I sensed at my back along with it.

At the stroke of midnight, Carly picked up her selenite athame and closed the circle around us. "We call upon The Morgana to protect those here and our other Sisters where they are. Hide us and defend us against anyone who tries to harm any of us. Guide our way as we banish this malevolent Spirit we are seeking. We call upon the Archangel Uriel to come into our circle to help and protect Liam as he takes the malevolent Spirit back to its rightful place in Tartarus. We ask Uriel to help Liam return safely to us once he has made his delivery."

The altar in our circle was the most beautiful and intricate I'd seen Carly and Katy make. At the top of the pentagram on the altar cloth, Carly had put a statue of The Morgana, who she'd described as a warrior and protector. At the top right, symbolizing Air, she'd placed her coven's precious grimoire because they were all participating in tonight's ritual. In the bottom right a dragon statue represented Fire and helped protect us. The bottom left had three large, smooth river stones for Water. The top left point of the pentagram contained a bowl of mud mixed with salt to represent Earth. According to Katy, it could hold Micajah's spirit if it became necessary.

In the center, Katy placed a large pentagonal mirror spelled to reflect anyone's eyes away from what we did or said within the circle. According to her, anyone attempting to scry or peer into tonight's ritual would see nothing but darkness.

All the careful preparation seemed like so much, and yet somehow not enough.

Parchment-scented witchy magic swirled around us, building steadily in power until I thought my hair would stand on end. Sean had offered his magic and Carly had accepted the offer, so golden shifter power stirred as well, along with my own magic drawn from my blood garden out back.

After her third time walking around the perimeter of our circle, Carly returned her athame to the altar and sat beside Katy, where she could intervene instantly if something went awry.

Katy had murmured to herself while Carly closed the circle. Now she spoke aloud. "I call upon the God Thor to protect and hide me in my workings here tonight. I call upon the Muse Calliope to help me to See what I must to help stop this necromancer and malevolent Spirit and return him to where he belongs."

As Katy bent her head over her bowl, waiting for a vision of the necromancer, Carly took a torn strip of parchment from the altar and dipped a quill into a pot of Sean's blood. Slowly and painstakingly, she wrote *Micajah "Big" Harpe* on the parchment, incorporating spellwork into the lines that formed the letters. The spellwork was designed to add power to the summoning. Micajah was sure to be protected by the necromancer's magic. We needed every advantage we could get.

The spellwork would begin to lose its potency the moment Carly finished drawing it. As soon as she completed the last symbol and letter, she set the quill aside, dropped the strip of parchment into a shallow clay bowl, and placed an amulet on top of it.

Carly rested her index finger on the red stone in the center of the amulet. In a tone that gave me chills because I'd seldom heard her sound so cold, she commanded, "Micajah Harpe, called Big Harpe, I summon you to this place."

I'd summoned spirits before. I'd stood before demon lords as they roared into being in our world from their realm. I'd faced a sorcerer and Valas and Dark Fae and whatever the hell Vlad was. I'd encountered countless ghosts in the form of everything from wraiths to poltergeists and shades and even the odd haint. And I'd already come face-to-face with the rage of Wiley Harpe, one half of a deadly duo who might have been America's earliest known serial killers—though that term seemed inadequate to describe the reign of terror the Harpes had waged on nearly every man, woman, and child who'd crossed their paths.

None of these encounters prepared me for the arrival of Micajah Harpe.

He exploded into our midst and into Carly's binding circle as a hurricane of wrath, dark magic, and enormous power.

However tall Big Harpe had been in life, in death he manifested as a giant well over seven feet tall, with wild, shaggy black hair and the same style of threadbare shirt and trousers Wiley had worn. Like Wiley, his feet were bare. Other than his attire, I saw little resemblance to his cousin. Perhaps the most unnerving difference was while Wiley had rope marks on his wrists, ankles, and throat, Micajah's neck showed that it had been sawed raggedly through and then stitched back together with thick threads of black magic.

Our research indicated he'd been killed and decapitated by vigilantes in 1799. Apparently, the necromancer had reassembled him.

This monstrosity of a man suddenly made my basement feel claustrophobically small. Even his hate was too big for the room.

"HOW DARE YOU!" he roared. Black magic surged, and foul smoke rolled across the floor from inside Carly's binding spell.

Witchy spellwork fractured and broke.

In the time it took for me to realize the binding spell had gone kablooey and think *Oh, shit,* he'd already smashed into the perimeter of the circle a half-dozen times, moving faster than my human eyes could see. Each impact sent a rumble through the house and strained both Carly's power and my wards, but the circle held...for now.

We'd trapped him, and now we got to deal with the consequences.

His rage and hate fell on us like a rain of hammer blows. I got a close-up of Micajah's huge snarling face just before what felt like a truck smashed into me and sent me tumbling. Maybe he'd tried to jump into me and been repelled by Carly's protective amulet, or maybe his intention was to take us all down one by one like a wrecking ball. Either way, he was *way* more powerful than Wiley had been, and *way* more angry.

I ignored the pain of both the hit and the tumble and staggered to my feet just in time to see Sean suffer a similar fate. To my relief, he rolled to his feet smoothly and took a fighting stance.

Micajah ignored Sean and instead plowed through Carly's altar, sending most of its contents flying. A burning candle landed in Katy's lap, but her trance was so deep that she must not have seen it. Sean grabbed the candle and set it upright on the altar cloth.

Meanwhile, Malcolm and Liam flew at Micajah and hit him at the same time, driving him back toward the circle's now-sizzling wards. In response, Micajah tried to rip my sidekick and the man he loved apart with his bare hands.

Instinctively, I made a gesture like tossing a pair of dice and manifested my earth magic whip. I pushed blood magic through the whip and lashed at Micajah. Even if the whip couldn't damage him, I hoped he'd flinch. Sure enough, he dodged the crackling whip, giving Malcolm a chance to grab Liam and get them both clear of his hands. Malcolm appeared intact, but Liam's ghostly form looked partially disintegrated. Malcolm put himself between Liam and Micajah.

Rather than attack the ghosts, Micajah redoubled his efforts to smash through the circle's perimeter with brute force. If those wards failed and we lost this chance, I didn't need to be clairvoyant to know there would be hell to pay—probably literally. Micajah would take his thirst for blood and vengeance out on everyone he could get his hands on.

I didn't want to drop my house wards because we had no idea whether the necromancer was twenty miles away or on the front damn lawn, but the circle *had* to hold until Liam got a chance to recover and make his move.

I spooled earth magic, grabbed the closest ley line, and slapped my palms to the floor. "*Stand*," I commanded.

Power flooded through me into the circle's wards. I choked back a scream as pain whited out my vision. I hadn't had time for finesse when I grabbed the ley line, so I was just going to have to white-knuckle through it.

A shout of fury and a surge of shifter magic made me raise my head just in time to see Sean drive his shoulder into Micajah's chest and shove him back from the circle's perimeter and away from Katy. Screaming curses, Micajah beat Sean with his massive fists, but Sean didn't back off.

Meanwhile, Carly dropped a piece of chalk and stood. She'd scribbled something on the floor that I didn't get a chance to see before she planted her bare feet on top of the spellwork. The air crackled and filled with the scent of burned paper and ozone.

Before my eyes, I saw silver-white vines spiral up and around Carly's feet and ankles. They climbed her body, blazing so brightly that I saw them even under her cloak. I'd never seen any witchcraft like that before. What the hell was she doing?

She and Sean locked gazes and some kind of message passed between them, one warrior to another. I'd seen that look before between Matthias and Arkady, and from Ronan to Lucy in the Broken World.

Sean lowered his head and drove Micajah toward Carly.

The vines reached her shoulders, and her eyes glowed silver-white. I heard a *snap* like a boat's sail in the wind and the scent of the sea swept through the circle.

I recognized that smell instantly and got the urge to back away. Instead, I held my ground and kept my palms flat on the floor so the flow of power to the circle's wards didn't break.

Maybe Micajah sensed the threat behind him was now much greater than the one in front, because he twisted in midair to face Carly. His face appeared dark gray with the force of his fury and hate.

When he got within arm's length, she raised her hand where it had been hidden at her side and drove her obsidian dagger hilt-deep into his gut.

His howl shook our house. He tried to pull out the dagger but his hand passed through it. How a dagger could wound a spirit, I didn't know, but it was yet another reason to respect Carly's magic.

"Creature who calls himself Micajah Harpe," Carly's voice sounded like a thousand voices speaking at once. "Your presence here is an abomination to all Creation."

"I don't obey the laws of any god or man," Micajah snarled into Carly's serene face. "I am my own mighty god."

In response, she twisted the dagger deeper into his belly. "You are neither mighty nor God," the Archangel Uriel said through Carly. "You are damned."

Micajah grinned and straightened, his shoulders back and head held high. "The cursed and the damned are rising, witch woman. Can't you hear it on the wind? Don't you see it in the sky? Don't you feel it in your blood?"

My sense of awe at being in Uriel's presence turned to dread. "Carly—Uriel—that's not Micajah talking."

"I do not speak to Micajah," Uriel said without sparing me a glance. "I speak to the one who uses his mouth."

In other words, he knew damn well this was the necromancer talking to us.

"Send this one back where he belongs," the necromancer said of Micajah, his tone dismissive. "I don't have any use for him anymore. I need men and women with intelligence and patience. Cunning people who'll take orders and aren't more interested in slaughter and rape than power."

"Why?" I asked through gritted teeth. The pain from the ley line was excruciating.

Like Uriel, Micajah didn't bother to look at me, but he answered my question. "A new king rises, and I intend to be one of his generals."

Sean and I exchanged glances. *Charles?* he mouthed.

That wasn't an unreasonable guess, but my gut said Charles wasn't the would-be king the necromancer seemed so enthusiastic about serving. I shook my head.

Sean's scowl deepened. The only thing worse than this kind of looming threat was to not know who was behind it.

We did have some clues, though. I slid a peek at Katy, who still hadn't looked up from her bowl. *Something woke up*, she'd told Carly. Black magic practitioners were gaining power *and* boldness, if this necromancer was anything to go by. And it looked like the killing spree of Micajah and Wiley Harpe was only one of the *little rumblings* Katy had mentioned.

I went back to my thought from a few days ago about the timing of Valas's apparent death and the waking Katy had described. What kinds of evils had the evil we'd known held at bay?

Micajah began to laugh. It was the same laugh I'd heard just hours ago on the black plains of Tartarus, coming from the hooded necromancer.

"Be gone, abomination," Uriel said. "I return this foulness to his eternal torment."

Again, our basement filled with that snapping sound. Micajah vanished. Malcolm and Liam flitted in alarm.

The silver-white magic vines around Carly faded. She slumped into Sean's arms, conscious but clearly dazed.

Meanwhile, Katy nodded slowly at the surface of her bowl as if responding to someone who'd spoken to her. Her unfocused eyes moved from her bowl to the floor on her right. She picked up a piece of chalk and scrawled words on the concrete.

I craned my neck to read the message: *Tomorrow morning at 10. Fields Park, north gate. Come alone, Alice Worth.*

Katy dropped the chalk, blinked several times, and focused on what remained of the altar she and Carly had set up so carefully. Her shock turned to dismay and then her face crumpled. She scrambled to her feet and ran into Carly's waiting arms. Sean held them both.

"He called me his *dark angel*," she sobbed into Carly's shoulder. "He had no right."

I wasn't sure what about that phrase Katy found so upsetting, but it must have evoked something from her past.

Carly stroked Katy's long pink hair. "No, he didn't have the right to call you his anything," she said, and held Katy's head against her chest.

With the danger apparently past, I let go of the ley line. The sudden absence of pain left me lightheaded. Everything went hazy.

I half rolled, half flopped onto my back with my knees raised to catch my breath and let the pain, dizziness, and nausea pass. The circle's power faded until only Carly and Katy's parchment-scented witchy magic remained. Even that normally reassuring scent didn't do much to ease my anger and worry.

At least Liam hadn't had to take Micajah back to Tartarus after all, thanks to Uriel. That was about the only silver lining I could see out of this whole mess.

Also, we'd just been in the presence of an almighty archangel and how was that *not* even in the top ten things I would remember about this day? How did a day that started with an exorcism go downhill from there?

"Alice, you okay?" Malcolm sounded as unhappy as I felt, but he was holding Liam's hand and they were so cute together that it was a balm for my aching heart.

I wasn't, but I said, "Yup" and sat up with a groan. I looked around my basement workshop, at the scattered contents of Carly's altar, smeared and broken spellwork, and five ritual participants who all wore nearly identical expressions that asked the same question: *What now?*

My gaze went to the piece of parchment on which Carly had written Micajah's name in Sean's blood. The parchment had turned dark brown with blackened edges, as if something or someone had tried to burn it but not quite succeeded.

What now, indeed?

In the end, it was Carly who answered our unspoken question. "It's time to clean up," she said, her voice brisk. "And then we will sleep. Thanks to Uriel and Hecate, we've survived to fight another day."

FORTY-THREE

THE CLOCK ON MY NIGHTSTAND READ *2:25 AM* WHEN SEAN AND I CRAWLED into bed.

I barely had enough energy to take off my clothes and throw them in the direction of the bathroom before I collapsed naked on top of the covers. Sean put our clothes in the hamper and got me settled in under the sheet and our spare comforter. I hadn't bothered with sleepwear, so neither did he.

Sex wasn't happening tonight, as much as we both wanted the intimacy. My exhaustion was bone-deep and my heart felt sick. He wrapped his arms around me and I rested my head on his chest.

"This wasn't a failure," I murmured, more to myself than him.

He answered anyway. "No, it wasn't a failure."

"Then why does it feel like one?"

It was the question that had haunted me from the moment Carly opened her tattered circle and put us to work cleaning the basement. And if the others' expressions and the grim silence were anything to go by, I wasn't the only one who thought so.

"We didn't get the identity of the necromancer like we'd hoped," he said. "We came face-to-face with real monsters, but instead of a demon or some other creature, Micajah and the necromancer are human. Humans aren't supposed to be monsters, but some *are*. I think that's harder to process than when the monsters have a thousand arms or a poisonous barbed tail or a body made of snakes."

"Not to mention we all put a lot of time and effort into preparing for the ritual, and then..." I shrugged wearily. "It didn't go according to plan at all. What a letdown."

"We also found out there's a much bigger danger we didn't know about before. All these things weigh heavily on everyone." He nuzzled my hair. "Don't lose track of what we *did* accomplish, though. We got Micajah and Wiley Harpe sent back where they belong, and that will save lives. You and Malcolm returned safe from Tartarus. And even though we don't know who the necromancer is yet or who this mysterious 'king' he talked about might be, knowing there's a dark force who is marshaling forces and seeking power is crucial information."

"Yeah, but who do we tell about that?" I asked. "Charles? The Council? The local police? SPEMA? They'll want know what we know and how we found out. We'll be the center ring of a three-ring circus, and we don't want to be."

He nuzzled my hair again and didn't reply.

"Right?" I raised my head. "We don't want that?"

"That's a complicated question, Miss Magic." His expression was thoughtful. "We have information and information has value. These are uncertain times—more so than usual. Charles Vaughan wants to solidify his position as head of the Court *and* move it in a new direction that expands its reach. The Council has serious concerns about its own relative political position and sphere of influence. Moses has already shown he's not the quiet businessman Darius Bell was. He's not content to simply pull strings behind the scenes and keep his head down as money rolls in. I get the impression he wants to be as much of a visible factor as the Court and the Council."

"That's how he operates in Baltimore," I said. "It's the worst-kept secret in town."

"On top of all that, the new police chief still has a lot to prove, especially when it comes to bringing mages, shifters, and nonhumans to justice. And you know the feds always have their own agendas. The district attorney's office *and* the federal courts won't like Charles's plan to make the Court a more visible and active participant in judicial matters. It's a lot of wheels in motion and everyone's toes are feeling vulnerable."

"And now here comes some mysterious 'king' who wants his piece of the pie." I yawned hugely. "Or maybe the whole dang pie. So what do we do?"

"We're going to think about the information we have, see what else we can find out, and then figure out what to do with it." He kissed my temple. "Speaking of which, what have you decided about this ten o'clock trap in Fields Park?"

I laughed softly at the phrase *ten o'clock trap*. "Well, first of all, obviously I'm not going alone. I'm sure he doesn't expect me to."

"Then why make that demand in his message?"

"Dramatic effect?" I shrugged. "*Come alone, Alice Worth,*" I said, making my voice spooky and deep. Sean chuckled. "He knows I'm not dumb enough to meet him face-to-face by myself. Dude's a drama queen. All necromancers are. Necromancy is all about showmanship. Well, and power."

"Put that way, he sounds less scary."

"Oh, no, he's absolutely very scary." I rubbed my nose on his chest. "Just because he's flashy doesn't mean he doesn't have the goods. I'm not taking any chances at this meeting." I yawned again.

"Babe, let's go to sleep. You've had a long, terrible day." He pulled me closer. "Good night, my love. Try to dream of beautiful things."

"That's a big ask," I murmured, and closed my eyes.

At least with Valas out of me I wouldn't have to relive her memories anymore. Then again, while I could have done without the horrors I'd witnessed in those dreams, it had been an unprecedented chance to get information about her that we never would have access to otherwise. A silver lining.

Dream of beautiful things.

Well, it was worth a shot, anyway.

AT NINE FIFTY-FIVE THAT MORNING, I got out of my SUV, stuck my phone in my back pocket, and headed for Fields Park's north gate.

I didn't bother looking for my backup—I knew they were all close by. Most of my pack was here. Katy and Carly were here. Malcolm and Liam had stayed at the house, safe behind my wards. They were vulnerable around the necromancer and I couldn't afford to divide my attention.

My pockets contained several amulets, including Carly's most useful spell, *Return to Sender*, which rebounded any magic that came at me back on whoever threw it. It worked on necromancers just as well as mages and witches. I also had some spellwork drawn on my skin hidden under my clothes. I was as protected as I could be, and I was ready.

On an ordinary day, the north gate was the park's busiest because it was close to the largest playgrounds. Today, the lot was nearly empty and the equipment unused. The mayor had lifted the curfew between six a.m. and six p.m. but clearly most people had stayed home. That was just as well. I didn't want to meet the necromancer near a playground full of children.

I spotted a few mid-morning walkers and joggers on the trail that looped around the park. Other than that, the area was quiet.

About twenty yards from the gate, I came around some tall bushes and spotted a dark-haired man in a suit sitting on a bench facing one of the empty jungle gyms, his back to me. I'd walked on the grass rather than the gravel path, but I had no illusions that I could sneak up on a necromancer.

Black magic tingled on my arms. He'd deliberately let me sense his power—not only so I knew I was in the right place, but as a not-so-subtle reminder of who I was dealing with. As if I didn't know.

Shifter magic prickled on the back of my neck. Sean and the others had probably felt that little surge of black magic. I was walking up to one of the most dangerous kinds of human occult practitioners by myself, and nobody watching liked it at all. I didn't like it much either, but it had to be done. I wanted to know who this man was and how I knew of him so I could move on to the question of how to deal with him.

I walked around the bench to look my quarry in the eye—

—and immediately knew two things: why I'd had a notion of him working in a corner office, and that nothing about a plan to deal with him would be simple.

District Attorney Gregory Pierce smiled up at me. "Hello, Alice." He gestured grandly at the other end of the bench. "Won't you have a seat?"

That was the voice, all right. I'd heard it at the occasional press conference and in campaign ads during the most recent election cycle. Hell, he'd even stood next to SPEMA agent Trent Lake at the press conference last year during the announcement of the arrests of the West-Addison harnad.

I tried to imagine telling Diaz the necromancer we'd been chasing, who'd caused the deaths of so many people, was the freaking district attorney. There was no version of that conversation that ended well.

No wonder Pierce looked like he thought he was untouchable in this scenario. He pretty much was.

Unlike our earlier interactions, Pierce didn't appear threatening at all. That put me more on guard, since in my experience playing nice hid more malicious intent than violence and threats. But the amulets in my pocket didn't signal the presence of spells or even dormant spellwork. And that initial little surge of black magic aside, I hadn't felt so much as a tickle of power from him. That could change in a heartbeat, of course, but I sensed he wanted to talk...at least for now.

I sat on the bench, turning sideways so I could keep a close watch on his every movement. "You don't have enough power running the D.A.'s office?" I asked.

He smiled. He had a really nice smile. I could imagine liking it if I'd met him socially instead of like this. His eyes even sparkled. Easy to see how he'd run a successful election campaign against the long-time incumbent. District attorneys tended to run on charisma as much as legal acumen and politics and he clearly had that in spades.

"I enjoy my job." He relaxed back against the bench, his ankle resting on his knee, and brushed some dirt off his shoe. Designer, of course, to match his tailored suit. "I've worked hard to get where I am in all aspects of my personal and professional life. I didn't come from a privileged background, unlike yourself, but we've both faced a tough uphill climb in some of the same ways. You enjoy the power and influence of the positions you hold and the alliances you've made. We're not that different."

"I'd say we're *very* different," I countered. "I don't go around killing innocent people using spirits I dragged here from Tartarus. I don't want to make the public too afraid to leave their homes. I don't use fear to get people to worship me or fall in line, or to curry favor with some mysterious 'king.'"

He chuckled. "Saint Alice, so comfortable on her moral high ground. We all think our own way is the right and noble way. How many times have you used your magic and power to intimidate someone into doing what you want? How many times have you decided what justice should be and appointed yourself the prover-bial judge, jury, and executioner without giving much thought to what actual judicial process looks like? Nothing's as simple as good guys and bad guys, white hats and black hats."

"I know that," I snapped. "More than most people, I understand all the shades of gray between good and evil. But I know good and I know evil, and I know which I'm sitting next to. What I *don't* under-stand is why you brought the Harpes into this. You had to know how evil they were. And I know you controlled what the spirits did and how, at least in the beginning. It takes real malevolence to do that.

There's no shades of gray involved in the murder of innocent people."

"I don't know these Harpes," he lied smoothly. "But I don't think someone like you describe would summon the spirits of killers and use them to commit crimes just to make people afraid. That seems like not quite the right answer."

"Then why?" I asked. "Why go to all the trouble?" *Why did all these people have to die?*

"Maybe they like causing fear, but they also want the thrill." He gave me an elegant shrug. "It's hard to say, since I obviously don't look for that kind of stimulation myself, but maybe a person who can control spirits and make them kill craves the rush. As a prosecutor, I've talked to many murderers. A lot of them say there's no rush like killing."

My stomach churned at the casual way he described his motivation for summoning the Harpes and destroying so many lives.

"Serial killers say their first is always the biggest thrill," he continued with a smile. "After that, they're just chasing that first big high. They have to up the ante every time to get the rush they want. But in this scenario you've imagined, where someone uses murderous spirits to control people who've never killed before— never even *thought* of killing—both the spirits and the person controlling them would be able to feel that first-kill rush over and over. Every killing would be as terrible and thrilling as the last. If the spirits were already killers themselves, they would enjoy it as much as their master. Everyone gets what they want. Hypothetically."

Everyone not counting the victims and the people who cared about them, about whom Pierce clearly did not spare one single solitary thought. And of course he'd framed it all as a hypothetical situation, careful not to incriminate himself in any way.

This man was *evil*. Pure evil in designer shoes and an expensive suit. A true psychopath.

"Too bad the whole spree came to an end last night," I said. "And now everyone will find out the truth about who is really responsible."

"I imagine any evidence of what you're envisioning would be hard to come by, though." He picked at some imaginary lint on his pant leg. "The physical evidence and eyewitness statements against your client and the other perpetrators are some of the strongest I've ever seen in case. Surveillance footage clearly shows who perpetrated these crimes—and in several cases, the crimes themselves. A district attorney such as myself couldn't hope to have better evidence for trial. You never think of any case as a slam dunk, but..." Pierce waved his hand. "I expect quick verdicts across the board."

"There's more potential evidence and testimony than what you've got," I pointed out. "Plenty to give the defense teams. Enough for reasonable doubt."

That elicited his baritone laugh. "I have no doubt you'd like that to be true. I'm sure Oliver Hensley is paying you good money to try to come up with something to help him and you have to justify your hourly rates. But even if your imaginary situation were real, there just isn't anything you can put in front of a jury, is there? Besides wild accusations, I mean. And maybe magic trace that humans can't really see, feel, or hear. They'd have to take one mage PI's word over the mountain of physical evidence submitted by the prosecutor. I just don't think it's likely, Alice."

This cannot be happening, I thought. I *cannot possibly let this man get away with framing Oliver and the others for murders they didn't commit and walk away scot-free.*

Pierce, meanwhile, wasn't done taking his victory lap. "I'm sure the Hensleys will pay you even though you have nothing to show for your time. I can't imagine Philippa giving you any references, though, which is a shame. She could have been a lucrative connection for someone like you. I wouldn't mind facing you in court someday. I think getting you on the stand would be a real treat for me."

My eyes narrowed. Oh, I would be a *treat* for him, would I? A dozen sarcastic responses welled up, but I just stared at him instead, my expression flat.

I suddenly understood Arkady's claim that sometimes she wanted to punch someone so badly her knuckles itched. Not only did my knuckles itch, but my blood magic tried to surge too. I was close enough and fast enough that maybe I could get my blood magic blades into his heart before he had a chance to fight back, but I couldn't very well kill someone in broad daylight in the park.

Besides, killing him—assuming I even could—wouldn't solve anything because all that evidence he'd mentioned would still exist. And obviously he wasn't going to own up to jack shit. So far, this entire tête-à-tête was just to make it clear he had all the cards.

Having made his point, or thinking he had, Pierce put both feet on the ground and leaned forward, his forearms on his knees. To a casual observer at a distance, his demeanor would have probably appeared honest and earnest, but from my vantage point I clearly saw how hard and cold his eyes had become.

"You know, you're intriguing to me," he said. "The Were Ruling Council doesn't know what to do with you. The Vamp Court doesn't seem to either. Despite what I think we can both agree is a questionable past, you've done well both personally and professionally. Your business is growing and you have a good reputation as a thorough and dedicated PI. And you've managed to land yourself the most highly respected alpha werewolf in the region."

That wasn't the first time someone had described my relationship with Sean that way, as if I'd sought him out for power and nothing else, and I liked it less every time. "Greg, if I were you, I'd keep my opinions about my personal life to yourself."

"Duly noted." His smile turned indulgent, as if my objection to his words was adorable. The itch on my knuckles increased. "Professionally speaking, then, you're interesting. It makes me wonder if we might find a way forward where our interests are aligned."

"That does not seem likely." This conversation was deadly serious, but I couldn't help but smile at the amount of understatement in my words.

"It might seem that way now," he countered. "Despite my initial impressions of you, I don't think either of us are going anywhere soon."

Huh. So he didn't want my heart anymore? Or he did, but he wanted to lull me into thinking he'd changed his mind?

"I'm a logical man," he said in reply to my frown. "Don't forget that I weigh pros and cons, evidence, and conflicting interests for a living. Situations change rapidly. People like me always have to think ten steps ahead. In the future, I see a lot of potential for people like you."

"What, when your 'king' takes over and you're one of his generals, you mean?"

"What a vivid imagination you have." He chuckled. "Have you ever thought about becoming a writer? That might make a good fallback career if you get tired of PI work."

Become a *writer?* How much of a masochist did he think I was?

"What did you mean by people like me?" I asked, genuinely curious to hear his answer.

"People who see the world more clearly than most." Pierce tilted his head thoughtfully. "You see all those shades of gray you talked about earlier. You know who wears a black hat, who wears white, and who just tries to blend into the woodwork and not be noticed. And either by accident or design, you have the range of connections most people would either kill to have, or avoid at all costs." He smiled. "Like I said, intriguing. The fact you've survived all these conflicting interests and...misadventures...is really remarkable. It speaks to your character and strengths more than anything else."

"So that's why we're sitting here?" I demanded. "You think I'm *intriguing?*"

"We're sitting here because you've involved yourself in cases my office is handling," Pierce said, which was certainly one way of putting it. "But I'm having this extended conversation with you because, as I said, we may find ourselves allied in the future, and I like to know who I want on my team."

It was my turn to smile. "Professionally speaking, you mean."

"Professionally speaking."

Sorting through all the lies, evasions, and vague references, I got the impression he was feeling me out in more ways than one. He used the word *ally*, but in my experience that was code for "person I want to use until they're no longer useful to me."

I was powerful, and I had powerful friends. No doubt he'd seen the darkness in me and my aura, from the strength of my blood magic to my willingness to take a spirit back to Tartarus because it was what needed to be done. Maybe he knew about some of the shadier situations I'd found myself in recently, like the death of Spencer Addison, or had heard the less-than-savory rumors we knew some members of the Council and the Anderson pack had spread about me. It made a kind of twisted sense that he might think I was closer to "bad guy" than good. And maybe he wasn't wrong.

But all I could see when I looked at him—like, *really* looked at him, past the designer clothes and perfectly barbered hair and seductive smile and superficial psychopathic charm—was a vision of him roasting on a spit in Tartarus.

The question was, what was the best way to get him skewered on that spit? And what about my client and all the others Pierce had framed?

And what about this triple-damned, mysterious, would-be king?

It occurred to me that once again I found myself talking in circles with someone who thought they were in charge even when they needed or wanted something from me. Maybe it took me a couple times around the block to learn something, but I *did* learn. Eventually.

"Here's the thing, Greg," I said, and gave him my best smile. "I *am* still alive despite everything, as you've noticed. And I assure you that what you know of me is such a tiny fraction of the whole truth that it's kind of funny that you think you've got a handle on who I am.

You must have an inkling of that, or you wouldn't be here on this bench talking hypotheticals with me. I've been in conversations like this before. And you know what I've learned?"

"What's that?" His gaze had turned dark, and for the first time since I approached him, I felt a tingle of black magic.

"I've learned my own value." I let my smile widen. "If you're looking for allies, I don't come cheap. And I don't play amateur games, get off on power trips, or go looking for cheap thrills."

Judging by the way his eyes narrowed, that one got him right where it hurt. He'd told me he killed people for thrills just to see my reaction. Well, my reaction was that he was trash, and someone like Gregory Pierce was not used to being dismissed as trash.

"I play hard, I play dirty, and I play to win," I went on. "That goes for allies and adversaries alike. Just ask the vamps and the Council and whoever else around town you think might have an educated opinion on the topic."

"Do I hear a proposal coming?" His expression turned calculating. "What would your terms be, I wonder?"

He'd bitten that hook so fast that I would have high-fived myself if it wouldn't have given away the game.

"Great question. I'll let you think on it." I rose. "I have somewhere I need to be, so if that's all—"

"We're not done." Scowling, he reached for my arm, maybe intending to yank me back. To his credit, he instantly thought better of it, but his expression didn't change. "Nobody walks away from me before I'm done talking."

There was that menacing voice I remembered—the one that had promised to come for my heart. Shifter magic prickled on my neck again. The wolves had heard it too.

"Is that so?" I raised my eyebrows. "Maybe in your courtroom or your office or your *circle*—" I put emphasis on the word so he knew what kind of circle I meant "—but you're just a guy in a suit to me."

Not really, because even someone who liked playing with fire had to respect the power of a necromancer, but I'd found his sensitive spot and I felt like jabbing it a few more times.

"You've said your piece; I've said mine." I made a show of checking the time on my phone, then stuck it back in my pocket. "We each know where we stand and what the question marks are. Make your next move, and I'll make mine. And now this is me walking away from you, Greg."

And that was what I did. I left him on that bench, and I walked away.

FORTY-FOUR

I HIT THE *STOP* BUTTON ON THE RECORDING, STUCK MY PHONE IN MY POCKET, and scanned the grim faces gathered around our kitchen island. "So that's the situation," I said.

"The flippin' D.A. is behind the whole thing. I did *not* see that coming." Malcolm crossed his arms. "Are you gonna let Diaz hear this recording?"

"I don't know." I took a long drink of coffee, which I'd spiked with a hazelnut liqueur because it felt like the situation called for it. "Pierce doesn't say anything incriminating. What's Diaz supposed to do, go after the D.A. on my word alone? He probably wouldn't even believe me. He might be open-minded, but there's open-minded, and then there's *your boss's boss's boss's boss is a serial-killing necromancer.*"

"I see your point." He floated back and forth. "So what are you going to tell Diaz? He's already texted twice, and you can only stall so long. He'd show up on our front porch right now if he thought he could do it without anyone finding out he's talking to you."

"I know." I slid onto one of the tall kitchen chairs and scrubbed my face with my hands. "Pierce is right about the evidence. Everything points to the alleged perpetrators. I have magic trace and shadows on video and my own testimony, but it isn't enough. And it's not like Pierce will confess. Even if Diaz could get a search warrant for his home, odds are that's not where he practices. He'd never risk someone finding his workshop or sensing black magic in the house."

"What if you found where he practices?" Matthias asked. "At a minimum, that would be corroborating evidence. He had to have something of the Harpes' to summon them, right? Like bones?"

"Even if I did find where he does his magic, it wouldn't exonerate Oliver or anyone else, much less be enough for anyone to convict him of the assaults or the murders," I pointed out. "Unless he kept a diary of everything he did, which isn't likely."

"Serial killers tend to take trophies," Sean pointed out. "Would he have trophies of some sort that could connect him to the victims or the crimes?"

I shrugged. "Maybe. But again, he's a prosecutor. He would know that would be a dangerous thing to do, in the unlikely event someone *did* catch on to what he'd done."

"He's arrogant, though," Matthias said. "Most serial killers and psychopaths are. They think they're smarter than everyone else. Ninety-five percent of that whole conversation was Pierce telling you how smart he is. I wouldn't be surprised if he *did* have trophies he can admire. The question is, where are they?"

"Probably the same place he practices his rituals," I said. "And that's going to be tough to find."

"Could you bait him into lashing out in public?" Liam asked, his voice tentative. "Get him to show his magic in front of witnesses?"

"I could try, but he'd probably figure out that's what I was doing. I might end up just getting arrested."

Matthias's phone buzzed. He checked the screen and glanced up at me. "Pierce just released a statement that his office has upgraded the charges against Oliver Hensley to first degree murder with special circumstances. He's requested another bond hearing to ask that bail be revoked."

"Just Oliver?" Sean asked as I processed that information. "Or the doctor too?"

"Just Oliver."

My phone rang in my back pocket. The screen read *RKD Calling*. I swiped the green button and put the phone on speaker. "Yeah?"

"Shit just hit the fan over here at the Hensleys' house," Arkady said. I heard her boots walking briskly on pavement and a loud commotion in the background. "The neighbors and a bunch of the victim's friends have gathered on the sidewalk. The cops are here to make sure nobody throws rocks but they're not making anyone leave. Philippa Grayson's inside with Oliver and Gracie. Have you heard about the upgraded charges?"

"Yes." Rage made my voice clipped and my chest feel tight.

Was this my fault? *Make your next move, and I'll make mine*, I'd told Greg, right after punching him a couple of times in his ego and then turning my back on him. Maybe the timing was coincidence and he'd planned to upgrade the charges all along, but this felt like a retaliation *and* upping the ante.

"Also, Grayson kicked me out of the house," Arkady said. "Oliver and Gracie told her what happened last night, and she blew a fuse. She gets real quiet when that happens, by the way. That is not a sight for the faint of heart."

I could well imagine.

"So the Hensleys are still Team Alice since you probably saved their asses last night, but if Grayson has her way, you're off the case. I heard the words 'restraining order' as I walked out the door. I got the impression she's suddenly gotten the notion from somewhere that you're not to be trusted, on top of being royally pissed that nobody called her after Oliver got possessed again and nearly killed his wife. The word *clusterfuck* was invented for this situation specifically. What do you want me to do?"

My phone buzzed with another incoming call. It was Diaz.

I got that skull-about-explode feeling again.

Sean, Matthias, Malcolm, and Liam watched me with a combination of wariness and concern, like they thought I might be about to do something unhinged like level the house or jump in my car and drive straight to Pierce's office, or both.

I was perfectly capable of utterly unhinged scorched-earth tactics, but this situation called for a scalpel, not a nuke.

Make your next move, and I'll make mine.

"Leave the Hensley house and get back here," I told Arkady. "I've got another call coming in."

"Uh-oh," Malcolm muttered. "She's got *that look*."

"And *that tone*," Matthias said.

"Copy that, boss," Arkady said and ended the call before I could remind her we were partners.

I hit the green button again. "I heard," I said by way of greeting. "I'm still working on putting a case together, Detective."

For a beat, Diaz didn't reply.

When he spoke, his voice was quiet with fury and very deliberate, with pauses during which I imagined he was trying not to explode. "Do you...have any idea...*how far*...I stuck my neck out for you?" he asked.

"Yes," I said, as calmly as I could. "I do know. And I'm doing everything I can to make sure you didn't do it for nothing. Are you all right? No one's caught on that you were the source of the leak, have they?"

"No, but you've been giving me the run-around since last night and I'm through with it. You need to tell me right now what you know. *Right the fuck now*, Worth. Or I don't ever want to hear your voice again."

I'd run through this conversation in my head more than dozen times since I left Fields Park, envisioning how it would go if I told Diaz about Pierce and let him listen to the recording I'd surreptitiously made that ended up being of zero evidentiary value. I'd played out the possible scenarios of whether he'd believe me or not and how that might go for me *and* him. And no matter which way I looked at it, even if he did believe me—which was a mighty big *if*—the odds of him successfully going after Pierce were basically nil. He'd just end up torpedoing his own career and losing everything he'd worked for and believed in.

If he didn't believe me, he might actively interfere with any attempts I made to bring Pierce to justice, and I didn't want that either. Pierce had to pay for what he'd done, and Oliver and the others deserved exoneration in both legal and public eyes. How I was going to pull that off, though, I had no idea—yet.

Maybe Diaz deserved to make that decision of whether to go after Pierce for himself. But I knew that if he believed me that he'd go after Pierce with everything he had because it was the right thing to do. The fact he'd committed felonies to bring me the murder weapons and give me those autopsy reports proved it.

I didn't have any business making this decision for him, but I was going to anyway. Maybe I'd get to apologize for it later if he ever decided to speak to me again.

My brain kept going back to my words to Pierce: *Make your next move, and I'll make mine.*

He'd made his move, all right. So now I had to make mine. But what move did I have? Pierce had me backed into a corner.

A wash of clarity came over me.

When Valas's Colorado mansion collapsed on top of Matthias, Daniel, and me, I'd held up the rubble by magic, power, and sheer force of will. I'd done the impossible because it had to be done. To do so, I'd dug down deep into who I was and what I was capable of doing and pulled off a *bona fide* miracle.

And that was who Gregory Pierce, district attorney and necro-mancer, was calling out. Not so much Alice Worth, mage private investigator, but the woman who'd held up four thousand tons of rubble and then turned most of it to vapor and pebbles to save her own life and two others.

If he thought I was *intriguing* now, I looked forward to what adjective I'd hear from him the next time I saw him. I had a feeling it wouldn't be nearly as flattering.

At the moment, however, Detective Ernie Diaz was waiting for my answer. So were Sean, Matthias, Malcolm, and Liam, whose expressions had gone from concern to something more like curiosity. I supposed my moment of clarity had shown in my facial expression and the way my shoulders relaxed.

"I need to ask you a question," I said to Diaz. "It's justice you want, right? You want the person who killed these people to pay for what they did, and for those who are innocent to be exonerated?"

"What the fuck kind of question is that?" He nearly shouted it. "Of course that's what I want. What kind of games are you playing?"

"No games," I stated. "I don't play games with people's lives. I never have and never will. I became a mage PI for the same reason you became a cop: to help people and make sure those who do wrong face justice. But I stay on this side of the badge because sometimes justice takes a different path."

"What does that mean? I told you no more run-around."

"I'm not giving you the run-around." My chest ached because I was about to blow up our alliance. There for a while, I'd almost seen him not quite as a friend, but a colleague. Someone I could work with, at least in an unofficial way. "I just want you to know where I stand because maybe it will make a difference in the end."

"You're not going to tell me what you know, are you?" His tone became cold and dangerous. "Even after you gave me your word, and I risked *everything* for you. I knew I shouldn't have trusted you."

I flinched at that, but forged ahead. "You risked everything for Madison Fernell and the others. That's what matters. Because you're a great detective and good man."

"Fuck you, Alice Worth," he snapped. The call ended.

Sean put his hand on my lower back.

"Sorry, Alice," Malcolm said quietly.

I checked the time, scrolled through my contacts, and started texting.

Matthias crossed his arms and studied me as I typed. Malcolm, meanwhile, flitted around the kitchen. "Start talking. Don't type. Talk. I don't like it when you get all quiet and crafty-looking. Tell us what you're thinking, or so help me, Alice, I will do something very unpleasant."

"I'm not sure this is the moment for threats," Matthias said, eyebrow raised. "Even in jest."

"*Even in jest?*" Malcolm put his hands on his hips. "I swear sometimes I think you're from another century."

I finished my text and put my phone face down on the counter. "When Arkady gets here, I'm calling a Team Alice meeting. I'll lay it all out for everyone at once and then you can tell me if you think I'm a genius or if this is the single worst idea I've ever had."

"Was that a genuine attempt to make us feel better?" Malcolm asked. "Because if so, you whiffed like a toddler playing T-ball."

"What is T-ball?" I asked with a frown.

Muttering, he disappeared through the floor into the workshop. Liam followed, leaving me alone in the kitchen with Sean and Matthias.

I had not had one spare minute until now to follow up with Matthias about what Bryan and he had talked about yesterday. The rest of today—and tonight—might be just as busy as the last few days, so I didn't want to put it off again. Arkady wouldn't arrive for at least fifteen minutes, even as fast as she drove.

"I'm sorry if it's a painful subject," I said to Matthias. "But I'd like to know what Bryan said to you in private last evening."

He clasped his hands behind his back, but he didn't adopt the formal, emotionless pose he'd favored before. "Bryan informed me that my *geas* has conditions I wasn't aware of."

"What do you mean? The fact Charles knew that you'd told us he found out about my ability to help shifters transition?"

"That was part of it." Matthias's expression darkened. "The more troubling part is *how* he knew. Bryan revealed that the *geas* doesn't just harm or potentially kill *me* if I violate it. It's designed to do the same to someone whose well-being I cared about very much at the time the *geas* was placed upon me."

"Oh, no." I sank onto the tall kitchen chair. "So Adri Smith—"

"Went through the same pain and injuries I did." Muscles in his face twitched. I wasn't sure if he was fighting fury or grief or both. "Except she isn't a shifter, and she isn't a dhampir. She's human."

I thought of all those broken bones and the excruciating pain Matthias had chosen to go through to give us the information about Charles.

I started to tell him he hadn't known his decision would affect Adri—because who the hell would have thought that might happen? —but of course he knew that. I imagined how I would feel if I'd unknowingly done something that caused Sean that level of suffering. Matthias might not love Adri anymore, but I couldn't imagine he felt much better than I would in a similar scenario.

Damn the vampires. Damn *Charles*. He had to have known the provisions of Matthias's *geas*. Why hadn't he told him a violation would harm Adri too?

I answered my own question a moment later: because it would have been much more of a shock for Matthias to find out the hard way. It was sadistic and cruel and entirely on-brand.

"I'm so sorry," I said. "Does that mean you don't want us to try to unravel the *geas?*"

"For now, I would prefer if you didn't." He glanced at Sean. "I understand it puts you all at a disadvantage not to have access to what I know. My allegiance is to our pack, not the Court, and not to Adri. But trying to remove the *geas* could kill me and Adri. She didn't ask for this any more than I did."

"Yes and no. Adri took an oath to the Court of her own free will," Sean pointed out. "She knew what that meant and what vampires are like. I'm not unsympathetic, but she had to know she'd be at their mercy. Ultimately, as your alpha, the decision of whether to try to unravel the *geas* is mine. If the time comes when I feel we have no choice, we'll revisit the subject. In the meantime, I'll ask Arkady to examine the document for clues about the wording of the spellwork but not attempt to break it unless we tell her to do so. Agreed?"

"Agreed," Matthias said.

I didn't like that Sean had taken the decision out of Matthias's hands, but Matthias didn't seem to object. And at the same time I recalled Arkady's admonishment from days earlier that I had to let Sean be an alpha and lead us. That went for good times and bad, and in the making of decisions that had complicated, far-reaching, and potentially deadly consequences—like the one I was about to propose.

Arkady arrived not long after that, just as I finished brewing a fresh pot of coffee. She parked her Harley out front, stomped inside still muttering about Philippa Grayson, poured a cup of coffee, flopped on the couch, and propped her boots on our coffee table.

"Well?" she said, looking around the room. "What's the plan to un-fuck this bullshit salad?"

My text message to Charles's super-secret phone, sent the moment I got off the call with Diaz, had read *Call me when you wake up*.

That evening, a full ninety minutes before his normal rising time at sunset, and less than an hour after Team Alice had finished hashing out our plan, he called.

And then it was game on.

FORTY-FIVE

I'D BEEN RIGHT ABOUT PIERCE'S CORNER OFFICE AND FINDING HIM SITTING comfortably in the daylight, but wrong about him not having a house deep in the forest. Still, two out of three wasn't too bad.

The house wasn't crumbling, though—it was a lovely two-story renovated California Gothic. The home and its woodsy acreage had been a foreclosure, snapped up for pennies on the dollar by a real estate investment company with a half-dozen properties currently under renovation. The paper trail linking Pierce to the company had been as twisty and hidden as the path I took through the woods from an adjoining property, but not hidden enough to escape the skilled researchers at the Vampire Court. Not many things were.

Pierce's wards around the property demonstrated his power and skill. My skin tingled when I got close to the perimeter he'd created a full hundred yards from the house. I smelled damp earth and decay —and fresh blood. He'd added new spellwork to his wards just hours ago, judging by the scent and the sharp metallic tang in the air. My blood magic let me know most of the blood he'd used was human. Some was from animals, but I didn't like that either. Necromancy wasn't limited to humans and human spirits.

Normally, I wouldn't be able to pass through the wards unnoticed; they were too well made, and Pierce's magic was too different from my own for me to unweave the spellwork or create spells of my own to trick it into letting me pass.

Good thing I knew someone willing to do bad things for good reasons, whose coven High Priestess let her do so under careful supervision. Someone who was no one's "dark angel" and thus highly motivated to help take Pierce out before he tried to make good on his threat to possess her.

The other day, Malcolm had told Matthias that he and I didn't mess with occult or black magic, even when the situation seemed to demand its use. Neither of us wanted to start making exceptions that might turn into new rules. Black magic was never not insidious. It would never just be used once and then go away. Like my addiction to the designer drug Black Fire, there was no permanent recovery from its lure.

And yet here I was, standing six feet from Gregory Pierce's wards, holding a cup of blood in my hand.

I was living proof that no matter how dangerous one might know black magic to be, once one has used it, there would always be situations that justified its use again. And again. And again. The abyss would never not beckon. The road to its edge was paved with desire for justice and its bricks held together by a mortar made of desperation.

If anyone understood the dangers involved, it was Carly. She'd reassured me about what I was doing and the kind of magic I'd asked Katy to provide. "You're self-aware about these choices," she'd told me as I watched Katy brew the potion I needed. "You understand the danger on a deep level. There's a big difference between taking a deliberate step after contemplation and jumping ahead hoping for the best."

What about taking a deliberate step after contemplation and hoping for the best? I'd thought, but hadn't said aloud. But she'd smiled and patted my arm, so I knew she knew what I was thinking. She was witchy that way.

Now more than ever I wished I had Malcolm with me, but I'd had to leave him safe at home because of the threat Pierce posed. Nothing was more dangerous to a ghost than a necromancer.

I took a deep breath, chanted the spell Katy had written for me, and dumped the cup of blood and herbs over my head.

Despite the hour or so that had passed since Katy made the potion, the thick liquid remained warm thanks to the magic it contained. That made the sensation of it running over my face so much worse, somehow.

I closed my eyes and forced myself not to flinch or wipe it away from my eyes, nose, or mouth as the foul-smelling mixture streamed down my body. The potion formed a coating of spellwork that rolled over me from the crown of my head to my feet. Katy had promised it would dry quickly. I hoped so.

Once the last of the spellwork tingled to indicate it was ready, I crouched and quickly buried the empty cup. I would have just incinerated it with my earth magic, but I didn't want to risk Pierce or his wards sensing my presence.

I dusted damp dirt off my hands and rose. Unbidden, an image of a one-eyed black cat slipping through the woods appeared in my mind's eye. The cat was Basil, Katy's feline familiar, the donor of the blood in the potion. Katy had assured me it wasn't nearly as much blood as it looked like and taking it from him hadn't caused him any pain, but the thought of what I'd just poured on myself made me nauseous. I'd just have to deal with that later. I had to get moving.

With a deep breath, I made sure all my magic was hidden under my shields, and then I walked through the wards.

They slid over me like a smooth, silky caress, without flaring or even buzzing on my skin. That was what stray animals felt if they crossed my perimeter wards at our home, which were designed to alert me to interlopers but let neighborhood cats and dogs and the occasional coyote stroll through the yard unbothered when Esme wasn't outside guarding her territory.

So as far as I could tell, Katy's spell had worked and tricked the wards into letting me pass as if I were a cat or some other small animal prowling in the woods.

Meow, I thought, and made my way toward Pierce's house.

Somewhere in these woods, Sean and the others were waiting and watching as I slipped through the trees. This was one of the parts of the plan nobody liked but me: sneaking up on Pierce in his oh-so-secret lair, outsmarting him and his wards along the way. At least Sean and the rest of our pack understood, even if they didn't like that I was going in alone. Wolves had a deep appreciation for stealth and hunting.

In black clothing, covered with dried blood and moving from tree to tree as I got closer to the house, I was doing my best to channel shifter-level stealth and cunning. Maybe it helped that I'd recently gotten to spend a week in wolf form, hunting and playing with Sean and practicing disappearing into my surroundings like a real wolf. The memory of that precious week made me smile, even as I got close enough to Pierce's place to sense his house wards.

They sizzled on the edge of my senses, but like his perimeter wards they slid against me in that silky, caressing way. I didn't think I could cross them without being noticed, however. A cat wandering through the woods, sure. A cat wandering into the house? Probably not.

As it turned out, I didn't need to get into the house to find Pierce at work.

Like earth mages, necromancers liked dirt all around them: beneath their feet, in their hands, and even under their nails. But while mages like Malcolm and me drew power, energy, and even security from the natural magic of the earth's pulsing life, necromancers drew theirs from decay. That in itself wasn't inherently evil or malevolent; life and death were two sides of the same coin, after all, and the universe and all its workings demanded balance. But necromancers, as Carly had pointed out, had allied themselves with Death itself and chosen to embrace black magic, the occult, and death magic for power and control above all else. Life and growth sustained an earth mage; death and suffering nourished a necromancer.

I found Gregory Pierce in the backyard of the house, wearing a black hooded robe with red along its edges, conducting ritual magic in an open-air cathedral unmistakably dedicated to Death. A half-dozen torches provided light in the garden while also ensuring plenty of shadows and dark corners to add to the overall creepy feeling of the place.

His version of a blood garden and altar area were hidden from view from above by a peaked pergola roof choked with black, thorny vines with drooping purple blooms and the scent of rotting flesh. All the king's horses and all the king's men couldn't have made me touch one of those thorns. I recognized instant death when I saw it.

In fact, everywhere I looked, death lay in wait.

It wrapped around the structure in the form of those nightmarish vines. It flourished in raised beds full of mushrooms, all of which I figured would either kill on contact or if eaten and were probably growing on corpses and blood within the soil. It dripped in plant and flower form from the heads of the garden's dozen statues depicting death and suffering. It hung in the air as an odor that made me want to sneeze and back away when the breeze shifted, and it slithered along the ground as venomous snakes that had gathered around Pierce and his altar like acolytes.

I squeezed my fist around the amulet Carly had given me to wear around my neck and fought the urge to leave this place and never come back. Her parchment-scented magic banished the stench of the garden, at least for the moments it took for me to regain my resolve.

I recalled a line from Malcolm's new favorite movie, in which a character suggested dropping a nuclear device on their location from orbit, describing that drastic action as the only way to ensure the terrible threat it contained could be destroyed. But looking at this garden and its caretaker, I wasn't entirely sure the equivalent of that dropped nuke would be enough. This infestation's roots would go deep. Pierce had owned this property for more than a decade. The garden had the feel of an established and powerful place of practice and worship, much like my grandfather's blood garden back in Baltimore.

Son of a bitch—this was going to be a nightmare.

Well, of course it is, I thought, and almost rolled my eyes at myself. What had I expected when dealing with a necromancer? Whimsical topiaries?

Without Malcolm nearby, I had to provide my own comic relief. I missed my ghost.

I'd never seen a necromancer's blood garden before. I hoped my first time would also be my last. It wouldn't do to make a habit of straying into them.

Pierce had something in a cauldron on his altar. As I watched from behind some bushes, he stirred it with what looked like a human femur, then dropped the femur in. He repeated the process with another bone. This one appeared to be a humerus, or upper arm bone. Black oily smoke swirled out of the cauldron with a sound that reminded me of a thick, wet cough.

I recognized this ritual from a long-ago lesson on the darkest of dark magic: Etruscan in origin and steeped in ancient rites I doubted more than a few had seen, much less practiced, in millennia. That lesson had taken place fifteen years ago at my grandfather's compound in Baltimore, but my memory of what I'd learned might help me survive. Hopefully.

Where had Pierce learned his practice? The vamps were looking into that, along with the rest of Pierce's background. There couldn't be many practitioners of this type of magic around. The list of suspects had to be pretty damn short. At least I knew it wasn't the necromancer I'd encountered back East. Her practice had been entirely different.

Wait—did those bones belong to the Harpes? Was he destroying evidence while I watched? Or cooking up something worse?

Either way, I was going to have to step into a place where not only would angels fear to tread, but they'd avoid at all costs.

Years ago, on the night we'd first met, I'd told Charles Vaughan that I became a mage private investigator because I was addicted to danger. I was being flippant at the time, but that didn't make it untrue.

I didn't want to go into Pierce's garden, but I did. I wanted to face my fears and come out the other side. I wanted to beat him on his own turf. I wanted him in awe of me—not because of my ego, but because the conceited asshole needed to get knocked down a few pegs.

There was a fine line between showmanship and a necromancer's everyday magical practice. Pierce was ringed by venomous snakes and wearing a black hooded robe while doing magic alone in his own backyard, away from prying eyes, for crying out loud. Who was he showing off for?

I could almost hear Pierce say *If it's not showy, what's even the point in doing it?*

I'd learned when dealing with bad guys like Pierce, whether they were Dark Fae, sorcerers, blood mages, or scam callers, the thing that made them tick was almost always their Achilles' heel.

The question for me now was: how would knowing Pierce was a psychopathic show-off help me take him out for good? And could I do it without wading knee-deep into freaking snakes?

And that was when the army of the dead arrived.

FORTY-SIX

Small animals, all in various states of decay, burst from the ground, dropped from the branches, and lurched out of the bushes and trees, as if the forest itself had come alive to attack me.

But it wasn't the forest. And the animals didn't attack—they *assembled* silently and in an orderly way. Which, I decided almost immediately, was worse than a frenzied attack because it was so eerie.

Dozens of dogs, cats, rabbits, squirrels, mice, foxes, raccoons, possums, skunks, and deer, and a few bobcats and coyotes too, gathered *en masse* around Pierce's garden. All were extremely dead, some little more than bones and fur and some sinew. Many were eyeless, but they moved with purpose anyway. My skin crawled.

The odor of death and rot grew so strong that I came perilously close to losing my dinner of a hastily snarfed PB&J. I swallowed hard and focused on watching Pierce.

If there was a silver lining to the assembly of dead things, they helped hide my presence. And they paid no attention to me whatsoever, even brushing past me as if I were nothing more than a tree or branch. I worried about those snakes, though. They weren't dead, which meant their senses were perfectly acute. Hopefully they stayed in thrall to their master and didn't notice something alive lurking in the shadows in the midst of all the decay.

Pierce threw back the hood of his robe and smiled at the sight of all the dead things that had gathered around him, and probably all the deadly things in his garden too. He seemed to have the same level of joy in this moment as I felt in the midst of my pack or when I played with Baby Daisy.

Necromancers. I just...didn't get it.

My plan for how this would play out had *not* included an army of undead critters, much less venomous snakes.

I didn't know if Sean and the others could see this nightmare, but they had to be able to smell the stench of decay. I pushed love and trust through our nascent bond and felt warmth in response.

I'd fought hordes of monsters in the Underworld and the Broken World, and plenty of other terrible and creepy things over the course of my life. The dead animals around me didn't frighten me as much as their presence was just unnerving. Not as unnerving as the amount of pleasure Pierce apparently got from this nightmarish tableau, though.

And not *nearly* as unnerving as when Pierce suddenly looked straight at me...and all the snakes gathered around him turned and looked too, their tongues flicking out to taste the air in my direction.

I definitely did not almost wet my pants.

I did, however, step out from behind the bushes and give him a little wave. "Evening, Greg. Nice place you've got. Very homey."

"It is for me." His smile widened. "I'm flattered you went to so much trouble to find me and get past my wards unnoticed. Courtesy of your pretty witch friend, I see. All that dried blood must be uncomfortable. Would you like something to wipe your face? Though I do love a beautiful woman covered in blood and black magic. It's...alluring."

Well, ew. But if he found me *alluring*, I could work with that. I wasn't above using my feminine wiles, such as they were. Whatever got the job done.

"Blood never bothered me much," I said with a shrug. "But to be honest, I'm not a fan of snakes. Any chance you and I could talk without your slithery little friends?"

He *tsk*'d. "My familiars? You'd ask me to dismiss my most cherished and devoted companions?"

"Call it a favor."

Now Pierce appeared thoughtful. "If I ask them to leave, will you allow me to give you a tour of my garden?"

"Why? Would that be a *real treat* for you?"

He laughed at my reference to how he'd described the prospect of getting me on the witness stand. "It would, actually. Maybe it would be a treat for you too. No other human has ever stepped foot on this ground. You're a blood mage. I know it calls to you."

It *did* call to me, because all blood gardens did. And to get close to him, I'd have to venture into that den of death and decay. I just needed to not seem too eager.

I put my hands on my hips. "Lose the snakes and I'll think about it."

He made a series of odd sounds like a cross between whisper and whistle. One by one, the snakes turned and slipped away in different directions, disappearing into the darkness.

"You know, that's less reassuring than I thought it would be," I said dryly. "I guess at least in the light I knew where they were."

"They'll stay clear. I wouldn't waste your beauty or power on a snakebite." He gestured grandly and even bowed. "Welcome to my paradise, Alice."

He was laying it on thick with the compliments tonight, as if I was susceptible to flattery with this level of danger close by. But I gave him a smile as if I liked his attention.

Once I ventured inside the garden, I'd be out of sight of my backup. Sean and the others would have to wait for my signal to know when to act. That, or for disaster to strike. One of the two.

I stepped over and around the dead critters and eyed the garden's deadly vine-covered doorway. "You wouldn't waste my beauty and power on thorns or poisonous mushrooms either, would you?"

Pierce laughed. "Hardly."

He'd kill me any way he could if I gave him a reason, but I pretended to take his assurance at face value.

It took every ounce of willpower and courage I had to step through the garden's doorway and past those dripping thorns.

Inside, Pierce's garden smelled of decay, leafy growing things, rich dark earth, and black magic. And blood—so much blood. Somehow both its smell and appearance were less unpleasant than I'd expected. The thing I liked least were all the little dark openings and shadows where I suspected his damn snakes had taken refuge.

His altar was simple: a massive stone base with a pillar, another flat stone like a tabletop inlaid with glyphs that glowed red, and a cauldron. Around the cauldron he'd placed red and black candles that had black flames and a variety of bones, including a few skulls. One skull and several of the bones were human and very discolored with age. The rest of the human bones looked recently added.

"Have you seen this kind of altar before?" Pierce asked. He sounded genuinely curious. "You don't seem surprised by what's on it."

I shrugged. "I've been around a lot of occult and black magic practitioners. Dealt with a sorcerer fairly recently even." Two, actually, counting Vlad, but he'd never believe me if I said more than one. And besides, Vlad's existence *and* final death were still in the category of top secret.

"You survived a sorcerer." His eyebrows shot up. "I take it the sorcerer is dead?"

"Super dead," I confirmed. "Made a big boom when he went. Very satisfying."

I hadn't said it to impress him—well, not *entirely* to impress him —but the news certainly appeared to elevate his assessment of me.

Mission accomplished there, since I wanted him to think I was here to talk about an alliance.

Since he didn't seem to object, I took a peek in the cauldron. Skull, femur, and humerus, all old, bubbling in a foul liquid with oils and herbs floating on top.

I pinched my nose, mostly for show. "You know that's gross, right?"

That elicited an indulgent chuckle. "It's all in the eye of the beholder. That's beautiful to me. A lifetime of learning and discipline in what looks to you like bones in a pot. All magic is beautiful to some and ugly and terrifying to others. All types of ritual practice, including yours, require ingredients and tools. These are mine."

It took serious mental gymnastics to equate human bones with the implements I kept in my workshop, but I didn't argue.

He led me to his beds of mushrooms, the source of most of the rotten smell that pervaded the garden. Some of the mushrooms were pretty, some were strange, and some were downright scary in appearance, like the ones we stood in front of first. They had gray corpse-like flesh, black edges, and long black fringes that reminded me of icicles.

"*Coprinopsis atramentaria*," he said, caressing their tops. "Commonly known as the inky cap. Perfectly safe to eat unless you drink alcohol before or after consuming them. One of my favorites because of their colors and how they love to grow from rotting wood. The smell is divine."

He clearly had a much different definition of *divine* than me. "All the mushrooms in these garden beds are deadly?"

"All of them," he confirmed. "But they vary widely in their manners of death. Some show you the mysteries of the universe before you die. Others introduce you to levels of agony virtually unknown to humanity. A few offer death in an almost painless way, guiding you through the veil in your sleep. Side by side, they're like a symphony of death."

The variety next to the inky caps was wholly unremarkable:

white tops and stems, some with pink or yellow in the center of their tops. Unlike most of the other mushrooms in this garden, I wouldn't have paid them any attention, but Pierce stopped to admire them. "*Amanita bisporigera*, or destroying angel. Such a beautiful name for such an unremarkable killer. One of the deadliest mushrooms in existence and yet easy to miss on first glance. Foragers frequently mistake them for safe, edible varieties. Looks can be deceiving, can't they?"

Even *I* could recognize that metaphor. Pierce probably thought of himself as perfectly safe in appearance but incredibly deadly in reality.

We moved to a more colorful bed. Unlike the deathly gray of the inky caps or the plain white of the destroying angels, the tops of these mushrooms were a deep red, the color of arterial blood. On closer inspection, their white spots were not just bumps, but bore a resemblance to screaming faces. I recoiled.

Pierce's body language changed, becoming almost reverent. "My treasures," he murmured, almost lovingly, his fingertips hovering over the surface of the mushroom. "*Amanita demonica*. They only grow from the body of a slain demon. The souls that demon claimed remain trapped in the flesh of the fungus, pushing to the surface but unable to escape. While its brothers and sisters in the *Amanita* family will merely kill you, this beautiful fungus will pull your soul out of your body. Would you like to touch one, Alice?"

His smile was almost tender or sensual, as if we were on a second date discussing after-dinner plans over wine instead of talking demons and death over Hell's own mushrooms. Then again, maybe for necromancers this sort of thing counted as flirting.

"Tempting," I said. "But I think I'll pass."

As he watched, I took my time wandering around the rest of the garden, surveying the plants and flowers that filled it. Most were dark green or black, making this by far the most gothic garden I'd ever stepped foot in. The only pops of color were mushrooms and the fire on the torches.

Here and there I spotted bones protruding from the soil. Most appeared human, but some clearly belonged to the kinds of small animals who'd gathered outside, silent and watchful.

"Your garden is beautiful," I said when Pierce moved so he could see my face in the torchlight. "Surprisingly so. Not what's on the altar or the snakes, of course, but the rest is lovely in its own way."

"You don't find death evil? Or ugly?"

"Death isn't evil or ugly in itself," I said. "But the way you deal it out, and use it for power and fear, and try to control it, *is*." He stood close enough to me that I had to look up to see his face, but I wasn't going to step back. "You realize with your ability and dedication to your practice, you could be powerful without dealing in death, right?"

"What use is power if it doesn't make people fear you?" He seemed puzzled by the concept.

"What use is power if all it does is make people fear you?" I countered. Hadn't I just had this conversation with Moses the other day? "What if your power and how you use it made people respect and follow you instead? If it's power you want, there are other ways to get it and keep it. Ways that let you keep your soul and not end up in places like Tartarus. I've been there. It's not nice."

"Death is not nice." He touched my cheek, his fingertips tracing a streak of dried blood. He smelled like smoke and rot. "Death comes for us all. It's an unbeatable foe for anyone who refuses to make it an ally."

Fear of death and the instinct for survival were the most powerful and fundamental forces I knew. And for people like Pierce, they overrode nearly everything else, making them willing to do anything to hold death at bay.

His hand trailed down my arm and raised my hand so he could inspect my inner wrist. "I noticed this scar earlier in the park. You've met one of my kind before."

"Yes." I took my hand back. "A long time ago. I barely remember."

He smiled like he knew that was a lie, but he let it go.

"I hate to break it to you, Greg," I said, to redirect the conversation back to where we'd left off. "But death comes for those who think they're its ally too. I see it happen all the time. Didn't we just talk about that sorcerer I killed? You can't defeat it—all you can do is put it off. And then when it catches up to you, in whatever form it chooses, you go all the way down to Hell's subbasement. Don't you fear that? Because I gotta be honest—if I were in your shoes, I would."

He smiled. "Are you trying to save my soul, Alice Worth?"

Was I? Since I'd arrived, I'd pretended, played along, almost flirted, waiting for a chance to spring a trap. But this last bit of conversation hadn't been fake. I'd come here wanting to send Pierce to Tartarus, only to find myself sincerely making an argument against black magic and necromancy to a serial-killing psychopath with buckets of innocent blood on his well-manicured hands.

"I could have been you," I said, which startled us both. "If I'd taken a different path and given in to the temptation to make the fantasies in my head reality. But as much as I've strayed over that line, and as many times as I've wanted to embrace the kind of power you love to have, something always held me back from the abyss."

"Fear of eternal damnation?"

"No, not really. My conscience, I suppose. And I saw the people around me, who were powerful but evil and hated and enjoyed making others suffer, and I knew I didn't want to be that kind of person. Maybe that's what makes you and I different: conscience and a difference of opinion on what power is for."

He tilted his head. "You don't think I have a conscience?"

No sense lying to him. "No, I don't."

"And yet I haven't killed you," he mused. "I wonder why."

"Because you think I might be useful." As I talked, I walked around Pierce and then in a circle, looking over the garden again. "I don't have value to you except for what I might be able to do for you. Those who are useful get to live. Everyone else, you don't care if they live or die. You can go through the motions as the D.A. and fake caring because you know you have to act like you have normal emotions, but people's suffering doesn't really *reach* you, does it?"

"No, it doesn't." Pierce frowned. "But somehow I do care whether you live or die, and not just because I think we would make a formidable team. I think it's because you seem to understand me better than anyone."

I've been around a lot of psychopaths, I wanted to say, but didn't. Carly's counseling sessions had helped me understand that I recognized psychopaths and their motivations at least partially as a result of my traumatic past. Spotting those behavior patterns was a matter of survival.

"I do understand you, at least somewhat," I said. "And I respect your power. I recognize ability and dedication to practice when I see it. But at the end of the day, you've killed a lot of innocent people and put more innocent people in jail for the crimes you committed. I don't know if there's any redemption for you even if you wanted it."

"Part of me wants to want it," Pierce said quietly. "But I'd only ever be pretending."

Suddenly the charming smile was back, as if he'd flipped a switch or realized he'd made himself a little too vulnerable and returned to his favorite persona—the one that got him elected district attorney, among other things.

"That doesn't mean we can't be allies," he said. "Unprecedented times call for unprecedented associations. We both know this is the calm before the storm. You'd be wise to find the strongest boat you can."

"I prefer my own boat," I countered. "That way I know who's on it and how seaworthy it is. And I prefer to steer rather than be taken for a ride."

His smile turned sardonic. "And yet you've chosen to be the consort and future mate of an alpha werewolf. Do you steer your own course, or does he take care of that for you?" He glanced meaningfully in the direction of the woods. "I'm sure he's out there somewhere, waiting for you or getting ready to lead his pack in an attack on me. Did he send you in to distract me? Or to try to sweet-talk me into giving up my evil ways?"

"Neither. He *is* here with our pack, in case you were less than hospitable when I arrived."

His smile became a grin. "Instead we've had a nice chat and you got a tour of my private blood garden, all out of his sight. What will he think of that, I wonder?" He slid his hand from my shoulder and down my arm. "What will he think of my scent all over you?"

My eyes went to something behind him. "I dunno. Why don't you ask him?"

CHAPTER

FORTY-SEVEN

PIERCE SPUN AND SENT A BLAZING BALL OF BLACK AND RED MAGIC TEARING through the night air. I'd sold it so well that he couldn't help it. Yay me.

By the time he realized Sean wasn't behind him and his fireball had done nothing but burn a hole through the foliage, it was already too late.

Never trust an earth mage with blood magic in your blood garden—and for the love of coffee, don't give her a tour and the opportunity to drop her own blood everywhere she went. But Gregory Pierce was a cocky bastard trying to impress a woman, and so he had.

The soil, plants, and fungi, so perpetually thirsty for blood, had gulped mine down without hesitation.

I grabbed a ley line, spooled earth and blood magic, and attempted to steal Pierce's prize garden right out from under him.

"*Rise*," I commanded, pushing blood magic into the word to make it even more irresistible.

The entire garden heaved up in answer to my call. The sheer dark power of its soil, plants, and fungi turned my world silent and my vision crimson around the edges.

Oh, the power was pleasure, and the pleasure washed everything else away. My knees damn near buckled.

This is why I don't use dark magic, I told myself, fighting the overwhelming urge to lose myself in the almost carnal bliss of the garden's magic and strength. I'd told Matthias black magic was both insidious and seductive but I hadn't meant the latter literally. Come to find out, this power *was* literally erotic.

Places on my body that had no business doing so were throbbing with desire. If this was how Pierce felt in his garden, no wonder he called it paradise.

"Fucking *bitch!*" Pierce shouted, and flung a fiery snarl of spellwork in my direction.

Nothing will bring you back to earth from an unexpected near-orgasm like a blazing ball of black magic designed to kill you where you stand.

The dark soil moved beneath his feet, roiling under my command to rise. That should have spoiled his aim, but the magic curved through the air straight at my chest. I made a gesture like I was tossing a pair of dice and my fiery green earth magic whip coiled out of my hand. Black and red blood magic crackled along its length, signifying how much of the garden's dark magic I'd absorbed. I tried not to love the sight of it.

I lashed the magic he'd thrown. It blew apart in a burst of power and sizzling lightning that left the odors of ozone and burned blood in the air. Another deadly ball followed right behind it. My whip missed it by inches.

Pierce's magic hit me with the force of a heavyweight boxer's punch, sending me staggering as it rebounded with a puff of parchment-scented witchy magic—Carly's *Return to Sender* spell. The ball hit Pierce straight on, the entire exchange taking less than two seconds. It was his own magic, so it didn't hurt him, but the important part was that it hadn't hurt *me*. Much, anyway.

That ball of deadly magic would have been the end of me, and he could throw that kind of power without being able to draw much on his garden's energy. I couldn't afford to let my guard down around him, not even for a second. And I had to continue to go on the offensive, because sooner or later—and probably sooner—that strategy would get me killed, or worse.

With my earth magic, I pulled at the soil beneath Pierce's feet. Moments ago I'd walked a slow circle around him while I pretended to look over the garden again, and he'd been so busy talking about himself he hadn't realized the significance of that circle. The soil swallowed him to above his knees before he realized what was happening and fought back.

Pierce yanked hard on the garden's power, trying to wrench control back from me. I abandoned my attempt to bury him and instead turned the earth magic under and around him to cold fire that burned his legs. He screamed in pain.

"*Alice Evelyn Worth*," he shouted, his voice resonant with magic.

There it was again—my name that he'd turned into a spell. But unlike when he'd used it in Tartarus, this time he put real power into the words.

The voice and the magic it held wrapped around me with the sensation of an enormous serpent squeezing its prey. At first Carly's spells held, but the magic didn't let up. It squeezed and squeezed until the *Return to Sender* spell broke. *Shit.*

The black coils tightened around me. I couldn't move. Couldn't even take a breath.

All I had to do was give the signal and Sean and the others would come running, but I wouldn't do that until either I had no choice or Pierce was no longer a threat because the wolves had no real defense against a necromancer's magic.

Pierce smiled and reached out. Black magic coiled around his fingers. I had no doubt what he intended to do: pull my heart from my chest and add it to his triple-damned staff. The odors of damp earth and decay grew until they filled my nose and I couldn't smell anything else.

The magic dragged me across the dirt toward that deadly magic and my doom.

My options had rapidly dwindled to almost nothing.

I had to stay alive, and I had to keep him alive. I needed him to prove Oliver's innocence. That made everything a million times more difficult.

I still had control of his garden—or most of it. And thanks to my own blood garden, I knew just how powerful and useful hungry plants could be, especially when blood was on the menu.

Unfortunately, that meant I would have to let his magic drag me really, really close. Close enough to be within reach of that magic-wrapped hand that flexed in eagerness to relocate my heart.

When it doubt, go for surprise.

Lack of oxygen had made my head swim, but I leapt straight at him. Smug son of a bitch did not see that coming.

With a cry, I knocked his magic-wrapped hand aside and drove blood magic blades from my fingertips into his muscular shoulders. I wanted lots of blood, and I wanted to take some of the fight out of him. Severed tendons and broken bones tended to accomplish that.

He screamed again as blood spurted from the wounds. The crushing magic wrapped around my chest broke. I twisted my blades in his shoulders to maximize the damage, then hit the dirt and rolled away, spooling air magic until I came to rest against one of the mushroom beds.

My blast of white air magic hit him in the chest and sent him flying back into a raised bed of hungry plants. They fell on him, wrapping him in their leaves and stems, sucking and slurping at his blood. The more he thrashed, the more tightly they wrapped themselves around him.

The ground rumbled and heaved again, but this time it wasn't my doing.

Pierce might be temporarily immobilized and wounded, but he

wasn't down and he wasn't out. And he wasn't powerless. I'd only bought myself a little time.

The army of dead animals converged, hopping, dragging, stumbling, and crawling across the churned soil. The air filled with the hair-raising sound of bony jaws clacking in simulated hunger. And perhaps worse, I spotted four of Pierce's serpentine familiars emerging from their hidey-holes.

Pierce was arrogant, and that had allowed me to take advantage of his inattention and turn this into something close to a fair fight. Sometimes I was cocky too, but even *I* knew there were about a hundred of these dead creatures, eight venomous snakes, and only one of me.

But before I called in the cavalry, I needed to put Pierce somewhere that reduced the amount of danger he posed to the people I loved most.

So I spooled earth magic, grabbed the soil beneath him, and *pulled*.

The plants groaned and thrashed in protest as a sinkhole opened beneath Pierce and swallowed him, along with a few of their brethren. I heard him gasp in air before his head disappeared into the churning earth.

I formed an air bubble around him as I pulled and pulled, rolling him down and around beneath the surface until I hoped he couldn't tell which way was up. Down, down, *down*. In moments, he was too deep for me to hear, but magic couldn't be buried.

Coils and fiery balls of black magic rolled from the ground in every direction. Some destroyed members of his undead animal army; others came perilously close to hitting me, and I had no *Return to Sender* spell for protection now.

I let go of most of the earth in the garden to focus on pulling Pierce deeper underground while avoiding the wild magic he continued to throw.

A rumble grew under the garden, shaking the earth hard enough that the windows of the house rattled. The plants swayed. Pierce's altar fell over, spilling the contents of the cauldron. The skull and other bones sank into the earth as if drawn down by something.

Whatever he wanted these bones for, I didn't want him to get them. I dove for the skull and grabbed it just in time to keep it from disappearing. It felt like it weighed fifty pounds in my hands.

When the skull spoke, I nearly dropped it.

"If I were you, I'd choose one of the mushrooms." Pierce's breathless voice emanating from the skull managed to sound smug somehow. "You're about to die very, very slowly, and very painfully otherwise. I suggest the death caps. I've made them particularly strong. One bite is all it will take."

The irony of being named Alice and someone telling me to eat a mushroom might be funny later—if I got to have a *later*.

Also, I didn't believe him about the one bite and a quick death. I did, however, believe that the army of dead animals and those freaking snakes *would* kill me. One of the snakes—a slim black one—raised up and hissed. I saw no sign of the cobra, and I didn't like that one bit.

"*Sean!*" I screamed.

Thanks to my hijacking of the garden and some of its power, I felt when my pack rushed through the wards. The ground rumbled again, throwing me off balance. Maybe that was Pierce's rage.

Bony mouths chomping eagerly, the army of dead animals attacked en masse.

Please let Pierce be buried deep enough, I thought. I tossed the skull into a bed of destroying angels and manifested earth fire whips tinged with black magic from both my hands.

One battle paused while another began.

With practiced aim, I spun and lashed the attacking carcasses, but there were simply too many for me to hold back. Teeth sank into my legs from all sides as I kicked, stomped, lashed, and broke them into pieces. Hot blood ran down my legs and pooled in my boots.

I remembered fighting the hordes of monsters in the Underworld and how I'd used my dark magic there to kill them. Would that work here? Only one way to find out, but it meant drawing in more of the black magic I liked way too much.

No choice.

I sucked in Pierce's dark magic, closed my eyes, and reached out to the dead things around me.

The pleasure of the power blended with the sickness of decay and rot. My stomach rebelled. I hit my knees in the midst of the attacking horde, heaving violently.

Through the overwhelming sickness, I wrenched the power of their undeath away from Pierce and ripped the corpses apart. The animals closest to me crumbled to bones and lay still. Dozens more clambered over the fallen to get to me. The snakes stayed away, though. Maybe the mindless attackers would have just as eagerly taken a bite out of them as me. I'd take all the favors I could get.

Then my pack mates arrived with snarls, teeth, and claws.

Six enormous werewolves, with Sean's beautiful black wolf in the lead, tore through the dead creatures, sending bones and decaying flesh in every direction. As many times as I'd seen my pack mates in action, the carnage they created left me in awe once again.

Ben, a tawny brown wolf with a patch of white on his chest, plowed straight through the dead creatures to reach my side. He sniffed me all over and let out a little questioning whine.

"I'm okay," I said, knowing damn well it wasn't true, but that it was true enough. "Just please keep them off me."

Snarling, he ripped apart every creature that came within reach. The extreme prejudice with which he did that revealed just how much rage he'd built up waiting for his chance to join the fight. Judging by the others' frenzy of destruction, they shared his feelings.

Now protected by Ben, I dug my fingers into the soil, searching for confirmation that Pierce remained buried and had enough air. He was, and he did. Hopefully the couple of plants that got buried with him wouldn't drain him dry before we could bring him back up.

That damn skull had started to sink into the mushroom bed. *Shit.* I stumbled to my feet. With Ben at my side, I made it to the bed, pulled the skull out of the dirt, and held it tightly against my chest with both arms.

One of the snakes went for me and promptly died in Ben's teeth. Several others were already dead courtesy of the other wolves. One was in pieces after being attacked by the small dead animals. I'd been right about that, anyway.

Around me, the wolves tore apart the rest of Pierce's dead army. The ground continued to rumble, but no magic emerged.

Exhausted, I plopped down in the dirt. Ben guarded me ferociously, his teeth bared. The soil still nearly boiled with Pierce's black magic and blood, now all mixed together with my own. My jeans were in tatters from the creatures' bites and blood oozed from more than a dozen burning wounds. I was so, so tired, in so much pain, and so freaking sick to my stomach that I longed to curl into a ball. But there was still a lot of work to be done.

My earth magic told me Pierce was more than twenty feet down and in a bubble with enough air to keep him alive for at least a few more minutes.

I put the skull on my lap and stared into its empty eye sockets. "Can you hear me, Greg?"

He laughed.

The sound unnerved me almost as much as the dead snakes and the crunching of animal bones in my pack mates' jaws. Ben's ears went flat against his head and his lips curled to show all his teeth.

"What's your endgame, Alice?" Pierce asked, chuckling. "You've given me air to breathe, so you must want me to live. Are going to call the police and hand me over to them? They'll laugh in your face. We've been *over* this."

His *you silly girl* tone made me irrationally itch to punch the skull in its nasal cavity.

"Or do you plan to execute me yourself?" he continued, still mocking. "You know this doesn't end well for you *or* your client. No court will set him free or put me in prison. You know you have nothing. Even the existence of this garden doesn't prove anything."

"Well, I think your public image will take a pretty big hit when the fact you're a necromancer becomes common knowledge." I settled in more comfortably, sitting cross-legged with the skull in my lap. Was it only this heavy when Pierce was using it to communicate? Necromancy was *so* weird. "And yes, I give you full credit for cooking up a perfect plan. Well, *almost* perfect, anyway."

"What do you mean?" Now his voice became suspicious. And he coughed. The air must be getting thin down there. "You still have no evidence you can present to a jury. No confession. All the evidence points to Oliver and the others. You've got *nothing*."

"Nothing your replacement could use, no," I admitted. "But as you know, rules of evidence vary depending on the court. And that's where you screwed up. You forgot your court wasn't the only game in town."

"SPEMA has the same evidentiary rules," he wheezed. "Do you think the feds are going to swoop in and save the day?"

"No, I don't." I glanced up. "But I know someone who is."

Charles had appeared out of the darkness to stand about twenty feet away where Sean and the other wolves besides Ben had gathered. Bryan stood behind him, accompanied by a group of about twenty Court enforcers.

All the wolves showed Charles their teeth in case the vampire had forgotten he had no friends here except his own people.

"Did you bring the cage?" I asked.

Charles smiled. "Of course. May I approach?"

My aching body protested the movement, but I gestured grandly at the remains of Pierce's garden of death. "Be my guest. I'm sure our host doesn't mind."

Charles strolled across the upturned earth. A small wrinkling of his nose was his only acknowledgement of the stench of blood and rot. His eyes darkened at the sight of my wounds, but he didn't comment on them or otherwise react to the scent of my blood.

And he took his damn time getting over to me too. Maybe he didn't want to startle the wolves by moving quickly, or maybe he wanted the last words Gregory Pierce heard before passing out to be his. Fair enough. I didn't have to get the last word. Pierce knew who'd won this round—or he was about to find out.

The vampire crouched beside me and addressed the skull in my lap as nonchalantly as if he talked to skulls regularly. "Mr. Pierce, I am Charles Vaughan, head of the Vampire Court of the Western United States. It is my very great pleasure to arrest you on six counts of murder, three counts of grievous assault, and one count of attempted murder and involuntary non-corporeal enslavement for this attack on Alice Worth."

Such a shame I'd had to bury Pierce, because I would have given a lot to see the expression on his face in the silence that followed.

"I take from your lack of response that you're displeased with this development," Charles said, showing his fangs. The vampire looked entirely too pleased with himself for someone who came strolling in after the battle was over. "Or perhaps you hope SPEMA and the local police will fight for jurisdiction or intervene on your behalf. I will save you the trouble and tell you they will not. Jurisdiction has already been settled. Justice found you after all, Mr. Pierce— if only much later than it should."

"This is not...a matter...for the Vampire Court," Pierce rasped.

"You might be correct if not for two things," Charles said smoothly. "First, the nature of the evidence against you, which meets our standards for admissibility. And second, the fact you attempted to kill and enslave Alice, who is a longtime most valued associate of the Court. Trying to murder her was a grave error on your part—*one you will surely regret.*"

Up to now, Charles's tone had combined his signature haughtiness with smug satisfaction, but the naked menace of that last bit belied his real fury. What percentage was a result of Pierce's murderous rampage and how much came from his attempt to kill me and bind my spirit for eternity, I wasn't sure, and I didn't care to speculate.

"This....will not...." Pierce began, and then his voice faded. The skull in my lap suddenly became much lighter, signaling that it no longer served as Pierce's creepy walkie-talkie.

Whatever he was about to say, he'd apparently run out of oxygen before he could finish what I could only assume had been a threat. Time to haul the bastard back up before he died.

"Bring the cage," Charles said over his shoulder.

As a group of enforcers approached carrying a heavily warded and spelled four-foot by four-foot cage between them, Charles said, "Well done, Alice. This is a brilliant solution to both our problems, indeed."

"Indeed." Exhaustion left me barely able to sit upright. Perhaps sensing that, Ben let me lean against his side. "You saw and heard everything?" I asked.

"I did." Charles smiled. "The testimony of myself and other witnesses will surely be incontrovertible evidence when added to what you have gathered and what we will find here. Please deliver the defendant to us for imprisonment."

I had just enough strength left in me to push my fingers into the dirt and bring Pierce's unconscious body up to the surface.

The soil boiled and turned until he emerged, caked with dirt and unmoving except for the shallow breaths that showed he was alive.

When the roiling earth rolled him over, the sight of Pierce's unconscious body came with a very unpleasant bonus: the damn cobra.

Only ten feet away from where I sat, the enormous snake slithered out of its hiding place in Pierce's robe and raised up about four or five feet. It spread its hood, its glowing eyes locked on me as its tongue flicked the air in my direction.

In a heartbeat, Sean's wolf bolted toward the cobra. But before he could reach it, Charles put himself between the snake and me, and Bryan pulled a gun and shot the serpent in the head.

My ears ringing, I staggered to my feet, one hand on Ben's wolf to steady myself. My legs trembled with pain and exhaustion as a new fear gripped me. "Was Pierce bitten?"

Bryan holstered his gun and ripped Pierce's robe and other clothes from his body in a half-dozen purposeful tears that made me think he'd torn clothing from an unconscious or dead body enough times to get good at it.

"I don't see a bite," he reported, to my relief. "He might have intended the cobra as a surprise for you when he returned to the surface."

Given the way the cobra had eyeballed me, I suspected he was right. Nice. I resisted the urge to kick Pierce in the ribs, but only barely.

I gave the cobra's body a wide berth and joined Charles and Bryan at Pierce's side. The necromancer's skin was pale from lack of oxygen and blood loss. Dirt caked his face and the wounds I'd made in his shoulders trickled blood, but he was breathing.

I'd done my part to capture him alive. Keeping him alive to stand trial was the vamps' problem.

"Probably need to put him under a suicide watch," I said.

Charles shook his head. "He is much too arrogant to take his own life. He will believe he will be acquitted until the moment the gavel comes down. After that, it will not matter what he does. Justice will be served either way."

It *did* matter, but I didn't contradict him. He wouldn't change his opinion and I was too tired to argue anyway.

Bryan locked stout spell cuffs around Pierce's wrists and threw him naked, dirty, and bloody into the cage.

The spellwork on the cage flared as soon as Bryan shut and locked the door. The dampening spells were so strong that even from six feet away my own magic felt muted. That spellwork was not playing around. Whoever had built and spelled that cage had made damn sure Pierce couldn't so much as reanimate a fly. I wondered if one of the Silver Thorn witches had made it.

With Pierce in his cage and in the Court's custody, the wolves finally shifted.

Sean went directly to me and wrapped his arms around me from behind. "Miss Magic," he said, and kissed my dirty, blood-matted hair. At least that blood was Pierce's and not mine for a change.

I leaned against him, letting him take most of my weight because my legs shook so badly. Moving around had caused blood to run from the bite wounds. I needed to use a healing spell as soon as we wrapped things up.

Charles glanced at us. His eyes tightened at the sight of Sean's arms around me, but he turned his attention to his enforcers as they carried Pierce's cage around the house to wherever their transportation waited.

Pierce's nasty blood garden, or what remained of it, belonged to the Court now as evidence. I had to trust Charles and the Court to do their part from here on. Using the words *trust* and *the Court* in the same sentence was tough to do, but we'd made a deal and Charles had sworn to uphold it.

At my suggestion, he'd traded his case against us for an even more high-profile case—one that could cement both his new vision for the Court *and* his leadership. That was enough for me to give him a chance to do what human courts could not: exonerate my client and the others and ensure Pierce paid for his crimes.

"Many more monsters lurk among us," Charles said, his dark, softly glowing eyes sweeping the garden and woods. "I would like my Court to bring them to justice with your help." Finally, he met my tired gaze. "But we will discuss that another day. For now, you must return home to heal and rest."

I could have drawn power from the garden to regenerate my magic and banish my exhaustion, but I didn't. The temptation burned so fiercely that I had to steel myself and focus on breathing in Sean's forest scent.

The black magic knew it had lost its master and wanted another. It also knew I had bathed myself in its pleasures and made myself vulnerable to its siren call. The magic beckoned like fresh-ground coffee, blueberry scones warm from the oven, and Sean's touch combined, times a hundred.

Carly would understand, but no one here knew how difficult it was for me to deny myself that magic. Having not only used it, but *enjoyed* it, now I had to walk away with it whispering seductively in my ear, promising pleasure and power and everything my heart desired.

It promised Moses's flayed body at my feet, and Kade's and Nora Keegan's too.

I had to slam the door on those promises, lock it, and throw away the key, and that was *so hard* because there were few things I wanted more in all the world than to be rid of my grandfather and his cronies.

Before I lost my will to do what needed to be done, Sean helped me kneel so I could push my trembling fingers into the dirt one last time. I found the familiar tingle of my blood and the magic it contained and unleashed my air magic burner spell. *"Burn."*

With a *whoosh*, powerful white magic swept through the garden and deep into the soil, incinerating every trace of my blood and leaving nothing but fine ash behind. The Court might get the garden, but they didn't get my blood. And the garden itself sure as hell didn't get to keep it.

A gust of cold wind blew through us, carrying with it black magic and an audible howl—Pierce's garden reacting to the burning of my blood and my rejection of its lure. The stench of rot grew to an almost unbearable level. Goosebumps prickled over my entire body. Charles hissed. Sean snarled and braced himself, but there wasn't anything or anyone here for him to fight.

"I don't want you," I whispered to the swirling magic, my words so soft I doubted even the wolves or Charles would hear me. "I know what you are. You're nothing but lies."

With another howl, the magic lashed out, knocking me back into Sean's arms. Bone-chilling cold swept through me, followed by searing heat. Sean snarled again. His golden shifter magic enveloped us, pushing back at the garden's power.

The air turned almost sooty with the stink of decay and black magic. Red and black tendrils of magic crackled across the upturned dirt to converge on the place where Pierce's altar once stood, then disappeared into the ground. The sensations of heat and cold in my body faded.

Everything went still.

But not *still* as in defeated or gone. Still, as in waiting.

"Alice." Charles crouched to bring himself eye level with me, but wisely kept his distance. Sean didn't want him near me at the best of times, and this was *not* the best of times by a long shot. "Please say something."

"Something," I rasped. "I'm hurt, but I'm okay."

Sean nuzzled my hair and then got me back on my feet. I could barely stand. He slipped his arm around my waist and held me close.

"We need to go now." His voice was edged with a growl. "Vaughan, we're leaving this mess for the Court to sort out."

"It will be thoroughly sorted." Charles gave us a half bow, but his gaze was on me, not Sean when he added, "You have my word."

For whatever that's worth, I thought, but didn't say. I didn't need to. I felt certain he saw it in my face.

With Sean's warm arms around me and his body pressed to mine, I could have fallen asleep right there on my feet, but rest wasn't in the cards for me—at least not for a while.

Once we made it home, I had some very important calls to make: one to Oliver and Gracie Hensley, one to Philippa Grayson, and one to Ernie Diaz. I hoped at least one or two of those conversations would go well.

Then I'd heal my wounds, burn my clothes, and shower for an hour to wash all the blood and dirt and death down the drain.

Only then would I be able to crawl into bed and sleep.

FORTY-EIGHT

G RACIE HENSLEY HAD A HELL OF A HUG.

She barely let me get past the threshold of their hotel suite before she threw her arms around me and squeezed so tightly that I swore my ribs creaked.

Pain nearly took my breath away.

A full fourteen hours after my battle with Gregory Pierce, I hurt all over, and no healing spell and no amount of ibuprofen made any difference. Almost as bad as the pain were the waves of extreme heat and cold that swept through me in turns without warning. I had no appetite and could barely drink water. Even the thought of coffee turned my stomach.

I'd been on the receiving end of a necromancer's black magic and the aftereffects might last for days, or weeks. Or longer. Katy was making me potions to soak in, but they weren't ready yet. Sheer determination alone kept me upright and putting one foot in front of the other.

I'd only left my bed because I wanted to meet the Hensleys in person to wrap up my case. I also wanted to see how they were doing. Not well, judging by how grim and pale they both looked.

"Alice," Malcolm muttered. Only Matthias and I could hear him, but he spoke in an undertone anyway. He'd been subdued all day because I was suffering and he couldn't do anything to help. "Get in there and sit down before you fall down."

Beside me, Matthias rumbled. He probably wanted to put an end to Gracie's enthusiastic and extended hug—forcibly, if necessary.

I gritted my teeth, rubbed Gracie's back, and extricated myself as quickly as I could without seeming unkind. "Hey, Gracie."

The room wasn't cold, but she wore a long-sleeve turtleneck, presumably to hide the healing bruises and cuts on her neck. I doubted that prevented Oliver from thinking about them, but she was doing her best. I supposed we all were today.

I looked past her at Oliver, who was sitting at a table by the sliding glass door that led to the suite's balcony. "Hi, Oliver."

"Hi, Alice." He managed only a brief smile. He'd noticeably lost weight in the few days since I'd seen him last. He no longer wore his ankle monitor, but that didn't seem to offer him much solace.

Gracie turned to Matthias, who'd accompanied me to the meeting. "Can I hug you too?" she asked, a bit timidly.

In answer, he opened his arms. She gave him a quick hug.

In the meantime, Philippa Grayson stood next to Oliver with one hand on the back of his chair as she studied Matthias and me. Her poker face gave little away, but I saw some sympathy in her gaze. She probably thought I looked like hell because of the wreck. I planned to let her think so, at least for now. They'd hear the truth soon enough, and more to the point, this meeting wasn't about me.

"I must say, Alice, I didn't expect this case to go in this particular direction," Philippa said. "I really can't decide if this change of juris-diction is pure brilliance on your part, or the biggest mess I've ever found myself in, legally speaking."

I started to shrug, then thought better of it because I ached so much. "We can go with both, if that helps."

Philippa chuckled. Actually *chuckled*. I got the impression that didn't happen very often. She eyed my companion, her expression more curious than apprehensive. "And who is this?"

"Matthias Albrecht," I said. "Beta of our pack. My driver, for the time being."

"He helped us the other night," Gracie added. "He was very kind."

"Nice to meet you, Matthias." Philippa gestured at the table. "Shall we sit?"

Moving slowly, I made it to the chair opposite Oliver's and sat, all without Matthias's help. I'd hear about it in the car on the way home, in addition to agreeing to meet rather than staying in bed, but I still had some pride left—though it was mostly in tatters after being carried everywhere lately and so much fussing. Matthias scooted in my chair and leaned against the wall behind me.

"So," Philippa said, folding her hands on the table. "Where should we begin?"

"I have a lot to tell you all," I said, and wasn't that a hell of an understatement. "But if you'll bear with me a moment, I have something I need to do first." I reached across the table toward Oliver and held out my hand palm up. "Please."

Clearly surprised, he took my hand. I held on gently but firmly, the way Sean always did when I needed to hear something important, and because I wanted him to feel how much I meant what I was about to say.

"I need you to listen to me." I met his gaze, but with kindness and not aggression. "You did nothing to deserve what's happened to you and Gracie. Nothing at all. You are not at fault for any of it. I understand if you can't believe me right now, or maybe your head knows but your heart hasn't gotten the message yet."

I'd guessed right; Oliver did blame himself. He wore his guilt in his expression as plainly as the shadows under his eyes.

I had never felt more like Carly in my life than I did in this moment. The only things missing were scones and a pot of tea.

"I don't know exactly how you're feeling right now," I continued.

"But I do know anyone can easily end up thinking they're complicit in their own victimization, even when they know who the real culprit is. They can internalize the blame because deep down I think a lot of us feel that bad things only happen to bad people, and because the bad guy seems so distant and big and almost unreal. There are a lot of factors, but they all lead to the same place: guilt you don't deserve to carry."

"It all feels like stones on my shoulders." He swallowed hard. His hand in mine turned cool and clammy. "Not just because I don't know why he picked me. I want to know why I lived and so many others didn't."

Survivor's guilt was another terrible burden I understood all too well.

"I don't have those answers yet, and honestly, I don't know if we'll ever get them. Even if we do, though, it won't magically make it all go away." I took a deep breath because every word I said applied to me as much as Oliver, and I'd had versions of this conversation with Carly more than once. "We can't control what happens to us, and I think that one shitty fact is at the root of most of self-blame."

"How so?" Gracie asked.

"Most people don't want to believe they aren't in control of their lives." I explained. "We'd almost rather think we're to blame when bad things happen than accept that. Everything I just said, I know from experience. I don't normally tell anyone that, but I want you to know I have some idea of how you feel right now because I've been there."

Malcolm put his hand on my shoulder. I felt his love—and his worry—through our binding.

No one said anything for several beats. Gracie took Oliver's other hand and laced their fingers together, tears shining in her eyes. Even Philippa sniffed, though it might have been allergies that caused it.

When Oliver finally spoke, his voice was wry. "That's a lot to process on an empty stomach," he said, with a faint smile.

Humor was a necessary defense mechanism. Sometimes we needed it to survive.

"I know," I said, giving him a little smile of my own. "Does any of this sound like what you're thinking and feeling?"

"Every damn word. Every. Damn. Word." He took a deep breath and let it out for the first time since we'd arrived. A little of the hunch left his shoulders. "Gracie's been trying to get me to talk it out with her, but I didn't know how to describe how I feel until now."

"That's a common roadblock," I assured him. "I have that problem myself. But if I've learned anything about dealing with the bullshit in my head, it's that it's all like a traffic jam. If you leave those cars there, that highway will stay messed up. You need to get in and start moving those cars, but not all at once—one by one. Does that make sense?"

He nodded slowly. "What do I do?"

"You do what Gracie suggested: you talk. Or if you can't talk about it yet, you can do other things to help get you to where you can talk." With my free hand, I dug into my shoulder bag and took out two business cards and a stack of photos face down. I slid the cards across the table. "Here's a counselor for when you're ready to talk, and here's the number for a trauma therapist who specializes in non-speaking methods. Both are important."

Gracie and Oliver studied the cards for a long time, as if the answers were inscribed on the paper.

"Have you done this?" Oliver asked, his expression guarded.

I translated that question as: *Will this help me?*

"Yes," I said. "Not with these specific people, but with my own therapist. And it has changed my life for the better. They're both expecting your call, and they're each holding bookings for you both this week. You and Gracie can heal together. I do that too—healing together. It's a little easier to take that journey when you're not taking it alone."

His mouth turned down. "I don't know what to say to a counselor, though."

"That's okay, because they'll know what to ask, and there's nothing you can say that's wrong."

Gracie squeezed his hand and smiled at him with so much love that I could almost feel it. "We'll talk to each other, Alice, I promise. And we'll make the calls."

"I'm so happy to hear that." And I was, though my aches made it difficult to show it. "As for the bad guy being some kind of mysterious, bigger-than-life monster..." I slid the stack of photos across the table. "This is Gregory Pierce. He used magic to assault you and many others. He tried to kill me. He murdered Madison Fernell and five other people. He's not some shadow or ghost or demon. He's a human being. He's flesh and blood. And he's going to pay for his crimes."

One by one, Oliver and Gracie turned the photos over and studied them. I'd put together a little collection showing Pierce in college and practicing as an attorney, as the D.A., at formal functions, and posing in posts from social media.

The last two photos in the stack were of Pierce in custody: one in the cage, and one in his cell at Northbourne, where he wore a jumpsuit and spell cuffs on his right wrist and left ankle. In the latter photo, he was staring at the camera, unsmiling. I was just petty enough to enjoy that his once-perfectly styled hair was sticking out in all directions and he needed a shave. And his stubble wasn't even the sexy kind.

"This is the bad guy," I said, gesturing at the photo. "Not you."

Oliver let go of both Gracie's hand and mine so he could hold that photo of Pierce in prison with both hands. He looked at it for a long time.

Little by little, his expression morphed from despondent and almost hollow to rage. Gracie's tears became anger too. I was glad to see their reaction, because anger directed at Pierce might help them let go of their own misplaced guilt.

I knew because that was happening to me when it came to Moses. The more I saw him as a person and not some far-away, vaguely monstrous boogeyman, the less I blamed myself for everything that had happened to me in Baltimore, and the closer I came to forgiving myself for things that had never been my fault to begin with.

A wave of cold washed through me, followed by painful tingling in my hands and feet. With their focus on the photo, Oliver and Gracie didn't see me flinch or move restlessly in my chair, or bite the inside of my cheek to keep from making a sound.

Malcolm did, though. And so did Matthias. Their unhappiness was palpable.

Carly had warned me none of us would come away from our encounters with Pierce unscathed. As usual, she had been absolutely right. How deeply affected we were and how long those effects would last remained to be seen.

Oliver crumpled the photo and dropped it on the table. "Fucking asshole," he said, visibly trembling in anger. "Why did he do it?"

I took a few deep breaths until I could talk without sounding shaky. "I'm going to tell you everything I know," I said, because hearing the truth would be so important to their healing process. "More will probably come out at Pierce's trial. You're going to get some answers, but you need to know not all of them will make sense. It sucks, but we can't make sense of senseless things."

When Sean had told me that on the night we'd fought the *úlfhéðnar*, I didn't think I'd end up quoting him so many times, but it might have been one of the truest things he'd ever said.

Gracie touched my hand. "Thank you, Alice. You saved our lives. I can't imagine what you've been through to solve this case, but I do know we owe you everything. *Everything*."

"Speaking of which," Philippa said, with a surprisingly kind smile, "do you have an invoice for us?"

"So practical," Gracie said, also smiling. Even Oliver smiled a bit. The mood in the room had changed drastically for the better, and I was glad for it.

"Lawyers are always practical, at least in my experience." I dug my invoice out of my bag and slid it over. "This settles us up."

"Won't there be more to do?" Oliver asked, frowning. "You said on the phone last night that you'll be collecting evidence for trial and appearing as a witness."

"I—" I swallowed hard when another wave of cold hit. "Anything else I do will be at the Court's behest," I managed to say. "Compensation will come out of their pocket, not yours."

"But the rates we talked about don't seem like enough," Oliver argued. "You saved our *lives*."

I'd gotten into mage private investigator work to do exactly that: to save lives. To help people who had nowhere else to turn. Tough to put a dollar amount on that, though I had to quantify my services at an hourly rate for invoicing purposes. Not to mention when it came to paying taxes, the feds probably wouldn't react well to seeing "I did it all for the good of humanity" written on my forms.

"Call the therapists and we'll call it even," I said. "Really. That's all I need from either of you."

"I promise." Gracie looked at Oliver. "Are you ready for her to tell us everything about how she tracked Pierce down and what happens next, babe?"

"Yes." He still looked rough, but he was sitting up straight now and making eye contact, and that was a huge improvement from when I'd arrived. "Will I have a Vampire Court trial?"

I shook my head. "You're a victim and a witness, not a defendant. *Pierce* will be on trial. The district attorney's office has already dismissed the charges against you due to the change of jurisdiction. The Court hasn't filed anything against you and won't."

"I'm still guilty in the public eye, though," he said, and how much that hurt him showed in his expression and the way his shoulders hunched again. "We can't go home right now, Philippa says. Vandals broke into the house last night. We're not safe there. And my company has asked me to take a leave of absence. Unpaid, of course."

Damn it, I hated this for them. I wanted to yell from the rooftops that both he and the others were blameless and Pierce alone was the perpetrator. But the legal process had to run its course, and Philippa would guide them through the steps of rebuilding their public image, maybe through interviews with journalists. It would take time, but I had to believe they could regain what they'd lost.

"I know, and I'm so sorry," I said. "But by the time Pierce's trial is over and all the facts are out there, there won't be any question who's to blame for these murders."

Oliver's eyes shimmered. He blinked rapidly. "Thank you, Alice. You don't know what this means to me, to us."

"I'm a mage P.I.," I said, managing a smile despite how much I ached. "It's what I do."

THANK ALL the stars in the cosmos, by the time Matthias, Malcolm, and I returned home from meeting with Philippa and the Hensleys, Katy had been by the house to drop off a basket of potions.

The first thing I did when I got upstairs was pour one bottle into a bath full of hot water, throw my clothes at the hamper, and climb into the tub, sinking down until everything was underwater except my nose and mouth. The potion smelled warm and safe, like Carly's house. White witch magic—the purest power I knew.

I stayed submerged for a long, long time.

I didn't fall asleep, but I dozed, occasionally murmuring the incantation Katy had written on a scrap of cinnamon-scented paper. Each time I did, the water swirled around me and the scent of the oils and herbs floating on the surface filled my nose and lungs.

For as long as I remained in the water, no waves of hot or cold went through me, and I felt no painful tingling. Heavenly.

I drifted in the quiet. From time to time, tears of relief leaked out from under my lids.

He did it silently, and thanks to the magic and the warmth I wasn't quite fully aware of my surroundings, but I still sensed when Sean snuck into the bathroom. Something in my body changed when he was nearby, even before I caught his forest scent blended with Katy's potion. I felt safe and at home when he was near. I was truly, deeply, *loved*.

The moment he came into the room, the last of the tension in my shoulders evaporated.

Eventually, the magic in the potion began to wane and the water cooled. When I exhaled and started to sit up, I was stunned that it didn't hurt to do so. Well, at least it hurt way less than I'd expected.

Then Sean was there, helping me to sit up with one hand on my back. He gently poured a cup of clean water over my face and handed me a towel. Pleasant-smelling or not, witchy potions could really sting eyeballs.

"I love you," he said as I wiped my face.

I opened my eyes to find him kneeling next to the tub, his shirt wet in the front from where I'd apparently splashed him while sitting up.

He smiled at me, and the corners of his eyes crinkled in the way that had drawn me to him from the moment we'd met. "You look better," he said. "You don't smell like pain now. More like..." He sniffed. "Marjoram?"

I swirled the bathwater with my hand and watched the herbs and oils spin on the surface. "Looks like a spice cabinet in here, so probably."

He surprised me by unfolding a huge, fluffy bath towel almost the size of a bedsheet. "I got you a present."

"Wow. Thank you." I rubbed the towel between my fingers. "Ooh, so soft."

He winked. "Wait until you're in it."

Moments later, he had me wrapped up like a burrito and sitting sideways on his lap on the bathroom floor, tucked under his chin with my head against his chest. Katy's instructions said not to rinse off for at least thirty minutes after getting out of the tub, so I'd have to wait to shampoo the stuff out of my hair. At least I smelled nice.

"This towel is the best thing ever," I murmured. "We're going to have to chain it to the floor so Esme doesn't steal it."

"Forget Esme—*I* may steal it." He kissed my hair. "Or at least ask you to let me borrow it sometimes."

I smiled. "Big ol' alpha werewolf in a fluffy bath towel. Better not let Malcolm see you in it or you'll never hear the end of it."

"I don't plan for anyone to see me in it but you." Gently, he rubbed my back. "Better?"

"Better." I yawned. "I'm so tired. I don't even care if I go to sleep with wet hair that smells like marjoram."

"Daisy is already on the bed, ready to sleep next to you." He rested his chin on top of my head again. "I'll stay too for as long as I can, but I have work I need to do. Ben is coming over later to talk with Matthias and me, and then they're going to run together at the pack land."

Ben and Matthias, hunting and running together as wolves. As pack mates. As Sean's beta and third. I never thought I'd see the day.

As if he could hear my thoughts, Sean shook with silent laughter.

"Do *not* say I told you so," I warned.

He cleared his throat. "Wouldn't dream of it," he said, and I heard the smile in his voice.

I wanted to watch Ben and Matthias running together, but that would have to wait until another time. Judging by the heaviness in my limbs and eyelids, I'd probably sleep straight through until tomorrow. I needed to heal. Maybe Katy's potion would grant me a long, pain-free sleep, and I'd wake up tomorrow rested and ready to drink coffee and chow down on one of Matthias's breakfast casseroles.

"Coffee and casserole," I murmured as Sean rose with me in his arms.

"Are you putting in a breakfast order for tomorrow?" He chuckled. "I've been cast aside. You used to demand my breakfast burritos."

"We could do both, if you don't mind." I yawned again. "I think I'm going to wake up hungry."

"I don't mind at all." He kissed the tip of my nose. "Miss Magic, the words 'I'm going to wake up hungry' are music to my ears."

EPILOGUE

TWO WEEKS LATER

Weeding a garden proved tricky when all the plants in it liked to bite any living thing who came near except its creator. Still, I had dirt up to my elbows and deep under my nails, and I was happy.

Inside our house, Nan and Matthias were cooking dinner and the smells drifted out the open patio door. Daniel and Sean had settled on the deck with beers to play with Baby Daisy, who'd recently discovered the game of fetch. Their voices and laughter and Baby Daisy's happy little *woofs* and playful growls reached my ears inside the tall wooden fence surrounding my blood garden.

"Rrrrrrrr?" Esme asked from her perch atop a fencepost, her furry head tilted in curiosity. If she were anything but a pūķis, I would be terrified for her to be so close to the plants, but they kept their distance from her, regardless of whether she was in feline or dragon form.

"A garden doesn't weed itself, Ez, even one filled with carnivorous plants." I tossed another uprooted weed over the fence and wiped my forehead with the back of my hand. "It's a dirty job, but it's got to be done. And since this garden eats anything that *isn't* me, I'm the gardener."

She appeared unconvinced. Cats—especially cat-dragons—seemed skeptical as a general rule. She raised a tiny gray paw, licked it, and washed her face very deliberately while maintaining eye contact.

"Do I have mud on my face?" I wiped my cheek on my shoulder and saw a smear of dirt on my T-shirt. "Oh, thanks."

"Rrrr." She swished her tail and jumped down from the fence-post, presumably headed back to the house to cajole or steal food from the cooks.

I'd spent a number of evenings lately in my blood garden, for my own sake and the plants' well-being too. Even with daily soaks in Katy's potions, I still experienced waves of cold and heat and twinges of pain that came with whiffs of damp earth and decay. Other than during my witchy baths, the only time I didn't experience any such discomfort was here in my garden. I hoped the sensations faded in time.

The plants certainly seemed to enjoy my presence. They swayed contentedly as I pulled the weeds that peeked through the layer of mulch. In between weed-pulls, I caressed their leaves. The plants shivered in excitement, leaning into my touch and rubbing my hand gently like a cat. The gentleness was deceiving, though. These plants consumed whole human bodies and pig carcasses on a regular basis, and required a *very* stout fence to keep them contained.

When I finished weeding, I treated the plants to drops of my blood, which I turned into the soil throughout the garden. The plants shivered and swayed and sighed. Blooms burst open from several of the plants, filling the fenced area with light flowery perfume.

I would have liked to spend more time sitting in my blood garden with my fingers in the dirt, soaking up the euphoric feeling of its power and the plants' adoration, but dinner would be ready soon. This was our first family dinner since Nan and Daniel returned from their honeymoon. I figured the occasion called for clean hands and clothes.

When I opened the garden's heavy gate—which we'd equipped with a sturdy deadbolt lock because the dang plants had figured out how to open a latch—I found Sean on the other side holding Baby Daisy.

"Did you weed, or just roll around in there?" Sean asked with a grin. "Did you leave any dirt in the garden?"

"Hush, you." I swung the gate closed behind me, making sure not to catch any of the plants in the door when it closed, and locked the deadbolt. "Don't act like you don't like it when I'm dirty. You know you'll get to clean me up."

"I do like getting you clean." He wiped the tip of my nose, then kissed me there. "There—I made a clean spot. That'll have to do until we're alone later."

Not to be outdone, Baby Daisy wiggled out of his arms and into mine, where she licked my chin.

"It's a team effort with you," Sean said with a chuckle.

"It really is." I put Baby Daisy on the ground and took Sean's hand for the walk to the house. Daniel had already gone inside. I loved that he always wanted to be by Nan's side, and vice versa. "I like my team, though."

"Good, because we're not going anywhere." He kissed my hair, then wiped his mouth. "Good grief. How did you get dirt in your hair?"

"I have dirt *everywhere*, babe." I winked. "I'm going to need a very thorough scrub-down tonight. Maybe with a little dirty talk to go with it. You know I like it when you make me blush."

He smiled and squeezed my hand. "Your wish is my command, Miss Magic."

Just as we reached the deck, my phone buzzed. I glanced at the screen and raised my eyebrows. "I'll be inside in a sec," I told Sean.

He kissed my temple and took Daisy inside, shutting the patio door behind them.

I swiped the green button. "This is Alice."

"Ms. Worth." Ernie Diaz cleared his throat. "Am I interrupting something?"

"We're about to sit down to dinner, but I have a few minutes." I leaned against the railing. I didn't want to get dirt all over our patio furniture. We'd probably be coming out here later to hang out with our drinks. "Is something going on?"

"No, nothing in particular." He coughed, obviously uncomfortable. "I...uh, wanted to apologize."

I did not see that coming. "There's no need—"

"There *is*." He sounded more sure of himself now, as if arguing with me put him back on solid ground. "The last time we spoke, the night you turned the Pierce case over the Vampire Court, I said some things I've come to regret."

"I didn't take any of it personally," I said, which was mostly true. "I hit you with a lot of big news that night. I don't think I would have reacted much differently in your shoes."

"Even so, I had no business calling you—" He cleared his throat again. "Any of that. Or accusing you of being in the vamps' pocket. I let my pride get in the way. I wanted to haul the killer down to the jail myself, or be there when it was done."

"I know." I half-sat on the railing and swung my leg back and forth. "If there was any way for Pierce to face justice in human court, whether it was local, state, or federal, I would have done what I'd said I would do and drop him on the steps of the police station. But there was no way. It was the Vampire Court or not at all. It wasn't any easier for me than for you."

"I understand that now. You were right when you said we both got into our line of work to help people who needed us and to put the bad guys away. And you're right that sometimes justice has to take a different path. It just took me a while to see it. For that, and for all the rest, I apologize."

"Apology accepted, then."

He sighed. "Goddamn it, it's still hard to believe Greg Pierce is a serial killer. I voted for him. I shook his hand more than once. I've gone *drinking* with him. How did I not see it?"

"Many psychopaths are experts at hiding who they really are. Don't beat yourself up, Diaz. He fooled everybody. But not anymore. And by the time the trial is over, every last awful detail will be out there for the world to see."

He chuckled, the sound as dry as gravel on concrete. "That's going to be rough on his ego."

"The bigger they are," I said.

"The harder they fall," he agreed.

"Anything else, Detective?"

He cleared his throat again. "You can call me Ernie," he said gruffly. "Not around Ferguson, though. In fact, it would be a good idea for you to avoid him altogether. I'm sure I shouldn't tell you this, but he got a write-up for some stuff he said about you in front of our lieutenant. Also a week's unpaid leave."

What on earth had he said that was bad enough to net himself a week-long suspension? "Anything I need to be looking out for? Slashed tires? Flaming bag of dog poo on my porch?"

"Nah. He's all talk." He grumbled. "Or he *better* be. He's got a good brain for solving cases if he'd stop being a little shitweasel long enough to use it."

I covered my laugh with a cough. "Thanks for calling, Det— Ernie. Stay safe out there."

"You too, Ms. Worth."

"Alice," I corrected. "Good night."

"Good night."

I ended the call, stuck my phone in my back pocket, and took a deep, cleansing breath. Diaz's anger, while not unexpected, had weighed more heavily on me than I'd realized until we'd made peace and my shoulders felt lighter.

The night was still, the stars bright. We'd decided to leave up the string lights in the backyard as a permanent decoration, and their twinkly colored bulbs made me smile. My skin buzzed with all the power I'd soaked up from my garden. I could relax here, surrounded by the people and things that made me happiest.

With the Court dismissing all charges against us and the Were Ruling Council and Matthias granted asylum, we could worry less about censure by the Council. Meanwhile, Charles and I continued to negotiate terms regarding me telling him the truth about the deaths of Valas and Vlad in Colorado. That transaction remained highly complicated thanks to the fact Charles could sense deceit, and Valas currently resided in a pit accessed via a mirror stashed in my basement. Everything in my life depended on no one finding out where she was—most especially Charles or my grandfather.

We'd seen no further signs of the so-called Disciples of the Sun, and no more information about them had surfaced. Sean and I were debating asking Cyro to dig around, but it was a thorny proposition. I didn't want them to know I knew they existed, much less that I was curious about them. Moses said he had intel, but I no longer accepted anything he said at face value. After his attempt to make the Court our enemy went south thanks to the deal I'd made with Charles, he'd be looking for another way to force me to rely on him.

The vampires in the area, including Charles and the rest of the Court, rose each day ninety minutes before sunset and stayed awake until well after dawn. Dark magic ebbed and flowed more strongly and more frequently than anyone could remember. Little earthquakes shook the ground near Northbourne almost daily. And last week, for two nights in a row, the evening sky had turned unnaturally red on the horizon.

The calm before the storm, Gregory Pierce had called it.

Something woke up, Katy had said.

And I continued to wonder: had Valas kept something at bay that now felt free to rise? Something or someone who wanted to be king?

I didn't know. No one did, except maybe Valas herself, but she hadn't appeared in the mirror again. Its surface remained eerily dark and silent. Carly said Valas still resided in the pit and hadn't fallen to

Tartarus. Maybe she was in there plotting her escape. Or maybe she was just waiting.

Sean stuck his head out the patio door. "Food's on the table, babe. The wolves are getting restless."

"Sorry." I hurried inside to wash my hands and change.

A few minutes later, when I came back downstairs, everyone was waiting in their chairs, except for Daniel, who met me at the bottom of the stairs to give me a hug. I loved his signature scent that reminded me of a grassy meadow and sunshine.

"What was that about?" I asked as he rubbed my back and let go. "I just saw you five minutes ago."

He feigned disappointment. "I can't hug my daughter just because?"

I gave him another half-hug just for good measure. "You can hug me whenever you want, unless it interferes with me getting to my coffee."

"It's a deal." He smiled. He'd been doing that a lot lately. "You look good happy."

"So do you." I squeezed his hand.

We joined the others at the table. Sean pulled my chair closer to his as I sat down. "Everything okay?" he asked, glancing meaning-fully over his shoulder at my phone, which I'd put on silent and tossed onto the couch because nothing was going to interrupt this meal if I could help it.

"Everything's good." I squeezed his leg. "Diaz wanted to apolo-gize. He's coming around."

"Good." He leaned over to kiss my temple. "We'll call that another win for Team Alice."

When we'd all filled our plates, Sean stood, glass of wine in hand. "I'd like to propose a toast to Nan and Daniel, and to the love that brought you together." We clinked glasses.

"And to family, in all its wonderful forms," Nan added, smiling around the table as we tapped our glasses again. She raised her glass to the other end of the table. "And to Matthias, for what looks to me like the finest roasts that have ever graced this table."

Matthias actually flushed. We all focused on our food and pretended not to notice our new beta's embarrassment. Luckily Malcolm and Liam were out on a ghost date, or I was sure my sidekick would have teased him unmercifully about it at work tomorrow, which would be Matthias's first official day as my first-ever PI trainee.

Tomorrow evening, I would make a return visit to Merrum Manor for my second dinner with Moses. I thought I would worry about it constantly like I had in the days leading up to my first meal with him, but instead it barely registered. I'd actually forgotten about it over the past week until a calendar reminder popped up on my phone.

At the manor, at Moses's table, I'd eat gourmet, chef-prepared food and drink expensive booze.

When I sat down with Sean, or Malcolm and Liam, or Nan and Daniel, or Matthias, or Ben and Casey, or Arkady, or all of the above, those were *family dinners*. The two things were worlds apart.

And Matthias's roast, like the happy chatter around our table, was indeed divine.

THANK YOU FOR READING

Thank you for reading *Heart of the Damned*, the ninth book in the ongoing Alice Worth series! I hope you enjoyed the story. Book 10 coming soon.

Reviews are very much appreciated by all indie authors. Please drop a review on your favorite site(s) if you have the time to share your thoughts.

Please follow me on the socials, if you haven't already.
Facebook.com/AuthorLisaEdmonds
Instagram, TikTok, and Threads @LisaEdmonds.Author

ACKNOWLEDGMENTS

Well, here I am, writing the acknowledgements for my tenth full-length book, and as always, my heart swells with my love for so many people who helped me along the way.

First and foremost, I want to reiterate the sentiment on the dedication page of this book: **This one's for you, my lovely readers, without whom I would not be writing this.** Please know I am grateful for you every day, and I'm never not cognizant of how lucky I am.

Thank you to my editor, Friel Black of Grey Moth Editing, who enthusiastically took on the challenge of providing developmental edits on a manuscript so big it has its own zip code, and guided me to a finished product I am truly pleased to have written.

Thank you to my longtime beta readers Adrienne Foreman and Marie Guthrie for your insights and support. Also, as always, I owe an enormous debt of gratitude to Carla, a.k.a. Lady Beltane, for providing information and advice on my depictions of all matters related to the Craft, from rituals, blessings, descriptions of altars, and the daily ins and outs of Carly's and Katy's practice.

I would like to thank dear friend, author, and mental health advocate Elisse Hay for advising me on the content of Alice's final conversation with Oliver and Gracie, during which she encourages them to seek counseling and therapy as part of their healing process.

A special thanks to my Discordant Owl Squad for all their cheering, support, snark, laughs, tears, and Zooms during the process of writing this book.

Many thanks to Lilla Glass, author and friend, for her encyclopedic knowledge of magical lore and much, much more. And to Stacy Choi, also author and friend, for putting up with my nonsense and sending me 234,023 reels each day to keep my spirits up and make sure I never miss a video of a cat doing something ridiculous.

My undying gratitude to JeFF Stumpo, for all these wonderful weird years of friendship and the flamingo joke. And much love to author and editor Heather McCorkle, who took a chance on Alice and me and set this whirlwind in motion.

To my lovely close family and friends: thank you all so much for your unyielding support and patience with this stressed-out, short-tempered, over-caffeinated author. Looking at you, Stacey K., Antoinette, John, Felicia, Mike, Felicity M., Tony, Nick, Jess H., and Jen W.

A very special thanks to my sister Michelle and brother-in-law Josh, as well as my sister-in-law Amy, my father Mike and stepmother Teri, and my cousin Tom and his wife Pam.

Finally, all my love and thanks to my husband Bill, who suffers the slings and arrows of living with a neurospicy writer every day but somehow hasn't run for the hills yet. Twenty-five years together so far, babe, and I still love you more each day. You are my heart.

ABOUT THE AUTHOR

Lisa Edmonds was born and raised in Kansas. A graduate of Buhler High School, she studied English and forensic criminology at Wichita State University. After acquiring her Bachelor's degree, she considered a career in law enforcement as a behavioral analyst before earning a Master's in English from Wichita State and then a Ph.D. in English from Texas A&M University.

For ten years, she was an associate professor of English at a college in Texas, where she taught a variety of writing and literature courses. Now a full-time author, she shares a cute Victorian-style home called The Storybook House with her husband and their pets, and enjoys writing, reading, traveling, spoiling her niece and nephew, and singing karaoke.

Visit LisaEdmonds.com for information on all books, including future projects, and join my Reader Community for an opportunity to receive an ARC of the next Alice Worth novel.

www.ingramcontent.com/pod-product-compliance
Lightning Source LLC
Chambersburg PA
CBHW030329010826
48973CB00004B/936